The Cornishman

By

George Donald

The girl was not the first woman he had hurt, but she was the first that he killed. He stared into her eyes, now opened wide with shock, his left hand held firmly across her mouth to stop her crying out and the other holding the long blade that he slowly pushed and twisted into her soft belly. His brow furrowed as he stared with curiosity at her face, now stricken with fear, the pain of the knife in her abdomen showing in her widening eyes. Her hands were against his chest, thrusting up against him, but he was far too strong for her and the weight of his body as she vainly thrashed her legs under him wasn't enough to dislodge him. Her terror excited him and he forced himself a little deeper into her as breathlessly, he hushed her. She whimpered beneath him, her frantic struggle growing weaker as the life drained from her. He knew he was about to ejaculate and thrust deeper into her, pushing as he did so a little harder on the knife and felt the wet, warmth of her blood oozing from the wound across the handle of the knife and onto his hand. Her body gave one final shudder as he shoved harder, the tip of the knife forced upwards beneath her ribs and into her heart. Her eyes glazed over, staring at him as with a soft sigh, she lay still.

He exhaled deeply and for a few seconds, listened intently in the darkness for any sound, but other than the traffic travelling along Paisley Road West some three hundred metres away, there was nothing. He blew softly through pursed lips and rolled off the dead girl, her sightless eyes still open. With his free hand he held his now limp penis to prevent the condom from slipping off. He wanted a smoke, but decided against lighting a fag, conscious if there was anyone else in the park that the flare of the match as it was struck might be seen.

He sat upright and laying the knife down on the grass beside him, fumbled in his trouser pocket for the small, plastic bag. Carefully removing the condom, he placed it into the bag that he knotted it to flush away later and returned the bag to his pocket. He half smirked and thought it would not do to leave *that* to be discovered, when the girl was found.

He glanced at the dead girl; the cheap material of her light blue coloured dress rumpled and pulled up to her waist, her thin, bare legs vividly pale in the moonlight and with a soft smile, placed his souvenir in his other trouser pocket. He saw that she had kicked off one brightly coloured yellow shoe during her struggle and it lay almost four feet from her foot. He grinned, wondering why the skinny wee lassie thought she could resist him. He leaned over and carefully wiped her blood from both his hand and the knife blade onto her dress. That done, he lifted his right trouser leg to replace the knife in the sheath he had strapped to his calf. Time to go, he decided and rising to his feet, he cast a glance about him to ensure there was nobody about, then pushed out of the bushes and walked away without a backward glance.

CHAPTER 1 – Thursday Morning, 27 May 1982.

It was a bright and clear morning and just gone eight o'clock when Jean McConnachie locked the front door behind her. Sandy, her white coloured Scottie pulled excitedly at the lead held in her other hand, eager to get to the park for his morning constitutional. "Hold your horses, ya wee bugger," the elderly woman pulled sharply on the lead, "or you'll have me over."
"Morning Jean," Archie cheerfully called from next door at number twelve, newspaper in one hand as he unlocked his door with the other, "that wee devil still not settled down then?"
"Morning Archie," she called back. "Och, he's always the same in the morning. He's like the rest of us old ones, needs to get his business done before he settles down for the day."
Archie laughed and cheerfully waved 'Bye' as he closed the door behind him.
Walking along Airth Road, Sandy settled down to a more sedate pace allowing Jean to enjoy the fine weather and the occasional word with a passing neighbour. Cutting across Auldbar Road, she turned right toward the traffic lights situated on Mosspark Boulevard, her and Sandy's usual route towards the entrance gate of the Bellahouston Park. As she walked, she could see the workmen in the park further up the hill, already hard at work preparing the ground to receive the lengthy altar being set up for the arrival the following week of the Pope. Jean was not Catholic, but even she could feel the anticipation and excitement of her neighbours in expectation of the visit by the Pontiff. The streets all about Mosspark and the surrounding area was being readied with parking cones and freshly painted road signs to accept and direct the large numbers who were expected to attend the open air mass.
" Aye, Sandy" she glanced at the freshly painted renovation, "the council will find the money from somewhere when they need to, so just so long as they get a good day for it," she unconsciously muttered to herself.
Crossing the Boulevard, Jean entered the park gate and conscious of her arthritic hip, slowly bent over to let the small dog off the lead. With a warning bark to any who dare challenge the proud wee terrier, Sandy raced ahead to his usual tree, cocked a leg and presented it with yet another soaking. That done, the wee dog's nose twitched at an unusual smell and slowly he followed the trail, occasionally casting a protective glance back at his mistress to ensure he didn't stray too far from her.

Sticking to her usual route, Jean walked slowly along the gently curving path that led to her favourite bench at the top of the hill while Sandy cavorted back and forth; every smell needing investigated and in due course squatted to release his bowels. Shooing the inquisitive dog from his dropping, Jean fetched the plastic bag from her jacket pocket and leaned over to collect the faeces. Straightening up, she frowned when she saw the small dog standing perfectly still, his nose in the air. Without warning, Sandy took off at speed and raced ahead of her. Jean sighed and called to him, but he ignored her and with a grimace, she just knew the wee bugger was after a fox. What he would do if one turned to face him she shuddered to think for Sandy, for all his big-hearted bravery, was getting on in years and like his mistress, suffered badly from arthritis. The old Scottie would be no match for a wily and cornered fox and in her head, she envisaged yet another vet bill. "Sandy!" she sharply called out again, but the dog had disappeared from her sight into the bushes. Wearily, forcing her aching joints onwards, she left the pathway and walked across the freshly trimmed grass towards where she had last seen him, calling repeatedly for him to come to heel. Several minutes passed before the dog appeared, his tail wagging as he proudly laid a woman's yellow shoe at Jean's feet, then sat down to be patted and praised.

Jean looked curiously from the shoe to the dog and cautiously bending, lifted Sandy's prize to examine it. The shoe didn't seem to be new; indeed the short heel was well worn down and the leather slightly scuffed and unpolished. A feeling of dread overtook her, but with uncommon courage, Jean knew that she needed to push into the bushes to find out from where Sandy had recovered the shoe. She wasn't aware her breathing had become short rasping, breaths. She ran her tongue over suddenly dry lips and slowly pushed back the overhanging foliage. Bending low, she entered the dimly lit shrubbery.

When she saw the young woman's body, she almost fainted, one hand grabbing at an overhanging branch to steady her while the other reached for her throat. So shocked was she that Jean was unaware of the sharp thorn that cut deeply into her forefinger. Instinctively, she knew the poor lassie was dead.

On the footpath below the crest of the hill from where Jean staggered from the bushes, the overweight jogger who had finally succumbed to his wife's nagging was labouring badly when he startled at the old woman's scream for help.

The first police officers to arrive at the park were met at the gate by a heavy-set, red-faced man in a bright yellow coloured tracksuit who directed them up the hill to the elderly woman. The officers could just make out the figure sitting on a bench. Slowly, the driver manoeuvred the police van up the narrow path and stopped beside the old lady whose body shook as she dabbed with a bloodstained handkerchief at her right forefinger; the other hand tightly held the red leather lead of her small Scottie dog that lay on the grass beside her.

"Hello there," greeted Willie McConnell, the older of the two constables. "The gentleman down there," he flicked a thumb over his shoulder towards the jogger, "phoned nine-nine-nine and said you had found a body, missus?"

Jean, pale faced and close to tears could only nod. McConnell's partner, Valerie Broadfoot removed her police cap and, perching herself on the bench beside the woman, placed an arm about her shoulders. "I'm Val," she smiled at Jean. "I see you've cut your finger there, so maybe we'll sit for a wee minute and let you compose yourself and then you can show us what you found, eh?"

"I'm fine hen, really," protested Jean. Then taking a deep breath and with a firm show of resilience, said, "I don't want that wee lassie lying there herself for another minute." With one hand on the backrest to help her to her feet, she handed the lead to the young policewoman. "Can you maybe tie wee Sandy to the bench here, hen? There's no need for him to see her again, eh?"

McConnell, a veteran of twenty-five years dealing with the public and their various peculiarities, choked back a laugh and thought that was definitely a first. Not wanting the dog upset by a dead body.

Supported on one arm by the policewoman, Jean led the officers to the bushes and with a shaking hand, pointed and in a sad voice, quietly said, "In there."

Willie McConnell's radio message confirming that it was indeed a dead body and that circumstances seemed to suggest murder provoked a rapid response from the receiving officer in the control room at Govan police office. His first telephone call was to the Detective Chief Inspector's room upstairs.

"Where's the body located," snapped DCI Gordon McIntosh, telephone in one hand and pencil in the other, unconsciously nodding while he wrote and listened to the officer's directions.

"Right, I've got that. Tell the cops…it is Willie McConnell who's at the locus, is it?"

The officer confirmed McConnell's attendance in the park.

"Good," replied McIntosh "aware that the old, experienced cop would be on the ball and could be trusted to get things started. "Right, tell Willie and his neighbour to stand back from the crime scene and get them to try and protect the area as best they can. I'll organise some uniformed reinforcements up there as soon as possible and then the Forensics and some of my guys will also be up there pronto, okay? Oh, and while you are it, contact the on-call Casualty Surgeon and provide details of where the body is located. Thanks, hen," he nodded at the handset.

Replacing the handset in the cradle, McIntosh bit at his lower lip, a childhood habit that had carried with him through to middle age and thought for a moment, inwardly cursing his bad luck that this should occur just when the bloody Pope was due to arrive in the Division next week. Lifting the handset, he dialled a number for police headquarters at Pitt Street. In short, terse sentences, he requested the service of a photographer and Forensics' team to the Mosspark Boulevard east gate of Bellahouston Park.

McIntosh hurried into the main CID office where two detectives sat at their desks. "You two, with me," he ordered and without waiting for a response, returned to grab his coat from his office.

Detective Inspector Mark Renwick was sat at his desk at Pollok police office reading the morning edition of the 'Glasgow News' when the telephone call came in. Slowly, as he listened to the officer from the control room at Govan, he closed his eyes and shook his head. Bellahouston Park was, strictly speaking, the responsibility of the Pollok sub-division and that meant, as the senior CID officer at Pollok, the body that had been discovered was his to investigate, but he knew that Gordon McIntosh would be all over the inquiry like a bloody rash. Renwick didn't so much dislike McIntosh as hate him with a passion. He believed the DCI to be a glory-hunting bastard who was mistrustful of Renwick.

This mistrust, Renwick had already experienced, was reflected in McIntosh's annual assessment of the DI and would impact negatively on Renwick's future promotion prospects. That and McIntosh's recent refusal to endorse Renwick's application for a transfer to the Scottish Crime Squad, having the temerity to suggest in the application that Renwick was not only inexperienced in the rank, but lacked motivation and leadership qualities and concluded by further suggesting that a further two years as a divisional Detective Inspector might enhance a future application.

As good as fucking said I'm useless, he inwardly raged and stamped to his feet. Crossing from his own room across the corridor to the narrow cupboard that was laughingly called the CID general office, he stuck his head in and curtly snapped at the uniform CID clerk, "Jimmy, where are the troops at the minute?"

Jimmy Reid, in the twilight of his career and knocking on the door to retirement, didn't look up from his typewriter, but lazily replied, "Two on a warrant inquiry, one at the Sheriff Court and the young guy Simon Johnson the aide; he's out at the report of a housebreaking in Priesthill."

Renwick stared down at the balding head of Reid, sneering behind the older man's back. Another has-been that should have been retired years ago he thought and then said, "I've just taken a phone call from Govan control room. There's a body been discovered in Bellahouston Park. The DCI is on his way there with a team, so I'll be going there now. You can get me on the radio if you need me."

Reid didn't turn, but simply nodded in response, glad to see the back of the moody bugger if only for a couple of hours. It was jokingly whispered among the divisional CID, the reason Renwick seldom left the office was he worried himself sick he might actually get involved in an inquiry where he would need to make a decision.

Reid had a sly glance through the window that faced onto the small yard at the front of the office that served as a car park and saw Renwick climb into the Morris Ital, the CID car Renwick favoured and insisted was left for his personal use, regardless of what inquiries his officers might have to attend. He watched Renwick drive through the gate and out into Brockburn Road.

"Where's that clown off to in such a hurry?" asked the voice behind him.

Reid turned to find the burly figure of Gavin Wilson, the uniform Sergeant who was that day's station Duty Officer, arms folded and leaning against the doorpost.

"Word is there's a body been found in Bellahouston Park, a murder apparently." replied Reid. "He's worried DCI McIntosh will get there before him. God know what he thinks he'll add to the inquiry," Reid continued. "That plonker couldn't find his arse unless someone put his hand on it for him. Serve him right if McIntosh lets him handle the inquiry, but it would probably mean an undetected murder, eh?"

Wilson grinned in silent agreement with Reid's assessment of the young DI. It was common knowledge that Renwick's father was a District councillor with a constituency somewhere in the north of the city who was also an influential member of the Councils Police and Fire Committee, a fact that Renwick wasn't above reminding people. It was widely rumoured that Renwick's rapid promotion during his nine years service was accredited to the councillor's approval when it came to certain budget requests, particularly those, it was whispered, that approved expenses and 'foreign fact finding' trips for some senior officers.

"So, have you heard the latest news, Jimmy?" asked Wilson, the murder almost immediately dismissed from his mind as the two men spent the next ten minutes discussing the ongoing conflict that was taking place almost eight thousand miles distant, on a group of remote and wind swept islands.

Acting Detective Constable Simon Johnson, just four years in the job and five weeks into his six-month attachment to the CID completed, listened patiently as the irate complainer demanded the detective interview the downstairs neighbours. According to the angry man, the "fucking Paki's" as he succinctly described the young couple, must have been involved because, the increasingly furious man spat, "They're all thieving bastards."

Simon had heard enough of the racist rants and firmly held up a hand.

"Shut up!" he snapped at the man, his five foot ten inch frame hovering over the smaller man who stared back in surprise. "For your information," he leaned forward and stared steadily at the red-faced complainer, "it was your neighbours who alerted the police to the break-in and who chased the culprit from the close and Mister and Missus Ahmed downstairs, Mister Edwards, are born and bred in Glasgow, so they're as Scots as you or me, okay? You should consider yourself lucky to have neighbours that do phone us when there's a problem rather than the rest of your neighbours who didn't give a flying cuss when I knocked on their doors and weren't interested in your break-in."

The man continued to shake with rage, but said no more. Simon knew that because of the loss of his property, Edwards needed to hit out at someone and the young couple downstairs, because of their colour, were an easy target, but there was no convincing the angry man and that he had already decided the Ahmed's were in some manner involved.

Shaking his head at the narrow-mindedness of the man, Simon continued to note the details of the stolen items, concluding his investigation by arranging for a Scene of Crime fingerprint officer to attend the flat the following day and leaving his name and office contact phone number. With a final warning that if Edwards gave the Ahmed's any problem Simon would be back to see him, he turned away as a snarling Edwards slammed the door in disgust behind him.

Wearily he trod down the stairs then heard the radio in his jacket pocket activate and call his name.

"ADC Johnson, go ahead," he replied to the Govan controller, stepping out from the graffiti ridden close into the bright sunlight that flooded Ravenscraig Drive.

"Report of a code four-four," replied the controller, "You've to report to the DI at Bellahouston Park," then added, as though in afterthought, "enter by the gate at Mosspark Boulevard near to Dumbreck Road, over."

Johnson was slightly mystified. The duty controllers, as a matter of procedure, used the Strathclyde Police codes that were created to cut down airtime and thwart interception by groups such as the Citizen Band amateur radio enthusiasts and the local media, who could easily tune into the unencrypted police wavelengths. Simon knew the codes weren't that strictly adhered to and it was almost a standing joke that the codes were so easily identifiable, notably because controllers would send a unit to a "Code two," and then follow-up with an explanation such as, "two cars and a lorry at such and such a location." Simon knew that even the street kids were now as familiar with the codes as were the cops. However, what puzzled Simon was there was no explanation to what this particular call referred.

"Roger," he replied, his eyes narrowing. He knew most of the police codes, well the frequently used usual ones anyway, but a code four-four puzzled him. It wasn't one he had previously been sent to and fumbled in his police notebook for the small, laminated code card. Squinting in the bright sunlight, his eyes opened wide and he stared almost in disbelief. Five weeks into his acting detective rank and this was his first murder.

Brilliant, he grinned and headed for the unmarked CID navy blue coloured Austin Metro.

She woke with the hung over feeling that had become part of her life, the smell of her own body revolting her. Her tongue rattled in her mouth and the pressure on her bladder forced her from between the stained sheets of the dishevelled bed to her feet. Her head was sore where the punter had grabbed her hair while he had fucked her. Funny that, she never understood why some men got a thing for grabbing a woman by the hair when they were doing it.

She screwed her eyes against the thin stream of sunlight that forced its way through the crack in the flowery curtains and lit her way in the darkened bedroom to the door. In the hallway, she banged on the adjoining door and cried out, "Alice, it's nearly nine o'clock, time to get up hen," then stumbled into the bathroom, pulling on the string that operated the unshaded bulb. The room was a mess, discarded shampoo and hair conditioner packets littered the single glass shelf and the small pedal bin was overflowing too. The bath was long overdue a scrub with bleach and the hose that was their makeshift shower and attached to the bath taps had come loose from the hook on the plastered wall and lay untidily coiled in the bath. She lifted the flap and sitting on the toilet seat, sighed with relief as she peed, half listening for the sounds of her flatmate getting out of bed. She ripped at the toilet paper and gently dabbed at herself, still a little raw and mentally cursing the punter from the previous night who had so roughly fingered her before entering.

What had made a bad decision worse, she closed her eyes in silent anger, the sod had then stiffed her for the promised twenty quid and laughed at her protests, then threatened to hurt her if she complained to the cops. As if.

Still, one thieving bastard every few weeks didn't make all the punters bad guys was her way of dealing with her situation; her philosophical acceptance of the sexual abuse and the theft of the agreed payment.

She pulled her knickers up and slopping her hands under the cold tap in the sink, lifted the stained towel and grimaced; she'd need to remember to add that to the wash today. She filled the plastic mug with water and gulped it down, the water running down her chin and dripping onto the faded and stained nightdress.

Making her way back towards her room she hammered more loudly this time on Alice's door and getting no response, pushed it open.

Lizzie stared with surprise at the empty bed. Like her own, Alice's bed was crumpled and unmade with the blankets thrown so it was difficult to tell whether she had slept that night in the room, but then Lizzie saw the curtains were wide open. Alice wouldn't have slept with them open and never, ever rose before Lizzie. Her brow furrowed, but more with curiosity than worry. So where was Alice, she wondered?

Gordon McIntosh arrived at the park gate and was pleased to see the uniform had already created a physical cordon with officers standing at irregular intervals in a line about fifty metres apart and a distance of about one hundred metres from where he presumed the body lay. In addition, he could see blue and white tape circling an area that enclosed some bushes and walked towards it. As McIntosh approached, a little breathless from the steep climb, a slim figure wearing the encompassing all in one white paper boiler suit, the hood down exposing the pony-tailed fair hair and blue coloured slip-on plastic boots over her shoes emerged from the bushes. Behind her, he could see two similar suited figures, Scene of Crime officers he realised, bent over and working in the shrubbery. A camera flashed as he approached the young woman.

"Morning Doc," he called out in greeting, aware he was panting slightly and yet his lungs cried out for a cigarette. "Thanks for coming out so promptly."

Without a word being spoken, the two accompanying Detectives, their notebooks in hand, walked off, fanning out to speak with the old woman and the jogger who had discovered the body, both of whom were stood some distance apart and each in the company of a uniformed officer. He could hear and see a small dog that was barking loudly at the activity about the park.

The young woman nodded in acknowledgment. The slightly built doctor, her wire-framed glasses perched on the end of her nose who, besides being a GP doubled as a police Casualty Surgeons, was young for such a responsible post, but had proved her worth to the hard-bitten Glasgow CID. In tandem with her doctoring role, the young physician also served as one of the City's reserve Pathologist's when the Chief Pathologist, Mister Julian Hammond was for some reason unavailable. On occasion, her immediate insight at a murder scene had proven to be of such evidential value, it made the investigating officers job that much easier and indeed, at a recent murder in the Gorbals, McIntosh was aware that her initial findings at the crime scene had almost immediately set them on the track of the killer. Right now though, McIntosh could see the young woman, her blonde hair fiercely tied back into a ponytail and wearing the oversized white coloured Forensic boiler suit, seemed a little distracted. Stopping before her to catch his breath, he said, "So, what do you have for me?"

The doctor, her face flushed with anger, peeled off the blue coloured Forensic gloves and exhaled slowly, then stood with both hands on hips and shook her head. "Bloody shame," she spat out. "That wee girl in there can't be more than late teens or in her early twenties at the most. Not that it really matters what age she is. Any death in this kind of circumstances," she waved her hand vaguely about her, the vehemence in her voice taking McIntosh aback as she hissed "is just bloody wrong!"

She exhaled slowly and her rage subsided almost at once, replaced by a humourless smile as McIntosh watched her change from the angry woman to the professional physician.

"Stabbed once, an upper thrust under the ribs it seems that likely pierced the heart though of course you'll need to have that confirmed at the post mortem. The entry wound is very narrow, so I suspect a thin bladed weapon. Her dress was round her waist and no sign of underwear, so I must presume that intercourse occurred, but again the PM will confirm that. However, that said, there seems to be slight bruising round the vagina so I'm guessing the culprit was either very forceful or the victim was raped."

"Defence wounds?"

She shook her head. "Nothing that I can see at this time, but of course…"

"The PM will tell all," McIntosh finished for her. "What about the time of death?"

She cocked her head at the sky and shrugged. "There's little sign of lividity at this stage, but that might be because of the uncommonly warm weather we're experiencing," she replied. "I'm guessing from the rectal thermometer, sometime between nine o'clock last night and three o'clock this morning. Oh and there's some bruising showing up about the victim's lips, so I'm guessing that pressure was exerted on her mouth."

"To prevent her from screaming for help, perhaps?" suggested McIntosh.

"Likely," she nodded in reply and then added, "Oh, and one more thing that might or might not be significant. She has indications of puncture wounds on the inside upper thighs of both legs, though curiously not the arms. The punctures are on the vein lines and I'm of the opinion that she is an intravenous drug user. Not a lot of needle marks, but they seem to be reasonably recent and," she paused, though deliberating, "I suspect she just recently started, what do they call it again … shooting up? Of course as I said, once your Forensics has examined her blood sample from the PM it will likely confirm my suspicions. Right then," she began to tear at the paper boiler suit, "that's me finished here Mister McIntosh, so once your Scenes of Crime have done their bit, the victim can be removed to the Mortuary. I'll see the Certificate of Life Extinct and my statement wing their through to you as soon as possible, if that's all right with you?"

"Grand, doc," smiled McIntosh as the young woman, using his arm to steady herself, pulled off the overshoes and rolled them and the torn into a ball that she then shoved into a paper bag.

"Oh, and one other thing," she added, "Unless the victim made a habit of going without her underwear, it seems that her knickers aren't on her body or anywhere near the body. Of course, they might be lying about here," she waved a hand towards the undergrowth, "but just in case…."

"The killer might have taken them with him; a souvenir maybe," McIntosh finished for her. "Thanks doc, that could be very useful."

With a nod, she made to walk off, but then he remembered and called out to her, "I heard you got yourself hitched?"

She turned and smiled. "Yes, three weeks ago to Donald. I'm now Jane Robertson, so don't be surprised when my statement arrives with the new name."

"Belated congratulations," he called after her and watched as she cheerily waved a hand and made her way down to the gate and her car. As she strolled down the pathway, he saw Renwick moving upwards and nodding to the passing doctor. Just what I need, he grimaced.

He turned at the tap on his shoulder and nodded his thanks when handed a pair of blue coloured, plastic overshoes. Steadying himself with one hand on the woman's white paper shrouded shoulder he slipped the shoes on and pointing to the photographer, asked the Scene of Crime officer, "You guys got everything you need?"

"Yes boss," replied the SOCO and then she pointed to a few paper bags that lay to one side. "Sorry to say, sir, but there isn't a lot we found on or near the victim. I've conducted the low adhesive tape procedure from the exposed skin and her clothing, but my guess is it won't give us much. Willie here," she nodded to the bearded photographer, "has got all the photos that you'll need and we'll get those and a list of the items delivered to you at Orkney Street pronto."

"The doc mentioned there didn't seem to be any underwear lying about. Did you find any nearby?"

"No, nothing," the woman shook her head.

"Thanks guys," said McIntosh, running a weary hand over his brow. Just what I need, he inwardly thought, another bloody whodunit. Taking a deep breath, he moved into the space vacated by the SOCO's and stared down at the body. During his long career, McIntosh had attended a number of murder scenes, some of which did not faze him, he privately admitted; not when the victim was himself a violent criminal. But this, he stared with a lump in his throat, riled him like nothing else could. A young and helpless young girl murdered and left like this and likely just to satisfy some evil bastard's sexual urges.

Like most of his colleagues, McIntosh had an unequivocal opinion on the hanging debate. As he stared down at the victim, he sighed and not for the first time in his career, wondered what kind of man could have committed such a crime. The killer who had committed this evil deed had knowingly stepped outside the boundary of society's most basic rule; a man so morally bankrupt who with undoubted premeditation, had committed without conscience the worst of the capital crimes, a man who in McIntosh's view deserved to hang.

McIntosh was mentally exhausted; tired of the many numbers of murders, of the rapes and wanton violence he had through his career investigated. He shook his head as though endeavouring to clear his thoughts of rage and forced himself to concentrate on what must be done. Already, the practised and well-tried system for investigating major crime would be coming into play and back at his office his detectives would be readying themselves and preparing for the long hours that consumed much of their lives when investigating murders. McIntosh knew that he had to be stalwart; he must think of the girl as the victim, not someone's daughter or child, not a sister or girlfriend or perhaps even a wife, though no wedding band was visible, but as the victim and by doing so, he could perform as the professional investigator he was.

As he continued to stare at the victim, one thing became clear. Whether by choice or forced here, the killer did not intend his victim to leave this place alive and likely had chosen the area for its isolated solitude, bringing with him the knife that had ensured the victim's silence.

Did that mean the killer knew the area, he wondered; that he would be safe from disturbance when carrying out the murder?

He had seen enough.

Before leaving, he took one final glance at the dead girl, fixing her image in his mind and backing out of the shaded shrubbery, instructed the patiently waiting detective to go ahead and arrange to have her removed to the mortuary. He guessed that the undertakers tasked with the removal of the body would be standing by, probably down at the park gate, with the tin coffin that was universally known throughout the Force as 'the shell'.

Standing a few yards away, McIntosh saw DI Renwick and the duty Procurator Fiscal Depute, a pasty-faced young woman in her mid-twenties, who in accordance with Scots Law was obliged on behalf of the PF's Office to attend the location of any suspicious death. He could see that the Depute seemed ill at ease and guessed she baulked at the very thought of viewing a dead body.

He rightly guessed the DI was also nervous.

"What we got sir?"

"What we've got," McIntosh slowly replied, gesturing to the detective to wait for a moment before summoning the undertakers up the hill, "is a young woman, probably late teens or early twenties, more than likely raped and then stabbed to death. Initial indications are she was murdered some time within the last twelve hours."

The PF Depute wasn't previously known to McIntosh, but once introductions were made he was pleased that after a brief glance to where the victim lay, she mumbled her concurrence that it was indeed a murder and excusing herself, hastily made her way back down the hill. Inwardly he thought if the same young woman was to attend the post mortem he would need to ensure there was someone close by to catch her, suspecting from her shocked expression at the girl's body, the Depute might not be immune to the clinical procedure of an autopsy.

Watching her depart, McIntosh nodded to the waiting detective to proceed and remove the body. As he did so, it gave him that few seconds to consider his decision; he had to choose whether to allocate the inquiry to the DI or instead inform him that though the murder occurred in his sub-Division, McIntosh would retain primacy.

The dead girls face flashed before him and he realised that to have the inexperienced DI run the inquiry would be a mistake, that there was a much better opportunity of detecting the killer if he were in charge.

Taking a deep breath, he said, "I'll keep this one, Mark, if that's all right with you, though I'll need you to run the Incident room. How do you feel about running the inquiry from the Portacabin at the rear of your office?"

McIntosh deliberately posed the question in such a manner that he believed Renwick would not be offended at having the murder inquiry removed from him, but hoped the DI would seize the opportunity to learn the intricacies of running such an inquiry from the hub.

To his surprise, there was a tangible expression of relief in Renwick's face as almost with eagerness, he nodded and replied, "I'll get it started sir. Eh, do you want me to allocate the inquiry team or…."

"No, leave that with me. We'll begin with four of your guys; you can pick them and I'll muster half a dozen from Govan. Right," he began to walk down the path, "let's talk as we walk and we'll get started."

With Renwick trailing a step behind, it occurred to McIntosh that the DI had been so relieved at being unburdened with the murder inquiry he hadn't even glanced into the bushes to inspect the scene.

McIntosh and Renwick walked down the hill and nearing the park gate, the DCI fetched a packet of Woodbine from his jacket pocket and lighting up, drew deeply on the fag. The CID aide Simon Johnson had just arrived and was standing just inside the gate, in conversation with a uniformed cop.

"Johnson," Renwick imperiously called out and beckoned him over, "With me," then turning towards the DCI said, "I'll return to Pollok now sir and get the Incident room set up. Is there anything else?"

McIntosh almost laughed out loud. It was obvious to a blind man that Renwick was trying to stamp his authority over the acting detective and anyone else that was listening. "No, Mister Renwick," he formally replied, respecting the DI's rank in front of his subordinates, "just let me know when you've set up and I'll get the box up to you."

Listening to the exchange between his bosses, Simon Johnson wondered what the box was, but thought it prudent to wait and ask later.

As though in afterthought, McIntosh turned to Simon and asked, "Did you get here in a CID vehicle?"

"Yes boss," replied Johnson, "the wee Metro."

"Good," then smiling, turned and said to Renwick, "Is it okay if I hijack the young guy, Mark?"

Tight-lipped, Renwick simply nodded.

"Thanks, right son," he turned to Simon, "wait till the undertakers bring the body down from the hill and follow their hearse to the mortuary. Once you're there, stay with the body till I get someone to join you. I want you to be the continuity of the body being removed from here and arriving at the mortuary. I'll get someone sent over to neighbour you and both of you will be present when the body is stripped of clothing and anything else that might be pertinent, understood?"

Simon nodded, his eyes wide and alert for any further instruction.

"I'll see that production bags are brought along so that you can take possession of the lassie's clothing and anything that might be of evidential value. Got that son?"

Simon, his mouth dry, again nodded, realising that almost straight away, he was being pitched into the murder inquiry and felt a flutter of excitement in his stomach.

"Got that sir," he finally said.

McIntosh refrained from smiling, recognising the young aide's eagerness and waved him away to his car. With a final instruction that Renwick ensure the park be thoroughly searched by the uniformed Support Group officers in attendance, McIntosh wearily walked towards the detective waiting to drive him to Govan office.

CHAPTER 2

Lizzie McLeish was puzzled. It just wasn't like Alice not to return home after an evening on the Drag. Her left hand supporting her right elbow, Lizzie gnawed at the quick of her fingers where the nails had once been and worried that without Alice's contribution, Wingy might not come across with the wrap that they both so badly needed. Already Lizzie's skin was crawling and she knew that within the next couple of hours, the sweats would start and then it would get progressively worse, starting with the shakes then the cramps and she didn't want to even consider how much worse it would get after that.

She sat down in the dark of the lounge with the curtains pulled tightly closed and still dressed in the stained nightdress, wrapped her arms about her thin legs and, though the day outside was warm, shivered in the coolness of the room. She shook her head as though this would clear her memory, trying to recollect where she had last seen Alice. She remembered them sharing a spliff in a dark corner of Anderston bus station, but couldn't remember at what time. Alice had just finished giving a punter a hand-job and they had laughed together as Alice described the man's panic when the polis patrol car had routinely passed by and almost caught them, him with his trousers round his ankles and his hands under her flimsy top, feeling her tits.

She glanced at the cheap clock that hung at an angle on the wall. The clock ran a few minutes' fast and displayed almost ten o'clock, but with no way to contact Alice, she knew she had one of two choices. Wait till her friend turned up or take what little money she had earned and try to persuade Wingy to give her some smack on the drip.

Yeah, like that's going to fucking happen, she cynically thought in the sure knowledge the one-armed junkie would not even consider giving her any kind of time to pay off a wrap. Wingy was not known for his generosity.

Once again, she wondered where her flatmate had gotten to and it occurred to her that maybe Alice had pulled an all-nighter with a punter, perhaps a tourist. Yes, that would be it and seized on this thought rather than the alternative, the waking nightmare that haunted all the working girls in the city, the worst-case scenario. A sudden fear seized her and her thin arms tightened even more about her legs.

Following the unmarked hearse, in reality a grey coloured windowless Transit van that bore the legend on the side 'Private Ambulance', through the south side of the city towards the mortuary located beside the High Court at the Saltmarket, Simon could hardly contain his excitement at almost immediately being involved in the murder inquiry. When the hearse arrived at the mortuary and reversed towards the rear doors in the small receiving enclosure, he parked the Metro outside and watched as the undertakers carefully manhandled the shell onto a wheeled trolley, up the ramp and into the building. A mortuary attendant wearing a spotlessly clean brown dustcoat took charge of the trolley and shell and bidding the hearse attendants a smiling 'Cheerio', beckoned to the young officer to follow him. Simon had only visited the mortuary during his induction training and then in the company of fellow recruits. As the attendant pushed the squeaking trolley, it occurred to Simon the wheels could do with a spot of WD40 and he watched as the attendant pushed the trolley through a set of scratched, heavy-duty plastic doors. The first thing he noticed was the strong smell of formaldehyde that assailed his nostrils.

"Here we go then," the attendant turned and smiled at him, his soft Welsh accent at odds with the guttural dialect of the native Glaswegian. "On your own are you, boy?"

"Eh, I've a neighbour due to meet me here anytime," replied Simon, curious as to why the small, slightly built man made him feel nervous. Was it the place and the atmosphere, he wondered or the ghoulish nature of the man's occupation. The attendant led him through a narrow corridor that in turn opened into a long, spacious and brightly lit room, the daylight pouring in from windows set high in the walls on both sides. Five tables were spaced along the room at intervals while against one wall were built-in stainless steel sinks. Over each sink was a flexible hosepipe attached to a restraining hook that seemed to Johnson to resemble a hovering Cobra snake about to strike at its prey.

"You've time for a cuppa then, eh boy?" said the attendant, manoeuvring the trolley to rest against the first of the long, metal tables and applying the brake to the wheels. As he stared at it, Simon saw the table had a slight downwards camber towards the centre and at regular intervals, was pockmarked with holes each the size of a five-pence piece. A flexible hose similar to that attached to the sinks lay coiled on the table. With an inward gulp he realised he was looking at an autopsy table and could not resist a glance at the shell.

"Tea or coffee?" asked the attendant, trying not to smile at the pale faced young detective.

"Eh, am I not supposed to stay with the body?" he asked.

"I don't think she's going anywhere son. Besides, my room," he nodded with his head, "is the other side of the door there, so nobody can pass without us seeing them, eh? So, tea or coffee?"

"Ah, coffee will be fine thanks," replied Simon, the smell of the place catching in his throat and silently wishing that the other officer would soon arrive and get him away from this place.

The attendant led him through to a small sitting room, comfortably furnished with two armchairs and a small coffee table and, seemingly aware of Simon's reluctance to leave the body alone, pushed the door wide open to permit Simon a full view of the corridor outside. Upon a worktop in a corner sat a kettle and a small fridge, tea and coffee jars and mugs. The volume of a small, red coloured transistor radio was turned down low but Simon could just make out The Jam's 'A Town Called Malice' being played.

He lowered himself into one of the armchairs while the attendant introduced himself as Marty. "Marty the mortician, they call me," he laughed and as he spoke, Simon relaxed, realising the little man was trying to put the younger man at his ease.

Ten minutes of polite conversation had just passed, for the most part Marty regaling Simon with ghoulish but comical mortuary stories, when a female voice called out, "Hello? Marty, you there pal?"

The sitting room door opened and Johnson, with some relief, saw it was Glenda Burroughs, the Detective Inspector from the Govan office. In one hand she carried a large paper bag that itself contained further paper bags and labels. Setting them down on the floor beside the chair vacated by Marty, she sat down and said, "Ah, there you are young man. Feet up and cuppa in hand already? My goodness, young Simon, you're not slow are you?" she grinned at him and then turned towards Marty, "Taffy, my lovely wee man. Couldn't do an old girl a coffee, can you dear? Milk, two sugar."

Of course, Simon knew who Burroughs was and had seen her at the office throughout his service but still, he could not resist a surreptitious glance at her. Burroughs, suspected to be the wrong side of forty, though it was never admitted, was a five foot, ten inch statuesque and extremely good-looking peroxide blonde whose shoulder length, curly locks never lost their shape. Wearing a pale blue blouse and navy blue skirted suit with matching shoes and handbag, she dressed every day as though she were attending a fashion shoot and was the fantasy of many of her male colleagues, though she was not known to date cops. It was widely rumoured that Burroughs maintained a discreet, intimate relationship with a wealthy man, but had never disclosed nor alluded to her beau's identity. What was not disputed was Burroughs undoubted skill as an investigator and some said, had it not been for the glass ceiling that pervaded the hierarchy of the gender conscious police management, Burroughs would have long since been promoted to a more responsible rank.

"In case you're wondering young Simon at me being here to neighbour you, the simple explanation is decorum. The deceased is a young woman and the DCI quite rightly thought it would be proper to have a female officer attend the removal of the clothing from the deceased. As it happens, I was the only woman in the office at the time."

Sitting in the second armchair, Burroughs caught Simon subtly glancing at her long legs and inwardly smiled. Men were so predictable, even the younger ones, but she wasn't offended. Contrarily, she was secretly delighted that she could still retain their interest.

"So the deceased, presumably she is through in the long room?" she asked.

"Yes Ma'am," replied Simon, relieved at Burroughs arrival and blushing with the knowledge that she had caught him looking at her legs.

Marty handed her a strong, black coffee and said, "I took a call from your office earlier Glenda, about the time for the PM. I've checked the diary and Mister Hammond will be available at two o'clock this afternoon, if that suits your boss. Who is it, by the way?" he asked.

"Gordon McIntosh at Govan," she pursed her lips and blew cool air across the top of the mug, then set it down on a low table before getting to her feet. "I'll finish this later. Ready?" she asked Simon, already standing.

"Yes Ma'am," he nodded, inwardly praying that he wouldn't mess this up.

Burroughs smiled tightly at him, recognising his nervousness then both of them followed Marty along the corridor to the long room.

Gordon McIntosh sat at his desk, one hand running through his thinning light brown hair as he read again the notes he had scribbled and a half smoked cigarette held between the fingers of the other hand. His eyes narrowed as he marked a tick against the names of the officers he would deploy to the murder investigation and a cross against those who would continue to deal with the day to day criminal inquiries, what the city detectives called 'on the book.'

The desk phone at his elbow rang and he reached for it, answering, "DCI McIntosh."

"Boss," said the hurried voice, "it's the duty officer downstairs. That's the Assistant Chief Constable of Operations on his way up the stairs to see you, sir."

"Thanks for the heads-up, Iain," replied McIntosh and replaced the receiver.

Less than a minute later his door knocked and without waiting for a response, John Murray strode into the room. A large, heavy set and imposing figure, Murray was acutely conscious of his appearance and never seen outside his Pitt Street office without his short, senior officer's silver tipped bamboo cane and carrying brown leather gloves. Despite all his effort at pomp and circumstance, it was Murray's bulbous red nose that first attracted attention. His uniform tunic sported the blue and white ribbon of the Long Service & Good Conduct Medal; an award some unkindly said for avoiding street duty by dancing between office bound job to office bound job, rather than the true purpose of completing the first twenty-two years of his almost thirty-five years service without incurring any complaint against his character. Indeed Murray, without apparent embarrassment, had been known to boast that his career was that of an administrator and even brag he had never given evidence in any court, a fact that completely baffled those officers who daily risked injury or worse in the pursuit of criminals and offenders.

It was widely rumoured that his Operations and Planning Department personnel had the highest turnover than any other department simply because his bullying attitude towards his staff.

"What's this about a body being discovered in Bellahouston Park!" he thundered at McIntosh, pointing his stick accusingly at the DCI.

"Good morning, Mister Murray," replied McIntosh, rising slowly and respectfully to his feet and indicating the chair in front of his desk.

In his mind, McIntosh recalled as a young constable early in his service, his old Sergeant imparting the advice, '*Respecting the rank, son, doesn't mean you have to respect the man.*'

"Yes, of course," huffed Murray. "Good morning Mister McIntosh. Now, what's this about a body?" he repeated, sitting down and placing his cane and cap on the desk in front of him.

McIntosh related the circumstances of the finding of the dead girl, her removal to the City Mortuary and his initial setting up of an Incident room at Pollok police office.

"Tut, tut," Murray shook his head. "You are aware of course that the Roman Catholic Pope is due to celebrate their bloody pagan mass there next Tuesday, aren't you?"

McIntosh swallowed the laughter that threatened to engulf him.

Even with the advent of the progressive police and with the introduction of diversity and tolerance to police training, Murray made no secret of his pride in his Freemasonry as well as a regular attendee and Elder of the Free Presbyterian Church of Scotland. Murray's numerous critics alleged that both organisations had assisted his promotional career movement within the Force, culminating in his current rank and thereby avoided the trials and tribulations of real police work. "I am aware sir," McIntosh stonily replied, "however, this is a murder inquiry and regardless of whether or not the Pontiff is arriving next week, I must conduct my inquiry to detect the killer of this young woman. I mean, you wouldn't have it any other way, now would you sir?"

Murray's face turned pale at the inferred slight. "I understand the victim is a drug abuser," he replied, unable to hide the sneer in his voice.

McIntosh felt his own face turn pale. How the devil did he find that out and in such a short time, he wondered and almost immediately realised that he had a leak, that someone was directly feeding Murray information. He knew that he should question how Murray came by this information, but also knew that Murray would never divulge his source, for why would he give up his spy in the camp? No, he'd simply use the old polis adage, that he kept his podgy finger on the pulse.

"There is a suggestion," McIntosh reluctantly replied, "that the victim might have used drugs, but of course I'll need to await the outcome of the post mortem and blood analysis to confirm that suggestion."

Murray snorted his displeasure. "You do understand that I have committed a large number of resources to this Catholic Pope's visit, Mister McIntosh? I want this matter cleared up as quickly as possible. I will not have my…" he paused and McIntosh saw Murray's throat tighten. "I will not have the Chief Constable embarrassed by the discovery of dead….dead junkies," he almost spat the words out, "lying about the park when this Roman priest is due to arrive here with his followers, do you understand?"

"I understand sir, but I'm sure you appreciate the position that I find myself in," he smoothly replied, sensing that an opportunity had presented itself. "I've requested the assistance of Serious Crime Squad officers to complement my own team and await the response from their Detective Superintendent. However, I am restricted by my overtime budget and as you quite rightly point out, it is important we get this issue resolved quickly. Do I therefore have your permission to draw upon the Major Incident funds to resolve this issue? As you said yourself, I have less than one week to sort this out."

Murray baulked at replying, realising that by insisting the murder be quickly solved, he had more or less given the DCI *carte blanche* to do so. He inhaled and said, "I will ensure the Detective Superintendent at the Serious provides you with sufficient resources, however, as for extra funding, let's see how far you get first with the extra officers before we go down that road, eh?"

McIntosh knew there would be no arguing with the bigoted ACC and shrugging his shoulders, nodded. "Fair enough, sir. Now, is there anything more I can help you with?"

Murray stood and lifting his cane and replacing his cap on his head, simply replied, "Get it done, Mister McIntosh," then turned on his heel and left the room, leaving the door wide open behind him.

McIntosh stared at the open door and grinned. At least he had the extra officers. Turning to his notes, he re-read them and wondered, who are you hen and what dirty bastard left you out there all alone? Reaching for his phone, he dialled his home number and when it was answered, said, "Hi, it's me. Sorry love, the pictures are cancelled tonight. I've copped a bad one, a young girl."

Mary, his wife of twenty-four years sighed and asked if he was okay? He rightly guessed that the older he got, the more Mary worried herself about him.

"I'm fine. I'll see you when I get in," he concluded the call and made his way through to the general office to commence yet another murder inquiry.

Lizzie McLeish had almost arrived at the skin crawling state, but worryingly, there was still no word from Alice. She paced the flat, uncertain whether to leave and make her way to Wingy's place and try to negotiate at least enough of a wrap for a single hit or wait it out until Alice returned. Finally, the craving overcame her impatience. She hurriedly dressed in jeans and loose fitting sweat top, pulled on her worn training shoes and stuffed the too few crumpled notes she earned from the previous night into her pocket. With a final glance at the clock on the wall, Lizzie mumbled, "Sorry Alice," under her breath and closed the flat's front door behind her.

CHAPTER 3

The silence in the long room was almost as pervading as the smell of formaldehyde. The stripping of the young woman's few items of clothing from her body, conducted by Marty the mortuary attendant, was witnessed by both officers. Simon watched, surprised that though the victim in life had once been an attractive and shapely young woman, her body was tending towards being gaunt and wasted. He was surprised that he experienced no sense of feeling, nothing gratifying as her naked body lay exposed. Much later, in the privacy of his flat, he would examine his feelings as he recalled watching her clothing removed and surprised to find that retrospectively, he had been embarrassed and a little sad.

At the removal of each item in turn and with long practised routine, Marty handed the garment to Simon, who marked the description on a brown production label that all three signed before he individually placed each garment and the label into a plain brown, paper bag.

As he did so, Burroughs took a note of the item in her official police notebook. Once satisfied that each bag contained the correct item pertaining to the label, Burroughs demonstrated to Simon how to secure the top of the bag, first folding over the opening and then sealing it with a low adhesive, blue coloured tape. The clothing was now bound for the Forensic laboratory, but as a final measure against possible contamination or interference, Burroughs had Simon seal the top of each bag again by stapling the folded opening several times through the blue tape.

"There we are," she announced at last, "all done shipshape and proper, eh?"

"Yes ma'am," replied a bemused Johnson, slightly confused at the lengthy procedure and asked her why the clothing was not all just placed in the one bag. "Have you heard of Locard's Exchange Principle?" asked Burroughs.

Simon, carrying the production bags in his hand, shook his head as they returned to Marty's small sitting room to finish their coffee.

"Okay here's your first lesson in crime detection," she smiled at him, fetching her cigarettes and lighter from her handbag. He was uncertain if her very sexy, husky voice was natural or the result of her heavy smoking habit. What was obvious was the absence of any smell of tobacco adhering to her; just the faintest fragrance of scented perfume that he guessed was expensive.

"Probably the most basic and easy way to explain it," began Burroughs, unconsciously slipping into the role of tutor cop, "is like this. A Frenchman called Edmond Locard, who was an early twentieth century advocate of crime scene investigation, expounded the theory that when there is contact between two items and regardless what those items are, there will always be an exchange of material, no matter how small. Therefore, a good detective should always consider this at a crime scene and always suspect there will be some sort of trace evidence left. My understanding from DCI McIntosh is that the victim was probably raped. If indeed she was, regardless of any possible evidence of sexual activity, that suggests to me that the culprit has probably lain beside, perhaps on top of or at least brushed against her and if he has, there is most likely been an exchange of trace evidence between them both. It might be a thread, a hair follicle, a spotting of blood or whatever. If there is, we're fortunate in Strathclyde Police to have an excellent Forensic Laboratory and if it is there, they'll find it. That's why it's so important to individually separate each item of clothing."

She could see that while Simon understood most of what she had said, there was still a shadow of doubt in his eyes.

She smiled and continued. "Look, let's say for example a hair follicle is found on the outside of her dress and we match it, say to John Smith or whoever. His defence might be that he danced with the victim or bumped into her or she sat on a seat he had just vacated and that's how the transference occurred, how the follicle came to be upon her dress, yeah?"

Simon nodded.

"But let's say instead we find the same hair follicle on her underwear or the low adhesive tape swabbing by the Scene of Crime people at the locus finds a hair stuck to her skin under her dress, how does he explain that, eh?"

"Got it ma'am," he replied, feeling a little foolish.

She smiled patiently at him. "I've being doing this for a while now Simon. Don't try to take it all in at once. Besides, if you do well as an aide and apply for the CID, you'll get all this on your detective course at Tulliallan."

Privately he thought *if* he got through his attachment and *was* selected for CID. To be a fully-fledged detective was something that Johnson really wanted and aspired to be. Then her remembered and asked, "DCI McIntosh mentioned the box was to be taken up to Pollok to the incident room. What's the box Ma'am?"

Burroughs sipped at her coffee and grinned. "There's nothing particularly special about it. It is what it says it is; just a big, oversized cardboard box that is packed and held in readiness for any major crime that requires an incident room to be set up. It contains all the different inquiry forms and stationary items that the DI and his team will need when they're running the incident room. Oh, that and the tin for collecting the cash for the tea-fund," she grinned at him. "We mustn't forget the tea-fund tin. Right, Simon my boy, get those production bags up to Forensics at Pitt Street and a word of advice. When you hand them over, make sure at the handover you that you see that each item is *properly* logged and itemised. You are the continuity from the deceased to the Lab, so be careful that you mark everything down in your notebook. You might end up having a speaking part at court if we arrest someone for the murder and if this ever goes to trial." She stared him in the eye to emphasis her point, "There have been cases lost because the proper procedure wasn't adhered to, okay?"

"Yes ma'am," replied a chastened Simon and inwardly thought, no pressure then. Their coffee gulped down, they both said cheerio to Marty and headed for their vehicles.

The ground floor flat of the rundown tenement building located in Garscube Road had just one occupant.

John 'Wingy' Price cursed loudly as he tried in vain to get the Betamax video player to work. No matter what buttons he pressed the tape wouldn't turn and he angrily vowed to get even with the conniving bastard who had swapped the stolen machine for the half dozen spliffs.

Not yet reached his thirty-second year, Wingy was what the local police division recorded in their files as a minor drug dealer and resetter of stolen property. However, while in his late teens, he had been a prolific and elusive housebreaker. Several years previously and unfortunately for him, one dark and windy night, while climbing a drain pipe at the rear of a block of tenement flats, Wingy had reached the second floor and was precariously balanced on a ledge while attempting to prise open a bedroom window. According to the tenant of the flat who was wakened by a scraping noise, she pushed open the window only to see a white and shocked face. With a shrill scream from both her and Wingy, she ran for help while he plummeted backwards to the ground.

The attending police officers summoned by the tenant immediately recognised the thief and with some satisfaction, at first thought him dead and considered sticking a chamois rag in his hand and writing off the incident as a window washing exercise gone wrong.

However, Wingy exhaled, moaned and with some reluctance, the officers summoned and ambulance whose crew was later credited with saving his life, if not his left arm.

Hence his nickname, Wingy.

He startled at the tapping on the glass of the kitchen window and for one, heart stopping moment, thought the polis were coming again for him. Cautiously, he pulled aside the back bedroom curtain and sneaked a look outside, then breathed a sigh of relief when he saw the young woman with her head bowed and her arms wrapped about her thin body. It was only the prossie, Lizzie McLeish. He scanned the area round about her and satisfied she was on her own, knocked on the glass and with his one hand and raised the protesting sash window up a few inches.

Lizzie hurried over and head bent down to the gap, pleadingly whispered, "Wingy, can you sell me a wrap? I'm desperate here, man. I've only got ten quid to my name. I'll give you the rest of the money tomorrow morning, first thing. I'm working tonight, so I am and I'll get the cash easy, so I will. Honest to God, Wingy, I'll pay you back first thing in the morning. You know I'm good for it."

"I don't do credit Lizzie, you know that," he sneered back at her. "It's cash up front or nothing. If you've got ten quid, I'll do you a tenner bag, but no credit, understand?"

"Jesus, Wingy, you know me," she was almost beseeching him now, "I don't let you down, for fuck's sake. I'm one of your best customers, so I am."

His eyebrows knitted in curiosity and a sudden desire coursed through his nether region. "Where's your pal, the one with the funny accent? Where's she at, eh?"

"I don't know," Lizzie mumbled, now starting to hurt and then, as much as the very thought of him touching her sickened her, she realised she had no other option. "Look, if I promise to bring the money tomorrow you can," she hesitated and bit at her lower lip as though the very words would choke her, "have a wank now. For free. Then can I get wrap?"

Wingy grinned at her offer. The only birds he managed sex with these days were the prostitutes who came to him for their smack and their joints, the ones that could not meet his prices. He stared at Lizzie, enjoying the satisfying thrill of making her wait as though he was considering his decision though if he had the choice, he would have preferred her pal.

Sighing, he finally leered at her and said, "Hang on a minute, I'll need to get the door unbolted then we can discuss exactly what you can do for me, eh?"

CHAPTER 4

The teenager, sixteen on his next birthday, stood in the small, but neat and tidy galley and feet apart to counter the gentle sway of the boat, spooned two large dollops of cocoa into the once-white enamel mugs. When with a whistle the old brass kettle steaming away on the small gas stove finally came to the boil, he carefully filled both mugs two thirds full and then from a carton in the tiny cupboard, spooned in some clotted cream.

With a mug in each hand, he cautiously stepped over the doorstep and walked out onto the scrubbed decking and towards the tall man who stood looking over the port side towards the brightly coloured orange buoys that spread out for several hundred yards across the bay.

"Here you go, Mister Trelawney," said the boy, handing the man a mug.

"Thanks Jack."

Crispin Trelawney smiled at the young lad and turning, stared again at the buoys. "You seem a little worried, Mister Trelawney," said Jack.

He nodded in response and quietly sighed. "It's the weather, lad. The unusually fine weather that's got me a little concerned," he replied. "The last couple of weeks, the lobster pots have been overfilled and yes, I agree that can't be a bad thing for the sales, eh?" he smiled at Jack. "But what we don't want is to either exceed our Fisheries Department quota or over fish the stock."

"Can't you just throw back the smaller lobsters?"

"That's an idea," he smiled then turned and the smile developed into a wide grin and his dark eyes mischievously twinkled, "but where's the profit in that, eh?"

The two of them stood in comfortable silence sipping at their cocoa as the elderly, but sturdy forty foot fishing smack gently rocked beneath them, the white cross on the black background of the Cornish flag on the mast above them barely registering the slight breeze.

The slim young lad was on the threshold of manhood and stood erect beside the tall, muscular man, whose thick black hair, now showing a tinge of grey, curled over his collar, the dark colour matching his neatly trimmed beard. Both wore stained, navy blue coloured coveralls and tight fitting sea boots. The man's hands were large and calloused, his forearms and biceps bulging with muscle from working the nets that he dropped during the summer months and daily strung across the bay outside the small fishing village of Hayle. Sipping at their mugs, they both stared across the half-mile or so of sea to the shoreline, where whitewashed cottages were clearly visible in the bright sunlight and typical of those that dotted the Cornish coastline.

Trelawney placed a hand on the gunwale and leaned over the side to stare into the water. The warm air drifting in from the America's and the current of the Gulf Stream that without fail, annually guaranteed fine weather, was the main attraction for the large number of tourists to the area and who in turn, enjoyed the many seafood restaurants in the villages all along the coast. It was to these local restaurants that Trelawney supplied the lobster and other shellfish that provided him with his regular income. He inhaled deeply and once again, he considered himself fortunate to be part of a tight knit and caring community. A darkness flashed through his mind and briefly he recalled it had not always been so and as he breathed in the salty air, he gave an inward shudder at past memories.

"You okay Mister Trelawney?"

"Yes Jack," he smiled at the concern etched on the youngsters face, "I'm grand so I am, so let's be collecting these pots now and once that's done, it'll be the 'Pirates Cove' for a couple of pasties each, then a pint for me and a Coke for you, eh?"

"Grand, Mister Trelawney," the young lad grinned back and taking the mug from Trelawney's fist, returned them both to the galley before pulling on the heavy-duty working gloves.

It was just gone midday and the sun was unforgiving in the sky over Pollok police office. Within the narrow confines of the CID general office, DCI Gordon McIntosh faced the hastily assembled inquiry team, who either sat or stood crowded together. A pall of cigarette smoke curled towards the nicotine stained ceiling and though the old, metal framed windows were thrown open wide, more than one officer coughed in the fuggy atmosphere. A chalkboard behind McIntosh had been set up and upon it was sketched a rough outline of Bellahouston Park. In a short and concise recounting of events leading up to the discovery of the body, McIntosh outlined the duties of the assembled detectives.

"As you will already know, DI Mark Renwick will head up the incident room from the Portacabin at the rear of the office and will be ably assisted by DS Brian Davidson, who will act as action inquiry allocator and double up as statement reader. Most of you and in particular our colleagues from the Serious Crime Squad," he nodded to the eight officers who crowded together at one side, "will have experience working on a murder inquiry, so I won't try to teach my granny to suck eggs. DI Glenda Burroughs will act as the liaison between the incident room, the Fiscal's Department, Forensics and Scenes of Crime and will be responsible for all productions and, once we get the victim identified, also act as the family liaison."

His head swivelled as he searched the small room and he smiled when his eyes alighted on Simon Johnson, half hidden behind a portly detective.

"ADC Johnson, you'll neighbour DI Burroughs, so don't bring any money to work or she'll have you paying daily for lunch and let me tell you, it's not pie and chips with that woman, it's fancy coffee shops with fancy prices."

As he hoped, the room erupted in laughter and McIntosh smiled with a slight relief. Experience had taught him that one of the first difficulties bringing different officers together as a team was immediately binding them. Laughter, he knew, was always the best way forward and catching Burroughs eye, saw her slight nod of approval; that she too understood.

"Right," he continued, "you all know who you will be working with, but before you collect your action forms, is there any questions?"

A hand was raised from the back. "How close are we to establishing the victim's identity sir?"

"The victim was fingerprinted at the locus and her prints are with the Identification Bureau at Pitt Street as we speak, so if she has passed through our hands at any time, we'll find her. I should also say that I'm holding back meantime with a public appeal. I want to give the IB first crack at identifying her rather than posting information that I would rather retain for now." He paused and cleared his throat. "You will also have heard there is a suggestion she was raped. That suggestion, ladies and gentlemen, will not leave this room."

McIntosh deliberately did not inform his team of Doctor Robertson's observation that the victim was probably an intravenous drug abuser. He had discussed the issue with Glenda Burroughs and both agreed that human nature being as it is, some members of the inquiry team might privately make the decision that any dead junkie was no sad loss to society and thereby dilute their resolve in finding the victims killer. It was not an opinion held by either McIntosh or Burroughs, but both were long enough in the job to know that many officers considered drug abusers as second class citizens and not worthy of the attention bestowed on them by both the NHS and the police. Besides, McIntosh had argued, the injections might be for a legitimate medical condition, though both he and Burroughs knew this was probably unlikely.

When the briefing broke up and the team sent to collect their action forms, McIntosh called Burroughs and Simon into the privacy of the DI's room and closed the door behind them.
"I'm about to head over to the Saltmarket for the PM," he began and then turned to the younger man. "DI Burroughs will accompany me Simon, but I'll need someone there to convey the body samples to the Forensic Medical Faculty at Glasgow University. It's just as you did with the victims clothing, the continuity of evidence, eh? I am guessing you will not have previously attended a PM and it won't be a nice experience, but it is an opportunity for you, a kind of learning curve as it were if indeed you do have aspirations to join us in the CID. However, I won't think any less of you if you decide to refuse. Are you up for it, son?"
Simon gulped, realising that he was being offered the opportunity to participate in an important part of the investigation. He could hardly speak for excitement and simply nodded, but then he found his voice. "Aye sir, I'll not let you down."
"Good lad. Right Glenda, if you travel with me and if you, Simon," he smiled at him, "grab a set of car keys from DI Renwick and we'll meet you at the mortuary."

Safely back in her flat, Lizzie McLeish was becoming increasingly worried at Alice's absence. Sure, her friend had stayed away overnight before and she wryly grinned at the last time, when Alice fell for the promises and thought the punter was going to set her up in her own flat. Poor, stupid Alice, she thought, falling for the patter like that.
In the bathroom, Lizzie lifted the loose tile and with shaking fingers, probed in the recess beneath for the small tobacco tin that contained her works; the bent spoon, the short length of rubber tubing to tie round her arm and the syringe. Shit, she'd forgot to get the lighter and scrambling to her feet, hurried through to the kitchen drawer to fetch the cheap, disposal lighter they used to light the gas ring. By now she was sweating and anxiously returned to the bathroom and quickly prepared the heroin. Sitting on the closed toilet lid, it didn't take long for her to fill the syringe and tightening the rubber band, worked the syringe into a vein before releasing the powerful narcotic into her blood. Her body shuddered at the sudden shock as the drug swept through her system and eyes fluttering, her mouth open and unconsciously drooling, she slid unceremoniously to the floor. Now slumped with her back against the bath, she lay still and tried to ignore the nausea that overtook her, the powerful drug dissolving all thought of Alice from her mind.

While Glenda Burroughs drove, Gordon McIntosh recounted the visit earlier that morning from ACC John Murray and McIntosh's suspicion that there was a leak, that someone had informed Murray about the victim probably being a drug abuser.

"Don't get paranoid, Gordon," Burroughs replied, concentrating on the traffic that slowly crawled along Clyde Street. "It needn't be anyone in our department. It could just as easily be one of the Scene of Crime personnel or a cop that was in attendance at the locus. You know how these things get started. There's nobody gossips like the polis. Saying that though, I have to admit that we both know Murray's a political creature and he's tight with the Police and Fire Committee councillors and I needn't remind you whose father sits on that board."

Her brow knitted in concentration as to McIntosh's horror, she weaved between a lorry and a parked Mini, in his mind almost taking the paint from his passenger door. "Nevertheless," she continued, oblivious to his concern, "would Renwick be that stupid? I mean, just how far can you trust him without worrying that he's going to pass everything he learns to Murray. I mean, do you think he's capable of passing information?"

McIntosh softly exhaled and stole a glance at the mad woman driving and then replied, "He might if he thought that touting to Murray would advance his career."

He sighed and continued, "You're right. I just don't like the man and I particularly don't like having to watch my back, but he's a Detective Inspector and like it or lump it he's part of the inquiry. I just can't ignore him."

Burroughs nodded and turning to grin at him, said, "I bet he was delighted you gave him the incident room job."

"That was one of my better decisions today. He's far too inexperienced to let loose and God forgive me," he shook his head, "but I just couldn't trust him to competently handle the murder inquiry on his own."

"As you said though, like it or lump it, there will come the day when he will be thrown into the deep end and will have to deal with a major incident on his own. That said, don't you think it might be a good idea to have him shadow you, watch how you work and deal with things? I mean it's all very well putting him away for the time being into the Incident room where he can't do much harm, but somebody, some time will need to instruct him how to manage a major incident. Besides, that way you can keep a closer eye on him."

"I know that Glenda, but here's the thing. I really don't care anymore."

He rubbed at his brow and decided that given the length of time he had known his friend, he might as well take her into his confidence.

"This will be my last inquiry. I've got my thirty years in next month and to be honest, I'm tired. I had thought of maybe giving it an extra year, but with the annual leave that is due to me I could probably finish up today and just go, but I won't leave during a murder; that's just not my style. I've talked it over with Mary and we've both decided enough is enough."

Burroughs risked a glance at him and seeing he was serious, decided to let him talk.

He shook his head and said, "I've had a confidential chat with the head of Personnel and she's sending me pension details so once I've sorted that out and finished this inquiry, I'm off, no looking back, no regrets; just gone."

"Who else have you told, in the Department I mean?"

"I had a word with the ACC (Crime) and advised him that I intend leaving, but didn't mention a specific date. Of course, I want to keep it quiet meantime, you understand?"

Burroughs didn't get the opportunity to reply for the car radio activated with a message for McIntosh, requesting that he contact the Fingerprint Department at Pitt Street as soon as possible. He acknowledged the call just as Burroughs pulled up outside the mortuary. Turning to her, he said, "I'll make the call and join you in the long room. Give Mister Hammond my apologies and tell him I'll be as quick as possible."

DI Mark Renwick settled himself behind the desk in the Portacabin and without looking up from his desk, instructed DS Brian Davidson to, "Go and stick the kettle on, Sergeant, there's a good lad."

Davidson, Renwick's senior by almost twelve years and with over twenty-seven years police service, turned white with inward rage at the *"...good lad"* jibe. Among his colleagues, Davidson was considered a reserved individual and angrily considered telling the cheeky bastard to put the kettle on himself. Biting his tongue, he reconciled himself that day in and day out for the foreseeable future anyway, he would have to work with the sod and saw no sense in starting off acrimoniously.

Listening to Renwick's instruction to the hapless Davidson, the Serious Crime Squad officers standing waiting to be allocated their action forms, stared at each other. The DI wasn't known to any of them, though the word was that Renwick was well connected. As one, the common thought that run through most of their minds was a relief that he was the incident room manager and not in charge of the inquiry.

Davidson shuffled out of the room and inwardly smirked. Renwick wouldn't see what went into the mug of tea when it was delivered to his desk and slowly started to roll the saliva about his mouth.

Simon Johnson stood when Glenda Burroughs entered Marty's sitting room in the mortuary.

"The boss is making a phone call from the office," she told him, pleased at his courtesy, "and he'll be with us in a minute or two." She turned towards Marty. "Is Mister Hammond here yet, my lovely wee Welsh wizard?"

Marty grinned as the booming voice said, "Right behind you my dear."

Julian Hammond, now in the twilight of his tenure as the Chief Pathologist of the City of Glasgow, laid a fatherly hand on Burroughs shoulder as he nudged past her. Slightly stooped, as are many tall men, Hammond's thick, shoulder length white hair was swept back, wire glasses perched on the end of his nose and a ruddy complexion that betrayed his fondness for whisky. His age could have been anything between sixty and eighty years. Dressed is an old tweed jacket with leather patches at the elbows under which he wore a flowery, round collared shirt with a bright red cravat and crumpled brown corduroy trousers, his slightly bizarre appearance could not disguise the brightness in his eyes.

"Don't know who you are, young man," he addressed Simon, "but do an old man a favour and stick the kettle on, there's a good chap, eh? Coffee, just milk," he added, then turned to Burroughs, "Now, my dear where's that bugger McIntosh? You did bring him with you, didn't you? And the Fiscal's Department, have they sent their rep over yet?"

Burroughs nodded and replied, "Gordon's on the blower to Fingerprints, Mister Hammond, possibly regarding identification of the victim." Her head cocked at the sound of high heels clicking along the tiled floor of door. "I think that might be the Fiscal Depute now," she smiled as a young, dark haired woman hesitantly poked her head in the door.

"Well, let's hope Gordon is successful, dear lady, let's hope so. You must be the Fiscal depute, my dear," he greeted the nervous young woman. Cigarette?" he offered her, pulling a silver case from an inside pocket and revealing heavily nicotine stained fingers.

The Depute declined as did Burroughs and Simon, who handing Hammond a cup and saucer, recalled seeing the young, pretty Depute at the park earlier that morning.

They waited and chatted for a few minutes then McIntosh arrived at the door. "Hello Mister Hammond," he greeted the elderly pathologist and nodded to the Depute. "That was Fingerprints. They've identified the victim, an Alice Trelawney," he said to the room and then added, "We have a last known address Glenda, so when we're done here you and I have a visit to make."

CHAPTER 5 - Late Thursday Afternoon

DS Brian Davidson was bored. For the umpteenth time he checked the few actions he had assigned against the log, straightened his pencils uniformly on the pad, tapped idle fingers against the desk, cast a quick glance round to ensure nobody was near enough to hear then silently farted and sighed with contented relief. He knew it was always like this at the outset of any inquiry, the initial statements routine and mainly relative to the discovery of the body. Had the dead girl been found in a housing scheme or any kind of residential area, there would have been the opportunity for door-to-door inquiries, but discovered as she was in the isolation of parkland, nothing could be pursued until such time that she was positively identified. Then the team could start chasing down family and friends and local haunts she used, but until then he had to find some way to keep the team occupied and motivated. He glanced over to where Renwick sat reading the

'Glasgow News'. A much experienced incident room operator, Davidson had offered to take the DI through the procedure that was the backbone to the incident room; the logging of action reports, statements, the indexing of persons, vehicles, addresses and locations and the dozen or so other administrative duties that ensured a well run and orderly inquiry. Renwick had curtly declined, telling Davidson that was his job while Renwick would 'oversee'.

In other words, Davidson bristled, the skiving bastard didn't intend doing a hands turn, but would leave it all to him.

Driving slowly along Kelvin Way towards the Forensic Medical Faculty building at Glasgow University, Simon Johnson's thought were still filled with the post mortem procedure conducted on the young girl. Bloody hell he thought, his body shivering at the memory; have I led a sheltered life.

He hadn't previously considered the procedure of a PM; in his naivety simply imagining it was like something out of the popular American television programme '*Quincy, M.E.*' in which the actor Jack Klugman, who played the title role of a medical examiner investigated all kind of homicides. Watching the show like millions of other viewers, Simon assumed Quincy was cutting a small hole and peering in to the victim's body and from that deduced how the victim had died, but what Simon had seen at the young girls post mortem so shocked him he seriously doubted he would hold down any food for at least a week.

How anyone could stand that day in, day out was beyond him and holding the steering wheel tightly, he again shuddered at the memory. Throughout the procedure, the pathologist Mister Hammond had chatted away to the DCI and the DI, telling them of his recent holiday in France and of the wines the cheeses he had brought home. Hammond didn't seem at all fazed when the young Fiscal Depute fainted into Simon's arms. It had been a fortunate distraction and, if he was honest enough to admit it, a toss-up as to whether it was Simon or the young woman who was going to be first to pass out.

He grinned, recalling DI Burroughs and him carrying the Depute to Marty the attendant's office and she nonchalantly grinning as she asked if he normally picked up his women in that way. He liked Burroughs and was pleased that the DCI has assigned him to work with her, believing that she could be a fount of knowledge if he did apply to join the CID.

Driving along the tree-lined avenue, Simon was conscious that they were almost now in full bloom with the fine seventeenth century architecture of the University buildings creating the perfect backdrop. Students of both gender and all ages and race wandered along both sides of the road, mostly carrying backpacks of satchels and nearly always heavy with books. To his surprise he saw a number wearing small Union flags on their bags in what he guessed was apparent support for the troops who were fighting halfway across the world, in the South Atlantic and almost immediately his brother Peter's face popped into his mind.

He risked a glance at the brown paper bag that lay on the seat beside him containing the glass sample vials and a cold shiver went up his spine at the knowledge that in those vials were not just blood taken from the dead girl, but tissue samples of her liver and kidney's and…

No, I won't think about it, he decided, shaking his head; it's the stuff of nightmares.

The brief glance at the paper bag was almost his undoing. When he raised his head a flash of colour passed before his eyes, causing him to violently swerve the Metro to the other lane, but fortunately for Simon, there was no vehicles coming his way. In panic, he stamped on the brake and came to a shuddering halt in the centre of the road, forgetting in his haste to depress the clutch and the Metro engine immediately stalled.

The whole thing has taken just two or three seconds and snapping his head around, he saw the cause of his near accident; a young woman on her hands and knees beside an old, rust coloured bicycle that now lay on the footpath, its wheels still spinning.

SHIT! was his initial thought. He made to open the drivers' door, but saw a black hackney taxi slowing as it approached him, the driver flashing his lights to indicate Simon move the Metro onto his own side of the road. Starting the engine, with one eye still on the girl who now was standing staring at him, Simon drove the Metro across the carriageway and parked a few yards from the girl.

Hastily, he opened his door, but had just got his legs out the car and onto the ground when the multi-coloured demon descended on him.

"What the *FUCK* did you think you were doing, you idiot!" the girl hissed at him, her fists raised to shoulder height.

He thought she was going to strike him and raised both hands defensively, shaking his head apologetically and replied, "I'm sorry, I'm so sorry. I didn't see you."

"Didn't see me?" the girl was incredulous, her eyes widening. "Look at me! How could you miss me!"

A few young people, mainly students he guessed, were beginning to stop and stare at the confrontation.

To his relief, the girl was obviously uninjured, though he reckoned her pride had taken a knock and as for not seeing her? He bit his lip to prevent himself from laughing. How could he have missed her, dressed as she was. Her auburn hair was piled beneath her multi-coloured Bob Marley beret type knitted woollen cap and over her jeans and lime green sweater she wore a knee length bright yellow kaftan coat and carried a pink coloured backpack on her shoulders.

"Look, let me out of the car please," he replied. She stepped back and he stood upright, seeing her to be just a couple of inches shorter than he was and nor did it escape his attention she was very, very pretty.

"I'm so very sorry. I got distracted…"

"With what," she fumed. "You were the only car on the road. How the hell could you not see me?" she pressed home the question.

Simon wasn't about to disclose what he carried on the front passenger seat and lamely shook his head. Over her shoulder, he saw the passers-by, sensing there wasn't going to be a fistfight, were now losing interest and shuffling off.

"Your bike," he pointed towards it, "Is it damaged?"

The girl, in her early twenties he guessed, huffily crossed her arms and scowled at him. "Betsy's all right, it's you that needs some attention, you stupid git," she snarled and without another word, strode off, picking her bike up and straddling it. With a further backward scowl, the girl cycled off towards the University.

He watched her ride away and shook his head at the near miss. She was right. How could he have been so bloody stupid? He might have killed her. Exhaling deeply, he got back into the Metro, started the engine and drove off.

Finding a parking space around the University was itself a problem and after almost ten minutes, he finally found a space on University Avenue and dumped the Metro in an empty 'Reserved' bay, sticking the car's police logbook on the dashboard in the hope that it might dissuade the 'yellow peril' from sticking a ticket on the window.

As he walked towards the Faculty building, his mood changed at the sight of an abundance of pretty female students, mostly dressed for the hot weather and by the time he reached the door of the building, he was feeling a little better from his encounter with the shrewish cyclist.

Simon was just turned twenty-six years of age and remembered with fondness his own time as a student, having graduated not at Glasgow, but from Stirling University with a Degree in Sports Fitness. The Degree had interested the police recruiter, not that Simon intended pursuing a fitness position with the police, but it demonstrated that he had the ability to both assimilate and interpret information and went some way to easing his entry to the Force. Of course, it didn't do him any harm that he was extremely fit and throughout his short career, where the shifts permitted, he continued to play both football and squash.

It took him just ten minutes to lodge the deceased's samples with the receiving attendant at the Forensic Medical Faculty and a few minutes later, with the receipts clutched in his hand, he was back at the non-ticketed Metro and returning towards the incident room at Pollok police office.

As he drove he regretted that the divisional CID cars had their domestic radios removed and glancing at his watch, wished he knew from the hourly news bulletin what was going on. He thought of his older brother Peter, who had by now presumably arrived with the Task Force at the Falkland Islands and promised himself that after work tonight, he would call his parents. No, he quickly changed his mind; he would *visit* them and spend some time with them because he knew they would be worrying themselves sick about their sailor son.

He retraced his route along Kelvin Way, his eyes keenly alert for the girl cyclist and turning eastwards onto Sauchiehall Street, drove towards the motorway.

His thoughts again turned to Marie.

After almost two years dating, they had spoken of marriage, having first agreed to move in together after finding the flat in Hollybrook Street in Shawlands, a steal at the time that they later purchased together. He sighed, almost with regret and shook his head; her lies and betrayal still raw and painful. During the first few weeks, it had been hard for Simon to come to terms with her leaving, packing her suitcase with the few things that she could stuff in and telling him through her tears she would send for the rest. She needed some time to herself, she had said. He naively believing her at that time and bewildered by her decision, unaware that for several months she had conducted a quiet affair with her married boss, for whom she finally admitted she was leaving Simon.

That gut-wrenching confession came later, in her letter.

The first few months had been financially tough. During that time he bought Marie out of the mortgage, intent on keeping the flat. At the outset, even with his parent's small monetary support, there were no luxuries with all his income either going towards the mortgage or the few basic shopping items he needed. But it had been worth it, he smiled; proud of the standard that he had brought to the once shabby flat that was now decorated and fully furnished, albeit mostly with second hand furniture courtesy of the Sally Army shop in Dumbarton Road. In the last year, the recession began to ebb and he saw the value of his flat surely, but slowly appreciate.

Driving onto the west bound lane of the M8 across the Kingston Bridge, he grinned at the memory of his mother's protestations that he was losing far too much weight, that he wasn't eating properly and her over the top subtle hint that he give up living alone and return home. He argued that wasn't a good idea while his father Michael, behind his wife's back, silently nodded agreement with his son.

Simon suspected her reasoning behind her argument was his mother had a maternal instinct to be needed. Her life was devoted to her husband and her children, but now with Peter serving as a Lieutenant in the Royal Navy and Simon living away from home, Alison Johnson had far too much time on her hands. The spare flat key he had given his parents in the event of any kind of emergency, had in the recent past been used to his mother who occasionally 'popped over' from her home in Muirend or 'just passed by' as she termed it. He didn't complain too hard and truthfully, enjoyed finding his washing and ironing done and neatly piled on the lounge settee and the place hoovered and dusted; well worth a bottle of her favourite white wine, once a week.

While he drove, Marie again occupied his thoughts and he smiled. He had been too eager, thinking that what he wanted from life she would also want. A couple of years his senior, she had dazzled him with her worldliness, her appreciation of the arts and her outgoing manner, her zest for life in general. Through time he had come to recognise what he had at first mistaken as her charm and flirting was a desire to experience more than he could provide. His brow wrinkled recalling her short temper when money was tight and how she would petulantly flare at the slightest criticism so that without realising it, Simon had begun to walk on eggshells when she was in one of her moods.

After the split and the betrayal aside, he had come to realise that he didn't really miss her as much as he feared he might and if he was brutally honest, come to accept that her leaving was in some sense, a relief.

There had been a few dates since Marie had gone, but none of the women had held his interest and all mutually parted company with Simon on good terms. Ruefully, he knew he was settling into bachelorhood far too early in life and at the urging of his good mate and fellow copper Bob Speirs, once more agreed to dinner; a foursome with Bob and his wife Sheila on Saturday evening at their house, a dinner that would include Sheila's pal.

Simon wasn't particularly fond of the idea of a blind date and truth be told, had never actually been on one, but allowed himself to be persuaded by Bob, who blatantly lied that it was Sheila's pal who needed the date, not Simon.

Ah well, he turned into the office backyard and inanely grinned. In for a penny…

Across the city, DCI Gordon McIntosh stepped out of the passenger door of the CID car as Glenda Burroughs locked the driver's door behind her. Standing together on the pavement they stared upwards at the dilapidated tenement building and then McIntosh glanced again at his handwritten note. "Nineteen Raglan Street right enough," he sighed, returning the note to his jacket pocket. There was no front door and he led Burroughs warily into the darkness of the dingy close. Almost immediately both wrinkled their noses at the smell of urine, fried food and faeces that all combined to cause Burroughs stomach to heave. Instinctively, her hand reached into her handbag for a perfumed handkerchief that she placed against her nose. "How the hell can people live in these conditions," she shook her head.

McIntosh turned and grinned at her. "If it's all you know it very quickly becomes your way of life," he shook his head.

None of the scrawled scraps of paper thumb tacked to the ground floor doors bore the name Trelawney and they climbed to the first floor, both carefully avoiding the undetermined brown material that sat in a neat little pile on the half landing. It seemed obvious that someone had used the landing as a makeshift toilet.

Somewhere near the top of the tenement they could hear the loud barking of a maddened dog.

The first door they arrived at had no name attached and McIntosh, almost under his breath, said, "Bugger this," and hammered with a fist on the door. He guessed the occupant had been listening at the door, for almost immediately they heard a bolt drawn back and the door opened a few inches, a thick security chain a visible deterrent to any would be thieves. The pale and wizened face of an old man peered at them. "What you wanting? Are you the polis? I've no done nothing wrong. So why are you banging on my fucking door, eh?" he spat out in quick succession.

McIntosh took a deep breath and forced himself to smile. "Sorry to bother you sir," he began, "but my colleague and I are trying to trace a young woman who lives in the close. Alice Trelawney. Do you know what flat she's in?"

The man's eyebrows knitted together and almost with a snarl, replied, "If that's the lassie with the funny accent, she lives with that wee prossie in there," and nodded across the landing to the opposite side of the landing. Without waiting for a response, the old man slammed his door closed.

"Result, eh?" grinned McIntosh and turned towards the unpainted door that bore no name.

Lizzie McLeish, still lying on the bathroom floor, heard the door being knocked then a few seconds later, knocked louder again.

"Alice," she weakly smiled and forced herself off the floor into a sitting position. The door was knocked a third time and even louder and she managed to shout, "I'm coming hen, for fuck's sake, give me a minute, will you?" and wondering why the stupid cow didn't use her key. Using the side of the bath, she pulled herself to her feet and stumbled from the bathroom through the small hallway to the front door, her voice stronger now as she shouted again at a further knock, "I'm coming, wait a minute, will you?"

She saw her own key in the lock and in her befuddled mind realised that Alice's key would not open the door if Lizzie's key were in the lock. Grinning like an idiot, she fumbled with the key and pulled open the door.

She wasn't prepared for the sight of the man and woman who stood there.

"Who…who are you? Where's Alice?" and then to her horror, with a stomach churning realisation and her knees suddenly shaking, she recognised just who the well dressed man and blonde woman must be, for they had were quite obviously the CID.

It was all she could do to stop her bowels moving.

Lizzie, sitting bent over on the old couch with her knees together and her arms wrapped about her, her straggly fair hair hanging limply and covering her face, wept uncontrollably.

McIntosh, having seen the distaste in Burroughs face, elected to sit on the couch beside the weeping girl and with a little hesitation, slowly placed a paternal arm about her shoulders.

"I'm very sorry to have broken the news like that, hen, but now I really need you to be strong, to help me because there's a lot of questions that I need to ask you, do you understand Lizzie?"

Lizzie tried to speak, but an overwhelming urge to vomit almost choked her and staggering to her feet, she rushed into the bathroom and expelled what remained of her stomach contents into the already stained bowl. As she retched, she knew her bladder had released and she was pissing herself then became aware of a hand holding back her hair and a cold, wet facecloth being applied to her forehead.

"Just take your time there, hen," said McIntosh's soft voice and then, "Here, hold my hand."

She felt his hand reach down and clasp her left hand that she squeezed tightly as another convulsion shook her body.

A few minutes passed and she felt a bit better. Gently, McIntosh assisted her to sit on the edge of the bath and crouching beside her, discreetly pushed Lizzie's tin and her works along the linoleum out of sight behind the toilet bowl.

"Feeling a wee bit better?" he asked.

She nodded, the soft tears still falling though with sorrow or shame at peeing herself while she vomited, she wasn't certain.

"Right then," McIntosh gently told her, "get yourself cleaned and when you're ready, come through to the front room. Or would you feel better coming down to the local cop shop for a wee cuppa?"

He saw the panic that crossed her face when he mentioned visiting the local station and fought hard to stop smiling, guessing that the young woman would be more eager to speak and provide a statement in the apparent security of her own place, rather than a police station.

"Wash your face Lizzie and come through when you're ready, okay?" he repeated.

She nodded, still unable to speak and then to her horror, saw the tin and her works behind the toilet bowl.

Again he saw her near panic and said, "I'm not here about anything other than Alice, do you understand hen? I don't care about that," he stared at her, but nodded to the tin. "Just come out when you're ready, eh?" and left the bathroom.

A few minutes passed and they heard the toilet bowl flush then Lizzie, her head bowed and her thin arms still wrapped about her, slowly walked into the room. They saw she had quickly changed into a pair of grubby, yellow coloured tracksuit bottoms.

McIntosh and Burroughs who both stood by the window rather than use the stained and torn armchairs or couch, turned towards her.

"She's really dead?"

"I'm very sorry, but yes," replied McIntosh. "I take it you were not just flatmates, but really good friends?"

Lizzie nodded, her face betraying the emotion that again threatened to engulf her as she limply sat down on the edge of the couch.

"She, Alice I mean, was discovered earlier this morning over in Bellahouston Park. Do you know where that is, Lizzie?"

She nodded in reply. "Some of the punters," then glanced sharply at them both and as if an explanation was needed, said, "I'm on the game, you see. I'm a working girl. Some of the punters have taken me over there. At night-time I mean. It's the big park near to where the Rangers play football, isn't it?"

"That's right," replied McIntosh, then realising that the young woman was gradually becoming more relaxed, said, "Do you mind if I smoke, Lizzie?"

She shook her head and he fetched a packet of 'Players No 6' from his jacket pocket and offered one to her.

Herself a heavy smoker, but favouring her own brand of cigarette, Burroughs was inwardly grateful that the strong smell of the tobacco might mask some of the undetermined smells that lingered in the humid room. She saw the young woman shiver and knew it had nothing to do with being cold; that the heroin Lizzie had injected was reacting with her body and she guessed Lizzie would not be able to afford the purest of heroin. Whatever she had injected or smoked would have been poor quality and adulterated, though with what shite the dealer used to adulterate the heroin would be anyone's guess.

Choosing the armchair that seemed the least stained, McIntosh sat gingerly down on the green coloured velour material and smiling at the young woman, said, "Look, I'm guessing that you've not long had a wee hit, Lizzie, but like I told you…" he raised his hand, palm outward and hurriedly added to forestall her protest. "Like I told you, we don't care about any habit you might have. What my colleague DI Burroughs," he nodded to her, "and I do care about is finding out who murdered your friend. So, how long did you know Alice?"

It took almost forty minutes of McIntosh coaxing and cajoling Lizzie for him to be reasonably satisfied that the young woman had told him as much as she knew or at least remembered, about her murdered friend, Alice Trelawney.

In a well-rehearsed routine, he stopped halfway through the interview as though suddenly remembering and with a soft smile, suggested that while he and Lizzie spoke, the Detective Inspector might find something in Alice's room that would help their investigation. While Burroughs edged from the room, McIntosh distracted the nervous Lizzie with another fag and bade her continue answering his questions.

When at last Burroughs returned to the front room he saw she clutched a small notebook with a pink cover.

He smiled at Lizzie.

"I think I've got enough for now, hen. The worst thing is that while from her fingerprints we're quite satisfied that it is Alice, we still need someone that knew her to positively identify her. Do you think you're up for something like that?"

"No way," she violently shook her head, "I can't do that. No fucking way," she almost shouted, her arms again tightly binding her body and now rocking back and forth on the couch.

"Okay, okay," again he held out the raised palms of his hand, "Don't worry about it."

"Did she ever mention her family, Lizzie?" interrupted Burroughs.

"Eh, no, not really, but she did say she had a dad down in England somewhere, but that they didn't get on. Cornwall she said."

Burroughs flicked through the small notebook and glanced at Lizzie. "Did she tell you his name?"

"Aye, but I forget," she replied and then they saw her brow furrow and her eyes narrow. "No, wait, it was Chris, Christopher I think, but I'm not really sure. Sorry, I don't really remember."

"Could it have been Crispin?"

"Yes, that was it," the excitement obvious in her rising voice, "because I thought it was a funny name. Crispin Trelawney."

Burroughs turned an expressionless face towards McIntosh. "We might have a home address Gordon."

CHAPTER 6

Sergeant John Greatrex had just pushed his bulky body from the patrol car he had parked in the small courtyard that adjoined the office at Hayle police station, when he heard his wife rapping on the window of their house next door.

Using his handkerchief to mop his brow clear of sweat from the last of the midday heat, he was about to smile at her, but the smile turned to a grimace when she made a sign with her thumb and small finger that he was wanted on the phone and with her other hand, waved for him to hurry inside.

Just my bloody luck, he thought and hoped that it wasn't a call that might prevent his usual Thursday night's darts match down at the Ploughman's Rest.

He pushed open the kitchen door and asked, "Yes my love?"

"You've to phone Exeter right away," his portly wife replied and then her face betrayed her curiosity when she added, "John, the Inspector said it was very urgent. What have you done now?"

"Me!" he exclaimed with surprise, "nothing. I've not done a thing," or at least I hope I haven't, he thought and worried that word about that little night-time stalking on the Moor with his brother had somehow gotten back to the Inspector. I mean, he thought, who would miss one deer?

He took a deep breath to calm himself and decided it could not be that. Taking the phone from his wife's outstretched hand, he slowly breathed out.

So why is Headquarters calling me in this backwater with something that was very urgent, he wondered.

The eighteenth century 'Pirates Cove' pub, located on a short cobbled street just off the main road that runs through Hayle and caught between two whitewashed cottages was almost empty when they arrived. Susie the teenage barmaid greeted them almost as old friends and smiling, took their order while they climbed onto bar stools.

Her wide smile was enough to cause the younger of her two customers to blush, but his companion discreetly ignored the lad's embarrassment.

Twenty minutes later, Crispin Trelawney and his young friend Jack Davenport had just consumed their second pastie and ordered another pint for Trelawney and a second coke for Jack when a voice behind them said, "And I'll have a glass of white wine, if you're buying, Cris."

Both turned to see Jack's mother, Louise standing smiling behind them, her hands on her shapely hips and her shoulder length, jet black hair tied back in a severe ponytail by a white ribbon. Louise was soberly dressed in a cream coloured half-sleeve blouse, black pencil skirt to just above the knees and short-heeled black shoes that added little to her five feet seven inches. A heavy bag was slung over one shoulder and she carried a pair of sunglasses in her hand.

Trelawney smiled and waved to the young barmaid. "White wine for Missus Davenport, please Susie," he smiled, then turned towards Louise.

"Hard day at the office, ma'am?"

"Just the usual," she exhaled, her eyes betraying her tiredness and reaching over to ruffle her son's hair stood between them and said, "So, how did the fishing go then?"

"Lobsters, not fish mum," snorted a grinning Jack, and added, "We made our quota, didn't we Mister Trelawney?"

"We did indeed young Jack," grinned Trelawney, who likewise ruffled the excited youngster's hair.

"And were you wearing your lifejacket like I told you to?" asked Louise, a pretend frown on her face.

"Ah, well…" started Jack with a blush on his face and conscious that Susie was halfway along the bar and could hear him. He was interrupted by Trelawney who stared at the lad and said, "No, he wasn't wearing a jacket," and with a genuine frown said, "I think you forgot to remind me about your mother's instruction there, Jack me lad."

"Sorry mum," said Jack, then hastily added, "Sorry Mister Trelawney."

The last thing Jack wanted was to disappoint Mister Trelawney, a man who was quickly becoming his hero and whom he guessed his mum secretly liked. Well, that's what he thought anyway because every time she spoke of him or he was with them, she seemed really happy.

Fortunately, Jack saw that Susie had moved along to the other end of the bar to serve a customer and was apparently unaware of him being reproached.

Trelawney caught Louise's eye and both knew the young lad was genuinely contrite, that it wasn't his nature to be devious or untruthful.

"Well," she leaned toward her son, her brow knitted as though contemplating a great decision, "if you buy me a pastie with the wage that Mister Trelawney paid you today, I might just forgive you. But just this once, mind you."

Sergeant Greatrex returned the phone to its cradle and exhaled. The Inspector told him the Fax was shortly to be forwarded to the main office in Penzance and he would instruct it be delivered by Panda car to Greatrex, as soon as possible thereafter.

However, in the meantime, the Inspector suggested that Greatrex phone the CID in Glasgow and speak directly to the man in charge of the murder inquiry, "…sort of put him in the picture John, if you get my meaning. Bad, bad business, but I know that you'll be the man to deal with it."

Yeah, right, thought Greatrex. *The man to deal with it*, the Inspector had said. More like the man to get caught in the fall-out when he broke the news to Cris Trelawney, he sighed.

Seated at his desk in Govan office, DCI Gordon McIntosh read the paperwork that had just been couriered to the office.

He half smiled at Doctor Jane Robertson's neat, handwritten statement, thinking she could give some of the buggers under his command a lesson on how to present facts. Based on previous experience of the doctor he had come to respect her opinion and though it was yet to be proven, thought her conclusion interesting.

According to Robertson, her considered opinion was that the deceased had been stabbed while in the prone position and that the culprit had probably lain on top of the deceased to inflict the one stab wound. He noted with a smile that Robertson concluded her statement with a caveat; the autopsy would probably determine if her opinion was correct.

He relaxed in his chair, the ache in his back more pronounced as time went by and thought about Robertson's conclusion. Had the killer been having sex with the young girl and if so, why hadn't Robertson seen the presence of semen in the vagina? Of course, McIntosh drummed his right fingers on his desk, the killer must have worn a condom. He lifted the copy of the Support Unit Sergeant's search report and quickly glanced down the list of items discovered nearby and lodged as Productions.

No condoms.

Bugger, he thought and wondered if it was worth having the Unit return to make an extended search of the area.

But all that would prove, he realised was that somebody had sex and a disposed condom need not necessarily have been used by the killer. He recalled the girl Lizzie McLeish telling Glenda and him that Bellahouston Park was quickly becoming the favourite haunt of the punters who nightly took the prostitutes over there. That might mean any condoms discovered in the Park could lead the inquiry team on a wild goose chase.

He lifted the desk phone and dialled Mark Renwick's extension.

His call was answered by Renwick's number two, DS Brian Davidson who asked that he hang on while he fetched Renwick to the phone.

"Yes sir," said Renwick, half a moment later.

"Just before I head home Mark, anything else turn up?"

"Nothing at the moment sir, but I'll be here another hour or two and I have your home number if I need you sir," he formally replied.

Another hour or two, he inwardly grinned. That old chestnut, smirked McIntosh, knowing that Renwick was trying to impress him with his diligence, yet suspecting that it was a lie; that sometime within the next ten minutes, Renwick would be onto the Govan late shift to ask if the DCI had gone home so that he himself could then knock off.

You can't kid a kidder, he grinned.

He was reaching to lock his desk drawer and thinking of Mary's homemade steak and kidney pie that awaited him, when the phone rung.

"DCI McIntosh."

"Hello sir, my name's Sergeant John Greatrex, Devon and Cornwall Police. I'm calling from down here in Cornwall. My Inspector suggested that I phone you. About the body you found up there."

McIntosh smiled at Greatrex's slow accent. "Thanks for phoning John; if you call me Gordon that will maybe make things a bit easier, eh?"

There was nothing wrong with the line; a good connection, but McIntosh thought there was a definite pause and then Greatrex replied, "Right you are, Gordon. I understand that you're the Senior Officer investigating the murder of Alice Trelawney?"

"That's correct. I'm assuming you're phoning from," he glanced at the copy of the Telex message he had caused to be sent, "Hayle, is it?"

"That's right Gordon; Hayle. We're a small fishing village just short of Penzance. Do you know the area at all?"

"No, I'm afraid I haven't had the opportunity to visit Cornwall. So John, did you know Alice Trelawney?"

Again, he detected a pause before Greatrex responded.

"Hayle's a small place Gordon. Round here, everyone knows everyone else and his or her business. Not like a big city where you work. I knew the girl when she was at the secondary school in Penzance, round about the same time my son went to school there. She came here to live with her father about, oh, nine, ten years ago now I'm thinking."

"Can you confirm if the father," again he glanced at the Telex to confirm the name, "Crispin Trelawney…if Mister Trelawney has been informed of his daughter's death?"

"No, not yet. I mean, not by the police anyway. Let me explain. You see, I haven't received the Telex here at Hayle. It's due to arrive by courier from Penzance. I'm a one-man station here you see Gordon; nothing fancy like a Telex machine, so when I receive official notification, I'll visit Cris when I have all the details, as it were."

McIntosh was irked at the delay in informing the father, but with some reluctance had to agree. There was no point in Greatrex going off half-cocked and telling the father without the full information. Unconsciously nodding his head at the phone, he realised this was the logical move and asked, "Is there a Missus Trelawney, I mean, Alice's mother."

"No she's dead, died some years ago. In London I believe."

McIntosh startled. The Sergeant's reply was quick; too quick and for some reason that McIntosh could not explain, the hair on the back of his neck ruffled; his very own intuition indicator that caused him to suspect there might be a story there.

"So tell me John, is there a likelihood that Mister Trelawney might be in a position to travel here, to Glasgow I mean? We have identified his daughter from her fingerprints and I can tell you, in strict confidence, she was recorded a year ago by the Scottish Criminal Record's Office for a minor DHSS cheque scam. It didn't amount to much, just a group of University kids, Alice being one of the five, trying to rip off a discarded chequebook they had found in a rubbish bin. To cut a long story short, they all pled guilty and admonished. However, their prints were recorded by the SCRO and remained on file and that is how we identified the wee lassie. That said, I really need a family member or family friend for a positive identification, so unless Mister Trelawney can provide me with a local relative or friend…" he tailed off.

Again, a there was definite pause as though Greatrex was considering McIntosh's information before he replied.

"It's only my own opinion Gordon, but I think it's more than likely Cris, Mister Trelawney I mean, will travel to Glasgow himself."

McIntosh had been a detective for too many years not to ignore the gut feeling that was causing him to be suspicious and he was far too long in the tooth to be fannied about.

"How well do you know Mister Trelawney, John? Is there something you're not telling me here; something I should know?"

He could almost hear the intake of breath, the Sergeant's reluctance to divulge something, whatever the hell it was.

"Listen, Gordon. Cris Trelawney isn't like other men. He's got a bit of history, but not down here," he hastily added. "In Hayle, the man's well liked and respected. Has his own fishing smack and works hard at the lobster industry, does Cris. Keeps himself to himself and bothers nobody, do you understand? We, the police I mean, have no cause to be involved with him, none all."

McIntosh was taken aback, intrigued even. What the fuck was this guy Greatrex trying to say?

"But outside Hayle, outside your police area," he pressed Greatrex, "you're talking about his history; so, what kind of history does Mister Trelawney have John?"

Again, that damnable pause before Greatrex replied, "Look, even I shouldn't know this, but you hear things; things that the bosses don't want you to know, yeah? All I can tell you is that before he settled here, Cris Trelawney…well, I know he's Cornish by birth, but he came up from London some years ago. There was some talk, just talk mind you, that he might have been involved in something up in London; something to do with a gang there, a real bad bunch by all accounts."

"Do you have any details, anything at all John?"

"No, I don't really know much more…" there was the sound of a door banging and a woman's voice.

"That's the Telex arrived from Penzance, Mister McIntosh," he reverted to formality. "I'll need to be off now to deliver the message. When I've done that, will it be okay for me to provide Mister Trelawney with your phone number, just in case he wishes to speak with you personally?"

"Yes, John, that sounds like a good idea," McIntosh wearily replied and read out the digits of the incident room phone number. "I'm off home for this evening, but he can either call the incident room tomorrow and leave a message or get me here at my office," and read out his direct number.

"Thank you sir and good evening," replied Greatrex before calling off.

McIntosh rubbed a hand across his brow. Now what the fuck was that all about, he wondered, but more importantly, how might it impact on the inquiry?

CHAPTER 7 – Friday morning 28 May.

After a restless night, Simon Johnson awoke before the alarm sounded and tumbling at the digital clock, switched on the radio button. The six-thirty bulletin on Clyde Radio commenced with the news that British troops had reached Darwin in the Falkland Islands. Simon's ears perked up at the mention of the conflict, his thoughts immediately with his brother Peter who was serving aboard one of the support ships as a liaison officer. Due to the infrequency of the mail and the necessity of censorship, Peter was unable to tell his parents or brother the name of the ship. Simon sighed when recalling that earlier in the month the Navy had already lost personnel during the sinking of the destroyer *HMS Sheffield* as well as the loss of two frigates, the *Antelope* and *Ardent* and silently gave thanks that Peter was not aboard a fighting ship of the line.

While the commentator continued with local news, he rubbed his tousled hair and rose from bed. He trudged through to the bathroom, all the while with one ear listening for some update in the murder inquiry, but there was nothing, though Bellahouston Park did get a mention because of the impending visit of Pope John Paul II. The sun streaming through the window dazzled him and he knew it was going to be another blinder of a day.

Across the city, Mary McIntosh nudged her snoring husband awake and reminding him to let the dog out into the back garden for a pee, then turned and tried to return to sleep.

Gordon McIntosh grinned and with boyish devilment, slid from the bed, dragging the quilt cover with him.

"Bloody child," his wife moaned and threw a pillow at his retreating back as he made the safety of the en-suite.

In Hayle, sitting in the half-light that streamed through the small windows, Cris Trelawney sat at the solidly built wooden table in the large, whitewashed kitchen of his stone-built fisherman's cottage and stared without seeing. A bottle of Morgan's Rum, with no more than two or three drams remaining, sat on the table beside two drained glasses.

Louise Davenport lay snuggled under a heavy blanket on a low couch facing the large cooking Range and gently snored, her shoes kicked off and lying under the couch. In the small front room just off the kitchen, her son young Jack lay sleeping and similarly covered on the old stressed leather couch.

When early the previous evening, the news of Alice's death was broken by the village policeman Sergeant Greatrex, both had flatly refused to leave Cris on his own.

Louise stirred, for a second wondering where she was, why she was still fully clothed and aching at the cramp in her neck. Her mouth was dry but with sudden clarity, she remembered.

"Cris," she softly said, sitting upright, her eyes suddenly alert and staring at the man she was slowly coming to love.

"Cris," she called again, a little louder.

He turned towards her, his eyes betraying the weariness of a lonely vigil.

"I need to leave, fetch her home," he said, his voice dull and monotone.

Louise stood and stepping barefooted across the coldness of the flagstone floor and wrapped her arms about his shoulders, her hair falling across his face.

"Shall I come with you, the office can do without me for…" she was about to say a few days, but changed it to "…for as long as you need me."

He reached up with his right hand and held her arm tightly.

"No, stay here with Jack. I'll be fine, really, so don't worry about me. Honestly, I'll be fine," he repeated.

She laid her cheek against the top of his head and nuzzled his head against her breast.

"Whatever you want, my love," she softly whispered, for the first time in the three months they had been seeing each other, been romantically linked, finally declaring her affection.

He seemed not to notice and lay unmoving against her arms.

She took a deep breath, her throat suddenly tight and with reluctance released her hold on him, then said, "It's a long way to Glasgow. You can't travel without having slept and if I'm to let you go alone, I won't allow you to do so unless you get to bed and sleep. Go now," she gently pulled at him, "and I'll sort your car out for you and pack you a bag."

Unresistingly, he allowed himself to be gently pulled to his feet and tiredly made his way through the cottage to his bedroom at the back.

Jack, rubbing at his eyes, stumbled through the kitchen door.

"Is he all right mum? Is Mister Trelawney going to be okay?"

She tried to smile at her son, noticing and not for the first time how much he resembled his father and how proud her John, gone now almost eleven years, would have loved to see his son grow into the man he was to become.

"Cris…Mister Trelawney," she nodded, "will be fine, Jack. It will take a long time for him to heal, but as long as he has us, friends like us I mean," she quickly added, "he'll be fine."

Jack's eyes narrowed and with a wry smile, replied, "But you're more than just a friend, aren't you mum? You *really* like him, don't you?"

She hesitated and then slowly grinned. "Yes Jack I *really* do like him, now let's you and me get ourselves home and into fresh clothes. We've a lot to do and arrangements to make if Cris is to get away tonight to Glasgow."

DS Brian Davidson was the first of the inquiry team to arrive at the Incident room located within the rear Portacabin at Pollok police office. His first task was attend at the uniform bar to collect any Telex information that might have been received through the night; thereafter read it and mark or highlight those items that might be worthy of bringing to the DI's attention for later inquiry or dissemination to the inquiry officers. However, to his disappointment, not one Telex relative to the murder of Alice Trelawney had been received at the incident room.
Unusually he ignored the cheerful greeting of the uniformed bar officer who couldn't fail but notice the small slip of bloodstained toilet tissue stuck to Davidson's chin.
When he returned to the Portacabin Davidson found the only other occupant to be DI Mark Renwick, who was at his desk.
"Shove the kettle on Brian, there's a good lad," said Renwick from behind his morning edition of the 'Glasgow News'.
Davidson bristled and glancing about him to ensure that they were alone, snarled, "Here's a better idea, Renwick, shove the fucking kettle on yourself."
Renwick, his face white, lowered the newspaper and glowered at Davidson.
"What did you say?" he replied, his voice low and working hard to keep the tremor from it.
"You heard me, you lazy bastard," snapped Davidson, turning away from him.
"You forget yourself Detective Sergeant," blustered Renwick, "I'm a Detective Inspector; I outrank you and I'll…."
"You'll what?" sneered Davidson, who turned back towards him.
Renwick apparently for the first time saw that the former rugby playing Davidson was a lot taller and stockier than he had previously noticed.
"Go on, you'll what," repeated Davidson. "Just me and you here sonny," he hissed through gritted teeth, "so if you want to make something of it, we can drop the ranks and sort it out in the car park; just me and you, eh?"
The door suddenly opened to admit the CID aide, Simon Johnson.
"Morning," he cheerfully called out. The smile died on his face when he saw Davidson, his face red and leaning threateningly over the desk towards the pale faced DI Renwick.
"Eh, anybody for tea or coffee?" Simon hesitatingly asked.

Within ten minutes, all the inquiry officers were within the Portacabin, some munching at warm bacon rolls or crowded round the table helping themselves to tea or coffee while awaiting the first morning briefing. The more astute officers sensed an atmosphere between the incident room DI Renwick and the normally cheerful DS, Brian Davidson, who other than a curt response to their greetings, kept his head bowed at his desk.

Stuck seated in a corner and feeling a little like the odd man out, but with his notebook at the ready, Simon Johnson wisely decided to keep his mouth shut.

The door opened to admit Glenda Burroughs, again dressed in a fashionable black two-piece trouser suit, her hair and make-up impeccable and attracting the attention of more than a few of the male detectives.

"Morning," she cheerfully called out to the crowded room, then turning to Renwick, said "Excuse us please Mark," and catching Simon's eye, indicated with a nod that he follow her from the Portacabin.

More than a few pair of eyes watched her return back through the door.

Renwick's eyes followed Simon to the door, but Simon deliberately avoided eye contact, guessing that some time later, the DI would catch him alone and might want to discuss what the young trainee detective had seen.

In the short corridor outside the room, Burroughs turned and as if disclosing a confidence, told him, "I've had a phone call from the boss, Simon. He wants me down at Govan; has something to discuss so as you're my neighbour, I'd like you to accompany me, if that's okay with you?"

Simon was surprised. It was clearly an instruction, but expressed in such a courteous manner by the DI that it inferred he had some sort of say in the decision. His respect for Burroughs continued to grow.

"Fine by me, ma'am, shall I get us a car?"

"No, we'll use mine, so," she replied and turning on her heel called over her shoulder, "just follow me."

Simon inhaled the fragrance of her perfume and thought as he watched the shapely Burroughs walk off that no matter where the stunning DI led, he would most definitely follow.

Lizzie McLeish woke with a blinding headache, her mouth raw and body aching. She had not intended to go out looking for punters last night, but her addiction didn't take a day off and like it or not, she needed to earn money to satisfy the cravings that arrived like clockwork each morning. Reaching down from where she lay, she grabbed at the denim jeans lying on the floor and scrambled in the rear pocket, panicking slightly until she realised she was in the wrong pocket and then exhaled with relief when she pulled out the crumpled notes from within. Thirty-five fucking quid, she inwardly moaned. She did not need to be a mathematical genius to work out that with what she already owed that shithead Wingy, it didn't leave enough for a full hit and she would again have to be satisfied with a tenner bag.

Lizzie wasn't stupid and knew that the crippled wee bastard adulterated his smack with whatever shite that was the cheapest; suspecting the rumour she had heard to probably be true; that he was lately using baking soda. What she did know was that the tenner bags Wingy sold were enough for a short relief, but hardly worth the money. If it come to it, she inwardly sighed, she would probably give in and give the wee bastard another blowjob to get something from him.

She turned onto her back and closed her eyes against the throbbing in her head.

Her thoughts turned to her dead friend Alice. No, not dead, she corrected herself; murdered.

Lizzie had thought the cops would be haunting the 'Drag' last night like they usually did when a prossie was killed or badly assaulted. But never raped, she humourlessly smirked. I mean, she thought, we don't get raped or robbed, do we? It's not 'rape' to shag a prossie that doesn't want to shag and it's not 'robbery' to steal a prossies money or when a punter refuses to pay for his service.

How many times has a cop told her that, she bitterly wondered?

She thought of the visit by the two detectives, the man and the woman. The man had been…she hesitated to even consider the word, but he had been nice. The good looking woman, a bit cold, a bit aloof and probably judging me, she angrily shook her head, but that set off another bout of throbbing and again she forced herself to lie perfectly still.

The chat among the working girls that had been out last night was that some had heard about the body being found in the Bellahouston Park. Among themselves, some had guessed it was one of their own. She hadn't really wanted to talk about it being Alice, but knew that she needed to put the word out that somebody had taken Alice over there and killed her. The girls had muttered among themselves and passed the word down through the streets and the lanes; promised to look out for one another, but Lizzie knew it was a front. They would stand about in two and three's for a couple of hours, but then the punters would arrive and slowly, the prossies would all drift away, either with a punter to some dark corner or to stand alone, the better to attract a customer for many punters didn't like approaching two or more women standing together.

Even the punters worried about being caught.

The only thing that they all agreed was nobody was going anywhere near the Bellahouston Park, at least not until the cops caught Alice's murderer.

Fine chance, she bitterly thought.

No, none of them would agree to go to the park, Lizzie sighed. Not for a couple of days anyway… or unless the price was right.

Her brow creased and though her head hurt, forced herself to again reach down to the denims and from the front pocket withdrew the creased business card.

Detective Chief Inspector Gordon McIntosh, she read, with a contact phone number and the logo of Strathclyde Police embossed on the front.

She knew she was about to cry and swallowed with difficulty; her throat still hurting from Wingy's thrusting at her and made her decision.

Lizzie didn't have many friends or at least, none like Alice. But now Alice was gone, dead.

She would phone the nice man, the detective and ask him if there was anything that she could do to help; anything that she heard or saw when she was out in the Drag.

But first, just lie a little longer here; just until she felt better, a little while longer lying nice and still.

Gordon McIntosh read the twenty-four hour crime divisional bulletin compiled by his nightshift officers. To his relief, apart from a couple of housebreakings solved with the arrest of the culprits, the theft of two motor vehicles and a couple of minor assaults resulting from a pub brawl in a notorious hostelry in Govan Road, there was nothing that needed his immediate attention. He penned an addendum to the report, congratulating the uniformed officers who after a lengthy chase, had arrested the violent housebreakers and dropped the report in his 'Out' tray for the attention of the Divisional Commander.

The door knocked and he glanced up to see Glenda Burroughs smiling at him.

"Is the manager in?" she parodied a well-known banking advert that was currently featuring on the TV.

He smiled and waved his hand for her to enter, seeing that the young aide Simon Johnson hesitated at her back.

"You too, young man," he waved Johnson in.

"Morning boss," greeted Burroughs, pulling up a chair to face his desk and hanging her handbag on the rear.

Johnson stood, unsure whether or not to sit down.

McIntosh suppressed a grin at the young lad's hesitance and said, "Simon, I'd like a wee private word with the DI, if you don't mind," he winked at Johnson. "Think you could rustle up three cups of coffee in say, about five minutes?"

"Yes sir, no problem sir," said a relieved Simon, who turning to walk from the room stopped, turned and asked, "Sorry, what do you take in your coffee, sir?"

"There's a list on the wall by the kettle in the general office," replied McIntosh, "and if you could close the door on you're way out please, there's a good lad." Burroughs smiled at McIntosh.

"What you grinning at, you blonde hussy," he pretended to be annoyed at her.

"It'll be a sad day when you retire, Gordon McIntosh," she replied. "You might not realise it and even if you do, rank has never changed you. You are still the same courteous and polite man that you were when I met you and that must be what, almost fifteen years now," she smiled.

"Yes, well, manners don't make you a good cop," he replied, embarrassed by her compliment.

"Nor a bad one either," she smiled in return. "Now, what is it that you want to see me about?"

McIntosh pushed the copy Telex across the desk to her and while she read, in short terse sentences he related his previous evening's conversation with Sergeant Greatrex of the Devon and Cornwall Police and his suspicion that McIntosh was not being told the whole story.

"When you were in the Special Branch, did you not spend some time down in London?" he asked.

Burroughs nodded. "That was over ten years ago Gordon. I had a six-month attachment with the National Joint Unit, the NJU. I'm not sure if you're aware, what that is. It's an intelligence unit based at Scotland Yard and open for secondment to officers from most of the UK forces. The City of Glasgow, as we were then, always had an officer based there. Quite a plum job it was too," she smiled at him. "The hours weren't too long with plenty of time off. I shared a flat with a couple of Met girls and we had access to all the night clubs, tickets for all the West End shows and partying every night I was off duty and lots of attention from *unsuitable* men. All in all," she grinned mischievously, "it wasn't a bad time."

"Yeah well," he returned her grin, "your *unsuitable* social life apart, do you still have any contact with any of the people down there in the Intelligence field? The reason I'm asking…"

"Is you want to find out about this guy Crispin Trelawney, just in case he travels here to Glasgow you mean?"

"That's it in one," he stretched back in his seat. "I tried the PNC for any trace of a Crispin Trelawney, but there's nothing showing up," he pursed his lips, his eyes narrowing as he scratched at his nose, and then continued. "If his daughter was murdered by a random punter who picked her up for sex, well, that's a line of inquiry we can concentrate on, but if her death is anything to do with her father's history, whatever that history might be? I believe it's just something that we can't ignore."

"I'll get onto it," she assured him, slipping the Telex message into her handbag. The door knocked and was opened by Simon, carrying a tray with three steaming mugs. "You said five minutes sir?"

"Come away in lad," invited McIntosh with a smile. "So, how's your secondment to the Department been so far?"

CHAPTER 8

Hours after his confrontation with Davidson, DI Mark Renwick was still seething and now that the inquiry officers were dispatched to their tasks, it left him alone in the Portacabin with the sullen DS. By unspoken mutual agreement, each ignored the other and the atmosphere, to use the old Glasgow adage, was so thick it could be cut with a knife.

Renwick glanced at his wristwatch and reaching over, turned on the small transistor radio on the shelf by his desk in time to catch the lunchtime news bulletin. He listened as the main story commenced that a battle was underway at some weirdly named place called Goose Green, where British forces were apparently engaged in a gun battle with Argentinean troops. The second item was the arrival of Pope John Paul in the UK and continued with an update of the ongoing preparations currently underway in Glasgow for the Pontiff's visit the following week.

As the commentator related the story about the Pontiff's visit, Davidson heard Renwick mutter, "Fenian bastard", but assumed the DI was referring to the Pope, rather than the Partick Thistle supporting Detective Sergeant.

Curiously, Renwick thought, no mention of the prostitutes' body discovered in Bellahouston Park.

49

Renwick's desk phone rang and switching off the radio, he lifted the phone from its cradle and answered, "Incident room, DI Renwick."

Davidson, his head bowed and throat burning from his poor shaving that morning, listened as Renwick affably greeted the caller and concluded the call with, "Right then, see you there tonight, say about seven okay?" before hanging up.

The door opened to admit Jimmy Reid, the uniformed CID clerk who ignoring Renwick, walked directly to Davidson's desk.

"That was the DCI on the blower there Brian, your number was engaged when he tried to get through. He asked if you would give him a call at his office."

"I'll get that," interrupted Renwick, who lifted the phone and dialled McIntosh's direct extension number.

"Hello sir, Mark here. What can I do for you?"

With his back to Renwick, Reid shrugged and winked at Davidson before turning to return to his own cupboard like room.

Davidson pretended to examine a statement, but listening closely heard Renwick mutter, "Yes sir" and saw him make a note on his pad. "Right," he heard Renwick say, "I'll get DS Davidson onto it straight away sir, bye."

Tearing the sheet of paper from the pad, Renwick walked to Davidson's desk and handed him the paper.

"The DCI wants accommodation at a local hotel for this guy, the dead girl's father, who is coming up from Cornwall to identify her. He should be arriving some time tonight or in the early hours of tomorrow morning. If you don't mind," he said, the sarcasm evident in his voice.

Bristling, Davidson couldn't look at Renwick, such was his dislike for the man, but resignedly nodded and simply replied, "I'll get it done."

Almost five hundred and fifty miles away, Cris Trelawney shrugged into his green wax coat and smiled at Louise, then took her in his arms.

"Thanks for everything, both you and Jack I mean."

She wrapped her arms about his waist and stared up at him. "You are sure you're ready to drive now? Have you had enough sleep I mean? It's not too late to change your mind, I could come with you, share the driving."

"No, I'm fine," he replied, her nearness and her scent almost causing him to change his mind. "This is something I have to do alone. You know what kind of father I was, how I let her down, how much I…"

She tore her hand away from his waist and pressed a forefinger against his lips. "I'll hear nothing of that," she firmly told him. "You did your best. My God Cris, if anyone tried to make up for what happened, you did." She sighed heavily and shook her head, her hair now bound in a tight bauble, her ponytail flicking back and forth. "Alice was in bad place. You *know* that you did try, so you have nothing to reproach yourself for. Nothing," she firmly repeated.

Louise returned her arm about his waist and leaned her head against his shoulder as she hugged him tight, then stood back and stared into his face. "Three days, no more Cris Trelawney. Any longer than that and I'll be coming for you, okay?"

He smiled tolerantly at her.

"The man I spoke with, the man in charge, a detective called McIntosh. He's making arrangements for a hotel room. When I arrive I'll meet with him first, find out what the arrangements is for seeing her…body and he'll tell me more about what happened, how she died I mean." He ran his tongue over his upper lip and she guessed he was finding it difficult to compose himself. Tight-lipped, he smiled at her.

"Now, you've made the arrangements and…"

She cut him off with a reproving glance. "Like I told you; I've spoke with old Trevor and he's agreed to run the boat out to your nets till you return. Jack's here so with him helping, there shouldn't be any problems and I'll see to this place," she waved her hand about her. "I've fuelled the car and checked her over, so other than stopping for diesel and checking the tyre and oil, the car should be okay for the trip. I've packed a bag and it's in the boot along with a flask of coffee and sandwiches, so mind that you stop off and get something to eat, Cris Trelawney. Don't you dare try to make the trip without a break," she wagged an admonishing finger at him.

Even though his heart felt like a large stone in his chest, he could not help himself and grinned at her. Tenderly he run his hand across her hair and drew her to him; his need for her overwhelming him. She reached up and met his lips with hers, tasting his minty breath and smelling the freshness of his shower. God, she thought, how I love this man; still finding it incredible that she could be so lucky twice in one lifetime.

"One more thing," his eyes narrowed as he walked towards the door and turning towards her, grinned, "See that Jack wears a life-jacket when he's out on the boat with old Trevor."

Alone in the Detective Inspectors room that she shared with the DI who was off with a long-term illness, Glenda Burroughs sat behind her desk and scrolled through her desk Rolex. Finding the name she sought, she smiled at past memories then taking a deep breath, dialled the number.

"Hello, Detective Inspector Harley," said the Cockney voice in her ear.

"Hello Jim, it's Glenda Burroughs," she softly drawled. "Long time no speak. You still good with your hands?" she coyly asked.

While he waited for Burroughs to make her call, Simon Johnson sat with the Govan CID clerk Alex McCormick, grinning at the politely spoken constable's anecdotal stories of life as a beat officer in the City of Glasgow Police.

Now in his twilight year, McCormick had never lost his love for the job and was well known throughout Govan for his courtesy and good manners, even when dealing with the most uncivil or abusive drunkard.

"Aye, young Simon, it'll be a sad day for the polis when the likes of Gordon McIntosh retire," McCormick sighed, pushing his oversized reading glasses back from the tip of his nose. "If ever a polis was to call at your door for any reason, then it wouldn't be so hard if it was a man like Gordon; a true gentleman in every sense of the word and a fine policeman to boot."

"Am I interrupting or saving you from this old tearaway," said the voice behind them.

"It's yourself so it is Glenda," smiled McCormick, "a vision of loveliness if ever there was one. Have you considered my offer yet?"

Simon stared from one to the other, puzzled.

Burroughs grinned and explained. "Alex says that he'll leave his wife if I'll run away with him."

Simon blushed, though quite couldn't explain why and marvelled that the old cop had such a good relationship with both the DI and DCI.

Must be an age thing, he wryly decided.

"Right then young man," Burroughs glanced at her wristwatch, than at Simon. "That's lunchtime, so where are you taking me then?"

Throughout the late afternoon, the inquiry officers returned to Pollok incident room, most with their heads down, their respective tasks completed, but disappointed that none had anything new to contribute to the inquiry.

Davidson listened with increasing frustration as each pair of officers explained their negative result to Renwick and were rebuked in turn for what the DI perceived to be their failings. He had seen this type of management before; find fault and then find someone to blame.

After four pairs had been so treated, Davidson had had enough and impatiently waited until the Portacabin cleared, leaving he and Renwick and alone.

Pushing himself up from his desk, he approached the wary DI and visibly trying to control his temper, said, "Listen, it's no secret I can't stand you, but you need to know something; these guys are out there doing what they can with the limited information we're giving them. The last fucking thing they need is to come back here and have you berate them when they are obviously doing their best. For fucks sake, I know you're a dickhead, but at least act like a Detective Inspector and motivate them; if you need to be critical, try and be constructively critical, okay?"

White-faced, Renwick clenched his fists to stop them from shaking, so afraid was he that Davidson was really going to lose it and attack him. His throat was dry and he knew he must respond, but before he could do so, the door opened and DCI McIntosh entered the room.

"Afternoon gentlemen," he greeted them, "how are things going today then?"

The palpable silence that returned McIntosh's greeting didn't seem to faze him and he sat heavily down on one of the vacant seats and then stretched across Renwick's desk to pick up the statement file. Wordlessly, he began reading the recent inquiry updates or what little there was.

Davidson smiled tightly and returned to his desk. Both he and Renwick knew that the walls of the Portacabin were paper-thin and it was more than likely that McIntosh had heard Davidson's outburst.

A few minutes passed then sighing audibly, McIntosh returned the file and with a shake of his head and while still sitting, said in a low voice, "You two seem to have problems working together. Well gentlemen, here's the rub. I really do not give a penny shit what your issues are, but what I will say is that any issues you have are secondary to this inquiry. No, I'll rephrase that. They are of *no consequence* to this inquiry. The wee girl that was murdered deserves better than you two bitching and whining at each other like a pair of adolescent kids. So gentlemen, like it or lump it, you will find a way to work together or by God," the pitch of his voice began to rise, "I will ensure that you are both returned to uniform duties. I will then find myself some officers who not only should know better, but who will work in tandem to ensure this incident room gives one hundred per cent to the inquiry team. Do I make myself clear, Detective Inspector Renwick?"

"Yes sir," mumbled a chastened Renwick.

"Detective Sergeant Davidson?" McIntosh turned towards him.

"Sir," replied Davidson, a little more forcibly.

"Right then gentlemen, please bear in mind what I have just said," McIntosh rose from his chair and left the room.

It was a few minutes later in the silence of the room that Davidson startled; '*what I have just said*' McIntosh had told them. He inwardly grinned. McIntosh had ordered them both to ensure the inquiry team is given one hundred per cent support. Unless he was reading the situation wrong, McIntosh was agreeing with Davidson, though obviously couldn't be seen to do so by supporting a junior officer in an argument with a ranking officer.

Feeling a little better about the chastisement issued by McIntosh, Davidson returned to sorting out the next day's tasks for the inquiry team.

He did not want to use a phone at work, worrying that somehow the call might be overheard or that a later billing would indicate who the call was made to.

His coat collar turned up against the flurry of rain, he hurried through towards the pub round the corner and pushing his way through the early evening crowd to the lounge bar, saw the public phone wasn't being used.

He counted out two ten pence pieces and reading them to insert into the slot, dialled the number. After a few short rings, his call was answered.

"Yeah, it's me, 'Handy'….Jim Harley. Yeah, I know it has been a while. That name you told me to watch out for, it's popped up. Yeah, yeah, I know it was a few years back, but it's not a name I'm going to forget is it?" he hissed at the phone.

"I don't bleeding know where he lives, do I you twat? Look, I'm sorry, I'm sorry, awright? I did not mean that, it's just that I'm under a bit of pressure right now. The rubber heels and this graft operation they've got going at the Yard; this fucking Operation Countryman, it's got every bugger worried sick."

"Yeah, yeah," he glanced about him and hurriedly acknowledged the response. "I know, I know. Look, I'm doing this as a favour, big man. I know there's a backhander, but I'm not interested in the money; all I want is the photos, all of them, right? And the negatives too of course." He closed his eyes in silent prayer and wondered again how the *fuck* he had got himself into this situation.

"Right, you got a pen handy, have you? He's on his way to Glasgow."

His brow creased in amazement at the question and he replied, "Scotland, you…" he paused and drew a deep breath, not wishing to incur further wrath. "I don't know from where, all I can tell you is that his daughter got herself murdered and the muppets up there in Jockland somehow managed to contact him and have told him to get his arse up there to ID her, okay?"

"From who? A bird, just a bird that I used to shag; a Scotch bird that used to work down here at the Yard, years ago."

He listened patiently and again glanced about him, fearfully aware the pub was sometimes frequented by colleagues from the Intelligence team he commanded.

"I didn't have any fucking choice, did I?" he whined. "If she records making the call as part of her murder inquiry, I have to provide the info and if I don't, questions might be asked later, d'you understand?"

He thrust a second ten piece into the slot and heard it tinkle down into the cashbox.

"No, no, there won't be any comeback to you, I swear. Of course I will; anything else I hear you'll be the first to know. You won't forget about the photos now…." but the big man had already hung up.

He slowly replaced the receiver, conscious that a thin film of sweat was beading his forehead.

CHAPTER 9

Glenda Burroughs knocked on McIntosh's door just as he was slipping an arm into his jacket sleeve.

"Got a couple of minutes, Gordon?"

He shrugged the jacket off and slipped it back across the rear of his chair, indicating she sit down. "Where's the devil's apprentice, young Johnson?" he smiled at her.

"I gave him an early night, being Friday. Young as he is, there's likely a girl involved."

"Lucky sod," McIntosh grinned.

"Don't kid yourself, you're well fixed up with that raven haired beauty you married," she retorted and sat down, placing a cardboard file on the desk in front of her.

"Not so much raven haired these days as raving mad," he sighed, but grinned anyway. "So, what you got for me then?"

She reached down into the handbag at her feet and withdrew her cigarette pack and gold engraved, Zippo lighter.

McIntosh, suspecting it might take a while, lit one of his own fags.

"Like you asked," she began, "I contacted an old colleague from my days at the NJU in Scotland Yard and spent a good hour on the phone of which just a few moments were social," she smiled. "It seems that your man Crispin Trelawney isn't who he says he is."

McIntosh's brow puckered and he sat forward in his seat. "Go on."

"According to my source, back in the late sixties, early seventies time, a power struggle erupted between two prominent London east end gangs, both who were vying for the booming drug market trade that was steadily overtaking cannabis as the drug of choice."

"Heroin," nodded McIntosh.

"Correct, Heroin. One of the gangs was controlled by a local likely lad called Ronnie Kyle. Kyle employed a number of minders, enforcers if you like, to carry out Kyle's business, one of whom was a man called Crispin McGuire. At that time, Kyle's business was predominately the porn industry; seedy sex-clubs, brothels, pornographic shops, that sort of thing, but then Kyle saw a lucrative opportunity to muscle into the drug trade and he began importing Heroin that he distributed through his chain of businesses. Anyway, it seems that there was a dispute with McGuire about selling the drugs. McGuire argued with his boss, tried to dissuade him from getting involved with Heroin and warned Kyle that the cops would crack down on him a lot harder for drugs rather than turn their usual blind eye to the sex trade, as they frequently did at that time. According to my source," she managed a smile, "the sex trade was *unofficially* sanctioned because, believe it or not, the London councils were happy with the availability of casual sexual encounters for the tourist industry; the large number of paying tourists it attracted to what was, in essence, deprived areas of the city that had poor economic growth. The sex industry therefore created local income, employment and in turn generated more revenue for the local hotels and associated retailers; which in turn again meant more tax revenue for the council coffers."

"Bloody hell," he sat back, his hands clasped behind his head.

"However, the introduction of drugs was about to change all that. While Kyle was tentatively poking a toe into the drug trade, a rival gang of predominantly Caribbean types decided there wasn't enough profit for two drug trafficking gangs in the east end and made the decision to bring down Kyle's mob. It seems that the easiest way to do this was to kill off the competition and there began a shooting war. Not so good for the tourism trade," she theatrically shook her head.

"It started with a couple of Kyle's boys being found shot to death in their car underneath a railway arch and then Kyle seemingly retaliated with the shooting dead of the rival gang leader's brother. It escalated from there until one night, when Kyle was making his way from one of his nightclubs to his car, he was shot in the leg by a motorcyclist, who made off."

McIntosh reached for her pack of cigarettes. "Do you mind?" he asked, showing her his own empty pack.

Smilingly, she leaned across the desk and handed over her cigarettes and her lighter.

"To continue, during the following weeks, a tit for tat continued and the Met recorded a further half dozen shootings and at least three murders."

"At least three murders? What, you mean…."

"Three that they know of," she nodded. "Some well known faces just disappeared, so make your own mind up regarding that. My source says there are at least five thugs, two believed to be from Kyle's gang and three from the rival gang; none of whom have been seen since and are thought to be part of the M1 motorway that was being constructed, round about that time," she wryly grinned. "So, while both gang's main players were being whittled down, it seemed that Kyle was becoming increasingly paranoid about his personal security and took to wondering how the mysterious motorcyclist knew to be there at the exact time on the night that Kyle exited the nightclub and was shot. So, he organised a little internal inquiry and lo and behold, his first suspect was the man that had argued against him becoming involved in the drug trade."

McIntosh took a deep drag of his fag. "This Crispin Trelawney… . or McGuire as he was?"

"Yes. He became Kyle's prime suspect and knowing that no matter what he said in his defence Kyle was so paranoid that nothing would prevent him exacting some form of revenge on McGuire. So McGuire simply took off and went into hiding. However, what McGuire didn't bank on was that Kyle didn't intend just killing McGuire, he wanted to hurt him more than that."

"How so," asked a puzzled McIntosh.

"It seems that for about two years apparently, McGuire was living in a flat with one of Kyle's strippers," she glanced at her notes. "A Daniela Corbett, known as Danni and here it gets really interesting. It seems that Corbett had a daughter, Alice Corbett who according to my calculation would now be about twenty years of age."

"McGuire, I mean Trelawney's daughter; Alice Trelawney, the dead girl?"

"Alice Trelawney, the dead girl yes, but McGuire's daughter, no," she shook her head.

"McGuire and Corbett had been living together for a number of years and McGuire took care of them both. From what my source told me, it seems that apart from the fact that McGuire was an enforcer in the sex industry and the mother was a stripper at a seedy nightclub, they lived together as one happy family. Anyway, I digress. Let's return to the worthy Mister Kyle, who unable to track down his one time employee Mister McGuire then decided to revenge himself upon Corbett and her daughter. McGuire obviously underestimated Kyle's paranoia and believed that it was he that Kyle sought revenge upon. McGuire seemingly completely underestimated the extent of the man's hatred. Danni Corbett arrived one night to perform her gig at one of Kyle's clubs," she stared pointedly at McIntosh and said, "and this is conjecture at this point, not evidence. It seems Corbett was dragged into a side room by Kyle and his cronies where after she was multiple raped, Kyle slit her throat."

"Bloody hell," was all the wide-eyed McIntosh could say, the ash from his cigarette falling unnoticed onto his tie and shirtfront.

"Though my source couldn't say who, the assumption is that someone in the club contacted McGuire and told him of his girlfriend's murder. Before Kyle could get to the flat Corbett shared with him, McGuire collected Corbett's child and with the child and a lawyer in tow, handed himself into Scotland Yard, claiming that he had knowledge of Kyle's illegal businesses. From then on a deal was struck; McGuire became a Crown Prosecution witness and was protected by the Met's Witness Protecting team while Kyle languished in Pentonville Prison for nearly a year, awaiting trial. The sad thing is that though it was strongly suspected Kyle murdered Corbett, by the time the police got to the murder locus in the club, it had been bleached clean. From the outset there was insufficient evidence to connect Kyle to the murder of Daniela Corbett and of course, no witnesses came forward, hence no murder charge was libelled against him; just charges relating to his drug and pornography businesses with the evidence of those charges coming from McGuire's statement."

McIntosh sensed that something went wrong and asked, "So what happened?"

"It seems that somehow much of the evidence against Kyle mysteriously went missing and at least two witnesses went back on their statements, having obviously been got at. McGuire's statement alone was not enough to continue with the Crown's prosecution and the trial collapsed. Within hours, McGuire and Corbett's daughter Alice disappeared into the Witness Protection Programme."

"Well," he huffed, "the security of the programme can't be all *that* good if a Sergeant in the Devon and Cornwall Police can tell me that one of his neighbours used to be involved in serious gangland criminality in London, can it? You said the evidence went missing. How was that possible?"

She shrugged her shoulders. "It's the Met, Gordon. Right now they are undergoing a very public anti-corruption operation at the minute and from what I am hearing and what's on the news, they're arresting a fair number of police officers daily. Because we're the polis doesn't mean we're immune to temptation or coercion," she stared at him.

"You're right, of course. Well, this certainly puts the cat among the pigeons, Glenda and again begs the question; was Alice Trelawney," he glanced at her, "we'll stick with that name for now. Was she murdered by one of her punters or is her murder something to do with her father or step-father, whatever you want to call him, and his feud with this London gangster, Kyle?"

Simon Johnson stopped the car and switched off the engine, listening for the noise that had been rattling about now for some weeks. He wasn't mechanically minded and the standing joke in the family was when Simon heard a rattle in the car, he simply turned the radio up louder. Annoyed that the six year old Chrysler Avenger was probably going to cost him yet more money, he locked the car and glanced along Merryburn Avenue to his parents detached bungalow, the neat and tidy garden surrounded by a freshly painted wrought iron fence; testament to his father's recent retired status. The fence, he assumed was one of the 'get round to it' jobs his dad had promised himself when the 'great day' arrived. As he walked to the front gate, Simon hoped there were enough jobs about the house to keep his father Michael occupied and out of the hair of his house-proud wife, Alison.

"Hello son," his father ushered him through the door. "Have you had your tea yet? We're just about to eat but you know your mum," he raised his eyebrows, "makes enough to feed an army. Anyway," his placed his hand on his son's shoulder as he gently led him along the short hallway, "you're just in time for the BBC six o'clock news."

"Is that Simon," his mother called through from the lounge.

"Hi mum, it's me," Simon replied, pushing open the lounge door and joining his mother on the couch.

The three sat through the news headlines, watching the video footage of dirty and exhausted paratroopers herding Argentinean prisoners from the Goose Green battle site; the camera hovering over the bodies of the fallen soldiers, young men whose nationality in death meant nothing. The forefront of the news was the Parachute battalion's Commanding Officer Colonel Jones was among the British dead, shot while heroically leading his men against a dug-in machine-gun nest.

Simon felt his mother's hand in his, her other hand holding a handkerchief to her eyes as her worry and concern for her son Peter spilled over to tears.

He leaned against her and wrapped an arm about her shaking shoulders.

"Don't worry mum," he whispered to her, "Peter's on a supply ship. He'll be okay. Just you wait and see."

Lizzie McLeish used her left hand to steady her right hand that held the lipstick, the shakes already threatening to disrupt her evening in the Drag. Her hand slipped and smeared a gash across her cheek. Frustrated, she threw the lipstick into the sink bowl and wiping her face with a used tissue, loudly cursed Wingy for not giving her the wrap. The tenner bag was of no use to her, she had whined, reminding him that Friday night on the Drag was the best paying night when the city centre was busy and that she could pay double the next time she visited him, but he had point blank refused her pleas.

He had laughed from behind his window at her threats and abuse and it was only when the elderly wifie leaned out of her first flat window and screamed, "I'm sick of you people coming to this close at all hours of the night! I've had enough of it, so I have! Fuck off, ya wee prossie!" then waving her phone and threatening to call the polis, did Lizzie stumble away and home.

Now, wearing the suspender belt and short yellow coloured PVC skirt, the low cut yellow top and no bra, she knew that though she hated the thought, as long as any punter was holding cash, she was prepared to do anything that the punter wanted; anything at all.

Mark Renwick parked his white coloured Morris Ital outside the pub in Dumbarton Road and locking it, stood back to admire the vehicle. The car, just over one year old, had been a gift from his father, proud of his son's promotion to Detective Inspector after such a short time serving with the police. His father's Council connections had assured Mark a good price from the dealer, who coincidentally also provided the Council with a proportion of their business vehicles.

It didn't occur to Mark that owning a vehicle obtained by such a deal might be construed by some as bordering on impropriety, just as the word corruption never entered his head.

He pushed open the doors of the nearby pub, his nose wrinkling with disgust at the fuggy smoke-laden atmosphere and shaking his head, wondered again why his brother Davie, three years Marks senior, frequented such places. Clearly, as he glanced about him, the clientele were lower working class and the foul curses bandied about seemed to indicate the type of punter the pub catered for.

"Hey, there's my wee bro'," shouted a voice from the corner.

Mark turned and forced a grin. His brother Davie, a pint glass in one hand and a cigarette dangling from his lips, was pushing through the crowd towards him. Reaching him, Davie, who was obviously the worse for wear through drink, threw his free arm around his slighter built Mark's shoulder.

"Come and meet the boys," he bellowed unnecessarily into Renwick's ear, spraying Mark with a fine drizzle of phlegm. "They're a right good bunch. They're my lad's from the barracks."

Half dragged through the protesting crowd towards the corner, Mark was noisily introduced to Davie's pals; eight men sporting short or cropped hair, all of whom like Davie, wore army fatigue trousers and polished boots. The men differed in the selection of shirts they wore, from plain coloured sweat tops to one individual, who drunkenly propped against the back wall, seemed to be almost comatose and wore a Mickey Mouse cartoon shirt.

He could plainly see the men, whose ages ranged from late teens to early thirties, were all drunk and wondered how his brother Davie, whose stomach hung over his thick, leather belt, could possibly fit in with the obviously fit and athletically built group.

"My boys, my section lads," shouted Davie with a grin, then raising his pint glass in the air and spilling some of the lager down onto a protesting Mark, shouted loudly, *Four Para!*"

Mark saw some of the TA soldiers sniggering, but then to his embarrassment realised they weren't laughing with Davie, but at him. The sly winks and nudges among the group was a plain indication that his brother was no more than a joke among these young men.

As if to humour Davie, the motley crowd about the table tried to rise to their feet, but while some made it, two fell back down, colliding with the table and spilling their drinks on top of themselves. However, all managed an accompanying, but ragged cheer of, *"Four Para!"*

It did not escape Mark's attention that more than a few of the pub's customers cast evil glances towards the Territorial Army paratroopers. With a cold shiver, it occurred to him that with the current problems ongoing in Northern Ireland, it was not unusual for what might be perceived to be the slightest provocation, pub brawls to erupt in the religiously divided Glasgow.

Being a serving police officer, let alone a Detective Inspector, the last thing Mark needed was to be caught up in a pub fracas.

"Look," he grabbed at his older brother's arm, "I just popped by to say hello," then meaningfully glanced at his watch. "I've actually got to go. I've an early start tomorrow morning," and began to edge away, forcing a grin as he waved to Davie's pals.

"Hang fire a minute, for fuck's sake Mark," the big man whined and grabbing at Mark's arm, downed the remains of his pint in one gulp. "I'm done here anyway. These *wankers*," he shouted the insult with a grin, "had better be fit for parade *tomorrow morning*!" he banged the glass down on the table.

Mark shrunk back, expecting the glass to shatter and saw with some relief it remained unbroken.

"Right," called Davie, still clutching his brother's arm, "you and me are out of here," and propelled the unresisting Mark towards the door, pushing a path through the increasingly hostile crowd till they reached the safety of the door and were outside in the cool air. One arm about Mark's shoulder, the grinning Davie slurred, "Okay, little brother now get me home, there's a good lad."

Reluctantly, Mark led Davie to the car and then helped his older brother into the passenger seat, insisting that the drunken Davie use the seat belt to strap himself in. Davie protested, but Mark insisted. "This will be the law by next year, so you had better get used to it," he sighed, grunting as he leaned across to click the belt into the metal housing.

The drive to their parents' house in the affluent west end of the city took barely five minutes, all the time the drunken Davie raucously singing songs that belittled anyone who wasn't fortunate enough to be either a member of the armed forces or in particular, the Parachute Regiment. At one point, when stopped at a red light on Byres Road, Davie wound down the passenger window and loudly berated a group of youths standing outside a corner pub. To his brother's horror, some of the group angrily made towards the car, forcing Mark to stamp on the accelerator and speed through a red light to avoid confrontation with the youths, some of whom threw cans and at least one pint tumbler after the speeding car. Davie, laughing hysterically, leaned from the window and shouted loudly, "Wankers" at the fist-waving group.

Mark, his heart in his mouth, could hardly speak, so enraged was he at his brothers idiocy that might include Mark in an incident that most certainly would have involved the police.

Incandescent with rage, he drove in silence towards his parents' house in Cleveland Drive, ignoring Davie's attempts to engage him in conversation; drunkenly rambling to Mark about the pending invasion. If Davie was to be believed he apparently expected the Spanish army to first invade Gibraltar then land on the shores of the UK in support of the Argentineans.

Had he not realised that Davie was extremely drunk, Mark would have had serious doubts about his brother's sanity.

Outside the large, detached house at number sixty-eight, he stopped the car, his hands still tightly gripping the steering wheel to stop them from shaking. He watched as Davie stumbled from the car and made his way laughingly up the path to the front door, but before Davie got there it was snatched open by their father. Mark saw Davie stop and even in the half-light, watched as his brother's head drooped and his shoulders sag at the sight of their father.

John 'Dodger' Renwick, now in his sixty-second year, stood white-faced. Dressed in a dark coloured, silk dressing gown, the large man seemed to fill the doorway. Standing at six feet tall, in his youth Dodger had been an amateur boxer whose muscular frame had developed through his early, formative years working in the Clyde shipyards. However, as time passed the same muscle had run to fat and now he was almost clinically obese.

His son Davie had inherited Dodger's physique while Mark had taken after their slightly built mother, Martha, who was two years her husband's junior.

Dodger had earned his nickname from his Clydeside workmates who through the years, watched him dodge his paid occupation as a welder to ambitiously pursue his career in the Labour Party, rising from shop steward through to his current prestigious role as one of the leading members of the Glasgow City Council. More than one former workmate had been heard to comment that on a Friday pay night, Dodger would rather sit in some draughty community hall and listen to the Red Clydesiders, as the then Communists were commonly known, spout their shite than meet his mates for a pint. But the same mates knew that Dodger wasn't there to fight for and improve the conditions of the working class; Dodger attended the meetings to further his own political agenda and for Dodger in the long run, it had paid off handsomely.

Now the leading light of local Labour politics, Dodger was about to achieve his ultimate goal; his party's candidacy for one of the thirteen Glasgow constituencies and nothing, as far as Dodger was concerned, would interfere with his election to the UK Government. If truth were told, Dodger really didn't give a toss about which party won the 1983 election; all that mattered was that he won his candidacy and was elected to serve as an MP; for the prestige, highly lucrative salary and opportunities such a position offered were Dodger's true ambition. However, on that dark night, he stared at his older son staggering up the garden path toward him and could not disguise the disappointment that he felt as Davie shuffled past him and into the house. His second son Mark, locking the car and closing the garden gate, earned a huge smile from his father who grasped his hand and shook it firmly. "At least one of my boys turned out all right," he called out loudly as he slapped Mark on the back and led him into the house.

Entering the brightly lit hallway, Mark could not refrain from grinning at his brother's back as Davie wearily climbed the stairs to his bedroom. When both were children, Mark had been intimidated by Davie and suffered his older brother's bullying taunts and physical abuse; punches and kicks that their parents had not witnessed. His complaints at Davie's treatment soon stopped after his father's admonishment that Mark should '*stand up and be a man*'. Through their childhood and adolescence, Mark's revenge had been to lay blame at Davie's door for any small disappearance of cash, household breakage or unexplained misfortune that occurred in the house. Whether Davie ever discovered or suspected his brother's deviousness, Mark neither knew nor cared. As far as he was concerned, he had achieved what he set out to do; win his father's attention and support in anything that he did.

As for Dodger, he daily criticised Davie's lack of educational achievement, his son's inability to hold down even the most menial of jobs and his on-going dependence on his parents for both his accommodation and financial supplement to his meagre unemployment benefit. Even Davie's most recent venture, volunteering almost eight months previously to join the TA Para's, the 'Weekend Warriors', had evoked sneering laughter from his father who privately gave his son no more than a month before Davie once again whined about the difficulties and packed it in.

It surprised not just Dodger, but Mark too that Davie continued to attend and endure the hardships of the training regime. They could not know that the bulky, awkwardly unfit Davie continued to be retained by the TA simply to boost their personnel numbers; that his continuing presence at the training nights and weekends added to their resource allocation for both equipment and financial MoD support. What the TA instructors would not disclose to Davie was that his bumbling poor fitness meant it extremely unlikely he would ever be selected for the prestigious P Company and consequently, would never to be sent for parachute training to earn the coveted paratrooper wings.

However, none of his TA colleagues nor any his family suspected that the one thing in which Davie excelled was an overactive and very vivid imagination.

Dodger led his favourite son into the large front room lounge with its heavy, dark oak furniture and glancing round the large room, again inwardly smirked at his good fortune. The house was a far cry from the rundown two-bedroom council flat in Duntocher, where Dodger and his new and pregnant wife Martha had begun their married life. The room smacked of an affluence that neither could have then envisaged. The rich tapestry of the floor to ceiling curtains, courtesy of a deal with a grateful constituent; the tasteful décor, whose wallpaper was hung and painted by a team of council painters. The ornate furniture, purchased at an extremely discounted price from a retailer as a favour to Dodger in gratitude for the knockdown sale of a plot of council land and Dodger's influence in driving through the planning permission to permit the mans new store to be constructed. In fact, the room represented the house; an affluence gained through influence and power, however, the only thing that didn't fit into the lifestyle and was out of place was Dodger's wife, Martha.

Martha Templeton, or Missus Renwick as she was publicly referred, to appear to be a dowdy and timid woman, but it had not always been so. Through the years standing in the wake of her husband's rising political star, Martha had lost her identity and become a shadow woman; referred to by Dodger when in polite company as his loving wife and occasionally dusted off and brought out for public or civic functions when protocol demanded a united family front. However, Martha's bodily use to her husband had long since withered and Dodger no longer retained any real affection for her. He made no secret of it to Martha, delighting in privately humiliating her with his preference for the company of the women willingly provided by an associate who owned a string of brothels. Such favour was rewarded by Dodger with an occasional discreet word when, via his position on the Police and Fire Committee, Dodger learned that the police intended to take an interest in the man's brothels.

No, Martha was of no real physical use as a woman, but never would Dodger consider divorcing her, for a sensitive public did not look kindly upon a politician who abandoned a loyal wife and particularly with next year's General Election looming.

This then was Dodger's family.

Davie, who in Dodger's eyes was worthless and repeatedly failed in all he attempted.

His second son Mark, a rising star in the police, but rather more by courtesy of his father's influence than his own talent.

His wife Martha, whose life revolved round a house that was not a home and whose relationship with her husband, both physical and emotional had long since faded then died, but remained as his wife simply for political window dressing rather than any love or sentimental attachment.

From a pseudo Georgian drinks cabinet, Dodger selected a ten-year-old malt and poured two generous fingers into the heavy, cut glasses, then handed one to Mark.

"I've to drive home, Dad," protested Mark.

"Don't be a wimp," Dodger replied. "I'll get you a bloody taxi, if need be. Drink up with your old man," he chivvied his son as he settled his bulk into a large and comfortable armchair.

Mark was uncomfortable; the truth was he was nervous of his intimidating father and didn't relish being alone with Dodger. Worse, he dare not admit that he found the taste of whisky revolting.

"So, what's happening in you office these days, son?" asked Dodger, breaking into Mark's thoughts. "Anything exciting happening?"

Slowly, sipping at his whisky, Mark recounted the finding of the girl's body, but in his retelling of the tale, it was Mark who was the lead detective in the case.

Ronnie Kyle irritably tapped the stubby fingers of his right hand on the ornate desk, his face blank, but his thoughts on the betrayal by the man he trusted most; Cris McGuire.

Across the desk, the six feet three inch bulk of the former boxer Moses Parker lounged silently in the padded leather armchair.

Kyle glanced across at the huge man. Since the departure of McGuire, the large Jamaican headed up Kyle's team of enforcers and, he inwardly chuckled, with a ruthless efficiency that had been lacking in McGuire. His eyes narrowed; McGuire, thought Kyle? He glanced at the writing pad in front of him. Trelawney, apparently he was now calling himself and wondered why the name sounded so familiar.

He reached for the phone and dialled a number that he hadn't called for some years.

When the call was answered he grinned and said, "Eddie me old son, how's it hanging?"

For a few seconds, Kyle listened to the gruff Glaswegian before smiling and winking at Parker then continued, "Eddie, I need a small favour, pal. I'm coming up to visit you up there in Jockland, sometime over the next day or two," but then his brow creased and his need for instant and swift retribution kicked in. "No, make that tomorrow. Yeah, that's right," he nodded and grinned as he spoke. "Me and one of my boys. I need you to get me a pitch; nothing too fancy, somewhere in the city centre. No, not a hotel; a flat maybe? That and somewhere I can conduct a private interview," he grinned evilly. "Oh and Eddie, I'll need wheels, preferably a closed van, something reliable, but won't stick out and get a pull from the filth, know what I mean? Oh yeah and one last thing, Eddie, something long that's been shortened, if you get my meaning; a double one that can be ditched when the jobs done. And Eddie, I'll be happy to recompense you for your trouble, me old son."

Parker saw Kyle nodding his head before finally telling Eddie, "I'll give you a bell on the trumpet when me and my boy is on our way." He listened then replied, "Glasgow, Eddie and probably from Gatwick tomorrow."

He replaced the phone in the cradle and stared at Parker before telling him, "Pack a bag, Moses and arrange for a couple of tickets for you and me. It's time we settled an old score."

"I ain't been to Glasgow before boss," Moses looked puzzled, "and I know it ain't as big as the Smoke, but how the fuck are we going to find Cris is a city?"

Kyle cunningly smiled and tapped the side of his nose. "Don't you be worrying about that, me old son. My pal Eddie has his sources. He'll get it sorted, you wait and see."

In the privacy of his attic conversion bedroom, the door locked behind him, a drunken Davie Renwick reached to the back of his sock drawer and fetched out the small key, then stumbled to the bed. Using both hands on the mattress to support himself he bent down and on his knees, from under the bed drew a battered suitcase towards him. Grunting as he lifted the case onto the bed, he drunkenly fumbled at the lock, finally releasing both catches and throwing back the lid. He lifted out the magazines and pulling back the protective towel, grinned at the suitcase contents, tenderly stroking the dull, 7.62 copper-headed bullets that lay neatly in the belt of ammunition beside the four trip-flares and the three hand grenades, stolen the previous month by Davie during the weekend live firing trip to the army range in Northumberland.

I will be ready, he drunkenly thought to himself, when they need me, I'll be ready.

He took a deep breath, recalling the indignities showered on him through the years by his father. "I'll fucking show him," he grunted aloud, his teeth grinding as he fantasised, his thoughts vividly stark as he saw himself storming against the foe, whoever that might be. Enemies would run from him while his men followed the heroic Davie.

Tears formed in his eyes as he imagined the adulation of the crowds when he paraded through his native Glasgow, the medals he would win bouncing on his chest and glinting in the bright sunlight. The women, young women he smiled to himself, throwing flowers to celebrate the homecoming of their very own hero.

He exhaled and reached into the suitcase and brought out his prize possession, tenderly rubbing it against his cheek. It had cost just a fiver at the east-end market, the Glasgow Barra's; a relic of the last world war. It had been rusted and needed attention, but Davie had lovingly oiled and polished it, restoring it to its fighting condition.

Almost with reverence, he laid the thin bladed, black metalled commando dagger back into the suitcase and covering it with the towel, then closed the lid.

CHAPTER 10 – 5am, Saturday morning, 29 May

Cris Trelawney reckoned he had now been driving for over six straight hours and he decided for now that enough was enough and pulled off the M6 into a service station. After completing his toilet in the restaurant building he returned to the car and from the boot, fetched the flask of coffee and sandwiches Louise had thoughtfully made up. He smiled at the handwritten note that warned him to be careful, that she wanted him home safe and signed with a large 'X' for a kiss. He stood at the rear of the car, enjoying the cool of the night air, munching the food and sipping at the coffee, but his thoughts were on the events over ten years previously when his life almost completely turned to shit.

Daniela had been a few years younger than Cris; a single mother raising the eight-year-old Alice on her own, using the only skill and ability she had; her body. Her basic education, she used to boast, had resulted in a Degree in Life and though she hadn't meant to fall into stripping, the money she earned enabled her to maintain her rent and care for her daughter, as well as hiring a child-minder for Alice during the evenings she stripped at Ronnie Kyle's Soho clubs.

Cris inwardly smiled, recalling the first time he had met her. Daniela was performing at the Green Parrot Nite-Club and he had given her a line about how lovely she was, before asking her out for a drink. She had given him a dazzling, professional smile and told him to try one of the other girls, that she didn't date gangsters. So full of himself, he had been surprised to be rebuffed like that and standing leaning his back against the old Volvo, sipping at his coffee, wasn't aware he was grinning and shaking his head, remembered that in those days he thought of himself as a right Jack the Lad. My God, how she had intrigued him. Of course, that had made him even more determined to pursue her and after some discreet inquiry among her friends at the club, discovering that she had a child and didn't party; that she wasn't into night's out with the girls, but led a quiet life with her daughter.

It was the film that did it.

He caught her one night just before she went home and asked for a favour. She had been suspicious until he explained that he really wanted to see a film that had just been released, but needed to borrow someone's child to go with him because it was a Disney animated movie, 'Robin Hood'. That had set her off laughing and to his relief, she'd agreed.

He had met her and the shy Alice the following night at the cinema then after the movie, the three of them went for a Wimpey burger and chips. Two months later he moved them both into his upmarket flat in Hackney and they had lived happily for almost two years, before….

Cris exhaled loudly and threw the dregs of the coffee onto the nearby grass verge, then returned the remaining sandwiches and the flask into the boot of the car. For the first time in … God, he couldn't remember since when, he wanted a cigarette, but he resisted the urge and climbed into the driver's seat. He didn't immediately start the engine, knowing that he was at least for now, too tense to drive. He thought again of Alice, how hard it had been for him to tell her that Daniela was gone and the lies he had told to ease the pain of her mother's murder; lies that had finally caught up with him and for which he was again paying the price. He gripped the wheel till his knuckles showed white and his body shook with rage and frustration; experiencing an overwhelming urge to find and deal with the man who had caused him so much grief and heartache. He sighed and inwardly admitted that no matter what Ronnie Kyle had done, Cris knew that ultimately, he himself was to blame for much of the things that had gone wrong with his life. He had hurt people, some he knew and a lot that he did not; all for the sake of being one of the gang, one of Ronnie's boys, the prestige and money that enforcing had brought him. He had committed some dark deeds, things that would haunt him forever. He thrust his head back hard into the headrest and tightly closed his eyes, seeing in his mind the admonishing face of Daniela.

At the breakdown of the case, he and Alice had been hustled from London to their new life in Cornwall. The change of identity, the cottage, the one-off payment and the wiping clean of his past; it had seemed like a fresh start. It had begun for Alice almost like a game. A new name, a new school and '*let's keep our secret, sweetheart*' had lasted for a long, long time and she had kept the secret, just as she'd promised.

Gradually, the first year over, the questions about her mother had faded as he grew closer to his adopted daughter and her to him until finally, she seemed to accept that her father was the only parent in her life.

Even two years previously when, Louise and Jack had come into their lives, it seemed that everything was fine and he had never been happier.

She never questioned her parentage; at least not till recently.

He had known it was a mistake to keep the photographs and the few letters, all contained within Daniela's vanity case, but he had not been able to bear parting with them; one of the few things he had brought with them from London.

The month before she left had been hard for them both. At first he didn't understand, couldn't comprehend her moods.

Louise had tried to tell him it was a teenage thing.

He should have suspected it was more than that though, for unusually Alice seemed unwilling to speak with him and her sullen attitude confused him, but like most parents, he decided that yes, it was probably just teenage angst.

As the awkwardness between them persisted he was bewildered, unable to understand her reluctance to discuss and share things that had previously always been open between them. Even her refusal to accompany him lobster potting out on the boat, a pastime she had always enjoyed had confused him until finally, irked, he had snapped. Things had been said, words that couldn't be drawn back and to his horror, it had come out.

She had discovered the small case with the album of photographs and the letters – and the poster.

He had kept the small poster as a joke; a flyer really that had been printed to entice the punters into the club. He and Daniela laughed at the poster and it was forgotten, carelessly and stupidly left between the photo album pages. The album of baby photographs, of Alice and her mum.

Photographs for the first years that did not include Cris.

She had found the album and delighted in the pictures until she found the poster that advertised Daniela as the top billing stripper in Kyle's club.

Her initial shock that slowly turned to anger that finally descended upon Cris, reminding him of the lies that he had told her through the years.

Her decision to cancel her place at Exeter University and instead travel to Glasgow University had surprised him, but he recognised her need to get away, to calm down, to realise that above all else, her mother loved her as did he.

Fourteen long months she had been gone and not one word. Nothing; his letters returned, unopened and marked 'Not At This Address.'

He choked back a sob that threatened to engulf him; nothing till this.

Taking a deep breath, he turned the key and started the engine then smoothly drove with increasing speed towards the motorway on-ramp.

Gordon McIntosh's wife Mary, her dressing gown wrapped tightly about her, was slowly coming to terms with the imminent change in their lives. Turning the bacon in the frying pan, she flipped the eggs, knowing Gordon liked them turned, but her mind was on other things, primarily his forthcoming retirement. Had Mary any say in the issue he'd be on retirement leave right now and not investigating yet another bloody murder. A practising Christian, she unconsciously shook her head, ashamed that her selfishness so easily dismissed the death of a wee lassie. "Morning love," said Gordon from behind her, slapping playfully at her backside as he made his way past her to his seat at the kitchen table. "That smells good. Can I have two eggs please?"

"I always give you two eggs, you silly man," his wife pretended to growl at him, using the fish slice to scoop the bacon, eggs and fried bread onto his plate.

McIntosh rubbed his hands in delight at the breakfast laid before him. "Right I'll murder this then I'll be on my way," he joked, the pun escaping him, but not Mary who giggled.

"How are things going, with the murder I mean?"

McIntosh blew a raspberry through pursed lips and shook his head. "It's early days yet, hen. The murdered girl's father is arriving today from Cornwall, so Glenda will be taking him to the mortuary to ID the wee girl then I'll meet him at the office, break the news about her," he replied. "It'll not be easy," his eyes narrowed. "No man wants to hear bad things about his child."

His thoughts turned to his own three children, a son recently married, another making his way across the world and daughter and her husband expecting his first grandchild at the end of September.

McIntosh had no compunction about discussing his inquiry with his wife, reasoning that after all, Mary had lived with him as a detective's wife since his appointment to the CID, twenty-five years previously and had almost as much knowledge of his cases as did he. However, there was no reason that she need know about the Cornishman's chequered past for, he rightly believed, the less people who knew, the better.

She stood over him and laid a gentle hand on his shoulder. "I know that you'll say the right thing, Gordon. You're a father yourself, so you'll know how the man is feeling."

He reached up and laying his hand over hers, nodded.

He was thinking that with a normal father, he would generally agree, however, the man from Cornwall; he might just prove to be a little different.

Lizzie McLeish woke with her usual headache and craving, but what's new, she thought. She lay as still as she could in an effort to prevent the wave of nausea forcing her from her bed to the bathroom and thought of the previous night's work. She could not stop herself from grinning. Just one punter, her first for the night and it had earned her one hundred and fifty quid!

The punter, some Swedish or Danish guy, she wasn't too sure where he was from, had offered her thirty quid, but wanted to shag her in his room at the Central Hotel. Sneaking past the desk clerk had been a riot! The punter was almost shitting himself in case he was caught and turned out of his suite.

Lizzie involuntarily coughed and held her head in both hands, the pain crashing through her head like a bunch of drunken Celtic fans rushing the bar at closing time. She took a deep breath and forced her body to relax, shutting her eyes tightly until the pain subsided. Again, she thought of last night's punter; his insistence she washed herself clean in the en-suite, watching her while she did so. She didn't mind him seeing her pee and douse herself, having long ago abandoned modesty in favour of sterling.

She wasn't happy that he wanted to ride her 'bareback', that he hadn't wanted to use a condom, but the promise of the extra twenty quid had settled any argument she might have.

In the bed, he had thrust at her and come almost right away and she just knew that he was a virgin, but she didn't expect him to cry and apologise for shagging her, weeping like a wean and telling her he had a girlfriend back home, wherever the fuck that was.

She had felt a little sorry for the man and tried to make him feel better and offered to give him a free blowjob. He had all excited and when she told him to go and wash himself he had hurried through to the en-suite. Stupid sod. When he closed the bathroom door, that's when she'd nicked his wallet and fucked off. The cards in the wallet were of no use to her and she had chucked them away, regretting it now for had she thought about it, she might have been able to sell them to Wingy. Eyes tightly shut, she slowly breathed in; one hundred and fifty fucking quid! It was a fortune.

She risked opening her eyes and tried to ignore the pounding in her skull. She turned her head to glance at the bedside clock, anticipating the pleasure of the hit the money would buy.

I'll give it another five minutes she decided and then pay Wingy a visit.

Simon Johnson switched on the car radio in time to catch the nine o'clock morning news. The headline repeated the news of the victory at Goose Green, though tempered the report with the number of casualties sustained by the British Forces. The reporter then described the arrangements made for the historic visit later that day by Pope John Paul to Canterbury Cathedral.

The murder of Alice Trelawney, or according to the radio broadcaster more correctly, the body in the park, was now, Simon dryly noted, old news.

As he drove, he reflected on his previous evenings visit to his parents' house. His mother's worried concern for his brother Peter had caused Simon to be restless and he had barely slept through the night; Peter's anguished face haunting him in the wildest and craziest of dreams.

Turing onto Barrhead Road, he forced himself to concentrate on the inquiry and wondered what job the DCI would have for DI Burroughs today.

Glenda Burroughs, he inanely grinned. Now there's a woman he wouldn't mind…..the shrill sound of the car horn panicked him into swerving back to the inside lane. He sheepishly waved a hand at the irate fist-waving driver with whom he had almost collided, watching as the car sped away towards the approaching roundabout.

Bloody hell, he reflected; I nearly came a cropper twice in as many days.

Taking a deep breath, he unconsciously eased off on the accelerator and began humming with Paul McCartney and Stevie Wonders as the musicians belted out their hit, '*Ebony and Ivory.*' Now fully awake and a little chastened by his near miss, he continued towards Pollok police office.

DI Mark Renwick arrived at Pollok office to find that DS Brian Davidson was already at his desk. Neither man acknowledged the other and Renwick settled behind his desk, noting that nothing had changed and there was no new items waiting for his attention. He glanced at Davidson and asked, "Is there anything new in this morning? Anything at all that I should be aware of prior, to the DCI's briefing?"

"Nothing sir," Davidson, with emphasis on 'sir', curtly replied, his eyes scanning the report in front of him, but then, as if suddenly recalling and without looking up, added "There was a message from the nightshift clerk at the Blue Swallow Hotel on Paisley Road West. He responded as we requested and informed the uniform bar that Mister Trelawney, the dead girl's father booked in a couple of hours ago. Mister Trelawney was given the DCI's note and told to expect a call from the DCI, later this morning."

Renwick nodded, not trusting himself to speak, conscious that Davidson must still be bristling about their confrontation the previous day.

The door opened to admit DCI Gordon McIntosh who cheerfully greeted both his officers as he made his way towards the table that bore the tea and coffee makings. "Anything doing?" he addressed Renwick.

"Eh, yes sir," replied Renwick, joining McIntosh at the table, "Mister Trelawney arrived and is booked into the Blue Swallow Hotel. He's been informed to expect a call from you this morning, sir."

Renwick made no mention that it was Davidson who had received the information.

McIntosh nodded in understanding and holding a mug upright, inquired if Davidson wanted coffee, but received a curt shake of the head in reply. It didn't escape his attention that there still existed a tension between them both. Inwardly he sighed and thought that if these two idiots wanted to continue their playground spat, as long as it didn't interfere with the inquiry, he would simply ignore it.

The desk phone rang at Davidson's elbow and McIntosh saw his face startle. "It's for you sir," said Davidson, handing the phone to McIntosh, then in a whisper added, "it's ACC Murray."

Renwick and Davidson watched as McIntosh listened for a few minutes, then finally said, "Yes sir, of course sir. I understand," they heard him say and saw him replace the receiver.

"Well, gentlemen," he sighed and turned towards them, "it seems that Bellahouston Park for the foreseeable future will be off limits for anyone hoping to use the park for, how shall I put this," he smiled, "recreational purposes. The ACC has instructed that as of early evening today and in expectation of the *Papal* visit, our uniform colleagues will be mounting a watch at the locked gates as well as a roving dog patrol within the Park itself. In short, while no longer to be considered a crime scene and in agreement with the city council, the Park is now on lockdown."

Simon Johnson sat among the rest of the inquiry team as they joked and chatted among themselves, enjoying the camaraderie of the detectives and even more determined to make a success of his secondment. The light-hearted banter continued while the team awaited the arrival of the DCI to commence the morning briefing.

DI Glenda Burroughs, dressed in a lemon coloured skirted suit and pale green blouse, pushed through the door held open by McIntosh, who in turn led Renwick and Davidson into the cramped room.

McIntosh's briefing was brief and to the point. Bluntly informing the assembled team that there was no new information or developments, the DCI outlined his plan for the late hours of that evening. The team would be dispatched to the Drag area of the city and speak with the prostitutes who were working there, gleaning what they could about the victim or any punter that caused suspicion among the women.

While McIntosh continued his delivery, Simon's shoulders drooped, aware that he would have to cancel the dinner arranged for that evening with Bob and Sheila Speirs and Sheila's friend. He knew that as a fellow cop, Bob would understand, but the fiery Sheila would have to explain to her friend why Simon wasn't arriving and that he would be held to account later for his non-appearance. Inwardly grinning, he figured it would cost him a bunch of flowers and a box of Sheila's favourite chocolate, Cadbury's All Gold.

For that few seconds his attention had lapsed and he suddenly realised the DCI was relating that the dead girls father had arrived and was being accommodated in a hotel on Paisley Road West.

"So, after this briefing, I'll be attending with DI Burroughs to interview Mister Trelawney, though I think it highly unlikely that he may able to provide anything that will assist us in the short term. However, I know that DI Renwick has the actions for you guys ready, but what I want is for you to knock off about midday, get home and have some hot food and a rest, then meet here again tonight at five o'clock when we'll have a further briefing prior to you going out to the Drag."

There was a veiled murmur of protest from the officers and then McIntosh put his hands up, almost in surrender. The hush quietened.

"Look, I know that you would rather stay on and work through and that staying on duty would incur overtime as opposed to a split shift, but the reality ladies and gentlemen is that there is a very little money in the pot. There was a senior management meeting last week at headquarters and it was decided that due to the manpower and resources being deployed for next week's *Papal* visit, the cost will be met by cutting back on overtime."

"So, murder inquiries get humped then boss?" said a voice from the crowd.

"Look," snapped an angry and red-faced McIntosh, his finger pointing at the speaker, "I don't like this any more than you do, but just like you, I have to work within the budget restrictions imposed upon me," he finished with a growl.

A silence descended upon the room with a palpable atmosphere that was uncomfortable; each officer in the room ignoring their colleagues and all too intimidated to stare down the irate McIntosh.

McIntosh ran a weary hand across his brow, his tone now softer and more conciliatory. "I know the old argument folks; had it been a lawyer's daughter or a councillors or doctors daughter, it might have been different, that the money for the investigation would somehow be found. But as I said, the reality is that the wee lassie was a prostitute and there is some," he took a deep breath, "that might consider her to be one of the dregs of society. Well, I really couldn't give a toss what the wee lassie did to keep body and soul together. As far as I'm…." he stopped and glared at the officers, shaking his head as he did so, "as far as *we* are concerned, the victim deserves our very best effort to find her killer and that, ladies and gentlemen, is exactly what we will do, whether or not management give us funds. Is there anyone here has any other thought about this issue, because now is the time to speak up. No? Right then, let's get it done."

With that, he turned and stomped out of the room, followed by Renwick and Glenda Burroughs.

"Right guys," Brian Davidson took charge, "see me for your actions and I'll let you know what streets you are covering tonight at the drag."

Glenda Burroughs beckoned Simon to her as he came through the door.

"Grab a set of keys, young Simon. You're driving the DCI and me down to the hotel to meet with Mister Trelawney."

Simon nodded and turned back into the office. Explaining the request to Brian Davidson, he saw Davidson smile, then handed Simon the key of the Morris Ital, the CID car that every Pollok CID officer knew was favoured by DI Renwick.

"Can't have the DCI travelling down there is a shite-heap now, can we?" smirked Davidson.

Simon, tight-lipped, took the keys and thought why is it I feel like the man in the middle between these two muppets?

CHAPTER 11

The young, snappily dressed Ports Control Unit detective ambled through the Terminal, taking his time and deftly avoiding colliding with that morning's passengers. He had half an hour to kill before the Belfast security flight arrived and apart from the police warrant card that hung about his neck on a thin, blue coloured lanyard, he might have easily been mistaken for a business traveller arriving or departing Glasgow Airport. Hands in his trouser pockets, he casually ambled towards the airport shop where the young and pretty assistant worked, intent on catching her alone and persuading her to have dinner with him.

Discreetly, he removed the gold band from his finger and as he neared the shop, unconsciously straightened his already perfectly knotted tie.

The young woman was aware of the detective approaching her shop and with subdued excitement, pretended she hadn't seen him and subtly made her way to a corner of the shop where she rearranged a magazine display on the counter. She glanced up, her eyes fluttering in anticipation of her practised 'surprised look', but was puzzled to see him suddenly veer off towards the Domestic Arrivals gate. Huffily, she snorted at what she perceived to be her prospective new beau's indifference and made her back to the cash till, reflecting that the young guy might not be as interested as she had first thought.

What she could not know was the young detective had not dismissed the opportunity for a romantic encounter, but been distracted by the sight of a man who was notorious in the Glasgow criminal underworld.

Two years service as a detective in Gorbals CID had introduced the young officer to not only the routine criminality and endemic violence of the area, but taught him that at the top of the pile of shit he daily dealt with was the formidable and apparently untouchable Eddie Beattie.

Slipping behind a group of well-dressed, Dutch speaking business executives awaiting the arrival of their escort, the detective covertly watched as the tall and groomed figure of Beattie, impeccably dressed in a camel coat and wearing his trademark light grey coloured Fedora, stood with his hands clasped behind his back, his attention apparently focused on the overhead Flight Arrivals Board. The detective saw two younger, stocky built men; both casually dressed in denim jeans and black leather jackets, though curiously wearing ties, standing on either side, but slightly behind Beattie. One he recognised as a local Gorbals hard man, recalling the guy had more than once been arrested by the young detective and usually for crimes of violence, but the second man was not known to him. Then he remembered; Beattie never travelled anywhere without being accompanied by a couple of minders.

The detective's curiosity was aroused as he deftly removed the warrant card from his neck and slipped it into a pocket. He believed that with the number of people standing or walking about, it was unlikely Beattie or his minders would pay much attention to him; nevertheless, he took the precaution of walking to a better position from which to observe the trio.

He cursed his decision not to carry one of the PCU radios with him and wished that the new black and white close circuit photographic cameras recently installed in the Belfast arrival lounge to photograph incoming suspects, had been installed in all the arrival lounges in the Airport. Maybe worth a suggestion to the boss, he inwardly thought.

Ten minutes passed and he glanced at his watch, wondering how long this would take and knew there would be hell to pay if he was not at his post five minutes before the Belfast flight landed. Could he risk finding an internal airport phone and get someone to cover for him, he wondered, but that might mean losing sight of Beattie.

A swarm of passengers emerged from the Domestic Arrival's gate and his excitement rose when he saw Beattie, his arms outstretched, greet and embrace a swarthy, rotund middle-aged man wearing a dark coloured, three-piece business suit beneath a three-quarter length black leather coat. Beattie's minders stood respectfully back, then stepped forward to shake hands with a tall, powerfully built black man dressed in a three-quarter length black, leather coat who carried two overnight bags, but also wearing a black skipped cap and whose face, the detective saw, looked like it had lost an argument with a pulp hammer.

The tattooed minder took a bag from the black man and all five walked towards a Terminal exit door.

Exhaling softly, his mouth dry, the detective decided that the meeting seemed too interesting to ignore and conscious of his desire to impress his boss and transfer to headquarters Special Branch, took the decision to risk watching Beattie and his associates for another five minutes and risk making the Belfast lounge in time.

The five men crossed the road outside towards the multi-storey car, but then directed by Beattie waving an arm, veered towards the open, ground level car park.

Standing at the entrance to the Airport Terminal, the detective watched from behind a row of parked taxis and had a clear and unobstructed view as the five men stopped beside a black coloured Jaguar vehicle; the car he knew from his time at Gorbals CID as that favoured by Beattie. While he continued to watch, he saw Beattie and the two leather-clad arrivals shake hands. One of the minders pointed to something inside the Jaguar. The large black man reached into the rear of the car and, the officer was certain, opened his coat and placed something inside. That done, the black man shook the minders hand, but the black man's left hand held the object inside the coat.

Through narrowed eyes, his mouth suddenly dry and unaware he was holding his breath, the detective watched Beattie and the minders get into the Jaguar and saw the two arrivals wave goodbye as the car took off towards the car park exit. Both men then walked through the parked vehicles until they were out of sight.

The detective was confused, wondering why the two arrivals had not accompanied Beattie and the minders in the Jaguar, tight fit though it might have been, but almost immediately realised; there was a second vehicle.

Shit! he thought and then hurried across the road, narrowly avoiding being struck by a taxi whose irate driver waved an angry fist at the detectives back as he raced through the car park, his eyes cast back and forth as he sought to locate the two men, but without success.

Annoyed at his failure, he walked back towards the Terminal building, already formulating in his mind the report that he would later submit to the Special Branch Intelligence. Though the report was criminal rather than terrorist related, the young detective figured that once it had been noted and, he smiled at his own good luck, his diligence taken into account, the details would be passed by the SB to their colleagues in Criminal Intelligence. Then it was their problem. He had done his bit.

The detective had just reached the car park exit and was about to step onto the road, but almost in panic hurriedly stepped back onto the pavement when an old, rusting, white coloured Transit van was driven past and almost struck him. He almost raised a fist at the departing van and his near outburst at the driver turned to wide-eyed shock when he realised it was the black man driving with the middle-aged man in the passenger seat, neither of whom had given him a second glance. The rear registration plate was partially obscured by dirt, but with his hands shading his eyes from the bright sun and peering after the van, he was able to discern the last letter 'F' and the numbers… 917L

Grinning widely, he cast his eyes towards the sky and inwardly thought, seems there is a God after all.

Cris Trelawney had rested, but not slept. The room and bed was comfortable enough and though exhausted by the long drive, he still felt too pent up to fully relax. Still, after a shave he spent a good time under a hot shower then towelling himself dry, lay on the bed, his mind racing with questions and images of Alice as a child, a pubescent teenager and lastly, the angry young woman who with an old rucksack on her back, had finally stormed from the cottage. Unable to escape the thoughts, he decided to rise, dress and have some breakfast at the hotel restaurant. He was about to leave the room when the bedside phone rang.

The young receptionist at the front desk was calling to inform him that police officers were waiting to speak with him. They asked should they come to his room or would he prefer to come downstairs to meet with them?

"Please ask them to meet me in the restaurant and I'll see them there in about five minutes," he replied.

He had prepared for them and was already soberly dressed; a self-coloured light blue shirt, navy blue tie, charcoal trousers and highly polished brown boots. Cris didn't think it necessary to wear a jacket, but as a last thought, fetched the most recent photograph that he had, the head and shoulder photograph of a smiling Alice, her hair pinned back with a clasp and taken while she sat on the harbour wall that surrounded the small dock in Hayle.

Taking a deep breath, he made a final check of himself in the wall mirror and closed the door behind him.

Simon Johnson, sitting in the hotel foyer reading a magazine from the low coffee table, saw the tall, tanned and athletically built man descend the stairs and walk towards the restaurant door. Though he had no way of knowing it was Mister Trelawney, he had guessed correctly and turned back to the magazine.

Gordon McIntosh and Glenda Burroughs both rose from their seats as Trelawney entered the restaurant. Burroughs was surprised to find that she thought the dark curly haired and bearded Trelawney to be very attractive.

McIntosh introduced them both and said, "I took the liberty of ordering coffee, if that's okay with you Mister Trelawney?"

Cris nodded, his hunger forgotten as he mentally assessed both the Scottish police officers. During his time in London he had dealt with the coppers on numerous occasions and had little faith in their honesty. His closeness to Ronnie Kyle had introduced him to some of the corrupt ones, but he had no experience dealing with the Scottish police, other than the occasional Jock he had come across who worked in the Met.

McIntosh, he initially thought, seemed a little jaded; a little world-weary while the blonde detective Burroughs was, without a doubt, a stunning looking woman. His eyes narrowed as he stared at her. For her part, Glenda Burroughs was aware of Trelawney's interest in her, but it was something over the years she had become accustomed to and merely ignored it.

He broke the awkward silence by producing the photograph and held it for both the detectives to examine.

"Just to be sure," he began. "This is Alice. I the picture took it not long before she left; travelled here, to Glasgow I mean. There's no doubt?"

He already knew the answer and watched as McIntosh shook his head and reached for the photo.

"I'm so sorry, Mister Trelawney. Yes, that's the young girl who…. No," he breathed heavily. "There's no doubt."

He paused than asked, "Can I keep hold of this photo meantime?"

Cris nodded as McIntosh continued.

"Again, I'm sorry that we are meeting under these circumstances," began McIntosh, interrupting his thoughts, "and I know that you will be anxious to see your daughter. However, there is several questions I'd like to put to you, before we travel to the mortuary. Is that okay with you?"

"Ask away," replied Cris, beckoning that maybe they would be more comfortable seated.

McIntosh commenced with recent background questions about Alice; how long had she been in Glasgow, did Cris know any of her friends, where she lived, what income she had? Was he in regular touch with her?

Cris was halfway through answering McIntosh's questions, but then interrupted briefly by the arrival of the smiling, middle-aged waitress bearing a tray of coffee and cups. They watched as Burroughs poured coffee into the three cups and helped themselves to milk.

"So, to continue, Mister Trelawney, when was the last time you spoke with or heard from your daughter?"

Cris's eyes narrowed, recalling the anger and spiteful things said; her refusal to allow him to accompany her to the bus that in turn would take her to Penzance and the major train station there.

"Not for some time, I regret to say Mister McIntosh. To be frank, Alice and I argued over a year ago, in fact fourteen months to be precise; when she left to attend Glasgow University the argument had not been resolved and so…" he shrugged, the guilt still bearing heavily down upon him.

An awkward pause lay between them before McIntosh said, "I've a son in his early twenties. His mother and I provided everything for Calum, but he went off and decided to travel the world. We haven't heard from him for what," his brow wrinkled, "nearly two months and just pray daily that he's okay. Kids, Mister Trelawney," he slowly shook his head, "you do *your* best and then they think *they* know best, eh?"

Glenda Burroughs realised that McIntosh was being kind, that he was simply trying to bond with the obviously distraught Trelawney. Strange though, she thought, Gordon not previously mentioning Calum had not being in touch for that length of time.

"If it's not too painful, Mister Trelawney, can I ask what the argument was between you and your daughter?"

"Will it assist your inquiry Mister McIntosh?"

Cris saw the cop turn and glance at his colleague and realised something was not right, that they were keeping something back. "What is it? What aren't you telling me?"

McIntosh softly exhaled, preparing himself to deliver even more bad news on top of the worst news.

"It's difficult for me to break this to you Mister Trelawney, but for the last couple of months, Alice was soliciting in Glasgow city centre."

A cold chill ran through Cris and his eyes widened. Soliciting? Alice? His mind reeled with the enormity of what McIntosh said and his hand shook. He spilled some coffee onto the saucer as he laid the crockery on the table.

"That can't be right, you've got it wrong. There must be some sort of mistake," he heard himself whisper, fighting hard to keep his voice from breaking, his head violently shaking. "Oh my God, please no. Not Alice."

"I'm afraid it's correct Mister Trelawney. We've spoken with the young woman who shared a flat, a squat really, with Alice and she has confirmed what we believe to be correct. Our assessment is that Alice was…working," was the only word he could think of, "when she was either persuaded or abducted to go with her killer to a park on the south side of the city. She was discovered there on Thursday morning."

He fought hard to stop the tears, not wanting to display any kind of emotion in front of these strangers.

"How was she killed?" he asked; his voice dull and flat.

"She was stabbed. The post mortem confirmed this and, well, I'd rather not put you through any more pain if you don't mind."

McIntosh decided not to add to Trelawney's misery by telling him that his daughter was also using drugs.

"Do you have any suspects, any clues as to who killed her?"

McIntosh shook his head. "Not at the minute, but I have a full team working on the inquiry." He chewed at his lower lip. "This isn't easy for the Detective Inspector or me," he nodded towards Burroughs, "but there is a line of inquiry that I might have to pursue, Mister Trelawney, that could involve you. You must understand, I can't rule anything out."

Cris's ear perked up and his eyes narrowed with suspicion. "Go ahead, ask me anything you want."

"It's about your background. We, that is, DI Burroughs and me, have made some inquiry and we are aware that you had some… difficulties," was the best he could come up with, "a number of years ago. In London," he added.

Cris slowly nodded. So, they knew.

"Is there any likelihood," continued McIntosh, "anyway at all that your former associates might have known about Alice being here; in Glasgow, I mean. Any likelihood whatsoever that by harming Alice they might be taking some form of revenge against you?"

Cris did not immediately reply, his thoughts suddenly remembering all those years previously, a foul-mouthed Ronnie Kyle ranting at him while being dragged from the Dock at the Old Bailey by three prison officers; screaming abuse and vowing vengeance against Cris.

He shook his head. "If you are referring to my past history with Ronnie Kyle, that's old news," he replied. "Kyle doesn't know where I am now, let alone where Alice was. Christ, *I* didn't even know where Alice was," he suddenly burst out with pent-up emotion, banging a fist on the table and causing the three cups to rattle in the saucers.

A trio of elderly matrons a few tables away startled at his outburst, but discreetly looked away.

"Sorry," he apologetically shook his head, "no. Kyle wouldn't be involved; couldn't be." He blew through pursed lips, slowly sitting back in the chair, his eyes rose to the ceiling and shook his head.

"You have to understand, Ronnie Kyle was a nutcase, a psychopath who murdered Alice's mother. He hurt Alice and me more than I would have thought possible. He'd had his revenge and besides, other than his remand time, he walked free. He will have had more," he sought the word, "interesting ventures than trying to find us."

"He's still about and still causing mayhem down in London," said Burroughs. "I spoke with a former colleague who told me that Kyle continues to be heavily involved in criminality; drugs mostly, according to my source."

Cris felt the blood drain from his face and his head spun, but whether from what the blonde detective said or the tiredness finally taking its toll, he wasn't certain. He stared again at her, a nagging ache in his memory.

"Let me get this straight," he faced Burroughs. "You know who I am now, really am. You got this information from a Met cop with whom you discussed Alice's murder and that means that this Met cop also knows what you know, yeah?"

"I was getting some background on you, Mister Trelawney," she replied, uncertain where he was going with this and inwardly annoyed that she sounded defensive.

"But a Met cop? Jesus, I don't know about you people here in Scotland, but you must know you can't trust those people down there? Kyle had and probably still has dozens of cops in his pocket. Don't you read the daily newspapers, listen to the news up here? They're corrupt down there." He stared hard at her, his voice rising and attracting the attention of the few people who still sat at their breakfast. "Did you happen to mention to your Met pal that I was coming here to Glasgow to collect my daughter's body? Bloody hell love, you don't know it but you might just have tipped Kyle off that the man he's been looking for all these years is here."

He run a hand across his brow, the past suddenly starkly clear in his mind.

"Hang on Mister Trelawney," interrupted McIntosh, aware that what was supposed to be a meet and greet with a distraught father was now in danger of getting out of hand. "Nobody's saying that this man Kyle will find out you're here."

Over Trelawncy's shoulder, McIntosh saw the aide Simon Johnson standing hesitantly at the restaurant door, attracted by the raised voices and gave the young officer a subtle nod to stand down.

Cris abruptly stood, pushing the chair back from him. "Mister McIntosh, you have no idea of the web of informants that Ronnie Kyle has or the potential danger you have placed me in. Now, if you would be so kind as to provide details of where your city mortuary is located, I'll find my own way there."

Shit, thought McIntosh, standing now, as was Burroughs. This had not gone the way he expected. He rose to his feet with his palms held out in front of him and tried to placate the angry man. "Look, I know you're anxious to see your daughter and likely take her home, but that might not be immediately possible."

"What do you mean?"

"Well, if as I sincerely hope we do find and arrest Alice's killer, the defence team will no doubt demand their own post mortem examination. The PF, I mean, the Procurator Fiscal…" he stopped when he saw Trelawney's eyes narrow and explained, "It's much like your Crown Prosecution Service. Anyway, the PF will not release Alice's body until such time there is a defence post mortem or the PF is satisfied that nobody will be arrested in the short term. I am sorry, but there it is. It's out of my hands."

"So what you are telling me is that yes, I can see my daughter, but I can't make any arrangements to take her home; I can't bury her yet?"

"Yes, of course you can see her, but no; you can't take her home; at least not yet."

Cris lowered then shook his head. "Well, that completely buggers up everything doesn't it?" he wearily replied. "So, how do I get to the mortuary then?"

CHAPTER 12

After a couple of wrong turns, Cris Trelawney found the soot stained, ornate Victorian building that was Glasgow's mortuary. He parked the Volvo then presented himself to the attendant at the reception office just inside the large wooden doors and was surprised to be there met by a young detective who introduced himself as Simon Johnson. He recognised the dark suited younger man as the driver from the hotel foyer; the young man who had brought McIntosh and Burroughs to the hotel.

The young detective seemed nervous and said, "I've been sent to officially note your identification of the deceased….sorry, I mean your daughter, Mister Trelawney."

Cris nodded, surmising Johnson to be inexperienced. They both followed the brown-coated attendant to a small viewing room, one wall they saw covered by a closed curtain. Cris braced himself as Johnson stood respectfully back and nodded. The attendant pulled at a cord and the curtain parted in the centre, sliding soundlessly open. The muted light in the room shone above an open coffin sat upon two varnished trestles and in which Alice lay serenely within. A spotlessly white sheet was pulled up almost to her chin, leaving just her clear and unmarked face visible, her hair freshly washed, combed and framing her face. On the varnished wooden wall behind the coffin was a wall mural that depicted a calm, rural scene of sunny fields and a blue watered lake; the picture deliberately chosen to be non-religious.

Cris choked back a gasp. He had seen bodies before, but this; this was like nothing he had ever experienced, his child lying here in front of him…in a box. His hands clenched into fists and he felt an unreasonable and uncontrollable rage. He wanted nothing more than to hurt or destroy something… or someone.

"Mister Trelawney, sir. Are you okay?" asked the voice.

He turned slowly towards the young detective, seeing the face that was pale and concerned.

"I'm fine," he managed to croak in response. "I'm fine," he slowly repeated.

"Sorry sir, but I have to ask…"

"Yes," he snapped back, immediately regretting his anger. It wasn't the young cops' fault, that Alice was dead. If anyone was to blame, it was himself. He took a deep breath and calmer now, said again, "Yes, it's my daughter. Alice Trelawney."

He could not stand to be there, seeing her like that. He needed fresh air and immediately. Without a word he turned and left the room, walking rapidly towards the main door, his booted heels clicking on the polished surface of the wooden flooring.

Outside, in the cool breeze of the morning, he stood at the top of the stairs, rapidly breathing in and out, suddenly overcome with tiredness and eager to get back to the hotel.

"Mister Trelawney, sir."

The young detective had followed him out into the sunshine.

"Is there anything I can do? Do you want to get a coffee or something? You've had quite a shock."

He knew the young guy was being kind rather than simply doing his job, but right now all Cris wanted was to be left alone. Tight-lipped, he shook his head and walked briskly down the stairs and along the pavement towards the Volvo, but then stopped and turning his head upwards, stared at the bright sun.

A middle-aged woman carrying a heavy shopping bag in each hand skipped round him, wondering what the tall man was looking at and raising her own head, almost collided with a lamppost.

But Cris didn't see this for right then, his thoughts were on himself; wondering why he felt no emotion; why the tears didn't flow from him like they would a normal father; why the anger he had experienced in the viewing room had so quickly dissipated.

He stood motionless, seeing nothing and oblivious to the curious glances of the passers-by. Slowly he raised his hands and eyes closed, covered his face.

Behind him, Simon Johnson stood watching the burly man walking away and breathed out. He had been more nervous than he had realised. The DCI's instruction had seemed so simple; drop them off at Pollok then attend at the mortuary and obtain a positive identification for the deceased. He hadn't considered how upset the man would be.

He saw Mister Trelawney stop, but with his back to Simon, the young detective could neither see nor understand why.

Simon glanced at his watch. If he were going to give Bob Speirs the heads up for cancelling tonight's dinner date, he'd need to phone from the office when he got back there and likely in lieu of Simon's non-appearance, Sheila would probably roast poor Bob. Good enough for him, he wickedly grinned and with a backward glance at Trelawney, walked smartly to the Morris Ital.

Across the city, Davie Renwick awoke to the midday sun streaming through the partially closed windows. He rubbed at his forehead with the heel of his hand to ease the headache, his mouth raw and dry and reached for the bottle of water he kept under the bed. He tried to recall what time he had gotten home last night and then remembered; his brother Mark had met him and the lads in the pub then brought Davie home. Mark, he grinned humourlessly. Mark was Dodger's greatest success; or so his father kept reminding Davie.

He could hear his mother downstairs, busying herself in the kitchen and likely making Dodger some breakfast before his father went out for his usual Saturday midday golf. Dodger was crap at the game, but forever boasting that was where he got a lot of his business done; on the golf course.

Slowly to avoid the blinding pain in his head, Davie turned and got out of bed. He switched on the radio just as the crappy Madness number one hit, 'House of Fun' was finishing and in time to catch the midday news. He listened intently as the commentator confirmed the victory at Goose Green and heard that British troops were now advancing towards the Islands capital at Stanley.

He punched a clenched fist into the air, immediately regretting the action as again the pain shot through his head. He sat on the edge of the bed, his eyes closed tightly against the drumming in his skull and imagined himself to be there with the boys, fully armed and advancing against the Argies.

Most of Davie's wakened thoughts were daydreams; imagining himself gallantly leading his platoon against overwhelming numbers of the enemy, screaming as he charged towards them, his rifle pointing forward and plunging his bayonet into the warm bodies of the terror-stricken bastards. His eyes filled with unshed tears as he imagined how heroic he would be, his men loving him for his courage and his bravery; how they would follow him wherever he led. In his mind, he saw himself awarded the highest of honours, imagined the glory and medals he would win. His eyes snapped open and he stood, ignoring the headache pain as he knew he could ignore battle wound pain. He needed to get to the TA Centre. He needed to get more training under his belt for when the call came; the call to defend the country against the Spanish and Argentinean forces that he knew now must surely come.

He needed to practise using his weapons.

He needed more practise in the art of killing.

Lizzie McLeish was on a high; a happy high. She had half expected the coppers to kick her door down when the punter had discovered she had nicked his wallet, but then reasoned, how would he know to tell the polis where to find her? Lizzie never gave her real name to punters; those that asked anyway. Most of them just wanted the business done, a wham bam, thank you ma'am and then back to their sad, fucking lives. Her face fell. She had made the mistake of telling Wingy that when she was walking home from the Central Hotel, she had slung the wallet and credit cards over the wall into the canal at Speirs Wharf and he had called her a stupid cow, ranting at her that he could have gotten good money for the cards. It occurred to her that she might go back later and see if the wallet had maybe landed on the bank, but was almost certain she had heard the wallet splash and reckoned it was in the water. Next time, she promised herself, next time she would not be so stupid.

The stuff she had bought from Wingy had hit the mark and she felt *so good*; she had even made herself toast and beans and bought a big bar of chocolate with some of the money. Well, chocolate and milk, a full pack of fags and a bottle of Lanliq wine, just to see her through the evening until she went to the Drag. She drew deeply on her cigarette and picked some loose tobacco from her lip; tonight she would be out there with the other women and earn herself more cash. Maybe even another trip to the Central or one of the other city hotels, if she was lucky enough to turn up a foreign visitor again.

She searched out and played her favourite compilation tape on the small radio/cassette player and danced about the front room to Phil Collins rendition of 'You Can't Hurry Love', singing loudly off-key as she stumbled about the floor; the fag between the fingers of one hand and the half full bottle of Lanliq in the other hand. She turned the music up louder and arched her back, screaming the words out even louder.

The pensioner from the flat below banged up on the ceiling, but Lizzie ignored the old cow and continued to accompany Collins as she danced about the floor, imagining herself to be a member of the Top of the Pops troupe of dancers. The combination of drink and drugs made her dizzy and she fell giggling in an untidy heap onto the couch, spilling some of the cheap wine onto her blouse.

She lay there, for a time dazedly happy as the drug continued to course through her bloodstream.

The relaxed Lizzie's drugged mind was now occupied by thoughts of that evening's trawl for punters on the Drag.

Alice Trelawney, her very best and closest friend, was now a fast and fading memory.

The Incident room at Pollok police office was deserted save for DS Brian Davidson, comfortably seated with his feet up on the DI's desk, his tie undone, hands clasped behind his head and a cigarette loosely dangling from his lips.

Of course, he could have gone home for a few hours just as Gordon McIntosh suggested the team did and returned to the three-bedroom semi in Simshill that he shared with his whingeing wife, but what was the point, he sighed. The skinny harridan was likely out at her mother's again, moaning the face off the old bitch about the hours her husband worked to clothe and feed her and keep a roof over her head. He grinned when he imagined that if Terri's sister was also there, the three of them were likely standing round a big, cast iron pot and stirring it like the three Macbeth hags, colluding together for all sort of curses to fall down upon his head.

Their childless marriage, he drew deeply on his fag and stared at the glowing end, had failed years before and the only thing that kept his wife hanging on was the knowledge that if she left him, she would miss out in her share of his pension and lump sum final pay-out. His eyes narrowed and he sighed deeply. It wasn't the first time he had given serious thought to just kicking her out. The tension in the house since that time…he shook his head, refusing to recall even to himself what had occurred that night. It had been separate bedrooms since and now they barely acknowledged each other's presence, let alone speak.

Bitch!

He squirmed slightly to make himself more comfortable and expelled some trapped wind onto the seat, wishing that Renwick had been there to see Davidson defile his fucking chair. He hated Renwick more than he dared to admit and though he would never disclose it was jealous that the younger officer, who having hardly seen an angry man let alone arrest one, had been promoted over an experienced detective like himself. What angered Davidson even more was the six months that he had spent as acting Inspector, yet been passed over when the promotion list was later posted.

He wasn't naïve and like everyone else in the Division knew all about Renwick's councillor father and Dodger Renwick's connections within the Police Authority.

He flicked the ash onto Renwick's desk and slowly shook his head, reflecting on the unfairness of it all.

He sat brooding on his twenty-eight year career as a police officer. Things had changed since he had joined the City of Glasgow Police. He considered that this new organisation, Strathclyde was far too large; an amalgamation seven years previously of the City cops and the muppets from the adjoining rural forces; none who in his opinion matched the Glasgow cops that he knew of old. Coppers that would be there when the job needed done; cops who knew the difference between right and wrong and yes, he unconsciously nodded at his own thoughts, when it was required, bent the rules a little. As far as he was concerned, there was a vast difference between justice and the rule of law.

As for the courts and the judges, he grunted in disgust; don't even get him started on those bastards.

He grimaced that now there were too many of these county bampots in charge; too many 'by the book' buggers and not enough real police officers to do the job properly.

His thoughts turned to his current management team. He considered Gordon McIntosh who was himself a former City copper, to be a decent man and it was just a pity that McIntosh had landed the murder rather than Renwick. He guessed why the DCI had taken the inquiry on rather than let Renwick run it. McIntosh didn't trust the weasly little bastard to solve it and that, he furrowed his brow, might prove to be the DCI's undoing.

Like the rest of the Divisional CID, Davidson knew the DCI was in the twilight of his career and waiting for the opportunity to hand in his notice.

It was just a shame that likely he would finish his career without solving this one. The other DI, Glenda Burroughs; now, there was a woman that he wouldn't mind giving one to. He closed his eyes and envisioned the lovely Glenda lying naked beneath him. He breathed a little faster and felt himself become aroused at the thought of what he could do to her.

The sound of footsteps startled him and hurriedly, he lifted his legs from the desk, wincing as he dropped his feet to the floor and awkwardly twisted his erection at the movement.

The door opened to admit two Serious Crime Squad officers, who nodded 'hello' as they continued to laugh at a joke.

Embarrassed, Davidson quickly stood and turning his back to the detectives, nodded in acknowledgement of their affable greeting. He winced again and made his way to the table that bore the coffee and the kettle.

CHAPTER 13 – Early evening, Saturday 29 May.

Within the crowded room at Pollok police office, the atmosphere heavy with cigarette smoke, DCI Gordon McIntosh stood facing the assembled officers, one hand in his pocket and the other holding a fag.

"Right guys and gals, you've been allocated your areas of the Drag. It's a bit early to be heading out there at the minute, so I'll take the time to give you what little update there is. First, the uniform search of the Park turned nothing up of any evidential value. As you may have already heard the Park in no longer a crime scene, however, it will be secured and patrolled pending the *Papal* visit."

He paused and from the knowing looks, realised this information was already out there.

"The deceased's father Mister Crispin Trelawney arrived in the early hours of this morning and is being accommodated down at the hotel in Paisley Road West. DI Burroughs and I met with Mister Trelawney and informed him of the circumstances of his daughter's death. As you'll likely guess, the news wasn't well received." He unconsciously stopped speaking, aware that in some strange way he couldn't describe, he was observing some kind of solemnity about the interview.

He cleared his throat and said, "To continue. Mister Trelawney was not able to offer any information about his daughter's murder other than to inform us that following a family disagreement, he had no contact with the deceased for some time; an issue I'm sure you'll understand that under the circumstances, he now deeply regrets. Indeed, he was under the impression that his daughter continued to attend Glasgow University as a student, so the news of her recent…" he paused, searching for the correct word, "lifestyle, came as a double shock."

He saw a hand tentatively rise, but lifting his own hand forestalled the detective and said, "I'll take questions in a minute. To continue again, just half an hour ago, DI's Renwick, Burroughs and I decided that the focus of the investigation would concentrate on the premise that while soliciting in the Glasgow city centre, Alice Trelawney was murdered by a client who somehow conveyed her to where she was found, had intercourse and then stabbed her to death. That, ladies and gentlemen, is what we are investigating."

He turned to Davidson.

"On the presumption she was driven to the Park, Brian, please allocate two officers to make inquiry with the local taxi firms; black hack's, private hires, etcetera. See if any cabs were logged that night to run a couple from the town centre to the location of the Park and don't forget to include the nearby area, particularly the streets where Park entrance gates are located."

Davidson made a note on his pad and replied, "Right, boss."

He started at his team, each officer watching him for further instruction; eager for the leadership they needed to solve this murder and he inwardly shuddered; feeling for the first time the weight of his years on his shoulders.

He felt alone.

He swallowed hard, knowing that as the Senior Investigating Officer - the SIO - it was his decision, his responsibility, to disseminate what information and intelligence he believed necessary to solve the murder.

It was because the responsibility was his, he didn't disclose to his inquiry team that following a lengthy discussion with Glenda Burroughs, both had reached the conclusion that it was not helpful to the inquiry revealing the murdered girl's father, Cris Trelawney, had his own chequered history.

Privately, he had also come to the decision not to make Renwick aware of Trelawney's past, fearing that it might somehow thereafter become open knowledge.

Besides, he explained to Burroughs, but more to convince himself, the less that Renwick knows the better and while both agreed that there was no direct evidence that Renwick might be ACC John Murray's inside source in the inquiry, neither could they ignore Renwick's family connection and in turn, Dodger Renwick's close association with Murray.

McIntosh inhaled a lungful of tobacco and continued. "As far as we are aware at this time, there is no suggestion of a boyfriend or a pimp; tonight however, you will speak with as many of the women on the streets that you can and try to firm up on this assumption. If indeed it does transpire that there *is* a third party that was associating with the deceased, whether a boyfriend or a pimp, I do not need to emphasis how important that information will be and needless to say, it might take the inquiry down a different road. Lastly, Mister Trelawney was kind enough to provide us with a good photograph of his daughter and you will be issued with a copy of the photograph before you set off. Right, I'll take questions now, if you please."

The same hand went up and the detective said, "When we're speaking with the prossies boss, we might get their backs up if they think we're interfering with business. We could be looking at a lot of hostile witnesses."

"Agreed," replied McIntosh, who then smiled and said, "but that's when you use your charm. Convince the women that we are there to protect them, not judge them. Stress how eager we are to catch the man who killed one of their own. Get them on *our* side. Anything they tell us will be in confidence and if they are unhappy about speaking with us on the street, make the offer or an arrangement to meet with them elsewhere, whether it be at a police office or at some place they feel more comfortable; whether it be their home or a café, okay? I do not need to remind you ladies and gentlemen what we're looking for here; statements from anyone who knew the wee lassie; any punters that have been rough with them or threatened them, particularly where a knife has been seen or inferred. Any vehicles or even, if we're lucky, a registration number that they suspect might be used by a punter they think could be dodgy. Use your instinct," he emphasised as he cast an eye about the room. "You are all trained interrogators, well, most of you but I'm not sure about wee Sammy there," he nodded towards a red-faced detective and provoked hilarious laughter from the assembled crowd. It was now legend that Sammy had recently arrested a suspect and believing the man was both ignoring and refusing to answer Sammy's questions, arrested and took the man back to the place office, where it was fortunate that prior to the issue going any further, Sammy discovered the man was indeed a deaf mute.

Another hand appeared, this raised time by a Serious Crime Squad detective. "How long do you want us to give it boss?" she asked.

McIntosh pursed his lip. "I'm not up to date on the hours worked by ladies of the night," he said to muted laughter, "but I suspect the hours after the pubs shut will be the witching hour, so to speak."

He thought for a moment and then instructed, "I'll leave it to your discretion. The only thing I will ask is that each pair takes not just a copy of Alice Trelawney's photograph, but also a radio with you and ensure you maintain contact with DI Renwick here at the incident room."

Standing slightly behind him, Glenda Burroughs half smiled. It was typical of Gordon McIntosh that he could make an instruction sound like a request; a style that endeared him to the officers who served under him.

McIntosh cleared his throat and turned to the table at his back to stub out his cigarette into what had been a coffee tin but was now an improvised ashtray. "It's likely the weather will also be factor," he continued, "though looking through the window there, it seems it might be another nice, clear night. I suggest you travel in your own cars to Cranstonhill police office, leave your cars there and walk down to the Drag area. Once you believe that you have exhausted all options for the evening, there's no need to sign off here, just collect your cars and go home and we will meet again here tomorrow at say," he turned a querying eye towards Glenda Burroughs, "midday?" Burroughs nodded and he confirmed, "Right, unless anything of vital importance turns up tonight, midday tomorrow then. And yes," he smiled at the curious glances, "before you ask, I'll be occupying one of the chairs in the incident room too, ladies and gentlemen so the management won't be snug in bed while you're out on your toes. So, any further questions? No? Right, let's get to it."

The crowd began to disperse and make their way through the door when Simon Johnson saw Burroughs beckoning to him.

Standing to one side, she said, "Look, Simon, I know that you had to go to the mortuary to meet the girls' father and I'm aware that you came back here to submit your statement. That means young man you didn't get home for a rest, did you?"

He began to protest, that it was okay, that he didn't really need the time when she put her hand up. "I've spoken with the DCI. I'm going to be here anyway and we really don't need you hanging about like a spare part, so take the rest of the night off and I'll see you here tomorrow, okay?"

"Okay ma'am and eh, thanks," he mumbled.

She couldn't guess at his disappointment, that he really wanted to be out there with the inquiry teams.

As he walked to his car Simon saw the teams disperse to their vehicles, listening to the jocular comments being bandied about and inwardly cursed. He would have liked to be one of the team interviewing the women; after all, if he wanted a career in the CID he would need all the experience he could get in his six month secondment. Still, he sighed as he sat in the drivers seat, there might still be time to salvage something of the night.

Two minutes down the road, he pulled into a row of shops at Braidcraft Terrace and saw the phone box was empty. Fetching a ten pence coin from his pocket, he dialled Bob Speirs number. It was Sheila, Bob's wife, who answered the call. Quickly, he explained that quite unexpectedly, he had been given the night off and was there the chance the dinner date might still go ahead?

He guessed that Sheila was considering if her friend might still be on for the dinner, but then replied, "Look, get yourself here for seven anyway. I've already told Yvonne that tonight was off, so I'm not sure if she'll be up for it; well, not after you've already cancelled on her once that is," she frostily reminded him.

Simon had known Sheila since she had started dating Bob and as quick as she flared, was aware that she calmed down just as fast. He begun to explain why he had initially cancelled, only to be interrupted by Sheila who said, "Yeah, I know, Bob's told me all about it, Sherlock. Look, like I said, I'll do my best and whether Yvonne makes it or not, you'll have dinner with us, okay?"

"Great," he replied.

"Oh and Simon," she coyly reminded him before hanging up, "don't forget my apologetic box of chocolates … and I'm also fond of carnations."

Ronnie Kyle stood behind the curtain at the bay window in the tenement flat, staring down at the shoppers in the busy Duke Street below who were still enjoying the warmth of the fading sunlight.

Moses Parker had parked the van round the corner in Bellfield Street and was now fetching them some food. He glanced about the furnished lounge, pleased that his pal Eddie had at least come up with something half-decent and guessed from the décor that Eddie caused the flat to be used as a knocking shop; certainly seemed like that if the VHS videos in the cabinet were anything to go by, he inwardly grinned. That and the fact the two bedrooms both had king size beds and wardrobes that contained at least one French maid's outfit and other skimpy clothing that of course, was all female. He suspected that somewhere there might be cutouts in the walls to accommodate hidden cameras, but had neither the inclination nor the bad manners to go looking for the equipment. He gently ran a finger along the window ledge. At least the place was spotlessly clean, he mused and it was apparent that fresh clean sheets and pillowcases had been changed on the beds.

The sound of the front door closing caused him to turn. Moses Parker entered the lounge carrying a plastic bag of canned lager in one large hand and an aromatic bag of takeaway curries in the other.

"Grub's up boss," he cheerfully called and made his way back through the door and into the galley like kitchen. Placing both bags on the worktop, he pulled open the fridge to deposit the lager and said, "Your mate Beattie has seen us all right here boss. The fridge is stacked with milk, bacon, eggs and…" he hesitated, lifting out a clear plastic bag and stared curiously at it, "… I don't know what this is supposed to be."

"That's black pudding, you ignorant git," grinned Kyle, then added, "The haggis-bashers, they love that kind of stuff up here. That and the greasy mince pies and crap like that they all eat."

Five minutes later, they sat facing each other across the small gate leg table in the lounge, the empty tinfoil cartons to one side and the plates wiped clean, each on his second can of Tennents.

"Not a bad little ruby that," grunted Kyle, burping loudly.

"So boss, when is your mate getting back to you? About Cris I mean."

"Well," Kyle drew deeply on the cigar between his stubby fingers, "what he told me at the airport was that he had a source that could get information on why McGuire…" he suddenly grinned, "I forgot, he's calling himself Trelawney these days, ain't he? Anyway, Eddie has someone on the inside of the murder investigation team, so Eddie thinks he should be able to find out real quick where the filth have got our Cris holed up."

Trelawney, Kyle slowly rolled the name about his mind. It still bothered him where he had heard that name before.

Moses stared curiously at Kyle. "So when we find out where's he's at boss, what do you want done? I mean, apart from the obvious," he added, showing a perfect set of gleaming white teeth, a complete contradiction to the punishment that his face had taken in the ring.

Kyle didn't immediately reply, but deep in memory rolled the half-smoked cigar between his fingers.

"That bastard cost me a ten month lie-down at the Scrubs," he said with venom, "and I don't forgive betrayal. When we get him Moses, he'll have time to consider the wrong he did me; first betraying me to that fucking mob of Caribbean bastards, no offence mate…."

"None taken boss," Moses dutifully replied.

"…then firing me into the filth."

It occurred to Moses that maybe Kyle slitting Daniela Corbett's throat might have something to do with Cris McGuire's turning Queen's Evidence, but thought now was not the appropriate time to remind his boss.

"So, when I get me hands on that dirty bastard, we'll settle a long overdue score, eh? For now though my son, it's just a matter of sitting back here, enjoying the peace and quiet and waiting for Eddie to do his bit."

Moses tapped his can of lager lightly against that held in Kyle's hand.

"I'm with you boss," he quietly replied, but his thoughts were cast back to a night over a decade before.

Darkness had just fallen and the teams, stretched across the quarter of a mile of streets and alleyways had little success. When shown the photograph of Alice Trelawney, some of the women admitted having known the wee blonde girl by sight; the few who had spoken with her recalling her curious English accent, but none knew her enough to provide any information about a pimp and most opined the lassie worked the streets alone. A few of the younger women were afraid to speak with the detectives, mistrustful of the promise of confidentiality and instead suspecting their personal details might be recorded and their nocturnal profession later revealed to their family and friends.

Some of the older women were angry that the presence of so many police officers would scare off their regular clients and point blankly refused to speak with the 'fucking polis.'

Wearily, the detectives worked on, their efforts producing a few positive statements and from a small number of women, suspicious of a number of cars that trawled the streets, scraps of paper which were scribbled registration numbers with ballpoint pens, thick mascara pencils and on one occasion a lipstick. In general, the officers were of the opinion the drivers were probably voyeuristic; that strange type of male whose sexual release was achieved alone and in the privacy of their vehicles when watching the prostitutes, rather than engaging with them. Besides, joked the cruder member of the team, it saved the cost of a knee trembler in one of the dark and smelly lanes.

As the night progressed, the teams radioed in to DI Renwick at the incident room that they were signing off and finally, just after two in the morning, all were gone from the area.

The few prostitutes that remained to ply their trade were themselves already dispirited by the police presence and slowly began to weave their own way to wherever they called home.

Among the last of the women who decided to head homewards, shivering in the cold dampness of the night, was Betty Fisher, a thirty-year old unmarried mother of toddler twin daughters.

Betty, dressed in a short denim skirt, flowery green coloured blouse and high heels, her arms tightly wrapped about her against the chill, was making her way from her usual haunt at St Peter's Lane into Douglas Street and passing under a bright, halogen street lamp when a dark coloured car drew up alongside her. She stopped and stared cautiously at the driver, conscious of the warnings the detectives had earlier issued that night.

The driver wound down the window and smiled at her.

"Are you open for business there hen?" he politely asked.

Grateful for the last minute punter, she bent towards the open window and deliberately thrust forward her small breasts, subtly using her free hand to pull the loose and low cut blouse tight against the nipples that in the cold were now erect and almost protruding through the thin material. She smiled, her most beguiling smile; the smile that she had practised countless times in front of the bathroom mirror.

"I might be if the price is right," she answered, her teeth almost chattering in the chill of the evening and forced herself to sound as cheerful as she could. She figured another half hour would not make that much difference and besides, she reasoned, her mother who was childminding the twins would probably just stay over on the couch anyway. The man seemed to be okay, was clean-shaven and wearing a tie and the car was nice and smelled clean too. A little pine tree hung from the drivers rear view mirror. A frustrated husband, her experienced mind told her.

Mingled with the pine, her nose detected a polished leather smell from the seats. "Want to get in and maybe we'll come to an arrangement," asked the polite and smiling driver.

"No, I like to discuss a price and what you want me to do for you first and if we agree, then it's the money up front," replied Betty who had in her mind already decided that after an uneventful night, with the cops crawling all over the place, this was better than going home empty-handed. Besides, she knew that she needed to earn something tonight to put towards next months rent.

"I'd like to take you somewhere nice and quiet and have a wee ride at you and I'm willing to pay sixty quid for the privilege. So, what do you say?"

Betty's heart thumped rapidly. Sixty quid for a shag? The going price was thirty to forty quid, at best. She tried not to sound overeager and all caution went out the window at the thought of an easy earner. "It's a bit late. Will you drop me home when we're done then?"

"Of course I will," gushed the driver with a broad smile, his teeth white and even. "I'm a gentleman, hen."

He reached across and pushed open the passenger door as Betty rounded the car and got in.

"Right, not too far away, eh?" she said and sitting in the seat and as she had done dozens of times before, pulled up the short, denim skirt and gave the driver a flash of stocking top; just enough to keep him interested, she inwardly grinned.

The bleached blonde haired woman, stood shivering and silent, watching from the shadow of the building across the road. Slowly she shook her head and muttered, 'Shite' when she saw the car slowly drive off with the much younger lassie. Ella McGuiness was annoyed that the few seconds she had taken to reach the end of the lane, the lassie she knew as Betty had managed to pick up what Ella guessed was probably the last of the night's punters. Just as the car turned the corner out of sight, her eyes narrowed and her lips moving as she quietly mumbled the digits of the rear registration plate, yet unable to explain why it interested her.

With a sigh, she muttered, "Sod it," and turned to make her way home.

She cursed her luck that the polis had been out in numbers tonight. Dodging them had been a pain in the arse and put paid to her getting a punter or two.

Still, better that she missed out on tonight's earner than being caught. No way was she going back for another term at Cornton Vale; no way was she getting herself locked up again, not if she wanted to keep the weans out of the hands of they social work bastards.

With one wary eye open for the detectives that had been crawling all over the Drag, Ella bowed her head and began the long, lonely walk back to Maryhill.

In the car, Betty relaxed in the sudden, unaccustomed luxury of the leather seats. The heater was on and after the chill of standing for hours in the evening air, the warmth rolled over her like a warm blanket. Her eyes began to droop and she turned to smile at the good-looking man.

The driver returned her smile, glanced down at his passengers legs and then, as if to reassure himself, with his right hand reached down to gently pat his right calf where the knife was in the makeshift sheath, under his trouser leg.

CHAPTER 14 – Early Sunday Morning, 30 May

Simon Johnson woke with a start and reached across to switch on the bedside radio alarm clock in time for the seven o'clock news. The first item was the latest bulletin from the war in the South Atlantic with the laconic voice of the male broadcaster introducing a MoD spokesman who reported an unsuccessful attack by Argentinean fighters who had fired Exocet missiles at HMS Invincible, but no rocket strikes was recorded hitting the ship. Even though Simon knew that his brother Peter was serving aboard a Royal Navy fleet supply ship, he could not but help worry that Peter would somehow become embroiled in the fighting. In his minds eye, to the Argies a British ship was a British ship, regardless whether or not it was a fighting ship of the line.

In further news, the commentator continued, British forces were making advances towards the outskirts of the Falkland's capital, Stanley.

Simon listened as the commentator continued with some local items then finished with the latest update on the preparation for the *Papal* visit. He grinned as he listened to the planned counter demonstration by local Loyalists, wondering how they would cope against the large and implacable officers of Strathclyde Police Support Unit; not a group renowned for their tolerance.

Lying there, he considered again the previous night's dinner at the Speirs house in Baillieston. Simon had arrived twenty minutes early, catching Bob and Sheila slightly off guard and nursed a lager shandy while chatting to Bob as Sheila finished preparing the table. Their other guest, his blind date Yvonne, a teacher who worked with Sheila at the primary school in Shettleston, arrived ten minutes late, obviously nervous and with a cheesy grin plastered to her long face throughout the meal. Simon realised almost immediately there was no attraction, at least not from him. In fairness, the young woman was not unattractive; well, he smiled, not if you were into horsey laughs and school jokes. He just did not see himself being saddled with a woman who guffawed like a donkey on speed and whose main topic of conversation was the antics of the pupils in her primary three class. He sighed and guessed she was probably as nervous of meeting Simon as he had to admit, he was of meeting her.

Of course, as Sheila would expect, he was the perfect gentleman throughout the evening and aware that Yvonne had arrived by cab, offered to drop her home at the end of the night. During the half hour trip to her flat in Cambuslang, he hardly got a word in, presuming from her incessant chatter she was eager to impress him and merely smiled and nodded when required. Her invitation for a late night coffee, he guessed was made with the intention of agreeing some kind of future date, but he politely declined and got away without having to take a note of her telephone number.

He had little doubt Sheila would have quizzed Yvonne during that day and be phoning him that evening to find out his opinion of her pal. Well, sorry as he was to disappoint her, he could only be honest and tell her that he was not interested. Any half-hearted untruth might be misconstrued and he definitely did not want to give Sheila the impression that he might see Yvonne again.

Forcing himself to rise from his comfortable bed, he stretched and yawned then absently scratching at his rump, made his way into the bathroom, idly wondering what the day would bring and what progress the officers had made in their late night trawl through the seedy side of Glasgow.

The security corridor located within Police Headquarters at Pitt Street in the Centre of Glasgow housed among other departments, the Criminal Intelligence Department. Like other police departments, it operated a twenty-four-seven service, for the criminal fraternity like their nemesis the police, has no set working hours. During the traditional working week of Monday to Friday, the men and women dedicated to this Department are obliged to dress formally; suits for the men and similar smart attire for the women. For those unfortunate enough to catch the weekend shifts, however, the dress code is more relaxed and so Sunday morning found Detective Sergeant Anne 'Patsy' Cline at her desk. Holding a half-smoked Benson & Hedges fag between the fingers of her right hand, she fetched a police arrest report from her in-tray and with the in her left hand and a coffee at her elbow, was uncomfortably regretting wearing the old stone-washed jeans that reminded her she was carrying too much weight.

Patsy glanced at the report, reading the account of an arrest the previous evening by uniformed officers of a prolific housebreaker in the Shettleston area of the city. She grinned delightedly as she read that following a foot pursuit in darkness at the rear of the tenement area, the thief turned to fight the young WPC chasing him only to discover the lassie was no shrinking violet. Though the cop suffered a bloody nose, with her baton she inflicted a wound on the unfortunate culprit's head that required over thirty stitches. Patsy smiled at the female cops' bottle and grinned even more when she read the cops neat handwritten account of the thief's antecedent history, guessing the WPC was relatively inexperienced. According to the report, the arrested man was often subject to moods of depression and '…committed suicide regularly'.

Patsy placed the report to one side to remind herself to have a word the following morning with her DCI and request that he place a phone call to the young cops Divisional Commander. The arrest of the housebreaker was a real coup and the Divisional CID was now libelling at least thirty break-ins against the man; all of the break-ins committed through the night against private homes.

The next report Patsy lifted from her in-tray was just that morning internally received from Special Branch. As she read the report, forwarded to the SB by one of their Ports Coverage Unit officers, her eyebrows knitted and she bit at her lower lip. Pushing her heavy-set body up from her desk, she crossed the room to the Z File cabinet.

As a supervisor, Patsy was one of the few Departmental officers authorised to hold a key and access to the cabinet within which was stored the files of the Force's Z rated criminals; individuals who had been deemed either to be so criminally active and prolific, highly dangerous or whose activities indicated they were a major threat to public order.

Occasionally, the individuals recorded in the cabinet met all three of the Z criminal criteria.

Patsy pulled the thick and bound file of Edward Steven Beattie and returned to her desk. Eddie Beattie, now approaching fifty-five years of age and long known to Patsy and her colleagues, had for more years than she could remember been a thorn in the side of the police.

Opening the file, she flicked to the more recent entries and glanced through them, some of which she noted had been submitted by herself. She wasn't surprised that the recent intelligence concerning Beattie had dwindled during the last few years and read the entry marked 'Secret', dated over eight years previously that offered an explanation for the lack of intelligence.

The entry suggested that Beattie was being provided with information that allowed him to foil police attempts to arrest and fold up his criminal empire. The secret report concluded with the opinion that strongly suspected Beattie's informant was a serving police officer.

Turning the pages, Patsy read a similarly marked 'Secret' report, dated a year later that identified Beattie's burgeoning association with Glasgow City Councillor John 'Dodger' Renwick and opined that both were colluding in the mutually profitable sale and purchase of Council land. The report highlighted Councillor Renwick's position as being 'pivotal' within the Police and Fire Committee and the influence Renwick was able to exert from this post.

However, nothing in the report suggested Renwick was being personally compromised or unduly influenced by Beattie, but instead offered the opinion that Renwick was himself, simply corrupt.

An addendum stapled to the report highlighted the promotion to Sergeant of Renwick's son, Mark Renwick. However, nothing could be determined to indicate Sergeant Renwick was a) providing his father with any information of value or b) in a position to offer his father any information that might be construed as sensitive.

As Patsy read on, she sighed when she saw that a handwritten entry dated less than a year previously indicated Sergeant Renwick was now Detective Inspector Renwick and posted to the city's G Division.

"But that doesn't mean to say the lads a wrong one," she idly mused as sitting back in the swivel chair she drew deeply on the last inch of her fag.

Patsy turned again to the report submitted by the PCU detective and read of the meeting at the airport Arrivals gate between Beattie, as usual accompanied by his minders, and the two men who had just come off the London flight.

The reporting officer had diligently identified at least one minder and provided a description of the second man.

She smiled. The detective had been extra thorough. The partial registration number obtained by him that contained the two men, 'F 917L' had been useful and a quick speculative check on the PNC by the detective had turned up a white coloured Transit van with the registration number CYF 917L. Unfortunately, over a year previously, the van was recorded on the PNC as written off in an RTA. But Patsy was pleased to see the PCU guy had done his homework, for attached by a staple to the rear of the report was the passenger manifest list with the names 'KYLE, Ronald' and 'PARKER, Moses', each name marked with a yellow highlight pen. How the detective had identified the men was not explained, but Patsy guessed he must have spoken to the cabin crew for according to the description in the report of the man called Moses Parker, he would have been difficult to miss in a football crowd.

She marked the two names on a pad by her elbow and took the pad to the workstation that housed the Police National Computer. Signing onto the site, Patsy typed in the first name, 'KYLE, Ronald'. The information almost jumped from the screen. "Whoa," she sat stiffly upright and softly muttered, the burning fag between her fingers forgotten, but reminding her when she squealed in pain. Blowing on them and waving her smouldering fingers in the air, Patsy's attention was immediately taken by the information on her screen, noting that cross-referenced with Ronald Kyle was the second name on her pad; Moses Parker. She also saw a unique identifying tag attached to each name and jotted the details down.

"Time for a phone call," she muttered and returned to her desk.

Joe and Rosie, both now in their late-sixties, had been together for as many years as the local beat men in the Saltmarket could remember. Rosie, her gaudily painted face resembling a City Bakeries Halloween cake and Joe, bearing visible facial scars and with more tattoos than teeth; a visible indication of his hard and drink-sodden life, were local legends who when sober were inseparable, but when drunk, the bane of every beat man's life.

The beat cops had many years since given up arresting them for their drunkenness and their regular weekend strife; usually during which they inflicted some hurt or injury upon each other. Indeed, the duty Inspectors had made it clear to each of their shifts that on the occasion the beat men were summoned by weary neighbours to call at the flea-ridden squat the couple inhabited in High Street to intervene in their domestic squabbles, it was preferable the officers simply separated them. The unwritten instruction was the Division would no longer tolerate the regular cost of fumigating the cells following the arrest of the hygiene challenged pair.

If on the odd occasion the injury suffered by one required medical treatment, the officers were quietly instructed to either drop whoever was that night's victim at the Royal Infirmary casualty department, where both were known to the luckless staff, and scud the other round the ear, issuing yet another firm warning regarding his or her future behaviour.

It was widely rumoured that a small, gambling 'sweep' had been organised among some of the more cynical beat men to predict when and which one of the two would murder the other.

However, that bright and sunny Sunday morning, each suffering yet again the effect of another blistering hangover, Joe and Rosie, their arms linked in mutual support of each other, warily tiptoed across the rubble strewn waste ground that backed onto the nearby railway arches at the rear of the Bridgegate, locally referred to as the 'Briggait'. Eyes downcast to avoid tripping, they stumblingly made their way towards the nearby car park at the rear of Argyle Street. It was their fervent hope the volunteer staff of the Simon Community charity caravan parked there in the early morning to feed the homeless and residents of the nearby men's hostel might be inveigled to provide them with some tea and a bacon roll.

Muttering incoherently to each other, Rosie suddenly stopped dead and her eyes widened as with a quivering finger, she pointed to the partially clothed body that lay in a fold in the ground.

Her piercing shriek, Joe was later to comment to a detective, "…nearly made me shite myself again, sir."

Almost ninety minutes after the discovery by Rosie and Joe, Doctor Jane Robertson, clad and perspiring within an overlarge and encompassing white Forensic suit, knelt in the Forensic tent beside the body while a similarly dressed burly man stood over her.

"What do you think, Jane?" asked DI Morris Knox.

Robertson sighed and using the back of her gloved right hand, wiped away a strand of blonde hair that escaped the boiler suit hood and hung over her glasses. "Too early to tell yet, Morris," she quietly replied, "but if you want my opinion and mind, it's just my opinion because…."

"You can't commit till such times the post mortem examination is concluded," he finished for her, with a grin.

Robertson turned and stared at the large detective, a smile playing about her mouth.

"Am I that predicable," she replied, herself breaking into a wide grin. "But of course you're right. However, that said the apparent evidence of forcible sex, the shape and location of the entry wound on this unfortunate young woman's body is similar," her eyes narrowed in concentration as she bent forward and closely peered at the bloodstained wound, "very similar indeed, to a case I was called out to a few days ago. Have you got her identified or is it too early for that?"

"Uniform found a wee black handbag lying over there," he gesticulated with his hand towards waste ground beside the nearby arches, "that had a bus pass inside. The way she's dressed, the sussies and the…" he hesitated, just knowing that no matter how he said it, he was going to sound sexist and opinionated. "What I mean is the short skirt and that; it seems to indicate the wee lassie was on the game. So as we speak, I'm having the office records checked against the name

Elizabeth Fisher. If she's been cautioned for street soliciting at any time in the Central Division, she'll be on file and we will likely have a photograph as well." He saw her turn her head back and forth and eyes narrowing, asked, "What?"

"She's not wearing any underwear; knickers I mean. Did your guys find any?" Knox shook his head. "There wasn't any mention of underwear, any type of lingerie being discovered. I mean, with these lassies it's not *that* unusual, but I'll organise a search anyway," he said. "Is it significant?"

"I'm not certain," she raised a hand towards the detective who obligingly helped her to her feet. "You might wish to consider contacting DCI McIntosh over in Govan," she slowly continued. "Gordon has a murder inquiry ongoing at the minute and though again I must stress Morris, that this is purely conjecture at this time, I have a strong suspicion that the PM examination will conclude this young woman's murder might be the work of the killer of the girl, over in the Bellahouston Park. If you *don't* find her underwear, presuming of course she wore some," she pulled a face, "you might also consider mentioning it to Gordon."

"I know Gordon. He's a good man. He was my Detective Sergeant when we served in the old City of Glasgow Flying Squad together," the large detective unconsciously nodded. "Once I get this place cleared away and the body to the mortuary," he jerked a thumb over his shoulder towards the building that was located a mere two hundred yards distant, "I'll get back to Stewart Street and give him a bell."

They turned away and began walking towards the arches and the nearby Briggait, where uniform Traffic officers were manoeuvring the police Incident Caravan into a parking position by the side of the road.

"So, what's planned for the rest of the day, doc?" inquired Knox.

"Back home for a shower and some breakfast and then…" she stopped and turned thoughtfully towards the detective. "My hubby Donald is down in London at a conference and I've nothing on this afternoon, Morris. Can you arrange for the mortuary to be open and make inquiry to determine if Mister Hammond is available to conduct the PM done today, rather than tomorrow? If he's not available, I'll stand in and that'll leave me free Monday morning to get some of my own chores dealt with."

"Shouldn't be a problem, I'll make the call," he slowly replied, his attention taken by a female detective who had just exited a CID car and who quickly strode towards him.

With a courteous nod to Robertson, the young detective, her face flushed with enthusiasm breathlessly said, "I've just checked the local street prostitutes files, boss," she handed him a brown coloured cardboard folder. "Elizabeth Fisher. Also known as Betty Fisher, as well as a few other names she's used as aliases in the past. Her photo is in the file and she's been fingerprinted as well for a couple of DHSS benefit frauds."

The DI took the folder from the young detective as she hurriedly added, "I got a look at the body before I went back to the office, boss. I think you'll find it's a positive identification."

Knox glanced at the file, seeing the sombre face staring back at him; a face that would no longer smile, cry or laugh. He read the short and summarised antecedent history, dated just two months previously when Fisher had received her second street caution for soliciting. With a sigh, he read the file recorded the dead woman was mother to twin daughters. His shoulders slumped and with sadness shook his head. He hoped the address recorded in the file was current and knew it was going to be a long day.

Bidding farewell to Robertson and with a final instruction to the officers at the scene, Knox returned the file to the young detective and instructed her to drive him back to Stewart Street office.

Seated at his desk in the Pollok police office Portacabin, DS Brian Davidson leafed through the previous nights statement reports, sorting them into files and updating the nominal index with the names and addresses of the prostitutes interviewed by the team. He worked methodically, but his thoughts were elsewhere.

He drew deeply on his cigarette and reached for the coffee, remembering the open doors and empty wardrobe and cleared out drawers.

Well aware that he was at work, the bitch had returned to the house yesterday and removed all of her clothes. That and the spare chequebook from the kitchen wall unit.

Well, he savagely thought, fuck her; there was plenty of other women out there that would be glad of his company, he inwardly smirked.

Like many of his gender, Davidson believed himself to know women; their like and dislikes, desires and dislikes and credited himself with higher opinion of his attractiveness to women than was perhaps realistic. While he sat daydreaming, his imagination took over his thoughts and he fantasised of himself again being a single, unattached man. He thought of some of the women he knew, their faces flashing before him. Among them, the young redheaded detective, working as a member of the team from Serious Crime Squad; then there was the pretty, auburn haircd probationary cop with the big tits and he remembered her breasts straining against the fabric of the white police issue blouse, the outline of her bra against the material. He felt himself become aroused. His breathing laboured as he thought of the one woman that he would really like to bend over his desk…

Surprising him, the door suddenly opened and admitted Glenda Burroughs dressed in a bright yellow blouse and lemon coloured skirted suit, her hair tied back with a black coloured velvet ribbon and immaculately groomed, as always.

"Morning Brian," she smiled at him, crossing the floor to dump her bag onto a chair while inwardly wondering at his red face. It briefly crossed her mind he was embarrassed, but she could not for the life of her think why.

"Eh, aye, morning," he mumbled in return, suddenly busying himself with the reports and shuffling them together. "I, eh, didn't expect you in so early Glenda," he half coughed at her.

"Well, unlike those poor sods out all last night, I got a full nights sleep so thought I'd get in early, see if there's anything I can help you with."

Her eyes narrowed. "You must have been here till, what…midnight?"

"Nearer two," he replied then jokingly added, "or four o'clock if you're doing the overtime returns. The DCI was here until just after one this morning. Coffee?"

"Yes please," she returned his smile and rummaged in her handbag for her cigarettes.

"Anything interesting in last night's statements returns?" she asked, using her Zippo to ignite a Rothmans, her cigarette of choice.

Stood With his back to her, he stood at the table in the corner, spooning coffee into two mugs and shrugged. "One of the Squad guys drives past the office on his way home and dropped the statements into me. They're scribbled and a bit patchy and they'll need editing when the teams get in. That said, I have had a quick glance through them, but from what the guy told me, there was nothing of interest. The teams had a quick chat before they broke off for the night and as far as I'm aware, a couple or three of the prossies knew the victim to see. It seems her English accent was a bit of a stick-out, so that's how they remembered her."

He held up the milk carton and she nodded to him and said, "One sugar please." Stirring the coffee, he walked towards where she sat smoking, handing her the mug. As she bent her head to sip at the coffee, he stared down at her and a curious madness threatened to overcome him; a sudden desire to reach out and touch her breasts. His throat was unusually dry and tight and startled by his own crazy thoughts, he shuffled backwards and turned towards his desk, praying that Burroughs had not realised how close he had come to making a complete fool of himself.

She stared curiously at his back, wondering what the fuck he was thinking and inwardly sighed. Men, she thought; who could ever hope to understand them.

The door opened to admit Gordon McIntosh. "Well, well, and here's me thinking that I'd be the first in this morning. Morning Brian, Glenda," he nodded to each in turn.

"Boss," replied Davidson, while Burroughs smiled in response.

McIntosh walked towards the kettle, then pouring himself a coffee, turned towards Davidson. "Is there any new information, Brian?"

"Nothing fresh, boss," he shook his head. "The statements are ready for your perusal, but I've already glanced through them and there doesn't seem to be anything that connects the victim to a pimp or a regular customer, though some of the prossies, like I was telling the DI, knew the victim from seeing her on the street. However," he handed McIntosh a statement form, "one of the interviewees did mention that any time she saw the victim, she was in the company of another lassie. From the description the Squad guy took, it fits the description of the lassie that you and Glenda interviewed, Lizzie McLeish."

McIntosh sipped at the scalding coffee and shrugged. "Don't suppose that's too unusual Brian. After all, she did admit to Glenda and me that it was her that introduced Alice Trelawney to the Drag area, so it's not unreasonable that they would be seen there together. However," he sighed, "doesn't mean that we can't speak to her again, maybe try and elicit if there is anything else she can tell us. Tell you what, have one of the teams fetch her and bring her here to Pollok for interview. It might clear her head a little if she's not in the comfort of her own surroundings, eh? Polite and courteous, but with a little bit of pressure; just enough to worry her in case she is keeping something back, okay?"

He placed his coffee on a desk and patted his pockets, searching for his fags. "What about the taxi cab firms; anything back from them?"

"Nothing positive, boss, but the word is still out and if they hear anything, I'm assured they will get back to us. Just don't be holding your breath," Davidson shook his head.

The phone on Davidson's desk rung and they stopped speaking while he answered it. McIntosh saw his DS's eyes narrow as Davidson held the phone out to him. "It's for you, boss, DI Knox from the Central Division."

"Knoxy," McIntosh grinned into the phone, "how you doing pal?"

Burroughs, stubbing her cigarette into the ashcan, saw McIntosh frown and then replace the handset.

"Morris Knox," he nodded to the phone and then recalled that Burroughs knew Knoxy. "It seems he called Jane Robertson out earlier this morning to a body discovered behind the Briggait, a young woman who worked as a prostitute. The doc has hinted there is the possibility of some similarities to our inquiry and he has asked me to meet him in an hour at the mortuary. He's got Prof Harland called out for the PM."

He turned to Davidson. "Brian, the team are due to arrive here in what," he glanced at his wristwatch, "just under two hours. Keep them here meantime, but don't divulge what Knoxy has told us. We don't know for certain the inquiries are linked; at least, not yet w don't and I don't want them distracted if they think we might have two murder inquiries, okay? Glenda and I will meet Knoxy and find out what he's got."

Burroughs was shrugging into her coat when Davidson asked, "What about Ren... I mean, DI Renwick, boss?"

McIntosh didn't miss the scorn in his Detective Sergeants tone and took a deep breath. He frowned as he considered and then replied, "Same goes for the DI. I'll update him when I've got more positive information."

The phone on Davidson's desk rung again and both McIntosh and Burroughs hesitated while Davidson replied, "Hello, incident room."

They listened as he replied, "Yes sir, right away sir. I'll be sure to do that sir."

He replaced the phone into the cradle and grinned. "That was ACC Murray, boss. I told him that you are currently out of the office and he instructed you've to phone him at home at your earliest convenience. Oh, but I forgot to get his number."

"Right, good man Brian," McIntosh returned the grin, but silently wondered what the interfering prick Murray wanted now?

Across the city, Dodger Renwick stopped his car in Clyde Street and carefully reversed the gleaming, black coloured Mercedes 380SL car into a parking space directly outside the casino. Not the most confident of drivers, Dodger heaved a quiet sigh of relief and again wondered why he had bought such a small, tight sports type car instead of something roomier for his increasing bulk. Switching off the engine, he smiled and patted at the leather bound steering wheel. He knew exactly why he had bought the car; to remind him that he was still a player and to attract and impress the women.

Heaving his bulk from the driver's door, he stood in the quiet of the Sunday morning, staring at the sandblasted building. What had once been a rundown warehouse was now a fashionable nightclub frequented not just by the rich and famous, but anyone with too much money and not enough sense. He knew the casino never lost, for the odds were always with the house. As he walked to the main doors for his prearranged meeting with the owner, he slowly shook his head and again marvelled at the number of predominantly Chinese punters who filed out through the glass doors of the casino, chattering away in their own dialect. He braced himself to his full height, dwarfing the smaller group as he pushed through them; where they got both the money and the energy to gamble through the night never ceased to amaze Dodger. Twisting his bull neck in his shirt collar and pulling his brown suede coat tightly across his bulk, he strode confidently towards the doors. At the entrance, the two shaven-headed stewards, both formally dressed in black bow ties and dinner suits and as tall and as wide as Dodger, nodded an affable greeting. While one politely stepped aside the other pulled open the door to permit him entry, quietly intimating in a falsetto voice that always reminded Dodger of fingernails drawn down a blackboard, "The boss is in his office, Mister Renwick. He says to go straight up."

Dodger guessed the vivid scar across the man's throat to be the cause of his high-pitched voice. He nodded in response to the courtesy and imperially strode through the main foyer of the casino, smiling at the young, shapely and scantily dressed hostesses tiredly working at tidying the now empty tables. He had come to learn that some of the young women, employed rather for their nubile looks than their hosting skills, for a price also made themselves available for discreet private parties and squinting as he passed her by, was certain he recognised one from a previous late night visit.

As always, he marvelled at the grandeur of the place; the satin lined walls, fake art deco, the comfortable leather couches scattered about the floor area and knowing the owner, guessed all the fitments was either obtained at less than cost price while others somehow found their way to the casino from the back doors of stock rooms or warehouses.

Dodger walked through the room, surveying the wall to his left with an unbroken line of one-armed bandits while on the facing wall was located an extensively stocked bar. Interspaced on the large floor area were blackjack, roulette and poker tables while in the centre of the floor was a wide, central staircase that led upwards to a small restaurant and a number of private gaming rooms that also doubled for what the casino called 'select function suites'. Striding up the staircase to the backroom that was grandly designated the management suite, he recalled with pleasure the privately invited parties he had attended in the plushly appointed, softly lit function suites. The invited clientele were all male who were entertained by an equal number of the young, scantily clad hostesses who provided the guests with entertainment that included more than just drinks.

At the top of the stairs, he walked to a darkened rear corridor and self-importantly nodded to the two young men, no more than in their mid twenties and both similarly dressed in casual trousers, shirt and tie and wearing black leather bomber jackets. They watched him approach with dull eyes as they stood lounging outside the management suite door, the boredom clearly expressed on their faces. On cue, one of the young men whose predominant neck tattoos, in Dodgers mind, singled him out as no more than a thug, pushed open the door to permit the Councillor entry, then pulled it closed it behind him.

The room was wide and spacious, ornately decorated with the main feature being a large, highly polished oak desk sitting in front of a panoramic window through which could be seen the masts of the moored, nineteenth century clipper ship, the *Carrick*.

Though he assumed the man behind the desk had been at the casino through the night, Dodger saw him to be alert and clear-eyed and as Dodger entered, glance up from that morning's Sunday edition of the 'Glasgow News'.

Eddie Beattie, much documented by the Strathclyde Police Intelligence Department as a prominent Glasgow gangster, but now trying to reinvent himself as an entrepreneur businessman, stood and greeted Dodger with a warm handshake.

In the recent past a much photographed Beattie featured regularly in the media as a substantial donor to local charities; a philanthropist whose donations, his accountant assured him, would be taken into account by HM Inland Revenue and would prove helpful with his legitimate tax returns.

Of course, Beattie's lavish lifestyle and business interests easily afforded such donations for his true income comprised not just of his legitimate business interests, but included his many criminal enterprises.

Beattie's accountant, described by the police as a man so bent if he spat forward, the spittle would strike himself in the forehead, was very good at his job and was not just well rewarded for his loyalty, but knew the cost to both him and his family if he didn't do so well.

It did not escape Dodger's attention that Beattie's set was elevated slightly higher than the seat facing the desk, thereby inferring a dominance over the seated guest. "Thanks for coming this early in the morning. What's your poison then, Dodger?" he asked, making his way to a table set with drink.

Dodger settled his bulk into the comfortable chair and smiled in return. "Just a soft drink, please Eddie. I'm driving."

Dodger watched Beattie pour a Coke into a tall glass and himself a black coffee from a Thermos pot, into a china cup and saucer. Settled back into his chair, he lifted a wooden box from which he offered a thick cigar that Dodger declined. Lighting his own from a gold coloured lighter, Beattie blew an almost perfect circle of smoke and smiled at Dodger.

"So, what's the latest on my application?"

Dodger pretended to frown as though the question was difficult to respond to and let a few seconds pass, hoping to impress upon Beattie the gravity of the issue. Finally he replied, "The plot of land in Shettleston you're trying to acquire Eddie is adjacent to a plot marked already by the council as the proposed site for a small shopping complex and a Council run nursing home. There has been plenty of local support for the project, particularly as the construction promises to bring in local jobs and businesses to an area with a high incidence of unemployment and depravation. Crime is endemic there and besides that," he shrugged as though struggling with the difficulty of the situation, "there is also an ongoing protest from the local police Divisional Commander. The police argument is that you build another pub and bookie premises there and you're introducing the opportunity for the locals to plummet further into debt, not to mention the social problems it will bring."

Beattie wordlessly stared at the cigar as he rolled it between his thumb and forefinger, then turned to stare steely-eyed at Dodger.

"Do you honestly think I give a flying fuck about the social conditions these reprobates live in? I don't give a shit about their sad lives or how they choose to live them. I'm in business to make money and the acquisition of property to further my business, Dodger. I have plans for the east end that go beyond a pishy pub and bookies. It's the land that I want; the land that can be developed." He paused as if lost in his own vision. "The planning application required me to state the purpose the land will be used for and it's no secret I'm in the gambling and alcohol industry, so it seemed to make sense at the time that my application was submitted with those plans in mind. However," his eyes narrowed and his tone softened as he flicked ash into an ornate ashtray, "I'll take on board what you're saying."

"What if I consider the pub being run as a sort of family themed premises, maybe include a restaurant inside? Like one of these cheap food burger places that are springing up all over the place," nodding his head at his own foresight.

He stared hard at an increasingly uncomfortable Dodger. "But what I really need to know Dodger is if I do amend the application, you can assure me that it will be passed through the Council planning committee and that you have enough influence to sway the committee? I wouldn't be a happy man if you were to let me down, Dodger; not after having seen you all right through the years with cash and favours, if you get my meaning."

Behind the simple question lay a veiled threat and it occurred to Dodger that upon entering the warm room, he should have removed the suede coat for he suddenly felt a trickle of perspiration running down his spine. As much as the larger man liked to think he and Beattie were equal, his private thoughts forced him to admit the gangster scared him shitless.

"Of course, there should be no problem Eddie," he smoothly replied, anxious that Beattie did not detect the tremor in his voice. "We both know that my word is my bond when it comes to Council issues and as you rightly point out, I have enough support to push through your Shettleston application and of course, any further applications you might have in mind."

Staring at Dodger, Beattie's beady eyes seemed to bore through the larger man before he slowly nodded his head.

"Okay Dodger, I'll have my architect draw up an amended application and have it submitted before the end of the week. One further question; what's the time frame for these things?"

Dodger pursed his lips as he thought and said, "The next planning committee meet on the last Tuesday of each month, so we've missed this month and we're now looking at the end of June. It's a bugger having missed this month, but it does give me four weeks to ensure your amended application goes through smoothly."

"Nothing else for it then," sighed Beattie who reached into a drawer in his desk and withdrew a sealed, bulky brown envelope that he pushed across the desk towards Dodger.

"A little something to assist with your upcoming campaign to run for Parliament and Dodger," he stared again, "there might be more of that if my plans for the east end stay on track. All I ask is you don't let me down, understand?"

"Of course, Eddie," Dodger replied, but a little too eagerly he inwardly gulped.

"Right, I'd better let you get on with your business Councillor," smiled Beattie, dismissing the larger man.

Dodger rose from his seat, but Beattie raised a hand as if recalling something and said, "Your boy, the younger one. He's a copper, isn't he? Works over in the south side of the city; Pollok I believe, in the CID."

Dodger slowly nodded, wondering where this was going.

"There's a…" Beattie hesitated, seeking the correct word, "an associate has travelled north from England, a man called Trelawney. Up here to identify the young girl that was found murdered over that way, in the big park there. The cops likely have him stowed away somewhere and I'd take it as a personal favour Dodger if you were to let me know where Trelawney is being looked after; where the cops have got him billeted. Probably a hotel I'm guessing. You understand?"

Dodger's curiosity was scratching at his nose, but he knew too well that to express such curiosity might not be the best idea. With a fistful of Beattie's money in the envelope clutched in his corrupt hand, he could only nod his head as Beattie smiled humourlessly and added, "I'll expect a call then and Dodger," he paused, then said with meaning, "sooner than later, eh?"

Beattie watched as Dodger shuffled though the door, gently closing it behind him and reached under his desk to switch off the video camera, hidden in the wall above the back of his head. A video camera with the lens directed at the chair just vacated by Dodger. Rising from his chair, he was grinning as he rounded the desk to the reproduction mahogany cabinet from where he collected the video tape that had recorded the entire meeting.

CHAPTER 15

Following his early breakfast that saw him the last to leave the quiet hotel dining room, Cris Trelawney grabbed a newspaper from the front desk and returned to his room. He glanced briefly at the 'Glasgow News', whose prominent headline screamed out '*Our Boys On The Offensive*' and underneath the heading a grainy photograph of a line of heavily armed Royal Marines, impossibly laden with packs almost as heavy as themselves and yomping across a barren wasteland. He dropped the paper onto the small desk and sitting on the edge of the bed, lifted the phone and dialled the number.

A breathless sounding Louise Davenport answered on the fourth ring.

"Hi, it's me," he said.

"I'm just through the door," she replied in a rush, dragging a chair across the tiled floor and sitting down with her elbows on the kitchen table. "I haven't even got my coat off yet. Jack and I were at church and we've come home to get changed into our sailing gear. He's dead keen that him and old Trevor take me out on the boat. It's a beautiful, calm day here so we're taking a picnic and lying offshore for an hour to enjoy the weather." She heard him chuckling and then, almost shyly, she added, "I miss you."

He could not know that pleased though Louise was to hear from Cris, she did not want to ask him what was happening in Glasgow, how he fared with his meeting the police and worried that to discuss the true reason for his trip might upset him. She was embarrassed at her own selfishness, that she didn't want this brief communication with Cris to be marred by discussion about his murdered daughter. Her unsaid fear was unfounded for all Cris simply said was, "I've seen Alice, but the police won't permit me to bring her body home. They're still making inquires."

"Are you all right? I can still come up, you know; maybe catch a flight or a train. It won't be too difficult to get time off."

He bit at his lip. His whole being cried out for her, wishing she were here with him, but a part of him didn't want her to be involved in what he now thought of as his past life and like it or not, Alice had been a huge part of that life. No, whether consciously or not, he wanted to protect Louise and Jack from his sordid, criminal past; just didn't want them to be part of it.

"There's nothing I'd like more than to be with you right now," he smoothly replied, "but really, there's nothing much here that I can do and to be honest, all I'm doing is sitting about waiting for the local detectives to make their inquiries. They've asked me some questions and I know they want more answers, but there's not much I can tell them other than Alice's history with me. Her life during the last year and a bit is as much a mystery to me as it is to them."

He tried to sweeten the refusal of her offer and hoped she didn't take it as some kind of rebuff.

Almost a half minute of silence lay between them and he thought she might be annoyed with his refusal to let her travel north, but then she replied, "Do you have any idea how long they will want you to stay in Glasgow?"

She heard him inhale deeply and he replied, "No, but I think it might be till such times they release …" he exhaled again, "…Alice's body."

With her free hand she clutched at her throat, her eyes welling with unshed tears and her throat choked with emotion. She took a deep breath and forcing herself to be calm, said, "Right, well, I miss you Cris Trelawney and I want you home. Home to me; as soon as you can, okay?"

He smiled at the receiver and with a formal respect in his voice, replied, "Okay, ma'am."

He heard her sob and then chuckle and added, "I miss you too and …" hesitating now, took his own deep breath and added, "… and I love you Louise Davenport."

"Love you too," she hurriedly replied and replaced the phone in the cradle before the tears threatened to engulf her.

"Mum?" said the voice behind her. She turned to see Jack standing there dressed in a heavy roll-neck jumper, jeans and Wellington boots, looking every inch the seaman, but with concern etched on his face. "Are you all right? Is Cris, I mean, Mister Trelawney, is he okay?"

She opened her arms and he walked into them, wrapping them about him and reaching up, kissed his forehead.

"He's fine Jack, he's fine."

And so am I, she thought with a tear-stained smile then standing and ruffling her son's mop of thick hair, added, "So, Captain, are we having this picnic or not?"

Sitting on the edge of the bed, Cris Trelawney stared at the telephone and slowly breathed out. He really did miss Louise and wondered again at his luck, meeting two women he would love, in one lifetime. It was luck that he did not really deserve; not after some of the terrible things he had done.

The boredom of the hotel room had given him much time to reflect on the past. It had surprised him that the copper, McIntosh was aware of his identity, of his past in London and more worryingly, his association with Ronnie Kyle.

Cris had thought long and weary about how he had come to be in the employ of that bastard; his arrival in London looking for work. First finding himself doing a bit of door stewarding, then later coming to the attention of Kyle and moving up the ladder of the gangsters empire till he was the top dog; the leading enforcer.

It had been fun to begin with; the money easily earned, the nightlife and women at his availability. Living the life, every young man's dream. Sure, he had come a cropper now and then; the cops fitting him up on some trumped up charge or other, but always Kyle had the influence to get him out of trouble, so no conviction was ever upheld.

It worried him that the good-looking blonde cop, Burroughs had made inquiry about him with the Met.

It still rankled, wondering if he was wrong; had he had met her before? He shook his head as if to clear it but stopped. His eyes narrowed and then closed and he sighed.

Now he remembered.

Davie Renwick lay in his bed, one hand behind his head while with the other he idly rubbed at his flaccid penis. Slowly, wincing against the pain in his head, he raised himself and turning, supported himself on one elbow and glanced again through foggy eyes at the discarded clothes and remembered. His head throbbed from the whisky he had consumed when he had returned home in the early hours of that morning, creeping into the house like a thief in the night.

He glanced again to the bedroom floor where his clothes lay in an untidy heap and sighed. He needed to get up, get the room tidied and into uniform to head down for a couple of hours of physical training at the Drill Hall in Maryhill. Training? He grinned then almost immediately winced, the simple effort causing his head to ache even more.

The Pegasus Bar more like for a Sunday morning curer.

Gritting his teeth against the throbbing in his skull, he turned his head and saw his mother's car keys lying on the bedside table. Shit! He had forgotten to return them to the hook in the cupboard at the front door. Forcing himself to rise and fighting the bile that threatened to choke him, he swung both legs from the bed and staggered towards the chair where lay a pair of jogging trousers. One hand on the back of the chair to steady himself, Davie carefully slipped the joggers on and then quietly made his way downstairs. He could hear his mother working in the kitchen, the radio turned low. At the hallway window, he glanced out into the driveway at the side of the house and saw his father's car already gone. Almost with relief, he exhaled and gave up any pretence at silence and made his way downstairs.

Martha Renwick turned at the sound of her son entering the kitchen and with a smile, offered her cheek for a kiss, immediately detecting the stale smell of whisky on his breath.

"Drunk again last night, were you son?"

"Just a couple of wee snifters after the training. It's hard you know, mum. Learning all these tactics and weapon drills," he replied, opening the fridge and fetching out a carton of fresh orange juice that he raised high and tipped back and proceeded to drink from.

"Here, how many time must you be told, Davie. Use a glass," his mother chided him, lifting a tumbler from the cupboard below the worktop.

Davie grinned and with the back of his hand, wiped his mouth before pouring a generous helping into the glass then threw the juice down his still parched throat. He refilled the glass and opening a high cupboard, rummaged in the plastic first aid box for the Paracetamol.

"Where's Dodger off to this early on a Sunday, mum?" he asked, popping two tablets from the blister pack that he swallowed with a grimace, washing them down with more orange juice.

"He didn't say," she sighed, wishing for once Davie would refer to his father as 'dad'. "Just took a coffee and some toast and left half an hour ago." Her eyes narrowed when she saw her car keys lying on the worktop. "Have you been driving again Davie? You know you're banned. If you get caught …"

"Yeah, yeah, yeah," he reached down and enfolded his mother in his large arms. "Don't worry mum, they'll not catch me."

"It's not the polis I'm concerned about," she almost whispered. "If your father …"

"What he doesn't know won't hurt him," he interrupted her with a wide grin, almost feeling better and knowing his mother would never tell on him.

"Now," he eagerly rubbed his hands together, "before I head down to the base, how's about a lovely fry-up for your favourite boy, eh?"

On that bright Sunday morning while Davie was slowly wakening from a drunken sleep, his younger brother DI Mark Renwick pushed open the incident room office door and striding through, ignored the cheery greeting from the Duty Officer Gavin Wilson.

Angered at the brazen slight, Wilson softly muttered, "Wanker" at the DI's retreating back.

Renwick was well aware he was late and face flushed, pushed the door to the Incident room open to find Brian Davidson sitting reading the 'Glasgow News'. He breathed a sigh of relief that Gordon McIntosh had not yet arrived.

His relief was such that he felt almost sociable and making his way to the kettle said, "Morning Brian, coffee?"

Without taking his eyes from the newspaper, Davidson muttered "No thanks."

Determined he wouldn't be riled by Davidson's off-handed response, Renwick gritted his teeth and asked, "Any word when the DCI will be in?"

Davidson forced his voice to be neutral, but took perverse pleasure in replying, "The boss has already been into the office. He's away with DI Burroughs."

Renwick turned a shivery cold, the kettle held in mid air. Slowly, he turned towards Davidson. "Did he say where he was going?"

Davidson glanced up at the pale faced DI and shaking his head, half-smiled. "No, but he said he would see you when he got back."

McIntosh did not instruct that Davidson be specific about where he and Burroughs were going to, so Davidson didn't think it necessary to add that McIntosh and Burroughs were meeting Knox from the Central Division. His logic was that if Renwick had arrived on time at work, he would have been present when the phone call arrived, so let him imagine he was due a bollocking for being late and fuck him, Davidson inwardly seethed.

An uncomfortable silence descended on the room with neither man even acknowledging the others presence.

As the minutes passed towards midday, the inquiry team detectives began to arrive, most at first quiet and reserved, bemoaning their late night finish as they helped themselves to tea and coffee. Gradually the hubbub of noise increased as the more jovial among the detectives recounted some of the patter they had noted from the interviewed prostitutes.

"So I said to her, your brother-in-law is one of your punters? Really?" recounted a Squad detective. "Aye, that's what she told me," then to laughter added, "and she says the bugger had the balls to ask her for family discount."

At his desk, Davidson grinned at the story and furtively glanced towards Renwick, who head down, pretended to be reading a statement and did his best to ignore the arriving detectives.

He heard the phone on Renwick's desk ring and watched as the DI's face first registered surprise, then saw him stand and call out to the room.

"Can I have your attention please. That was the DCI. He and DI Burroughs are at the City Mortuary meeting with DI Knox from the Central Division. The DCI has new information and does not want anyone leaving the office until he returns with an update. He reckons he'll be about an hour, so if you want to organise some of you to fetch rolls in from the café in the Pollok centre…" he tailed off and sat down, his face flushed with realisation as he stared at Davidson.

He knows, Davidson inwardly grinned.

CHAPTER 16 – Midday Sunday, 30 May

The morning sun blasted through the bay window of the first floor flat that was located in Duke Street.

Ronnie Kyle, dressed in an open-necked shirt and casual trousers, sat comfortably in an old-fashioned easy chair, his legs crossed and a cigar lodged between the stubby fingers of his right hand. An empty coffee mug lay on a low table by his left hand. Months previously, he had at last surrendered his vanity and he wore a pair of silver framed reading glasses while he read the Sunday morning edition of the 'Glasgow News'. In the kitchen, he could hear Moses Parker whistling tunelessly to a Tambla Motown classis playing on the small transistor radio. He involuntarily salivated as the smell of fried bacon assailed his nostrils.

"How long till breakfast Moses, I'm bloody starving," he called out.

Moses poked his head out from the tight little kitchen. "Two minutes, Guv," he replied with a grin. "Sit yourself down at the table and I'll bring you a pot of char."

Five minutes later, both men were wolfing down Moses' fry-up. With a clatter, Kyle threw his cutlery onto the plate and loudly burped. "That hit the spot, me old son," he smiled while dabbing at his mouth with the back of his hand.

"So, what's on the agenda for today, Guv?"

Kyle exhaled and entwining his fingers at the back of his head, stared in reflective thought at Moses.

"I'll give it an hour for this food to settle, then I'll phone that Jock git Eddie Beattie, find out if he's made any progress in tracking down our old pal Cris's whereabouts." His eyebrows knitted and his face darkened. "I'm sick of sitting here in this shitty hovel, waiting for information. And another thing," he nodded towards the black canvas holdall bag that lay against the wall, "I want to be certain the shooter is working properly, so I think that you and me will take a drive into the country, Moses. Take in the sights as it were and find ourselves a quiet little place for a bit of target practise and somewhere, when we get our hands on him, we can take Cris and remind him what it means to betray his friends, eh?"

Moses slowly nodded and felt a shiver run down his spine. In all the years he had worked for Ronnie Kyle, he had seen and done some terrible things, but nothing, he knew with a sure certainty, would come close to the punishment that Ronnie had in mind for his former friend, the man Moses knew as Cris McGuire.

Simon Johnson, a pressed volunteer, carried a plastic bag laden with bacon rolls in each hand as he strolled towards the main door of the Pollok Shopping Centre and prepared for the five-minute return walk to the office in Brockburn Road. As he walked through the bustling shoppers, he turned to look at a display of televisions in the window of DER and collided with a flash of colour.

"Hey, watch where you're…" said the voice, then stopped. "You again!" accused the young woman.

Simon, wide-eyed could only stare. What were the odds? The girls auburn hair was once more piled beneath her multi-coloured Bob Marley knitted woollen cap, but on this occasion she was wearing a white blouse and a dark green skirt under her yellow kaftan coat, brown leather Jesus sandals and from her left shoulder hung a knitted, patchwork bag.

Angrily, she folded her arms and eyes narrowed and full of suspicion, accusingly stared at him. "Are you stalking me or something? It's not enough you try to run me over, now you're out to knock me down again."

Bemused, he could only stutter in reply, "Sorry… sorry, I didn't see you."

"Well perhaps you should consider having an eye test," she fumed, standing her ground and seemingly unwilling to let him move away.

He sighed and grinned, oblivious to the curious stares of his fellow shoppers. "I really am sorry, miss. I was too busy looking at those," he raised a hand holding a bag and pointed to the electrical shop window.

She frowned. "Well, no harm done, I suppose," then she again stared accusingly at him. "You're not really following me, are you?"

"No," he grinned. "I work over at," then hesitated. "Over in Brockburn Road," and held up the bags. "Look, I'm on a roll run."

She glanced at the bags and smiled and to Simon, it seemed her whole face lit up. "Well," she slowly drawled, "just try to be more careful in future, okay?"

As she made to step around him and without thinking it through, he said, "Wait, eh, can I get your phone number?"

She stared at him, surprised.

"Whatever for?"

"Ah," now he was thinking on his feet. "Well, I was thinking, maybe if I'm out driving or walking again, I should phone you and tell you where I'm going to. That way you can take a different route and I'll be sure not to run you down?" God, he thought. How lame does that sound?

She smiled again at him and he held his breath.

"Are you thinking of asking me out on a date?"

"Ah, yes," he slowly drawled. He screwed his face up, knowing that she had every right to tell him to bugger off, but the girl grinned at him.

"Well, I suppose it might be safer if I'm there to keep an eye on you," she glanced down into her bag and fished out a pencil and the stub of a receipt. On the receipt she scrawled a telephone number and stuck the receipt into the top pocket of his suit jacket.

As she turned away, he called after her, "What's your name?"

"You're the detective," she called back at him, "find out."

He stared after her, surprised at her intuition in recognising he was a police officer.

Only when she was out of sight did he realise he'd forgotten to remove his warrant card in the small plastic sleeve that hung on the lanyard, round his neck.

The hubbub in the incident room settled to a quiet whisper and died completely when the DCI and DI entered. McIntosh, his face grim, stared about the room.

"DI Burroughs and I have just returned from the mortuary where, with DI Morris Knox, we attended the post mortem of a young woman discovered earlier today in waste ground behind the area known as Paddy's Market. As you will have realised, this is the Central Division area and therefore, their inquiry. However, the Pathologist Mister Harland has almost conclusively determined the victim," he glanced at a sheet of paper in his right hand, "Elizabeth Fisher, who worked as a street prostitute, was murdered by the same killer who is responsible for the murder of Alice Trelawney."

An excited whisper enfolded the room.

McIntosh raised his free hand and said, "Quiet please." He took a deep breath.

"In light of this new information, ladies and gentlemen, it seems we have what the American police call a serial killer; two murders within a few days. What will happen now is it is my intention to contact the ACC (Crime) and suggest that we conduct both murders as the one inquiry. I have agreed with DI Knox that if required, he will arrange for a sub-office to be located within Stewart Street from where we will make inquiries local to the city centre. However, the main thrust of the inquiry will continue from here at Pollok."

He paused for breath. "As we speak, DI Knox and one of his colleagues from the Female and Child Unit are attending at the deceased's home address to break the news of her murder and glean what information he can."

"Mark," he turned to his Detective Inspector, "DI Knox is sending four officers over to assist with Actions. Please ensure they are brought up to speed on Alice Trelawney's murder so we are all marching to the same drum."

"Sir," replied Renwick, making a note on his pad.

"I'm sorry, ladies and gentlemen, but we're looking at another night down the drag," McIntosh announced to muffled groans, "So for the minute, while I'm meeting with the ACC and unless there is anything requiring immediate attention," he turned and glanced at Brian Davison, who shook his head. "Then, ladies and gentlemen, get yourselves away home for now and meet here again at say, six o'clock this evening when hopefully, I'll have some more information for you."

As the team began to depart from the office, McIntosh again turned to Davidson and asked if Lizzie McLeish been brought to the office yet?

"Two of the Squad guys fetched her about an hour ago boss. She's sitting in the detention room."

McIntosh was puzzled. "Why is she detained? Was there a problem?"

Davidson shook his head. "She was out of her face, boss. Smack, I'm guessing. The last I looked in on her was about ten minutes ago and she was sleeping. The bar officer has been giving her copious amounts of water to bring her back to her senses. But no, she's not officially detained. The doors not even locked. I just had her put in there to keep her out of the way."

McIntosh rubbed a weary hand across his face. "Okay then, see if you can bring her round and bring her into the DI's room where I can have a word with her."

Davidson moved off to instruct a detective to fetch Lizzie, while McIntosh beckoned that Glenda Burroughs speak privately with him.

"I promised Alice Trelawney's father we would keep him apprised of any developments. I do not want him to learn from the radio or the newspapers that there's been another murder, particularly when it becomes public knowledge that the woman worked as a prostitute. I'm almost certain the papers will put two and two together, then it will come out about his daughter plying her trade too, as a prostitute. Can you take young Johnson with you and give Trelawney the briefest of facts that it seems his daughter is not our only victim. I think it's only fair we give the man a heads up."

"Will do, Gordon," she replied, smiling at his thoughtfulness and waved for Simon Johnson to approach.

Briefly, she instructed the young aide to contact the hotel and determine that Mister Trelawney was there and to grab a set of car keys and accompany her to the hotel.

"Boss?" said the voice behind McIntosh and turned towards Davidson. "Just to remind you, ACC Murray has been calling all morning. He is still expecting a call from you," then seeing the anger in McIntosh's face, raised his hands palms outward and added, "Don't shoot the messenger."

McIntosh smiled and nodded. "Okay, Brian if he calls again, I'll be grateful if you inform the ACC that you're still trying to reach me."

Davidson had the good grace not to grin, but simply nodded and turned back to his desk.

Lizzie McLeish sat on the wooden, unforgiving chair. She wore the same dirty and dishevelled clothing, her skin waxy coloured, hair tousled and her body like that of a broken plastic doll as she stared into space, or so it seemed to McIntosh. He leaned across the desk and tapping at the bottom of the packet, offered her a cigarette. She stared at the packet and shaking his head, he withdrew two fags and lighting both, stepped round the desk and placed one between the bony fingers of her right hand. Automatically, Lizzie raised her hand and inhaled deeply.

He thought she looked ghastly, far worse than when he had previously seen her and privately considered that if she continued her drug taking, the young woman was not long for this life.

"Why am I here," she slurred, her voice an almost inaudible whisper.

"I need to know about Alice, just some more questions Lizzie. Then you can go home," he replied, his voice soft and sympathetic.

"Alice," she repeated. "Alice hasn't come home. I don't know where she is." She shuffled uncomfortably on the chair and asked, "Is it about the wallet, the foreign punter's wallet? The bastard wants his wallet; that's it, isn't it? I threw it away, didn't I? That bastard Wingy, he wasn't happy, wasn't pleased. He could have done something with the cards."

Confused, McIntosh let her ramble on. What the devil is she talking about, he wondered? What wallet and who is Wingy?

"Tell me about the wallet," he patiently asked.

Lizzie straightened in the chair and peered at him through a multicoloured fog. "He was just a punter," she whined, "just a punter. Stole his wallet when he was in the bog," she giggled. "Bastard was a virgin."

McIntosh blew out some smoke and realised Lizzie must be relating an incident that had nothing whatsoever to do with Alice Trelawney.

She stared at him and smile creased her face. She didn't know where she was, couldn't recall being brought to Pollok, but what she did know was that in front of her was a man, a punter and the possibility of an earner crossed her drug induced thoughts.

"Something I can do for you, mister?" she tried her to engage her most beguiling smile, but found it difficult to focus and even Lizzie realised she was out her face, her words difficult compose. "Maybe give you a wee wank or a shag, eh?" she slurred again. "No cost you much, mister." She waved her hand at him, the ash falling from the cigarette to the linoleum floor.

He stared at her, but not unkindly and exhaled. The poor wee lassie was too far gone to be of any use to him. Anything she did know had been learned at the first interview. Rising to his feet, he walked past her and gently, almost fatherly patted her on the shoulder as he opened the door and called down the corridor for the bar officer.

The uniformed officer arrived and McIntosh gave him his instructions; to see that Miss McLeish is taken home and to ensure that at least one of the officers conveying her is a woman.

The last thing McIntosh needed was a sexual complaint about one of his officers from the druggie, Lizzie McIntosh.

Stepping into the incident room, McIntosh instructed Brian Davidson to contact Criminal Intelligence at Pitt Street and request they conduct a speculative check into the nickname 'Wingy', adding there might be a possible connection with both Lizzie McLeish and the deceased Alice Trelawney.

"Got all that boss," Davidson noted the name on his pad. "Just to let you know, DI Knox called from Stewart Street. He has informed Elizabeth Fishers next of kin, her mother apparently, of her murder. Says to tell you there was no man in Fishers life; well, not one that lives with her or that she was seeing regularly, anyway. She lived with her two weans, but the mother has them meantime. He'll send the mothers statement over with his cops."

"Thanks Brian," he rubbed a weary hand over his face. "God, could I do with a coffee and a fag."

While Simon Johnson drove the Ital in Paisley Road West towards the hotel, Glenda Burroughs blew smoke through the partially open passenger's window and turning towards him, asked, "So young Simon, what's happening in your life, anything exciting?"

"No, not really ma'am, just the usual day to day stuff; work, doing up my flat, visiting the folks, that sort of thing."

"Where's your flat located?"

"It's in Hollybrook Street, just off Calder Street in Shawlands. I bought it with my then girlfriend, but she moved on so it's just me now," he replied.

"Oh, so you've got your own love nest then," she teased.

He was aware that she was staring at him and he could feel the heat of his blush and not for the first time was aware of the nearness of her; her scent and the quiet rustle of her stockings when she moved her legs. Uncomfortably and to his horror, he felt himself become aroused.

As if realising the effect she was having on the young detective, Burroughs turned her head away. "So here we go again," she said as Simon turned the car into the hotel forecourt.

Cris Trelawney had waited for them in the hotel foyer and indicated they follow him to the restaurant. They saw he had already arranged a table that bore a tray of cups and coffee as he beckoned that they sit.

"You have some news?" he began, his eyes betraying his curiosity while he poured coffee into the three cups.

In the briefest detail, but without naming the deceased, Burroughs disclosed the discovery of a body of a woman whom, she stressed in confidence, was previously recorded by the police as a working girl; "a street prostitute" explained

Burroughs, conscious her young partner was unaware of Trelawney's London history and maintaining the illusion Trelawney was simply a fisherman.

"DCI McIntosh believed it was better that you heard this from us, rather than learn it from the media," she continued.

Sitting beside her, Simon was a little disconcerted that Burroughs was being so formal with the man, showing neither sympathy nor any kind of sorrow for his own loss.

Cris nodded his head and asked, "I take it by informing me of this new development, you have some suspicion this woman's killer is the same person; the same man, who murdered my Alice?"

Burroughs hesitated and then slowly replied, "There is an indication both murders were committed by the same individual, yes."

"Well, there's nothing left to say other than I hope you have some luck catching this man before he kills again," he replied as he stood.

Both Burroughs and Simon got to their feet and bade Cris farewell.

As they made their way towards the restaurant door, Cris called out, "Miss Burroughs. Can I have a word please," then glancing at Simon, added, "a private word?"

Burroughs stared back at him, then turning to Simon, said, "I'll be a moment. Wait in the car, please."

He pushed through the restaurant door and made his way to Ital, feeling a little bit miffed that whatever Trelawney had to say was not for his ears. As he unlocked the driver's door, he grinned. Mister Trelawney was not a bad looking man. Maybe the 'private word' was to do with the DI's attractiveness.

Any thoughts Simon had on this issue was soon dismissed when Burroughs returned to the car, her anger obvious the way she slammed the door behind her. He saw her face flushed, her mouth set in a tight frown and she was breathing through her flared nostrils.

Wisely, he decided to keep his mouth shut, started the engine and smoothly drove out of the forecourt.

The return journey to Pollok was made in uncomfortable silence and stopping the car in the small front yard, hardly had Simon applied the handbrake when Burroughs was out the door and into the office.

"You're welcome, ma'am," he quietly said, wondering all the time exactly what Trelawney had said to so enrage the DI.

CHAPTER 17 – Sunday Mid-afternoon

Dismissed until six o'clock that evening, Simon Johnson drove the ten minutes it took to get to his flat, thinking of the girl he had met earlier that morning at the Pollok Shopping Centre. He smiled at the memory, surprised to see that she was even prettier than he recalled when he had almost run her over, in Kelvin Way. Parking outside the tenement flat, he pulled his suit jacket from the back seat and fetched the receipt she had stuffed into his top pocket and groaned.

It was not her telephone number.

She had written '*Find me if you are really interested,*' with the word 'really' underscored and had initialled the scrawl with the letter, '*G*'.

"Bugger," he muttered, then shaking his head at her cheek, grinned. Pushing open the heavy entrance door to the close, he made towards the stairs and thought, yes, I am really interested.

In the lounge, the telephone answer machine blinked with a recorded message. The machine had been a gift from Marie's sister that either she didn't want when she left or simply forgot. He had considered throwing it out, but reasoned it was not the machine's fault that Marie was unfaithful and besides, when every penny was a prisoner, it saved him the cost of purchasing a new one.

He pressed the button and listened to Sheila Speirs voice, requesting he give her a call back.

Later, he thought, making his way into the neat little kitchen, figuring his stomach right now had priority, his head full of thoughts of the very pretty and mysterious G.

Sat at dinner in one of the private rooms of his club with a bottle of his favourite German beer at his elbow, Eddie Beattie did not acknowledge Mickey's entrance when the younger of his two minders wordlessly entered the room, a telephone in one hand and the telephone cord coiled in the other hand. Swiftly, the minder plugged the cord into a wall socket and placed the phone on the table beside his boss. That done he stepped a few discreet paces away from the table and stood with his hands behind his back, staring at the Georgian framed prints on the opposite wall.

Beattie knew that Mickey would not have dared disturb his boss's dinner if the minder didn't believe the call to be important.

He dabbed at his mouth with a brilliantly white linen napkin and lifted the phone from the cradle.

"Yes?"

As he listened, Beattie smiled and unconsciously nodded, then repeated "Room 37, The Blue Swallow Hotel on Paisley Road West. Yes, I've got that."

He smiled again and sighing with expectation, concluded the call when he suggested, "Tonight, seven o'clock at the usual place. Bye."

He continued to smile and beckoned Mickey remove the phone from the table. When the young minder had closed the door behind him, he resumed his meal.

Mary McIntosh stood over the cooker while the tea brewed on the gas ring. She was worried about her husband. Gordon was so close to retirement and now this, a double murder. Damn! She closed her eyes against the throb in her forehead and asked God to forgive her callousness at the death of the two, unfortunate young women.

Still, she had her own priorities and worrying about her husband's health was foremost in her mind.

He didn't know she had seen him rubbing at his chest, pretending to her it was wind. The stupid sod. Of course she realised what it truly was; the stress of the job after all these years finally taking its toll.

"Penny for them," said Gordon behind her, startling her from her thoughts. "Thought my cuppa was on its way?"

"Yes, it's here," she replied, blinking away the unshed tears and sniffing, pretended to cough to fake the tightness in her own chest at her worst nightmare, the dreadful thought of losing her man.

"Here, here, what's all this then?" he asked, surprised at her emotion, his arms enveloping her as she turned into them.

"Oh, I'd say it was the time of the month," she leaned into his shoulder and half laughed, "but they days are long past. Thankfully."

He laughed with her and continued to hold her tightly, but still was worried that there was something amiss.

She shrugged out of his grasp and still sniffing, bade him sit at the kitchen table and turned to collect the teapot from the cooker.

"What time do you need to be back at the office?" she asked, pouring tea into the two mugs.

"I've got the team mustering at six o'clock, but I'd like to be there for about the back of five."

"So you'll have time for me to get you some dinner?"

He smiled at her, uncertain why she had seemed upset and then a thought occurred to him.

"Not expecting any visitors, are we?"

"No, why?" she replied, her face expressing her curiosity.

"Well," he slowly drawled and standing took her hand and drew her to her feet.

"If you are certain it's not the time of the month and we've got a couple of hours to kill and as I'm not really that hungry…"

Her curiosity turned with wide-eyed sudden realisation to a shocked grin and she replied, "Gordon McIntosh. It's the middle of the day, for heavens sake."

"Yeah," he grinned in return as he gently pulled her towards the kitchen door, "so when we're upstairs, we'll be able to see what we're doing then, won't we?"

The red-bricked Territorial Army barracks located in Thornbank Street in the Yorkhill area of Glasgow near to the Sick Children's Hospital, for now accommodated a Company of the Parachute Regiments Scottish TA battalion. Within the building's expansive gymnasium, the forty odd 'weekend warriors' groaned and screamed in pain as the battalions three training instructors, all regular army, pushed them to their limits around the makeshift assault course, screaming and kicking at the exposed bodies and urging the part-time soldiers to greater effort.

At one side of the gymnasium Davie Renwick half-lay propped against the wall, exhausted and totally spent, his body aching, his breath coming in gasps and his heart racing. A tanned, shaven headed and heavily tattooed instructor wearing the

117

white singlet of the Army Physical Training Corps, stood over him. The instructor's hands clenched and the veins in his muscular arms were prominent while the man screamed abuse and used expletives previously unheard of by the heavily built Davie. The instructors spit flew at Davie as the man derided him for even having considered being a member of the elite unit.

"Move yourself, you fat wanker!" screamed the Cockney instructor, angry that he was stuck here in this shithole with these worthless civvies while his comrades were earning glory in the Falkland's; angry with himself for losing it with this fat fuck and angry that there wasn't a fucking thing he could do about any of it.

Davie shrank from the abuse, not daring to even look up at the maddened instructor, uncertain if he was about to receive a beating at the soldier's hands. His fear of the belligerent man overtook his senses and to his shame, he lost control of his shaking legs and began to empty his bladder.

The instructor saw the pool of urine seep from beneath Davie's camouflage trousers and surprised, stopped in mid sentence. In disgust, he turned away and with a backward glance, ordered Davie to go and get himself cleaned up.

To his relief, Davie's comrades were too busy being beasted by the other instructors and none had apparently witnessed his shame. Still shaking from his encounter with the instructor, he slowly got to his feet, aware his trousers were soaking up his spillage and made his way to the door.

He stumbled towards the locker room and hastily threw off his webbing and ammunition pouches. From his locker he fetched a towel and was making his way to the showers, but stopped. The noise from the gymnasium had ceased, but then as he listened, he heard the men laughing and cheering uproariously.

He hung his head in further shame, his dignity now completely gone and knew that the men, his buddies, his comrades, were laughing at him and that the instructor had revealed his disgrace.

Turning, his head down, he made his way to his locker, grabbed his civilian jacket and abandoning his issued military gear, left the key in the lock and made his way to the exit for the last time.

He would never know that the instructor, in a rare display of sympathy and remorse for the fat civilian, had kept his secret; that the men laughed loudly with relief when at the end of the physical training session, the three instructors had congratulated and joked with them on their efforts.

Davie's father Dodger, dressed in a bright yellow polo neck shirt and matching sweater and tan coloured golf slacks, sat back in the soft armchair within the prestigious West End Golf Club and regaled the three fellow club members with gossip from the Glasgow City Council Chambers. The men, all involved in local businesses, as one barely tolerated Dodger, but dutifully smiled through his stories, each conscious that their association with Dodger, a prospective Member of Parliament, might at some future time be of use in their respective business.

"Your table is ready sir," smiled the club waiter at Dodger's elbow.

"Right then gents, off for grub," he stood and rubbing his hand together, he grinned at his three companions and followed the waiter through to the dining room, unaware that behind his back, the three men gave each other knowing winks and smirking, quietly shook their heads at the boastful Dodger. It was common knowledge among the membership that Dodger was a man who had never swung a golf club in his life, but joined for the prestige and influence the locally famous club offered its members.

The waiter led Dodger to his favourite seat by the panoramic window that provided the best view over the nearby eighteenth green. He ordered a bottle of his favourite red wine and sitting alone, cast an eye across the nearby tables. At one table, a Sheriff sat with his wife while at another table, two executives with whom he had previously done business sat with women who definitely were not their wives. He smiled and made a mental note for this little titbit, he reasoned, might just become useful at some future time.

A fellow City Councillor from the opposing Party sat in deep, animated conversation with two men not known to Dodger and whom he was certain were not club members. His curiosity aroused, he made a further mental note that before he left to ask the Club Steward who the Councillor's dining guests were. Such information might be worth a twenty in the Stewards grubby palm, for long experience had taught Dodger it was always wise to know with whom the enemy were consorting.

Staring across the immaculate lawn of the eighteenth green, his thoughts turned to his earlier conversation with Eddie Beattie. His long association with the gangster had through the years paid handsome dividends, but he realised that if he were to become… no, he inwardly smiled, when he became an MP, he would need to sever that tie. It wouldn't do for him to be associated with Beattie, regardless of what financial inducements Beattie might offer. Not when as an MP there was likely to be more rewarding and beneficial contacts to be made.

"Phone call for you Mister Renwick," said the young teenage waitress, disturbing his thoughts.

He smiled at the pretty, ponytailed blonde girl and rising from his seat, followed her towards the private members lounge to take the call. As they walked together in the narrow hallway, he placed his hand her shoulder. The girl stopped and surprised, turned towards him. He let his hand trickle down her slim back and let it lie there at the small of her back on her waist and just above her tight little arse; just that second too long and just long enough to make the young girl uncomfortable. Wolfishly he said, "It's actually Councillor Renwick, my dear." The girls face flushed. She muttered, "Sorry," and abruptly turned and walked off. He watched her walk away, admiring her pert little bottom in the tight black skirt and with a sigh, made his way to the telephone booth.

"Hello?"

"It's me," said his wife Martha, her voice on edge. "It's Davie. There's something wrong. He's very upset. Can you come home?"

"You called me because the lazy bastard's upset?" he thundered. "What do you mean, upset?"

"I …I don't know," she replied, immediately regretting her decision to phone her husband. "He came in … he's been crying," she softly said, her voice almost failing her.

"He's been crying? What happened, did someone offer him a fucking job," he sneered.

A woman passing by glanced reprovingly at his language, but he ignored her and continued, "Listen, you idiot. I've told you before. Unless it's an emergency, don't fucking phone me at my club, okay?"

He slammed the phone back into the cradle and turning to the woman, angrily said "What?"

White faced and tight lipped, the woman walked off.

Martha Renwick stared stunned at the phone. She cast a nervous glance upward at the kitchen ceiling and listened, as though able to see through two floors and hear her son Davie in his bedroom in the attic, but could not hear any sound.

It had been a mistake to phone Dodger; she realised that now. The selfish bastard wouldn't have come home from his golf club even if Davie had been dying, her bitterness at her callous husband overtaking her normal apathy at Dodger's movements.

She leaned forward with both hands on the kitchen worktop, her head slightly bowed and again wondered just what was the point of her *fucking* life? Martha was unaccustomed to using bad language, even in her thoughts, but there were times; yes, there were times when even bad language felt appropriate.

She was not an old woman, not at sixty; at least not by today's standards anyway. After all, didn't 'Woman's Own' even recently feature an article that said sixty was the new fifty?

Again she looked up at the ceiling, wondering what had so upset her Davie. Sadly, she shook her head. Even Davie these days had his own secrets. His night-time borrowing of her car, making her promise she wouldn't tell anyone, least of all Dodger and the lock he had fixed to his bedroom door. At first she thought he had found himself a girlfriend. As if, she shook her head. Not while he was drinking so much. She worried about Davie, not just his physical health, though she wryly thought, he had his father's genes and could certainly do with losing a few pounds and not like Mark, built like a whippet and who had taken after his mother. Ironically, Davie was just like his father, yet the two would never get on while Mark, the successful policeman, was more like Martha and the apple of his father's eye.

She shook her head at her son Davie's situation, realising that like Davie, she was trapped with an uncaring husband as he was with an uncaring father.

Her ears perked up at the sound of the upstairs shower electric being switched on and running. Right, she decided with a humourless smile; now that he was in the bathroom, she'd get the kettle on and have a nice cup of tea waiting for him when he got back to his attic room.

Cris Trelawney was becoming bored witless. Sitting about the hotel achieved nothing, he had decided and since there was little for him to do other than await further updates from the cops, he night as well get out and about and see a bit of the city, though likely Sunday probably wasn't the best time.

The receptionists' eyes sparkled when the tall, swarthy and bearded, good-looking guest from Room 37 approached her desk. His query about places of interest almost provoked her into referring him to her flat in the nearby Ibrox area, but with an inward sigh, she instead suggested the Kelvingrove Art Gallery and Museum of Transport, both of which would be open and free entry. If he wished some place to eat, she continued, the lengthy Byres Road was a short walk from there with its excellent variety of pubs and restaurants.

In a mental flash of recklessness, she almost confided that her shift was nearly over and considered offering her services as a guide, half hoping that she might be included in his day out. Swallowing hard, reason took over and she provided him with directions towards the Copland Road Underground, reminding him that as it was Sunday, the service concluded at six that evening. Watching him walk to the exit, she sighed with regret, wondering what a strong looking man like Mister Trelawney could do for her.

It took Cris just a few minutes to walk the short distance to the Underground and the elderly female station assistant, who sold him his ticket to Kelvinhall Station smiled and told him the next train would be but a minute or two.

Standing on the platform evoked memories of his time in London, of travelling upon the Underground there. He breathed in deeply and inwardly smiled, recalling his fascination with the subway system when he first arrived in London from his native Cornwall, a naïve and restless young man; handy with his fists, aggressive and confrontational. His brow narrowed. It had not taken much time before he had come to the attention of both Ronnie Kyle as well as the cops.

The train seemed to race through the darkened tunnel, shaking back and forth as it traversed beneath the city on its short journey to Kelvinhall Station.

The brochures in his room had described Glasgow's West End as a hive of activity, multi-cultural and teeming with life. On that warm Sunday afternoon, it was exactly as described.

Cris decided to forego the cultural foray to the museums and instead walked north into the nearby Byres Road, moving through the throng and feeling the heat upon his face, searching for a pub to quell his sudden thirst and happening upon Tennents Bar. Almost half the bar area was crowded with Sunday drinkers, with a smattering of women adding to the friendly atmosphere. A hubbub of chatter drowned out the juke-box that tried vainly to belt out The Human League's: 'Don't You Want Me.' The cheery barmaid suggested the local Tennents lager and pint in hand he found an empty table and sat down on the bench seat against the back wall.

He reached across the seat for an abandoned edition of the 'Glasgow News.' The front-page headline bore the latest news of the Falkland's conflict and he glanced over the story and then turned to page two. The second column on the page featured a story about the murder of Alice, whose smiling face stared at him. He felt his chest constricting and his throat dry. The cops had issued the newspaper with a copy of the photo he had given McIntosh and an appeal for information. As he read on, he was grateful the article didn't disclose at the time of her murder, Alice had been working as a prostitute and assumed that was down to McIntosh, giving silent thanks to the detective. The very word 'prostitute' made him shudder. Even with his background and the things he had seen and done, he still could not attribute that word to his daughter.

Slowly, he sipped at his lager and contemplated just how much longer he would remain in Glasgow. According to McIntosh, his boss, this PF guy, could keep a hold of Alice's body for a week, a month; any bloody time. The truth was Cris had to admit that his finances would last just so long and he would need to return to Hayle and get back to work. He could not remain in Glasgow indefinitely. He had already done the hard part; travelling up here to identify his daughter. When this PF guy did release Alice's body, it would be a simple matter then of making an arrangement with a local undertaker to convey the body to Hayle, even if it again meant Cris having to return to accompany her.

Thinking of funeral arrangements brought to mind Daniela's simple service. The small crematorium in Hackney, close to where they had lived had seemed the most suitable venue. The few friends he had made refused to attend, fearful and conscious that any further association with the man they knew as Cris McGuire, would invoke the wrath and retribution from the banged-up Ronnie Kyle. He smiled when he thought of the girls, though; Daniela's mates and fellow strippers all of them. Heads held high, the six of them clinging close together had sat in the second pew behind Cris and a tearful Alice.

He hadn't needed to turn his head to know the pews at the rear of the room had been occupied by plain-clothes detectives from the Met's Serious Crime Squad; all armed and watchful while outside, uniformed officers carrying Heckler Koch MP7 machine pistols patrolled the nearby roads, such was the clear threat from Kyle and the money he could spend to have his revenge on Cris.

As promised, the Superintendent in charge of the Witness Protection Squad, a decent man Cris later had to admit, forwarded Daniela's ashes that he later and very privately, scattered from the small harbour at Hayle.

His eyes narrowed. Perhaps that would be the best solution for Alice. When her body is released, a local cremation here in Glasgow and a private ceremony at Hayle where with dignity, he could scatter her ashes to join her mother in the sea that she had loved.

He closed his eyes, his decision made and opening them again, finished his pint and prepared to travel back to the hotel. Tomorrow morning, he would contact DCI McIntosh with his decision and return home.

Mickey, Eddie Beattie's tattooed minder banged upon the door of the second floor tenement flat and waited, using a hand to slick back his gelled hair. The big black guy, Moses something, opened the door and with brilliantly white teeth, grinned at him.

"Hi me old son, you got something for us?"

"Mister Beattie said you've to get this," and handed Moses a sealed envelope. "Says he's sorry he didn't come himself, but that he's got something on. Told me to ask if there is anything that you and your boss need, Moses?"

Moses looked curiously at the envelope and turned it over. Back and front were blank, but it was bulky enough to indicate there seemed to be something inside.

"Right, thanks…Mickey, ain't it? Nah, we're cushty for the minute my son. Tell your boss we're doing okay," and giving Mickey thumbs up, closed the door.

"Who was that Moses," Ronnie Kyle called from the bathroom, pulling open the door and wafting a newspaper about his head. "Want to give that twenty minutes to clear I think," he grinned at the big man and then eyes narrowed, asked "What you got there, my son?"

Moses handed the envelope over to Kyle.

"It was one of Beattie's boys. Asked if we needed anything else, but I told him we were fine, boss."

Kyle tore open the envelope and found it to contain a sheet of paper with a typed note and a page torn from a Glasgow A-Z map that had the letter X scrawled on it. Reading the note he smiled.

"Looks like Eddie has come across after all, Moses. We've got an address and," he smiled at the large man and held up the map page, "somewhere to take him for a chat. After our little chat, Eddie's made an arrangement about where to take our Cris so that he'll never be found."

CHAPTER 18 – Sunday evening.

Simon Johnson had a plan.

During his time working as a uniformed cop, he had attended a number of calls to the Pollok Shopping Centre, mainly arresting shoplifters detained by the in-house security during which he had not only gotten to know some of the security guys, but also developed a friendly rapport. Some of them, the younger ones anyway, were wannabe cops and eager to assist their local beat men for the cooperation also worked in their favour; the more shoplifters they caught, the better to impress their bosses with their diligence.

Simon's plan, well, as far as he was concerned, was quite simple.

The girls' multi coloured Bob Marley hat was a real stick out and if she *were* a regular visitor to the Centre, he would simply ask the security to keep an eye open for her and try to find out who she was.

The only fly in the ointment was what reason he would provide to the guys. He could hardly call her a suspect for a crime, yet to admit he had an interest in her would only confirm what she had suggested when they last met; that he was stalking her.

Alternatively, he could simply ask them to provide *her* with *his* phone number and leave the contact up to her. Of course, that would leave him open to some good-natured abuse from the security guys, but it was worth it if his plan worked out.

He decided if he was going to do this he would travel to work an hour early and call in to the Centre's security office before attending the six o'clock roll call at Pollok office.

He shrugged on his suit jacket, grabbed a raincoat and feeling unusually confident, headed for his car.

DCI Gordon McIntosh pulled into the bay at Pollok office and was dismayed to see ACC John Murray's staff car already parked there, the civilian driver with a newspaper spread across the steering wheel.

McIntosh thought it unlikely Murray would be working on a Sunday, but almost immediately realised that with the Papal visit due in a couple of days on the Tuesday, 1 June. It was therefore reasonable to suppose that Murray, who as Venue Commander for the visit and the Pope's safety while within the Force area had overall responsibility, would likely be almost living out of the Planning Department's incident room at police headquarters. The Glasgow Councillors had almost worldwide promoted the Papal visit as an advert for tourism to the city and McIntosh guessed the last thing Murray would need was for any sort of balls-up; not on his watch, anyway.

Pushing through the rear door he was immediately greeted by a nervous Mark Rankin, who with eyebrows raised and hushed whisper informed McIntosh the ACC awaited him in the Rankin's room.

Taking a deep breath, McIntosh knocked and walking into the DI's room, saw Murray had planted himself at the DI's chair, his cap and swagger stick on the desk in front of him, elbows on the arm of the chair and his fingers making an arch in front of his bulbous nose.

"Caught him yet?" was Murray's opening comment.

McIntosh didn't fail to catch the sarcasm in the comment nor the lack of invitation for him to be seated, but wisely chose to ignore both the veiled insults. After all, what was the point in arguing with a man who had hardly ever caught a cold let alone a violent, raping murderer? Murray, as far as most of the Force's CID was concerned, would not know a criminal from a boil on his arse.

Drawing upon his tolerance and dwindling reserves of patience, McIntosh replied, "No sir, not yet, but that's not to say my team are not making the best effort. As you will be aware…."

"As I am aware, DCI McIntosh," thundered Murray, "you now have two murders to solve. That is twice the opportunity to catch this culprit and plenty of men with which to do so. My God, when I think of the money and resources that are being

124

wasted on these two….two…. individuals," he spat out, the disgust evident in his voice.

A palpable silence descended on the room as both men stared at each other. McIntosh, white faced, stood shocked. Never in all his service had he broken the discipline code. Never had he doubted that as a police officer it was his duty to regard all individuals without fear or favour. He had always prided himself that he treated colleagues and members of the public with the same courtesy that he himself wished to be treated. He had, throughout his long and distinguished career, acted with honour and to the best of his ability.

But now, listening to the bigoted anger of an excuse for a police officer, his patience already worn thin by the bullying attitude of Murray, he broke his silence and quietly asked, "Will there be anything else, sir or do you have anything of value to contribute to my inquiry,"

Had Murray been an astute man or even the ability to listen to his subordinates rather than the sound of his own voice, he might have recognised that now was not the time to provoke his Detective Chief Inspector.

"Are you being cheeky?" he scowled.

McIntosh slowly shook his head, a red rage overcoming his usual good sense and replied, "Cheeky? No, I'm being serious. I am a police officer, a detective, and I have a job to do; to solve the murder of two wee lassies. Two young women who had families. You," he could feel his face burning with anger and unable to control his anger, retorted, "you're nothing but a fucking accountant!"

He turned sharply on his heel and flung the door open wide.

"Come back here, McIntosh!" screamed Murray, rising to his feet and rounding the desk, but the DCI ignored him and continued through the corridor to the incident room, throwing open the door and surprising the assembled team.

He sensed rather than saw Murray hurrying after him.

The assembled team that included Glenda Burroughs and Mark Rankin and DI Morris Knox, numbered over a dozen officers, all of whom were taken aback by the DCI's sudden entrance and even more so when the red-faced Assistant Chief Constable, John Murray burst through the door.

Much like a Kelvingrove Art Gallery tableau, not a word was spoke nor did anyone move. The team simply stared at McIntosh who could see on their faces that they could not have failed to hear the shouted command from Murray.

Just inside the doorway, the furious ACC pulled up sharp and waving an arm to the team, shouted, "Get the fuck out!"

So irate was Murray it didn't occur to him that his overweight girth blocked the only exit, but still nobody moved.

McIntosh slowly turned towards Murray. "If perhaps you were to calm down sir?" he smoothly suggested.

Murray, by now almost apoplectic with rage, swept his arms round the narrow room and screamed at the team, "I gave you an order, get out now!"

One or two of the team started shuffling towards him, their eyes on McIntosh, but no one left the room, fearful to pass by the large Murray. Others stared curiously at both men, while some with their eyes evoked sympathy for the DCI's obvious predicament.

Murray pointed a shaking finger at McIntosh and such was his vitriolic hate for the DCI that it overtook sound sense. "You're suspended!" he cried out. "I'll have your fucking job!"

To his wide-eyed amazement, McIntosh smiled and softly replied, "Fair enough, Mister Murray. I believe it is unlikely you'll cope, but good luck sir. Let me see you solve two murders. It's all yours," and turning, he smiled and nodded to his team, then politely stepped round the visibly shaking Murray and past him out through the door.

The ACC, breathing heavily, stared menacingly at the team, who with the exception of an older, portly detective standing at the rear of the room, avoided his glance.

"Detective Inspector," he bellowed at the pale faced Mark Rankin. "As of now, you have overall charge of this inquiry and will report directly to me. Do you understand?"

Rankin could only nod, his eyes wide and shoulders slumped at the sudden responsibility thrust upon him. "Sir," was all he could manage in response.

The portly detective at the rear of the room continued to stare at Murray, whose eyes narrowed and who shouted at him, "Do you have a problem, officer?"

The detective screwed his face, scratched at his nose with a nicotine-stained forefinger and nodded.

"Aye, sir, it seems I do, sir. I'm Detective Constable Willie McNee from the Serious Crime Squad. I also have to inform you that I am the constables' representative for Headquarters Division of the Police Federation and I am appalled in the manner which Mister McIntosh, being a Federated member, has just been suspended by you."

McNee, refusing to be intimidated by Murray, sniffed loudly and again idly scratched at the irritation on his nose.

"Frankly, according to Federation rules as agreed with management," he paused and smiled and pointing a finger at Murray, said, "and that's you sir; you being an ACC and all," he reminded Murray. "Well, according to the rules, not only was your language to my Federated colleague highly," his eyebrows narrowed as he sought for the correct word, "unorthodox, but it was extremely inflammatory and particularly as the suspension you issued to DCI McIntosh was conducted outwith the proper procedure as agreed by the Federation and management. You again, sir," he smiled at the perplexed Murray. "In short, Mister Murray sir, you're bang out of order," then, with a half smile, added, "if you get my meaning."

In the room, the other officer's heads swivelled faster than a Wimbledon crowd, switching from McNee to the ACC, then back to McNee.

But McNee was not finished. His voice neutrally calm and face expressionless, he continued. "Of course as I am certain you are aware Mister Murray, I am duty bound to report the full circumstances of DCI McIntosh's *public* suspension to my committee members." Waving a hand about him, he continued. "I should remind you that my colleagues here, who are also Federated members, will be obliged to provide me with statements. Thereafter I will present the facts to the Federation Committee, who I am certain will take this issue up with the Chief Constable," he paused and added, "Sir," with mock politeness, his face blank and his eyes locked to Murray's.

Murray's mouth fell open and an icy claw grabbed at his spine, the full horror of the last few minutes now settling upon him. His loss of control in front of these….these…

With a sinking feeling, he realised that he had left himself wide open to a formal complaint from that bunch of fucking lefties, the Police Federation.

Aghast, he stared at McNee, his mind unwilling to accept it, would not believe it; the fat wee bastard was threatening him!

Drawing himself to his full height, he wordlessly whipped about and strode through the door, pulling it closed behind him with a petulant bang.

Stunned, the detectives stared at the smiling McNee, unable to believe what they had just witnessed, then the room thundered with raucous laughter and much backslapping.

"Keep it down, keep it down," shouted Glenda Burroughs, using her gold Zippo to light a much needed cigarette. When the noise abated, she turned to Renwick and, inhaling deeply on the fag, nonchalantly picked a strand of tobacco from her tongue and her calm voice belying the tension she felt, asked, "So Mark, what now?"

Pushing open the bedroom door, Davie Renwick rubbed at his wet hair, his dressing gown wrapped about him and belted with the old cord. Shocked, he did not expect his mother to be sitting on his bed when he entered his room, her face pale and draped between her hands, the belt of machinegun ammunition. His discarded, soiled uniform trousers lay bundled in a corner, but to his horror, the opened suitcase lay at her feet. The grenades were on the floor beside the trip-flares and the commando dagger upon the opened towel.

To his horror and worse than the discovery of the munitions, she had found his porn magazines.

"What's this Davie?" she quietly asked.

He swallowed hard, his mind racing. Could he fool her? He tried to smile and continued to rub at his wet hair.

"It's my back-up mum. You know what's going on over there, in the Falkland's. My team have been issued with personal equipment; you know, just in case."

He grinned at her. "Don't forget mum, I'm in the military, now. It's my job," he shrugged his shoulders as if it was no big deal.

Martha's education was no more than the basic three R's and she had left school at fourteen, but she wasn't stupid. Her older brother had completed his National Service, well, eventually when he wasn't going AWOL that is, she wryly recalled. She guessed the army would be very possessive of their guns and their bullets and, she glanced down at the small green coloured bomb things with the round pins attached, whatever the hell *they* are. No, these things here, she was sure; these would probably be accountable.

No, she unconsciously shock her head, this wasn't right; not right at all.

"Did you steal these Davie?"

"Steal them?" he tried to look shocked and pretended not to have heard her correctly, for repeating it gave him time to think. "Of course not, mum," he scoffed with a half-laugh. "It's like I told you; the sergeant said we had to keep some stuff at home so that if we were called out in an emergency, we'd be ready."

"So how would you use these bullets," her eyes flashed in anger, "if you don't have a gun?"

He was thinking on his feet. He stooped and took the belt of ammunition from her. "It's for the machine gun, mum; the GPMG. One of the other lads stores the machine-gun in his place. We all carry a belt like this for him. Honest."

She knew he was lying and her heart ached. Her son was treated like a pariah by his father, barely tolerated by his brother and but for her, Davie would have nobody. She sighed and wearily got to her feet. Reaching up, she gently stroked at his cheek. "If your father knew you had these things in the house, son, he would go off his head. Don't let him catch you with them, okay?"

She stooped and lifted the camouflage trousers and his shirt off the floor. "I'll put these through the wash. Come down when you're dressed and I'll get you some dinner," then gently closed the door behind her.

Davie exhaled with relief, certain he had fooled his mother.

He thought of what she had said, about his father 'going off his head.' Too late mum or hadn't you noticed? The bastards already off his fucking head, he growled.

Simon Johnson missed the confrontation that occurred within the incident room. To his annoyance, his plan, his 'great idea' had come a cropper and landed him with a prisoner and a shoplifting case to report; the last thing he needed when he was part of the murder inquiry team.

IIc shook his head and turning in the passenger seat, glanced at the woman sat beside the female cop in the rear of the patrol car. How the hell was he going to explain *this* to DI Burroughs?

This afternoon, his idea had seemed so simple. After a quick snack and a shower, he decided to leave an hour early, travel to work but first call in to the security office at the Pollok Shopping Centre and speak with the guys there.

So bloody simple and yet it had gone so bloody wrong, he bitterly thought.

It was fortunate that Jimmy Clark, a former cop and all round good guy who had left the Force early because of angina problems, was the duty supervisor. Simon had begun by explaining to Jimmy about the girl and her brightly coloured hat. As expected Jimmy, who was as wide as the Clyde, had seen right through him and good-naturedly got it out of Simon; that the young detective had a romantic interest in the girl.

"Aye, I've seen her loads of times," he had teased Simon with a grin. "Always wears that hat. It's like her badge, her symbol. Nice looking wee girl," he had nodded with approval, "Does her shopping at the Asda store; well, her and an older woman, her mother I think it might be." Jimmy's eyes had narrowed. "In fact, I think… no," he nodded his head, "I'm sure her mother works in the Centre."

Without another word, he reached for the desk radio and called one of his guards. "Bobby, the wee lassie with the bright coloured hat, the lassie whose mammy is called Babs and if I'm not mistaken, I think Babs works in the Shaws the chemist shop. Do you know the woman; over."

The radio cackled and Bobby's response came through almost immediately.

"You mean Babs McTear? Her man Alex is a member of my bowling club. What about her; over."

Jimmy grinned at Simon and pressing the transmit button, asked, "What's the daughter's name, over."

"Young Gracie, over," was the immediate response.

Simon took a deep breath and smiled in delight. "Don't suppose you've got her phone number too?" he joked then stared in happy surprise when Jimmy grinned at him. "If you don't ask, you don't get," the older man said and withdrew a cardboard folder marked 'Alarm/Keyholder File' from the desk drawer.

"I was right about her mother working at Shaws, so chances are she might be listed with us as a keyholder in the event we need to call somebody if an emergency occurs, during the hours the shop is closed. If she is," his fingers danced down the list as he quickly scanned through the pages, "we'll have her contact details. Aye, I was right. Here it is."

He glanced up at Simon. "You'll not be telling anybody where you got this phone number now young Simon, understood?"

Simon shook his head. "She set me a test Jimmy; to see if I could find her if I was really interested in her," he confided with a smile. "If you keep that secret, I'll keep yours."

"Agreed," replied Jimmy and wrote the digits of the McTear's home phone number onto a scrap of paper.

Yes, Simon reflected as the patrol car travelled along Orkney Street and turned into the rear yard. It had seemed so simple. He had almost been out the door with the telephone number in his hand when the radio message had come in from two of Jimmy's guards reporting they had detained a female shoplifter and were bringing the woman to the office.

His heart sank. Having secured Jimmy's help with his problem, he could hardly walk out and leave without offering to assist, particularly with him being a police officer.

A few minutes later the distraught woman had been led into the office with one guard carrying the bundle of children's clothing she had tried to conceal beneath her heavy coat.

It was the coat that had given her away, the younger guard had eagerly told Simon. Who would be wearing such a heavy, baggy coat on a sunny and warm day like today?

Once he had collected the guard's statements and taken the children's clothing as evidence, Simon phoned Pollok office for a patrol car to assist him only to learn the prisoner would need to be taken to Govan office, that there was no female turnkey at Pollok.

Now here he was at Govan office and watching the woman being booked at the charge desk by the duty Inspector who frustratingly laboured at entering her details into the large, black bound journal. To make matters worse and add to his foul mood, the Inspector had left his half-eaten fish supper to process a previous prisoner who, drunk and belligerent, was being forcefully manhandled by two uniformed cops who struggled with him through the metal gate that led to the cell area. Fighting for all his worth, the middle-aged prisoner was screaming at full volume and berating the grim-faced cops in the foulest of language as well as casting doubt upon their parenthood.

Impatiently and conscious of his absence from the briefing at Pollok, Simon drummed his fingers on the wooden desktop, but stopped when he caught a warning glare from the Inspector.

The cops who had brought Simon and his prisoner from the shopping centre to Govan grinned at each other, delighting in his discomfort and pleased it wasn't them being subjected to the increasingly bad tempered Inspector's scowl.

"As the arresting officer *acting* Detective Constable Johnson," the Inspector at Simon, I'll expect *you* to complete the Criminal Record Form and fingerprint the prisoner and while you're here at Govan."

Simon could almost swear the bastard was enjoying himself.

"And while you are here you can dictate the case for custody at the District Court tomorrow."

"Custody, sir? She's being kept in custody?" he said, aghast. "Is she not being reported then sir? I mean, it's a simple shoplifting case …" Simon began to argue.

The Inspector raised a hand to quiet him. "It *was* a simple shoplifting case," he smirked, "but the PNC has thrown up a couple of arrest warrants for this woman. Isn't that right, Ella?" he turned to the pale faced and silent prisoner, ignoring her quivering lips. "So after the District Court, she'll be detained again for custody to appear on Tuesday at the Sheriff Court, DC Johnson. Now get her fingerprinted and let me know when you've got the case recorded for the typists."

With that, the Inspector slammed the journal closed and turned away to return to his desk.

Simon, now utterly defeated and envisaging the bollocking that awaited him upon his return to Pollok, shook his head and tapping her on the shoulder, said, "Please come with me Missus McGuiness."

With one hand on her elbow, he led the weeping woman through the metal gates and upstairs to the fingerprint room.

CHAPTER 19

Gordon McIntosh sat numb in his car, in the driveway of his house. He could not believe what had just happened. Suspended. Never in his police career had he been treated or even spoken to like that, not even during his time as a junior cop. His drive home had been almost in a daze, his thoughts a jumbled mess.

The sudden knock on the driver's window startled him and he turned to see Mary's worried face peering at him.

"Gordon, what's wrong? You're as white as a sheet. Are you ill?"

He took a deep breath and as Mary stepped back, he opened the door.

Cris Trelawney sat on the edge of the bed, staring at the telephone. He had already filled the suitcase with the few things that he had brought with him and all that remained to be packed were his nightclothes and washing bag and earlier informed the receptionist at the hotel desk of his intention to depart, the following morning.

Strangely, he felt more at ease this evening than any time since learning of Alice's death. He reckoned his decision to return home and await word about the release of her body, given the circumstances, was the best decision that he could make.

He thought about phoning and informing DCI McIntosh of his decision, but figured that could wait. There was a more important call to make first.

He dialled the number and when the call was answered, smiled and said, "Hello Jack, it's me. Is your mum there?"

In the car park outside the hotel main doors, the rusting van came to a halt and the driver switched off the engine and the headlights.

Ronnie Kyle, sitting in the passenger seat, glanced up at the hotel windows and turning, took a deep breath and said, "Okay Moses. We know where he is so let's you and me find ourselves a nice little takeaway for now and we'll come back later, when it's dark."

DI Mark Renwick beckoned that Glenda Burroughs follow him into the DI's room.

"Look," he nervously began, his voice low and hesitant, "I know that I'm in charge now, but Glenda, I've never dealt with a murder case before and now that bastard Murray has put me on the spot…"

It took all her willpower to restrain from laughing at the useless git. Detective, she inwardly seethed. Renwick couldn't find his arse unless somebody placed his hand there for him and if she was honest, it rankled that even though she was the senior Detective Inspector in the division, the chauvinistic Murray had not even given her a second glance.

To refrain from immediately answering, she used a well-tried delaying tactic and reached into her jacket pocket for her cigarettes, taking time to light one with her lighter while Renwick watched her with hopeful eyes.

"The thing is Mark," she replied, "let's face it. You're no Gordon McIntosh."

"Now wait a fucking minute…"

"Let me finish," she chopped the air with her hand and cut him short. "What I'm trying to say is that Gordon has far more experience and can lose you when it comes to running a major inquiry. What you might consider is forgetting what Murray said."

She could see in his eyes that Renwick was prepared to grasp at any straw; anything that might get him through this waking nightmare that had been thrust upon him.

"How do you mean," his eyes narrowed, "forget what Murray said?"

"Well," she drawled, confident now that Renwick was on the hook, "what Murray doesn't know won't hurt him. All he is interested in is a result. It's the old adage of bring me solutions, not problems. All Murray wants is the killer of these two women caught and before this Papal visit, right?"

"Yeah, right," he slowly agreed, uncertain where this was leading.

"And don't forget, after that little debacle in there," she nodded her head back at the incident room, "it's likely that the guy from the Serious, DC McNee, will carry out his threat and report Murray for his outrageous and very public suspension of Gordon McIntosh. Let's not forget too, he did that in front of a number of junior ranking officers. In anyone's book, that is completely unacceptable."

She paused for breath, seeing in his eyes that she had not yet won the younger DI over to her way of thinking, but still, she pressed on.

"That means Murray will likely have to explain himself to the Chief and he won't want that, will he? So, the way I see it, the answer is simple. Gordon McIntosh continues to run the inquiry from home, but you are the lead of the inquiry at the office."

"Wait a fucking minute," his eyes widened in understanding, "You're suggesting that I run to McIntosh every time I need a decision made? No way," he scoffed, violently shaking his head, his hands making scissor cuts in the air.

"I'm not suggesting you run back and forward to his house, you idiot," she hissed, "I'm suggesting you use the telephone. Think of the benefits for you," she soothed. "You use Gordon's talents and *when* there is an arrest, you get the credit."

His eyes narrowed as he contemplated her suggestion, as if suddenly realising the immense boost that detecting the killer would bring to his career, not just from the senior police management, but the media too. However, as quickly as this thought entered his head, the shadow of doubt crept back like a thief in the night.

"What if Murray finds out?" he whined at her. "He'll screw my career like he intends screwing McIntosh's."

"How will he find out? Who's going to tell him? You?"

Renwick breathed hard, reluctant to make such a decision, but realising that Burroughs spoke sense. In his heart, he knew he was not experienced enough for the task; one murder was bad enough, but two murders?

No, he shook his head; it was far too risky. "You're asking me to risk my career," his voice now reduced to almost a whisper. "No, I can't do it. I won't do it," and turning on his heel, left her alone in the room.

The first floor cell used as a fingerprint room was unlocked. Simon Johnson bade the sobbing woman sit on the one wooden chair and removed his suit jacket. During his time as a uniformed cop Simon had fingerprinted dozens of individuals and knew well the folly of getting the black fingerprint ink on clothing, for it stained the material and was almost irremovable. Hanging his suit jacket on a wall hook, he turned to the high, narrow table and opened the small can of 'Brasso', pouring some onto the soft cloth and scrubbed hard at the bronze plate affixed to the table. Satisfied that it was as clean as he could get it, he squeezed a small dab of ink from the paint tube onto the plate and with a hand roller, spread the ink across the face of the plate.

He fetched a fingerprint form from the untidy stack on the wall shelf and folded the form so that the ten boxes for each digit were uppermost on the table beside the plate.

"Missus McGuiness?" he beckoned the woman to stand and reached for her right hand.

Ella had stopped crying and now, eyes red-rimmed and hands clenched, looked fearfully at Simon.

"You have been fingerprinted before, Missus McGuiness," he softly smiled at her with encouragement, "it won't hurt. I promise."

"Is there anything I can do to get out of here?" she sniffed at him.

Simon startled, as if becoming aware of the vulnerability of his situation; conscious that he now found himself alone in a room, albeit a cell, with a woman who was a convicted prostitute. If she made some kind of allegation against him…

"Eh, no Missus McGuiness. Look, I appreciate that you aren't happy that…."

Ella half laughed, having also realising that the young blushing copper thought she was offering him a wank or a blowjob to get her out of here, but even she knew that would not work. Her eyes narrowed. If she *had* thought that it might help her….she shook her head.

"Look, it's about the lassie that was murdered. Wee Alice, the English girl. I heard on Clyde Radio this morning that there was another girl found. If it's true and she was murdered, I might have some information that might be able to help you."

She stared hard at Simon, all signs of her previous despair now gone and a desperate, but determined glint in her eye.

"But it has to work both ways, son. I need to get back to my kids. So, who do I speak to?"

Cris Trelawney lay back on the bed watching the BBC evening news on the wall mounted television, his boots kicked off and his hands clasped on the pillow beneath him. He felt rested, relaxed now that he had made his decision. Louise had cried, relieved that he was coming home. Now it only remained for him to inform the detective, DCI McIntosh of his decision.

It happened that as Cris was thinking of informing McIntosh of his decision, the detective was at that time explaining to his increasingly angry wife what had occurred shortly before in the incident room at Pollok.

Knowing her to be a woman not normally given to expletives, he was surprised at his Mary's reactions, at the oaths she uttered and all regarding the parentage of ACC Murray. As Mary McIntosh ranted and raved, the phone in the hallway rung, interrupting her flowery dialogue.

"I'll get it," he jumped from his armchair, grateful for the distraction and fearing that had Mary answered the phone, she might vent her wrath on whoever was calling.

"Boss," said the quiet voice of Brian Davidson, "I'm in the Superintendents room, using his phone. Nobody can hear me from here. After you left it was a bit of a hornets nest here. One of they lads from the Serous Crime Squad, a guy called McNee; he went off on one at Murray. Threatened to call in the Federation because of the way Murray treated you in front of the troops, I mean. Told Murray that what he did, suspending you like that I mean, was against all the regulations or some shite like that. Anyway, the word is that McNee *does* intend going to the Federation and there will be an official complaint made to the Chief. Anyway, cutting a long story short, Murray fucked off sharpish, not long after you had gone and then McNee left on his own to contact some bigwig in the Federation. I don't know if it's going to help you at all, but McNee seems to think Murray had no right to suspend you."

McIntosh brow creased and he drew a deep breath. Willie McNee had been known to him for a number of years and he had always considered the man to be a quiet, unassuming type; solid and dependable, but hardly the man to set the heather on fire. Though he had never personally worked with McNee, their paths had crossed through the years on different inquiries and he had heard good things about him, but was unaware that he was active within the Police Federation. Still, he was shocked at this new development.

"Are you telling me that Willie confronted the ACC about me?"

"Willie, yeah that's him. Willie McNee's his name and yes, he didn't half give Murray what for," he sniggered. "You should have heard the rest of the team. Cheered the wee guy like he'd scored the cup final winner."

McIntosh swallowed hard. That a man who really did not know him that well would stand up for him as McNee apparently had done. He had not realised how drained he felt, how much the encounter with Murray had taken out of him. He sensed Mary watching him and half turning, saw the quizzical look on her face and raised his hand to stall her before she spoke.

"Before he left, who did Murray place in charge? Glenda?"

The few seconds of silence almost answered his question before Davidson spoke.

"No, DI Renwick," he almost spat the name out.

McIntosh shut his eyes against the throbbing pain in his head and the ache in his chest, realising that if the team was to be held together, he was going to have to massage Davidson's ego.

"Brian, I know you do not get on with Mark, but he's going to need your support. He doesn't have your experience or your savvy so, as a personal favour to me, I want you to support him as best you can."

He listened for the outburst, but Davidson remained silent. He slowly continued, "I thought Glenda Burroughs would have been the obvious choice, but let's face it; Pollok Sub-Division *is* Marks' responsibility, so in my absence," he almost choked at his choice of word *absence*, "it's only right that he oversees the inquiry. I'm certain that Glenda will assist him all she can, but you are the man on the ground with the practical experience of running an incident room. Will you help him?"

There was an audible silence before Davidson replied.

"I'll help *you*, boss, so if that means doing as you ask then, yes; he'll get my fucking support," he almost hissed, the venom in his voice apparent.

"Good man Brian. I know I can always rely on you to come through," McIntosh almost sighed with relief. "It's more important that we catch the murder of the two wee lassies than worry about our own problems, eh?"

"If you say so, boss," was Davidson's laconic response and then he hung up.

Councillor John 'Dodger' Renwick slowly reversed the gleaming, highly polished Mercedes into the tight driveway adjacent to the house and carefully opened the door to avoid scratching the paintwork against the neighbours' boundary wall. Taking a deep breath, he squeezed his bulk from the drivers' seat and locked the car behind him, yet again taking that few seconds to admire its sleek lines.

His wife Martha was busy in the kitchen when he opened the front door and clattered his keys onto the small table in the hallway, seeing with satisfaction Martha's car keys already there. Not for the first time had Dodger warned her about lending the car to that useless waste of space, his son Davie.

He loudly called out, "When's my dinner ready?" and without waiting for a response, made his way into the front lounge where he poured himself generous measure of whisky.

Settling himself into his favourite armchair, he fetched his reading glasses from his shirt pocket and reached for the Sunday edition of the 'Glasgow News.'

Martha, wearing a wraparound red and white chequered apron, her greying hair untidily bundled up and held together by a number of kirby grips and wringing her hands on a dishcloth, stood in the doorway staring at him.

"John, I want to speak to you about our Davie," she began, biting at her lip and already guessing what her husband's response would be.

"Davie? What about him," he growled, half listening, his attention taken by the papers editorial that suggested a change of Local Government might not be a bad thing for the city.

Martha swallowed with difficulty, continued to wring her hands, uncertain if what she was about to divulge was the right thing to do.

"Aye mum, what about Davie," asked the soft voice behind her.

Startled, she turned to see Davie, dressed now and wearing his outdoor jacket, standing in the hallway and staring at her, his eyes betraying his disappointment that the one person in the world he trusted was about to betray him. Wordlessly, he shook his head and headed to the front door, quietly closing it behind him.

"I said, what about Davie?" growled Dodger, lowering the newspaper and half twisting in his seat to glare at his wife.

Martha turned her pale face towards her husband and met his stare, but then turning her Judas face away, returned depressed to the kitchen.

Simon Johnson ensured the prisoner was locked in the detention room and seeing the duty Inspector still at his desk finishing his meal, made his way unobserved to the CID offices on the first floor. The general office was empty and he assumed the late shift detectives were out responding to a call. Inwardly hoping that he wasn't about to make a fool of himself, he sat down at a desk and dialled the internal number for the DI's room at Pollok.

To his surprise, it was DS Davidson who answered the phone and learning it was Simon, his response was a terse, "Where the fuck have you been?"

Taking a deep breath Simon asked to speak with Glenda Burroughs and heard Davidson sigh, before loudly informing the DI and anyone else within earshot that her 'missing lamb' was on the blower.

Even at that distance, Simon felt his cheeks turn red.

"Well, well young man," said the silky voiced Burroughs. "I got the message from the control room that you caught yourself a shoplifter. Ready to return here and come out to play now, are you?"

He was uncertain whether she was joking or being sarcastic and swallowing hard, replied, "Sorry ma'am, but it seems that the woman that I arrested might have some information about the murder."

"Wait, what are you talking about? I thought you arrested a shoplifter?"

"Aye, she is a shoplifter, but she's also a convicted prostitute. The problem is she's currently wanted on a couple of Extract warrants and her non-payment means that after her custody appearance tomorrow morning at court, the warrants would take her straight to prison."

He took a deep breath and launched straight into his story.

"When I was about to fingerprint her, she told me that she wants to cut a deal. Claims if she is sent to the nick again, her kids will be taken off her by the Social. She refuses to divulge anything other than telling me that she has some information that might be useful; about the murders, I mean. She says she won't speak to me, but to the man in charge."

Burroughs did not immediately answer and Simon thought she was considering what he had told her, but could not know she was glancing about her.

"You haven't heard then?" she finally replied. "DCI McIntosh has been suspended. It's DI Renwick who is in charge now."

Simon caught his breath, What the hell happened he wondered and then asked, "What shall I do, ma'am? Do you want to tell the DI about the woman's offer?"

Again, there was a definite pause.

"Where are you phoning from?" she asked.

"The CID general office; at Govan, I mean."

"Are you alone? Can you be overheard?" her voice dropped almost to a whisper.

"No ma'am, I'm on my own. The late shift is out, covering a call I think."

He heard slight bump as the phone was laid down on the desk, then a door being closed and guessed she wanted privacy.

"Listen to me, Simon. I don't want to involve you in the politics of what is going on here, but I'm going to make a suggestion. You might find you have a decision to make and I don't want to influence you in any way in making that decision, do you understand?"

"Ma'am?"

"Whatever you decide, I'll respect your decision and not think less of you, understood?"

He didn't really understand and his stomach was already churning. Whatever Glenda Burroughs was about to suggest, he guessed was not what really he wanted to hear.

"In the short time you have been seconded to the CID, Simon, you must have realised the DCI McIntosh is not just a good man, but a very experienced and thorough detective, yes?"

"Of course, ma'am," he slowly replied.

"So it's fair to say that if anyone is going to solve the murder of these two women it will be Gordon McIntosh, yes?"

Again without hesitation he agreed with her.

"So, though you would be perfectly correct in telling DI Renwick about the woman offering information, would you consider that the information would be best given to the DCI?"

"Yes ma'am," he replied, his eyes closed and knowing now where this was leading.

"So if you *weren't* present at the incident room today and *didn't* hear the DCI being suspended, you would have no cause other than to believe him to still be in charge of the murder inquiry?"

"Of course, yeah."

"And having spoken with me and without telling me the reason for your call, you simply wish me to provide you with the DCI's home telephone number. Does that sound like something you would consider, Simon?"

He took a deep breath and fished a pen from an inside jacket pocket.

"Do you have the number there, ma'am?" he asked, wondering if this simple request might herald the end of his ambition to join the CID.

Returning the phone to the cradle, he sat back and stared at the phone number, the enormity of what he was about to do now hitting him.

"Bloody hell," he whispered aloud to the empty room, "I might even get sacked."

CHAPTER 20

Davie Renwick wandered the length of Byres Road almost in a daze. The bright, inviting lights of the pubs he passed beckoned to him, but he seemed not to notice, his head reeling from his mother's betrayal of his confidence.

Unaccountably, he found himself close to tears. The shock of peeing himself at the TA gymnasium and what he believed to be the ridiculing laughter from his former comrades still echoing in his ears.

He stopped and leaned against a wall then to his surprise, his stomach heaved and he vomited on the pavement.

"Dirty bastard," said a young woman wearing a short dress and high heels who arm in arm with her friend and a bottle of cheap cider in her hand, passed him by with a look of disgust on her face. They had barely gone ten feet when both erupted into teenage, giggling laughter at the unfortunate Davie.

His body shook and using the back of his hand to wipe at his mouth, Davie stared after her.

"Bitch!" he screamed at her. The young woman turned and giving him the middle digit of her right hand, carried on walking, laughing as she did.

He breathed heavily, his hatred for her, his mother and all fucking women causing his body to shake.

Thrusting a hand into his jacket pocket, he withdrew the set of keys and staring at them lying in his hand, smiled and turned his head upwards to the lit neon sign over the pub entrance.

Maybe a wee snifter, he thought and then home to collect his mother's Ford Escort car.

Mark Renwick sat doodling on writing pad in front of him. He was pleased with himself. The allocation of that evenings patrol duties to the inquiry detectives had gone smoothly enough and what surprised him more than anything else was that Brian Davidson had been overly helpful.

Ever suspicious, Renwick wondered if Davidson was angling for some sort of reconciliation now that ACC Murray appointed him as man in charge of the inquiry.

Well, the bastard can forget it, he angrily thought.

Renwick would not easily dismiss or forgive the threatening confrontation and disrespect from Davidson and for that, he intended making the bastard suffer.

Yes, he would have his revenge against the arrogant shit.

It didn't escape him either that in making Renwick the lead DI, Murray had ignored Glenda Burroughs seniority, causing him to consider that maybe the blonde bimbo wasn't as highly thought of as she considered herself. It irked him that she suggested he act as a front for the inquiry while running back and forth to that dinosaur McIntosh who would be the real power.

The more he considered it, the more Renwick began to believe himself capable of running the inquiry.

First thing tomorrow morning he'd order a complete revamp of the administration. The files were in a shocking state and the paperwork, though undoubtedly Davidson would disagree, required to be better cross-indexed.

He would also look at the hours the team were working, unhappy with the time off they were permitted during the day as some sort of pay-off for the hours they worked during the evening.

Yes, eyes bright now, he'd set a fire under their arses and show Mister Murray just how an inquiry should be conducted.

So animated was Renwick with his plans that he failed to consider the most important aspect of the inquiry; the apprehension and conviction of a double murderer.

In response to the phone call, Gordon McIntosh, casually dressed in a black coloured polo shirt, brown corduroy trousers and tan coloured sports jacket, arrived at Govan CID office to find a nervous Simon Johnson pacing back and forth.

McIntosh did not hold out any hopes that the prisoner would have relevant information, but the phone call from Johnson had, if nothing else, knocked the black mood from him and at the urging of his wife he had with some reluctance agreed to drive to Govan office. He realised that by phoning him, young Johnson, aware he was suspended from duty, had taken a considerable risk in phoning him rather than passing the information to Mark Renwick at the incident room.

Ah well, he thought, it shouldn't take too long. The media had gotten hold of the story about the discovery of a woman's body in the Saltmarket area of the city, but the police had not released any details, least of all the victim's name. Almost wearily, he climbed the wide, ornate stairs of the building to the former District Court rooms that were now the CID suite and found Johnson nervously waiting there for him.

"First things first, Simon," he shrugged off his sports jacket and smiled at the anxious, younger man, "what say I fetch us three cups of coffee to my office while you fetch your prisoner up for a wee chat, eh?"

"Oh, aye sir but I have to tell you, the duty Inspector has been giving me a real hard time about keeping her in the detention room. Sorry, sir, I told him that you were coming down to the office and had requested a word with her. That's the only way I could stop him from locking her up in a cell and kicking my arse," he added with a grimace.

McIntosh hid his smile and nodded.

"I'll phone downstairs, so leave the Inspector to me, son. You just rustle fetch this woman and I'll see you in my office in five minutes."

True to his word, Simon brought Ella McGuiness to the DCI's room and bade the woman sit in the chair facing his desk.

McIntosh, bearing a tray with three mugs of coffee, a bowl of sugar and carton of milk, followed them in then setting the tray on the desk between himself and McGuiness, sat down facing her in his swivel chair.

"Right Missus McGuiness, I'm Detective Chief Inspector McIntosh, but you can call me Gordon," he smiled at her in at attempt to relax the obviously anxious woman and beckoned that she help herself to milk and sugar.

"My young detective there," began McIntosh, adding milk to his own mug and nodding to Simon seated bchind her in a corner, "said that you might have information that can assist us with the murder of two young women. Is that correct, hen?"

"Ella," she nodded, "you can call me Ella. Can I get a fag, Gordon?"

"Aye, sorry, where's my manners Ella," he replied and offering her a cigarette from an opened packet of Woodbine, reached across the desk and lit it.

Ella drew deeply on the cigarette and nodding towards Simon, said, "I told him that if you can help me Gordon, I saw something that might help you. It's my weans you see. If I go to the jail, the Social will take them."

She sniffed loudly at what the poker-faced McIntosh perceived to be an obvious ply at extracting some sympathy from him. He reached into his jacket pocket, withdrew a clean white handkerchief and he handed it to her.

"I'll be straight up with you, Ella. I won't promise you anything, but if you have information that might assist me, then I can have a word tomorrow morning with the PF. Either way, you'll not get released tonight, but when you go to court…"

"But I need to get home to my weans tonight!" she cried out loudly, banging her fist on the desktop and causing her coffee cup to spill over into the saucer.

"Ella!" McIntosh sharply responded. "You should have been thinking about your children when you were out blagging clothes from the shop in the Pollok Centre. He took a deep breath and in a softer voice asked, "Who has the kids at the minute?"

"My mother," she mumbled.

"And I take it your mother will hang onto the kids until you get home?"

She nodded, not trusting herself to speak.

"Right then," he nodded. "Like I was about to say, if your information is of assistance to me, then I can have a word tomorrow with the PF; see if we can work out some sort of deal to get you a Fiscal's release in the meantime or at least till you sort out these outstanding fines. They'll not go away Ella. They will still need to be paid, you do understand, don't you? I can't have the warrants cancelled."

Again, Ella nodded.

"Okay, I don't want there to be a misunderstanding. The best I can do is get you a release tomorrow and you need to be clear about that, but only if your information is of use to me. Listen hen," he leaned forward on the desk, his tone more conciliatory, "I know you don't know me from Adam and you've no reason to trust me, but all I can say is if what you tell me pans out, I will do my best for you, okay? Let's face it Ella, what do you have to lose? You were set for prison tomorrow, but if I can help, you might just get out. So, what is it that you have to tell me, hen?"

Simon in the corner sat quietly, hardly daring to breathe and willing the woman to speak. Then he saw her nod her head.

"It was last night on the Drag. Well, sometime after midnight I should say. I'm not certain about the time. I've learned not to carry a watch when I'm working. Now and again you come across some thieving bastard that will steal your back teeth," she hissed with anger, not wishing confront McIntosh by adding that complaining to the polis was a waste of time.

"Anyway, I was out working, but the polis, they were everywhere. I didn't get a punter because I was worried that if the detectives spoke with me, they would check out my details and lift me on the warrants."

She sniffed and sipped at her coffee, then licking at her lips, again drew deeply on the cigarette.

"I hung about hoping that the cops would just fuck off, but it wasn't till later when the streets were becoming quiet that I took a chance and headed down to Douglas Street where you usually find the last punters turning up. That's when I saw her getting into the car."

Any hope that McIntosh had that Ella might have real information was dashed. Last night the place was flooded with his officers. He had made the mistake of allowing himself that little vestige of hope that the woman's information might be genuine. Alice was murdered late Wednesday night or in the early hours of Thursday morning and not Saturday night or the early hours of Sunday morning. He sat back and passed a hand across his face.

"Last night Ella? You're not talking about Alice are you; Alice Trelawney?"

Ella looked puzzled.

"No, not her. I heard about the wee English lassie getting herself murdered and her name was Alice, I think." Her eyes narrowed. "At least I think it was the same lassie that I had seen a few times round the Drag. I don't know what her second name was."

McIntosh stared curiously at her.

"You said not her, so not Alice Trelawney? So who did you see get into the car, Ella?"

"Well I know the lassie to see and we've exchanged a few words sometimes, you know, hanging about waiting on the punters and that. It was only this morning when I heard on the radio that another lassie had been found murdered. I just thought maybe what I had seen might be useful, you know?"

McIntosh inhaled deeply and tapped the ash from his cigarette into the ashtray. He didn't doubt that Ella had seen a woman getting into a car, but that was the stock and trade of the area. A sinking feeling overcame him, but still he had to ask.

"Did you recognise the name of the woman that got into the car, Ella?"

"Oh aye, it was wee Betty. Betty Fisher."

Shocked, McIntosh sat bolt upright and cast a quick glance at Simon Johnson, sitting quietly in the corner. Johnson had been present in the Pollok incident room when he had informed the team about the murder of the second woman and named her as Elizabeth Fisher.

To McGuiness puzzled surprise, he leapt to his feet and moved quickly round the desk, beckoning the young aide to follow him into the corridor.

"Simon," he turned and round on the younger man, staring intently at him. "Did you provide that woman with the name of the second victim?"

"No, sir, not at all," stuttered Simon.

"This is really, really important," he stressed. "Could she have heard Elizabeth Fisher's name from any of the other officers?"

Simon, now realising the implications of what McGuiness had said, vigorously shook his head, his eyes narrowing with comprehension. "No sir, I was with her throughout the time she was arrested and remember; she wouldn't even *tell* me what her information was, just said she wanted to speak to the senior investigating officer."

McIntosh was stunned and later, he would comment that he thought his heart had for that few seconds, stopped.

Apart from her killer, it now seemed possible that Ella McGuiness was the last person to see Elizabeth Fisher alive.

Martha Renwick sat alone in the kitchen of the huge house. Numbly, she twisted at her apron and stared at nothing, her thoughts a jumbled mess.

She had stopped weeping, but still tasted the salty tears that had coursed down her face.

Davie, my poor, poor Davie, she thought. She had not meant for him to hear. She had not intended to tell his father about what she had discovered in his room, only to plead with Dodger to give the boy yet another chance but knowing before she opened her mouth that he would rant at her; accuse her of being too soft and utterly dismiss her concerns.

And now Davie was gone out, probably to once more get drunk and….

She sat upright at the slight noise from the hallway, but could only hear the loud tick of the ugly old grandfather clock. Another gift to Dodger from a grateful constituent, she shook her head. She wasn't stupid; knew that Dodger's backhanders and 'gifts' were rewards for the favours he offered in his role as a City Councillor. She glanced about her at the newly installed kitchen with its modern equipment and horrid, square microwave; the latest thing, he had told her without asking whether or not she wanted a new kitchen or a microwave.

After all, she shrugged, what did her opinion matter?

As if these 'toys' would keep her happy, buy her silence.

Dodger had been gone now an hour or more and she knew from the manner in which he was dressed and the aftershave he favoured that he was visiting one of his whores.

She no longer cared. It was a game they now played; he pretending he was on council business and she pretending to believe him.

Their relationship had foundered a long time previously and if she were to admit it, she was glad that he no longer found her attractive; his thrusting at her and things he would make her do still caused her to blush, to be embarrassed.

She took a deep breath and decided she would take a bath. Switching off the kitchen lights, she was passing the hallway table when she saw her car keys were gone.

Her eyebrows knitted and then her eyes opened wide with understanding. The slight noise she had heard.

Davie had sneaked home.

Mark Rankin sat alone in the DI's room, which was much preferable to sitting with Brian Davidson in the incident room. He glanced about him, imagining himself as the new boss. He was realistic enough to know that it was unlikely that even though he might apprehend the murderer of Alice Trelawney and Elizabeth Fisher, such success might not immediately warrant his promotion, but again it would go a long way to enhance his chances if the opportunity for promotion occurred; particularly if he could get ACC John Murray on side.

It was no secret that the Catholic Pope's much-publicised visit that was to occur on Tuesday at Bellahouston Park was Murray's big project. The word at headquarters was Murray had hinted that if the day went off well, the likelihood of him being included in the New Year's Honours List was highly probable and might even enhance his opportunity for him to be appointed as the Chief Constable of one of the smaller Scottish or English Forces.

His thoughts were rudely interrupted by Glenda Burroughs pushing open the door and like an embarrassed schoolboy, he almost jumped to his feet.

"Don't be getting illusions of grandeur just yet, Mark," she grinned at him. "You had better come through to the incident room. Young Simon Johnson has just returned from Govan and he's brought a witness statement with him that I really think you should read."

Cris Trelawney opened his eyes. He had not intended falling asleep but at last, the long overnight drive from Cornwall and the stress of the previous day had finally caught up with him. The door knocked loudly again and tiredly, still fully dressed but for his boots, he padded to the door in his socks and pulled it fully open.

His eyes widened in shock and he swallowed with difficulty.

Ronnie Kyle, a cigar dangling from his mouth stood there with a solemn faced Moses Parker looming largely behind the smaller man. It didn't escape Cris's attention that beneath the black leather jacket folded over his arm, Moses held a sawn-off double-barrelled shotgun in his huge, right hand and it was pointed past Kyle and directly at Cris.

"Hello Cris," Kyle smiled evilly at him and removing the cigar from his mouth, said, "long time no see, my son."

Seated behind a desk within the incident room, Renwick read and reread the statement while Simon Johnson stood nervously in front of him.

"And you got this from the woman, this Ella McGuiness, the shoplifter you arrested earlier today?" he stared at Simon.

"Yes sir. I was about to fingerprint her at Govan office when she offered the information. After I noted her statement I thought it best to return here as soon as possible and inform the incident room."

He swallowed hard, not daring to glance at Glenda Burroughs who stood to one side of Renwick, her face blank but with a definite twinkle in her eye.

"Who else have you told about this," asked Renwick, squinting up at the younger officer.

"No one sir. I came straight here," lied Simon, staring straight into Renwick's eyes, trying with difficulty to stop his legs from shaking and wondering what the fuck he was doing, lying to the man who as far as the police were concerned, was now the Senior Investigating Officer in the ongoing murder inquiry.

"Where is this woman now; still locked up at Govan?"

"Ah, yes sir. The duty Inspector kindly agreed that as she might be a material witness in the murder case, he will ensure she remains detained in the detention room rather than a cell and will arrange to put her before the District Court tomorrow morning."

Unconsciously, he kept his fingers and toes crossed that the assurances DCI McIntosh gave the Inspector and the lie Simon was perpetrating at McIntosh's request would not come back and bite him in the arse or worse, get him locked up alongside Ella McGuiness.

"Good work," Renwick unexpectedly declared and smiled at him. "This registration number she gave us in her statement. How certain is she of the number?"

"She seemed reasonably sure sir. I quizzed her how she would remember and she said the letters rhymed with her favourite football club, RFC. I haven't checked the number on the PNC, deciding instead to get up here right away with her statement. When I finished taking her statement I asked her again about the registration number and she gave it again without hesitation."

"And you're certain you didn't mention to her the name of the second victim, Betty Fisher? That she gave you the name?"

Simon's face burned with embarrassed anger and he flinched; that was the second time he had been asked that bloody question. He might be just a bloody aide, but he wasn't stupid. As a uniformed cop he had taken more statements than he could remember and was not in the habit of feeding information to a witness. Tight-lipped, he replied, "No sir. She gave me the name."

Renwick either didn't notice or care at that his question caused Simon offense and turning to Brian Davidson, said, "Get onto the PNC, Davidson….eh, Brian, and check out the number."

"Sir," replied the stony-faced Davidson and left the room clutching the statement.

"Eh, good work Johnson," Renwick turned back to Simon. "It seems that you might make a detective after all, eh?" he forced a laugh.

"Sir," Simon quietly acknowledged the half hearted compliment and with a sideways glance at Glenda Burroughs, made his way to the table to grab a coffee. While Renwick impatiently drummed his fingers on the desktop and Burroughs lit yet another cigarette, Simon pretended to study the statement file.

The door opened and Davidson quickly stepped back into the room.

"Car's registered to a lease company with an address in Berkshire," he opened without preamble, his face already betraying his disappointment. "I checked the Police Almanac for the phone number of the local station and spoke to the duty sergeant down there who knows of the company and told me that they are quite a big outfit, locally. Apparently they lease their vehicles to smaller companies for a set period, usually three years and then just about when the lease is up and the cars are due the first MoT, they dispose of the cars at auction."

Renwick turned his wrist to look at his watch. "Damn it. There's no likelihood we'll get anybody at the company at this time on a Sunday night, unless," his eyes narrowed and he shot a glance at Burroughs, "we can get their keyholder to check their files for us?"

"I'd already thought of that," Davidson interrupted with a smug look on his face. "The sergeant checked the keyholder file for me. It's an alarm company that hold the keys during dark hours."

"Fuck!" Renwick spat out, his fists clenched as he banged once on the desktop.

"Even if we don't get the information tonight," Burroughs smoothly interjected, "it won't do any harm to put out a broadcast to all stations just in case the driver of the vehicle is on the prowl again."

Renwick, keen to seize upon any initiative, nodded his agreement and said to Davidson, "See to it please Brian."

While Davidson used the incident room phone, Burroughs turned to Simon and smiling, instructed him, "Contact the controller at Govan, and ensure the troops on the ground at the Drag are also made aware of the registration number. Wouldn't do for them not to be informed that there might be a killer out there in a car and us sitting here on our arses with the car's details, would it?"

"Ma'am," he nodded to her and left the room to find another phone.

Cris Trelawney, hooded with an old hessian sack and his hands bound behind at his back, was thrown about the floor in the darkness of the old van as it negotiated across what felt like rough ground.

He still found it hard to believe that after all these years Ronnie Kyle had found him.

Cris was under no illusion as to what Kyle had planned for him. Had it just been the bastard alone, Cris would have fought him and undoubtedly won, but the menace of the sawn-off held in the very capable hands of his former pal Moses Parker had put paid to any thought of resistance.

Even leaving the hotel, he had no chance to indicate to the young receptionist that anything was amiss, not when Kyle had warned Cris he would, "…cut her fucking throat if you as much as even look at her."

Now here he was, tied and helpless.

"All right back there are you Cris?" came Kyle's taunting voice.

The van stopped and he managed to turn his body to sit upright, his legs splayed in front of him. He heard the rear doors squeak on rusting hinges before being opened and then a pair of hands, Moses he guessed, reached for him and dragged him out. The hands pulled his legs until they dangled downwards and he felt himself being pulled erect to his feet. He could hear the sound of distant traffic and assumed wherever they had brought him to was close to a major road or maybe even a motorway. Without warning, a fist was driven into his stomach with such force he bent double and expelled the air from his lungs, coughing into the foul smelling hood that he guessed had once been used to carry grain or wheat.

"A little taster, Cris," Kyle joked, clearly enjoying himself.

Almost at once he had known it was the little bastard who had punched him. Had it been Moses, Cris would have been on the ground trying to breathe.

A pair of hands, Moses again he thought, took him by the shoulders and propelled him across even ground then he heard the scraping of a heavy metal door being drawn closed and banged shut. He guessed from the silence and echoing footsteps he was in some sort of large, high roofed building.

The hands roughly pulled him backwards and while he tried to retain his balance, his back slammed against what seemed to be an upright pillar or post. The hands fiddled at his wrists and he knew that he was being secured to a post or some kind of upright stanchion. A minute or two later the metal door was dragged open again and Cris heard the van slowly driven into the building. He figured that bringing the van in was an afterthought and when the blindfold was snatched from his head, he saw why.

Eyes blinking to adjust to the dim light, they had brought him to what looked to be a dark and derelict warehouse. The headlights of the Transit van remained switched on and seemed to be the only source of illumination; the beams cutting a swathe through the darkness and providing a ghostly hue in which dust mites danced in the air.

Kyle, a fresh cigar clenched in his teeth, stood grinning in front of him. Without warning, he half turned to his left and swung back quickly, striking Cris with his fist on the right side of Cris's face.

He felt the cartilage in his nose break and the blood from his ruptured nostrils run down into his mouth, through his beard and over his chin. Clenching his teeth, he blinked away the pain. It was not the first time his nose had been broken. Through watery eyes, he saw Moses standing to one side, his face impassive, the shotgun held loosely at his side.

Cris knew he was going to die. He had already accepted the fact. Bound and helpless as he was and at the mercy of Kyle, there was nothing he could do to prevent it. A rage overtook him and he sneered at the smaller man.

"That the best you can do, you fucking pervert?"

The insult didn't rile Kyle as he had hoped, not if the smaller man's smile was any indication. Instead, Kyle simply shrugged from his overcoat and handed it to Moses Parker, accepting in return a pair of black leather gloves that he slowly slipped onto his hands.

"I've waited a very, very long time for this," he smiled at Cris. "You wouldn't believe how many times I've thought about you, what I intend doing to you after you betrayed me, old son." His face wrinkled and he shook his head. "You were the best man I had Cris. I relied on you, trusted you. I would have made you my successor, but how did you repay my generosity? You turned your back on me for what, a fucking slapper and her kid!"

Cris flinched as Kyle raised his fist to punch at him, but then he inexplicably stayed his hand.

"No," he shook his head at Cris, "it's going to be a long night, my old son. I don't want to waste a second of it. You're going to die tonight Cris," he stared with maddened eyes and tightly gripped Cris's jaw in his gloved hand, "but I promise you, you wanker! It won't be an easy death; no by God," he sneered and shook his head, his face so close that his spittle struck Cris in the face. Then, as if remembering, his eyes narrowed and he said, "But first things first. Who was it that tipped you off I was coming for you? A name and I promise," his face now inches from Cris, "after I've had my fun, I'll let you die quick."

Cris stared down into the smaller man's eyes. He fought to stop his legs from shaking, conscious of a sudden need to pee that almost caused him to dribble into his trousers, but more than anything, the last thing he would ever do was give in to the little shit.

"A name?" he smiled and shook his head. "Here's something that will maybe help you even more, Ronnie. Try and do something about that fucking halitosis."

CHAPTER 21

Throughout that evening and past midnight into the first hour of Monday morning, the inquiry team contacted the incident room with their police radios; each team tiredly reported their lack of success then signed off for the night to wearily make their way home.

In the incident room, a bored Glenda Burroughs saw the time to be after 1pm and, herself half-awake, indicated to Simon Johnson to "…knock off and go home," instructing the young aide to return at nine o'clock that morning and with a wink and a grin, added that he try to avoid arresting any more shoplifters.

He didn't protest the order to go home and wondered if he would get any sleep, still worrying about his meeting at Govan office with DCI McIntosh and the consequence if he was found out in the lie.

Shrugging into his jacket, he nodded to Burroughs and Davidson, seeing that DI Mark Renwick had discovered a new energy and now fully animated, restlessly prowled the incident room.

As they watched him, Burroughs and even the unsympathetic Brian Davidson thought they understood Renwick's anxiety. The registration number of the suspect vehicle was in his grasp and yet, there was no immediate way to identify the user of the car. His and the rest of the teams worst fear was the killer might strike again before the information was acted upon.

What neither Burroughs nor Davidson could know or suspect was that the DI was not particularly worried about the murder of another prostitute. No, Mark Renwick's anxiety stemmed from his urge to apprehend and present the murderer to ACC John Murray. He was inwardly excited at the possibility of making an arrest and solving what until now had the hallmark of a real who-dun-it.

Titillated by the prospect of further promotion, Renwick's reluctance to leave the incident room was beginning to play upon Burroughs nerves. Yawning, she stood from the uncomfortable wooden chair and said, "Mark, there's no more can be done tonight. It's unlikely the Berkshire car lease company will open much before eight tomorrow morning and by the time they search their records for the current keeper of the suspect's car, it will be some time after that. We'll be lucky to get our suspects name and address anytime before nine o'clock. So here's what I suggest; we knock off and be back here tomorrow morning for, what…seven-thirty?"

Before Renwick could respond, Davidson jumped to his feet and grabbing at his car coat, echoed, "Seven-thirty it is then. Goodnight," before pulling open the door and without a backward glance, he was gone.

Renwick, realising that he was stymied, gruffly agreed and switching off the light, followed Burroughs out of the room.

Across the city, DI Mark Renwick's father Dodger was arriving home, physically a little the worse for wear following his evening sojourn at the brothel located on the second floor of the tenement building in Nithsdale Road. He was exhausted and knew that he should have requested a more 'comfortable' woman; someone a little older rather than the willowy teenager who had been gifted to him by the grateful owner.

Yet, smiling as he switched off the engine, for someone so young and barely out of school, Dodger found her initial youthful eagerness to please an exhilarating experience. Her later cries of pain had excited him more than he realised and but for his hand over her mouth, she might have attracted the attention of the Madam and the brothel's burly minder.

He was certain the extra twenty he bunged the weeping teenager would buy her silence and settle any complaint she might have.

Carefully, he reversed the car into the narrow space and opening the driver's door, vowed yet again that he would somehow contrive to have the elderly neighbours' wall knocked over and replaced by a wooden fence while ensuring that to provide

Dodger with a little more space the fence would dip that extra few inches into the neighbour's property. A quiet word with Dodger's man in the planning department should do the trick he inwardly smiled.

Locking the driver's door, he turned the corner towards the front door and realised almost immediately that his wife Martha's car was missing from the driveway. His head snapped up to glance at her window, but he already knew her habits. He saw the low glow of the bedside light and realised she must be in bed reading.

"Bastard!" he snapped at his absent son, his fists clenching and unclenching and a rage overtook him.

Davie wasn't getting away with it again tonight. Dodger's dream of a political career in the London Parliament was almost realised and that fucking idiot of a son of his could very well ruin everything; all it would take was for Davie to be arrested driving while banned from driving and worse, while drunk. The media would have a field day and there would certainly be a backlash at the polls. Shaking with rage, he stamped through the front door, needing to take his anger out on someone.

"Martha!" he screamed up the stairs.

Gordon McIntosh nursed a glass of Glenfiddich and finishing his tale, smiled at his wife Mary sipping at her sweet sherry.

"So that's that then," she smiled back. "If what the woman says is true, then the case is halfway to being solved. Your young man…." she hesitated.

"Simon Johnson, he's doing his aide in the Department at the minute."

"Your man Simon," she continued. "He took a bit of a chance didn't he? I mean, he really should have told that man, him that I don't like…."

"Mark Renwick."

"Aye, him. He struck me as being a sleekit git, that one."

"That's not fair," he grinned tolerantly at her, "you only met the guy once."

"That was enough for me," she sniffed theatrically. "I didn't like the look of him from the start. Anyway, shouldn't have this boy Simon have told *him*, seeing as *he's* now in charge of the inquiry?"

McIntosh slowly nodded his head, oddly touched that though he had barely spoken more than a couple of times with young Johnson, the lad had seen fit to pin his loyalty the DCI.

"Aye, you're right of course; he should have. However, it was bright enough of him to recognise that the woman he had arrested might have some bearing on the case, particularly as we weren't getting anywhere with it," he sighed.

"Given time, Gordon, given time," she gently rebuked him. "You yourself admitted that some of these cases take weeks, let alone the few days you worked on it. I mean, I've been a detectives wife long enough to realise that when a murder is committed, if it's in a house or anywhere there might be people around the area, then quite likely you've got witnesses; isn't that what you've told me?"

He nodded.

"Well then. The first wee lassie, she was discovered in a park in the middle of nowhere, wasn't she? I mean, come on Gordon. Where do you start with that kind of murder? My God, you didn't even have her name, to begin with."

He sighed and nodded again. "You're right. I suppose that given the fact it has just been a few days, we haven't done so badly," yet strangely satisfied that the case now had a realistic chance of being solved, regardless of who was in charge. His face clouded over and his brow knitted. "I just hope that we…" he sighed, "the team I mean. I just hope they can identify the driver of the vehicle and hopefully before he kills another poor young woman."

"My God, look at the time," Mary pretended shock and rose to her feet then threw her head back and finished her sherry in one gulp.

McIntosh's eyes widened and he laughed. "You trying to rush me into bed, woman?"

She smiled mischievously at him, her eyes playful but her mind conscious that in the darkness of the night, depression and anger can combine to thwart sleep.

"You know how reckless I can get when I've a drink in me, Gordon McIntosh," she whispered in her best seductive voice. "Why don't you chase me up the stairs and I'll show you what an old girl can do for you?"

Davie Renwick could barely focus. Mounting the edging of the pavement, he turned the wheel of the car into the driveway and standing on the brakes, stalled the vehicle when he skidded to a halt, sending stone chips flying from beneath the front tyres into the neatly trimmed lawn.

Mouth slackly hanging open, he almost fell giggling from the driver's seat onto the driveway, catching his fall by hanging onto the steering wheel then slowly lowering his heavy body out of the car till he was lying with his head and torso on the ground and his legs still in the well of the car.

When the front door of the house was snatched open, Davie was still drunkenly giggling. Lying awkwardly, all he could see beneath the car was a pair of legs moving round the vehicle towards him. Suddenly a pair of hands reached down and he felt himself physically dragged from the car and dumped unceremoniously fully onto the ground.

"You fucking waste of space!" hissed his father who then with his fist reached down and punched Davie on the side of the head.

A stunned Davie felt himself again dragged further from the car, this time by his jacket collar then kicked fully in the ribs by the enraged Dodger.

"Tomorrow," his father snarled at him, "you pack your bag and fuck off out of my house, d'you hear me you useless bastard?"

Shocked, Davie cowered on the ground, his legs drawn up beneath him and his hands and forearms instinctively covering his head in expectation of further blows, but to his relief, Dodger had walked off towards the house, slamming the front door behind him.

Breathing rapidly, his eyes glazed, a sober hatred overtook Davie and he stumbled to his feet. He staggered to the door and pushing it open, heard Dodger banging about in the kitchen and then the fridge door being slammed shut.

His breathing was erratic and glancing upwards, he knew then what he had to do and staggered towards the stairs.

In the quiet of the darkness in Netherplace Road, in the affluent Newton Mearns area of the city, Glenda Burroughs off the engine and wearily locked the car door before glancing upwards to her top floor flat. She smiled when she saw the lounge light was on. Walking along the path between the neatly tended ground floor gardens, she stopped and stood within the close entrance, her eyes closed and nose twitching and breathed in the fragrance of the flowers that filled the night air. It was so quiet, so peaceful and so calm after the bustle of the office.

Unconsciously, she reached into her handbag for her cigarettes, withdrew one from the pack and lit it with her lighter. Standing in the shelter of the porch of the close mouth, she inhaled deeply and reflected on what had occurred.

It had been a difficult day, not least for Gordon McIntosh. Her brow creased, recalling the uncertainty of young Simon Johnson at her suggestion he contact Gordon with information provided by the female prisoner.

Her eyes narrowed and her chest tightened, a sudden fear overtaking her that if Johnson, for any reason, decided to admit the collusion with McIntosh and it led back to her…

She softly exhaled and smiled at her own panicked stupidity. It was nothing more than her own tiredness and the cloying darkness of the night that caused her concern.

Johnson would not say anything; of that she was fairly certain, but the thought persisted.

So what if he did? After all, it would simply be his word against hers.

She glanced at the engraved Zippo, still clutched in her hand and smiled at the memory of the gift, wondering if he would still be awake.

Pushing open the close door, she wearily made her way up the stairs to her flat.

In her small bedroom, Martha Renwick lay awake in bed. She had heard the screeching of her car tyres when Davie returned home, her fingers nervously clutching at the quilt cover when she heard her husband Dodger scream at her son that he was to be gone by the morning. Fearfully, she pulled the cover up tightly about her and squeezed her eyes closed. The slamming of the front door when Dodger returned to the house was loud enough to startle her. Her breathing became irregular and, warm though she was, her body involuntarily shivered.

A few minutes passed and she thought that perhaps things had calmed down, but the squeak of the tread on the fourth step warned her that one of them was coming upstairs. She lay perfectly still, not daring to breathe, waiting for either the master bedroom door to be opened or Davie to continue up the narrow stairwell to his attic room. The seconds dragged past then while she listened, Martha heard Davie stumble up the narrow flight of stairs. She exhaled with a sigh of relief, pleased that the confrontation between her son and his father seemed to be over; well, at least for tonight.

She closed her eyes when from above her, she heard Davie dragging something across his bedroom floor. With a start Martha realised it must be the suitcase and her eyes opened wide with puzzled curiosity. Why would Davie….the suitcase that contained those… those things.

Her eyes darted towards her door. Should she get up, get out of bed? Her fear caused her to imagine Davie being so angry with his father that he might… she stopped, too afraid to even think *that*!

Martha sat up in bed and swung her legs over the side, her feet barely reaching the carpeted floor. She jerked upright when she heard the heavily built Davie coming back downstairs and reaching to the bedside table she switched on the lamp and stood upright.

She heard Davie now on the landing outside her door and called out, "Davie?" but he either ignored or didn't hear her and continued heavily footed downstairs. Surely he can't be leaving already, she fearfully clutched at her throat; not my boy, my wee Davie. Living with Dodger was just bearable, but only because Davie too was in the house. Without him being here, life she knew would be intolerable.

Grabbing her dressing gown from the hook behind the door, Martha rushed out into the brightly lit hall landing to call upon him, but Davie was gone from the bottom of the stairs.

That's when she heard the raised voices and, her stomach tight and legs shaking, she made her way downstairs.

Cris Trelawney was barely conscious. His knees had given way and he hung limply from the post to which he was bound, the blood and mucous from his nose and mouth dripping through his bloodstained beard onto his shirt and the concrete floor at his feet.

"I'm going to ask you one last time, Cris," snarled Kyle, the front of his silk shirt now spotted with Cris's blood, "who the fuck phoned you? Who warned you I was coming for you? Who else in my mob sold me out? Answer me, damn you," he vehemently screamed. Enraged, he reached up with one gloved hand to grab Cris by the hair and yanked at it, causing the back of his head to strike the post. Cris tried to smile, but such was the pain in his lips and at least two broken back teeth he could barely manage a wince. Through blackened eyes, he stared at the smaller man and tried to spit at him, but the saliva merely rolled with the blood down his chin.

"Fuck you," he managed to whisper.

Kyle, panting from his exertions, stepped back and slowly shook his head.

"No, Cris," he quietly replied, "fuck you," and without turning his head, reached behind him to Moses Parker, his hand outstretched, fingers snapping to be handed the shotgun.

He turned to take the weapon and his eyes opened wide. Too late, he saw the shotgun barrels held in Moses hands and the wooden stock swung towards him with such speed he had no time to cry out before the stock thudded against his forehead. The jarring force of the wood against skin and bone almost tore the weapon from the large man's hands. Kyle's head snapped backwards. The vans headlights, dimming as the battery run low, caught the spray of blood from his shattered forehead as it flew in an arc through the air, creating a vivid scarlet pattern in the half-light. Kyle, his mouth open, with eyes suddenly wide and betraying their shock, flopped like a broken marionette to the ground.

Still tied to the post, Cris stared through bloodied eyes at the fallen man and could only watch as Moses, continuing to grasp the shotgun by the barrels, swung the weapon from shoulder height and again Cris heard the audible thud as it crashed once more against Kyle's head, causing his body to jerk and bounce against the unforgiving concrete.

Moses staggered back and dropped the bloodied shotgun, his eyes staring down at his boss.

Cris could hardly breathe and his tongue felt twice its size in his mouth. He was thirstier than he could ever recall and the salty taste of his own blood and vomit caused him to gag repeatedly.

He tried to call out to Moses, but it was as if the large man was in a stupor and did not hear him. Again Cris tried to speak and finally croaked, "Moses."

Turning slowly, Moses stared for a few seconds at Cris then almost in a daze, stumbled towards him.

"Sorry," he mumbled and producing a lock-knife from his jacket pocket, opened it and with shaking hands began sawing at the rope binding Cris, accidently nicking the flesh at Cris's wrist and said, "Fuck."

"I'm so sorry Cris," he softly repeated and pulled away the rope binding Cris. Hugging the wounded man to him, Moses gently took Cris weight in his big hands and stared into his eyes. "I shouldn't have let him do this to you mate. I'm sorry."

The beating had been worse than Cris thought and his knees buckled, but Moses had a firm hold of him and gently lowered him to the floor, his back against the post.

Behind Moses, Kyle twitched and gave a soft moan.

"You got some water?" Cris gasped.

Moses nodded and headed towards the van, returning with a glass bottle of Irn-Bru.

"This do?"

Cris nodded as Moses crouched and holding the bottle against his lips, tipped some of the liquid into his moth.

Cris coughed as the bubbles of the carbonated Irn-Bru mixed with the blood and he spat thick phlegm out onto the concrete, nodding again that Moses hold up the bottle.

He was amazed at his own thirst and took a deep swallow.

"Thanks," he burped and then nodded towards the fallen Kyle. His eyes narrowed as he stared at Moses.

"What changed your mind?"

Moses returned his stare then shook his head.

"Guilt, I suppose," he slowly replied. "I couldn't stand it any longer, watching him beat you like that, man. It wasn't right." He sighed heavily. "Over the years, he had this thing, you know, about getting you. Finding you, making you pay for *betraying* him," he spat out. "All the time obsessed with finding out who had phoned you that night, to warn you that he was coming for you."

"He didn't suspect it was you, then? That it was you who had called me?"

Moses shook his head. "No, never even gave it a thought. Not Moses Parker, his tame nigger boy," he snorted, then his face clouded over with the bad memory of that night.

"I'd slipped away, gone upstairs to the payphone on the wall beside the cloakroom, you know the one?"

Cris nodded.

"That's when he was… you know, doing that to Daniela."

He sat back, his legs splayed out in front of him, his large hands flat on the concrete supporting his body. "Anyway, while I was upstairs, phoning you, I thought him and the boys were going to rough her about a bit. You know, slap her like. Not that I would have approved," he held one hand up, palms towards Cris, "but you remember what Daniela was like, man. She were no shrinking violet was that lady. I figured she could take a slap, even give it back," he grinned at the memory of her. Then his face clouded over, "I swear to you, it never occurred to me, Cris; I couldn't guess what his real plan for her was, honest man; I swear it, on my mothers grave."

Cris let him talk, to tell the story at his own speed. He guessed Moses needed to admit his part in Daniela's death, even if it was simply not being there when she needed him.

Almost unnoticed and unheard, Kyle gave a final sigh and eyes wide open, his mind unable to comprehend what had happened, he quietly died.

Moses swallowed hard, his eyes narrowed and glancing backwards with disgust at his former boss, took a deep breath.

"When I got back down to the basement level, the boys were coming out of the room. They were laughing, Cris," he spat out, shaking his head, his disgust evident in his voice. "Fucking laughing. The thing is," his expression changed to one of puzzlement, "they were laughing about Ronnie raping her, man. I don't think that even they knew he was going to…you know, kill her."

Moses used the same hand to wipe at his face as though trying to erase the memory of that night from his mind.

"I went into the room and he was stood there looking down at her, that fucking boning knife he kept in his desk in his hand. He had…he had killed her with it. She had fought him though," Moses nodded, recalling her courage. "He had scratches on his face and his neck. He told me to get rid of her, dump her body in the Thames."

He shook his head.

"I couldn't do that though; dump her like some bit of fucking garbage I mean."

"Is that why you left her in the park at Clapham Common?"

Moses nodded. "I guessed though when the coppers found her, he'd want to know why I didn't put her in the water, so I got my story in first. I told Ronnie that the cops were tailing me; that they must have seen me in the big car I had at that time, the Granada and that I had to dump Daniela on the Common. You know what it was like back then, Cris."

He adopted a falsetto voice and pretended to be a Metropolitan policeman.

"What's this then, eh? What's a big black bastard like you doing driving a fancy car? Can't have that now can we?"

He shook his head at the memory and shrugged.

"You'll remember I was always getting a pull by those bastards in the Met, wasn't I? Cost me a fucking fortune in bungs, it did," he grinned humourlessly, but the grin quickly faded.

"Ronnie didn't question me too much about where I put Daniela's body, because he was just glad that I had gotten her out of the club."

His face darkened. "Then he started a witch-hunt, trying to find out who had tipped you off. Broke a few bones he did; or rather I did," he sheepishly admitted.

They sat for a few minutes in silence, broken when Cris coughed and gesticulated towards Kyle's body.

"What we going to do about him, then Moses?"

The large man winked at Cris before pushing himself to his feet. He walked to where Kyle lay and bending down, rustled through Kyle's coat pocket and retrieved the map page.

Turning towards Cris, he waved the page and grinning, said, "If I drive and you direct me, we'll take Ronnie on a little trip," and grinned even wider, his white teeth shining brightly in the gloomy atmosphere, before adding, "his last trip."

Martha, her hand shaking, pushed the partially open door wide. Dodger, a whisky glass in his left hand, stood facing her from across the room. Davie stood a few feet inside the room, his back to her.

He was shouting at his father, his words slurred as he screamed, "I'm a man, you fucking old shit; a soldier. I'm trained and prepared to die for my country." He staggered, but almost immediately regained his balance.

She hesitated, wondering why Dodger stood so still, saying nothing, not abusing or cursing his son. It struck her that Dodger looked pale faced, almost frightened. That's when she saw it, when in her bare feet she took a further step into the room.

Davie was holding one of the green coloured grenade things, the small round bomb thing, in his right hand.

Martha knew real fear then and unable take her eyes off it and trying not to panic him, softly said, "Davie, it's me love. What are you doing son? What have you got there, Davie?"

He half turned towards her, staggering slightly on drunken legs, a sheen of sweat beading his forehead.

Davie desperately wanted to sit down and go to sleep, but this was his moment; the moment that he finally had his father's attention.

"Go to bed, mum," he ordered her, then almost pleading, added, "please."

From the periphery of her eye, Martha saw Dodger try to back away towards the French doors, but Davie also caught the slight movement and shouted to his father, "Stop! Don't you fucking move, not one inch!"

Dodger, his eyes now wide with fright, froze and stood still, the whisky glass falling unnoticed from his hand.

"Look son," he forced a smile, "you're a bit overwrought and you've had a wee drink tonight, so let's be reasonable, eh Davie?"

"So it's *Davie* now is it?" he sneered in return, "not 'you fucking waste of space' or 'you useless bastard'?"

Dodger swallowed hard, mesmerised by the hand grenade held in Davie's sweaty hand. What Martha could not see from her position by the doorway was the safety pin extracted earlier from the grenade by Davie and now held in his right hand.

Davie lurched forward and almost fell, but with his right hand, caught hold of the wing of an armchair and steadied himself.

Across the room, Dodger breathed a sigh of relief.

Martha tried again. "Davie. Listen to me son. This is not doing anyone any good," she shook her head, trying with difficulty to impose some sort of authority into her voice. "Now come on, there's a good lad. Give me that thing and get to your bed, eh?"

She stepped forward to Davie's left side, her hands reaching out to grab the wee bomb thing from him, but Davie, turning towards her, mistook his mother's concern for loyalty to his father and sharply, or as sharply as his drink-sodden mind allowed, pulled his arm out of her reach.

Almost as if in slow motion and to his utter horror, Dodger saw the grenade slip from his sons sweaty grasp and fly the short distance across the room towards him.

Unusually agile for such a heavyset and unfit individual, Dodger swiped at the projectile with his right fist and to his surprise, succeeded in batting the grenade back across the room towards Davie and Martha, seeing it bounce off the armchair by Davie and land almost at his feet.

Martha, who had no idea of the consequence of the removed safety pin, stared with curiosity at the small green bomb thing while Davie, his reactions completely inhibited by alcohol, stared with sorrowful eyes at his mother.

The panicked Dodger flung himself to the floor, fortuitously behind a large and well-padded sofa couch.

Neither Dodger nor Martha could know that the British military L2A2 fragmentation grenade is internally fitted with a 4.4-second fuse that is normally held from detonating the explosive the grenade contains by the safety pin that now, unfortunately, was clutched in Davie's right hand.

Most individuals will rightly consider 4.4 seconds to be a fraction of time, but to the three stunned occupants of the room, the 4.4 seconds seemed to drag out a little longer. The short distance that the grenade flew between Davie to his father and back to the carpet at Davie's feet was a little over twelve feet and time enough for the fuse to continue its deadly countdown.

Davie, staring down at the fallen grenade, looked up and with sorrowful eyes had just time to say, "Mum…"

At that point, the fuse detonated the black powder charge within the grenade and exploded it with a flash and ear-shattering bang. The approximate twelve hundred metal fragments flew in an unpredictable pattern of fragmentation, shredding the bodies of Davie and Martha, who both almost instantaneously died.

CHAPTER 22 - Early hours of Monday 31 May.

The uniformed officers who had spent the night patrolling the perimeter of Bellahouston Park were relieved to see the arrival of their colleagues who would mount the dayshift patrol. Together the dozen or so nightshift officers huddled by the Mosspark Drive gate within the small tent that served as the handover location, smoking as they sharing the final dregs of lukewarm coffee from the urn. The welcome arrival of the police personnel carrier bringing their colleagues from Govan office was greeted with hoots and good-natured jeers.

Once more, the nightshift-supervising sergeant informed his replacement that all was well, that nothing stirred and tongue in cheek, reported no fresh murdered bodies.

Piling into the personnel carried, the tired nightshift was driven off towards Govan office to later disperse to their respective homes and make the most of their twelve-hour break.

Over eight thousand nautical miles distance, the forces of the UK were that time engaged in land and sea battles with the forces of Argentina, whose Mirage fighter planes was armed with the deadly Exocet ship-killing missiles.

The six o'clock Clyde Radio broadcast of that morning opened with good news, hailing the success of the Royal Marines of 42 Commando who, supported by SAS troops and following a fierce battle, captured Mount Kent while their comrades of 3 Para and 45 Commando reached Estancia House and Teal Inlet.

In music and record shops across the UK, teenagers purchased Adam Ant's *'Goody Two Shoes'*; the song that after a short two weeks would topple Madness from the number one spot in the UK charts.

In Edinburgh, Lothian & Borders Police were anxiously gearing themselves for the visit of Pope John Paul II to the Murryfield stadium; however, unlike their colleagues in Glasgow, they did not have to investigate the murder of a young woman discovered at their venue.

The media, headlining the pending Papal visit the following day to Glasgow, had almost forgotten the murder of Alice Trelawney and not apparently yet made the connection with the death of Elizabeth Fisher.

Gordon McIntosh, wearing his old, threadbare, but favourite dressing gown and following a sleepless night, paced restlessly in the kitchen of his home. With a cigarette wedged between the fingers of his left hand and cup of coffee cooling on the table beside him, he scanned his early morning, delivered copy of the 'Glasgow News' for the report of Elizabeth Fisher's murder.

"Morning," yawned his wife Mary, herself wearing a dressing gown and leaning over to kiss the top of his head. "Thanks for last night," she coyly smiled at him.

"No, thank you," he returned her smile, then frowned, "Sorry, hen. Did I disturb you when I got up?"

"No," she tiredly continued to smile while she poured herself a coffee, "I couldn't sleep either so you tossing and turning all night didn't keep me awake."

"Sorry," he pulled a contrite face. "Too much on my mind I suppose."

Mary sat down opposite him and had barely sipped at her coffee when the kitchen wall phone rung.

She glanced at the wall clock and then with a puzzled look at her equally puzzled husband, rose from her seat, reached across and lifted the phone from the cradle. "Hello?"

"Good morning Missus McIntosh, It's the Chief Constable's secretary," said the crisp female voice, "is Mister McIntosh available please, ma'am?"

"Eh, yes," replied Mary, beckoning that Gordon should take the phone and whispering, "It's the Chief's office."

"Hello, Gordon McIntosh."

"Please hold for the Chief Constable, Mister McIntosh," said the woman.

A few seconds passed then the booming voice of Tom Muirhead greeted him.

"Good morning, Mister McIntosh. First, let me apologise for calling you at home at this time of the morning."

"Ah, that's not a problem sir. I was up anyway," replied McIntosh, but did not add that he hadn't slept because he had worried himself sick all through the night.

Thomas Muirhead, a gruff, six foot three Aberdonian with grey, wiry hair and piercing blue eyes, now in his early fifties but still built like the prop forward he once had been, was now in his fourth year as Chief Constable of Strathclyde Police. Not a man to mince words, he was well liked and much respected by the officers of his Force.

Known for his integrity and straight talking, Muirhead had been often been described by the media as a 'copper's cop'. His reputation was that of an uncompromising martinet who had three very basic and publicised rules; he would police without fear or favour, reward endeavour and hard work and lastly, he would never succumb to pressure, whether that be from organised criminal gangs, politicians or the media themselves.

"I had Donald McInnes call me at home last night," he thundered down the phone. "Told me some story about you being suspended by ACC Murray, is that correct?"

Donald McInnes, Chairman of the Scottish Police Federation, McIntosh mused. So DC Willie McNee had pulled out all the stops after all. He took a deep breath and replied, "Ah yes sir, I regret that's true. Mister Murray and I…"

"Mister McIntosh," Muirhead interrupted. "The wherewithal of the circumstances can be discussed at a later date, if they need be discussed at all for in the greater scheme of things, the last thing I want is that upstart McInnes hounding me at my home. At this time I have more pressing matters to attend than a spat between two of my officers, regardless of their rank." Muirhead's voice began to rise.

"I have the Pope and his overlarge entourage arriving tomorrow in Glasgow with an estimated three hundred thousand Catholics also converging on the city. My Head of Special Branch informs me there is credible intelligence that these damned Loyalist protest groups is colluding to disrupt the visit and intend stirring up some trouble at Bellahouston Park. The twenty-four hour incident report here on my desk informs me that a second young woman, a prostitute apparently, was discovered murdered in the Gallowgate area and there is a reasonable belief it might be the work of the same man who killed the young woman in the Park. Now," McIntosh could hear him take a deep breath, "I have just recently received information about an explosion in a private dwelling house in the west end of the city, with two dead. So I'm certain will you understand that I *really* do not need two of my senior officers to be at odds at this time; do I make myself clear, Mister McIntosh?"

"Crystal clear, sir," replied McIntosh. He waited for Muirhead to speak again. A few seconds passed and then Muirhead, now more composed, continued, "Mister McIntosh. As of this phone call, you will consider yourself reinstated to duty. You will solve both these murders and I require you to do so with the utmost alacrity, do you understand?"

"Yes sir, only," he paused and risked a quick glance at the anxiously waiting Mary, "what about Mister Murray, sir?"

There was a distinct pause and then Muirhead calmly replied, "You will leave Mister Murray to me. *I* am the Chief Constable and your reinstatement is *my* decision."

He listened and could clearly hear as Muirhead inhaled, then almost as if in a whispered confidence, continued, "Mister McIntosh, you must realise when I assumed command of this Force that I did not promote a number of my senior officers, that I… how can I put this? I *inherited* these officers. However, you will recall that one of my first decisions as Chief Constable was to promote you to your current rank. I did so because you earned and merited that rank. You have proven your ability as one of my most able senior detective officers and have to date, never let me down. Please ensure you do not do so now. My kind regards to your wife. Good morning to you."

The line went dead. McIntosh, stunned, turned to Mary.

159

"Seems I've still got a job, hen," he slowly said, then broke into a smile as he added, "What's the chance of you looking out my suit and a shirt for me while I grab a shave and a shower. I need to get to work."

The police, ambulance and Fire Brigade vehicles, parked variously about the street and the entrance to the driveway, had now switched off their blue lights. Scenes of Crime and Forensic personnel, enveloped in their distinctive white boiler suits, moved about the front of the building and garden area, occasionally stopping to exchange information in hushed whispers. The front door of the house was seen to be open and guarded by a nightshift police officer in a bright yellow coloured fluorescent jacket whose arms was folded and who impatiently wondered when his relief would arrive to permit him to get home to his bed. Plastic blue and white chequered tape bearing the now familiar logo, 'Police - Do Not Cross' stretched around the house to create a sterile area with a cordoned off perimeter and this tape was itself guarded by an officer at each aspect of the large, detached dwelling. Outside on the street, a horde of curious neighbours stood at the outside perimeter of the cordon. Among them was the nightshift crew from the 'Glasgow News', consisting of a reporter and photographer who had stole a march on their media rivals and now moved among the neighbours. The reporter eagerly pressed for information and quotable comments while the photographer snapped happily at the emergency vehicles attending the scene.

The sudden arrival of a bottle green coloured military vehicle that disgorged four soldiers in combat fatigues raised eyebrows and speculation as to what had occurred within to warrant such activity.

The reporter's eyes narrowed when he saw the blue light attached to the roof of the vehicle and immediately recognised it for what it was. These squaddies were the Bomb Squad.

"So, it's Councillor Renwick, his wife and their son that lives there then?" queried the reporter.

"As I understand it, yes," sniffed the retired head teacher, peering at the notebook and insisting the reporter correctly spell the old man's name.

"The 'Glasgow News', you said; so you're not the 'Herald'?" he sniffed again.

"Aye, buddy, I'm from the 'News'", the reporter replied, impatient to be moving on and trying to catch the eye of his snapper. "Ah, d'you know the wife's or the son's name?"

The old man stared disdainfully at the reporter. "My dear chap, they're not the sort of people that one mixes with, you must understand. The man is a …a…. well," he sniffed once more and with lowered voice, confided, "Let's just say I'm Conservative."

The reporter guessed the old man either had a bad nasal problem or more likely was a stuck up arse, but smiled dutifully and moved away; indicating with a nod towards the Bomb Squad team that the photographer obtain as many snaps as possible of the military vehicle and its occupants.

The soldiers split up, two towards the house and two to stand by and guard the truck.

At the doorway, the younger man, his hands on his hips John Wayne style, barked at the police officer, "Lieutenant Andrews, Royal Army Ordnance Corps. Who's in charge here?"

"That the army arrived?" said a voice from within the house.

A large man, bareheaded and wearing a white boiler suit over his police uniform, beckoned for Andrews and his much older corporal to come through the door and met them in the expansive hallway, his hand outstretched to shake both theirs and a smile on his ruddy complexioned, moustachioed face.

"Chief Inspector Bob Munroe. Thanks for coming out."

"So, how can we assist, sir?"

Munroe pointed towards a small anteroom next to the kitchen and replied, "Maybe we should speak in here."

The room, seemingly used as a cloakroom, contained an old gate leg table with four chairs around it. Indicating the soldiers sit, Munroe sat his large frame down and drawing a pack from inside his boiler suit, offered them both a cigarette. While Andrews declined, the corporal followed the army tradition of refusing nothing but blows. Lighting both his own and the corporal's cigarette, Munroe began.

"The house is owned by Councillor John Renwick who resides here with his wife Martha and son David. As we understand it, David is a member of the Territorial Army, based here in Glasgow at Yorkhill. The Para's I believe, if the wall posters upstairs are any indication."

"Yes, I know Yorkhill barracks. We occasionally provide the TA with support and lectures on demolitions," nodded a thoughtful Andrews.

"Demolitions," Munroe nodded in turn. "That's why we've asked you guys to come along today." He took a deep breath. "Our control room took a call earlier this morning from Councillor Renwick informing us his son had detonated some kind of bomb; a grenade we believe, in the front room of this house."

As if wishing to clarify the suspicion, Munroe produced a clear plastic bag with a brown label attached and within what could clearly be seen was a metal pin. He added, "We discovered what looks like a safety pin among the debris."

Andrews examined the bag and looked aghast. "A grenade you say? Here in the house? Where the fuck…pardon me, sir, but where did his son obtain a hand grenade?"

Munroe didn't fail to see the poker-faced corporal's eyes upturn and then, as though the light of dawn had forcefully struck Andrews, the Lieutenant slowly nodded. "He's filched a grenade from his barracks; that must be it."

"Yes," Munroe replied, swallowing while trying with difficulty to keep his face straight, "we believe he had *filched* the grenade."

"Anyway," Munroe continued, tapping ash into an ashtray on the table, "as a result of the grenade detonating, both the son and Councillor Renwick's wife Martha suffered fatal injuries."

He shook his head with sadness and slowly exhaled. "It's a real mess in there, however, Councillor Renwick fortunately survived without injury; other than shock, I should say and is now at Cranstonhill police office assisting us with our inquiries."

Andrews eyes narrowed and he slowly asked, "If the grenade has already been detonated sir, then why are we here? Surely, this is now a job for your Forensic and Scenes of Crime people."

Munroe nodded and replied, "Ordinarily yes, you would be correct. However," he rose from his seat, "I wonder of you gentlemen would follow me upstairs to the son's room. There's something there that you might be able to help us with."

Sat in the interview room at Cranstonhill police office, still robed in his dressing gown, but also with an NHS blanket wrapped round his shoulders, he leaned his elbows on the table in front of him and ignored the cup of weak tea that lay in front of him.

At Dodger's request, they had left him alone for ten minutes, acceding to his request that they permit him time to compose himself.

What they could not know was he needed the time to try to collect his thoughts, wondering how the hell he was going to talk his way out of this and how it would impact upon his Parliamentary ambition.

Martha and David were gone. He shuddered at the memory of the explosion; the smell of the black powder, the smoke and dust and the sight of their eviscerated corpses.

It was a miracle he had survived. When he had seen what that fucking bomb had done to the front of the sofa….

My God, he shuddered again and closed his eyes tight against what might have been.

However, the main question that worried him was, how could he turn this around to his advantage? What could he do to convince the police and in particular, the electorate, that he innocent of any wrongdoing; that he had no knowledge of grenades and bullets in his home, that it was all Davie's fault.

Almost four decades in politics had taught him that the Party and the public was a fickle creature; supportive when told to be but almost as quick to condemn. The bodies of Martha and Davie again flashed into his mind and, curiously, he found himself smiling.

It might just work.

The names of a couple of local newspaper reporters tumbled through his mind.

The door opened and the two detectives entered. The younger detective, a man aged about thirty with a blank expression, stood in one corner while the older detective, a heavy-set woman in her early forties with dark hair greying at the temples and bundled untidily on top of her head, wearing a black trouser suit and who called herself DI Paterson, smiled at him. "How you feeling Mister Renwick, is there anything that we can get you sir?"

Mister Renwick? It occurred to him that he should remind her he was, after all, a civic dignitary, a Councillor, but thought that might just get up her rather large nose and so instead, smiled wearily and shook his head.

"I'm fine. Just so…just so…."

Try as he might, he just could not induce any tears so adopting his best sorrowful face, simply lowered his head. If nothing else, politics had taught Dodger that when faced with uncertainty, body language and facial expression could be useful to deceive.

As if understanding his pain, the detective walked to Dodger's side of the table and laid a comforting hand on his shoulder.

"I'm so very sorry for your loss," she softly told him, "and I regret that I must ask you some questions during this difficult time. Do you think you might be able to help me understand what happened this morning at your home?"

A sudden chill run through him. With a flash of realisation, it struck him that this woman might be a little sharper than he had at first anticipated. He had to be very careful.

Without raising his head, he nodded.

"Right then," she replied to his nod and returning to her side of the table, sat down facing him. He refused the offer of a cigarette and while she lit her own, raised his face to look at her and rubbed a deliberately shaking hand across his brow.

"So," she softly began, "tell me in your own words what happened?"

CHAPTER 23

Simon Johnson had one of the worst sleepless nights that he could recall. More times than he could count, he had to get up to pee. Tossing and turning through the night, he could not even lay the blame at nightmares, for he hardly slept at all. He closed his eyes tight, trying to force sleep; got up sometime after two in the morning with the intention of boiling milk only to discover to his disgust he had forgotten to buy some; he counted sheep, but no matter what he did, nothing worked.

Rubbing at the sand in his eyes, he finally surrendered and got out of bed just after six o'clock and showered, surprising himself that following the shower he felt better. Getting dressed, he took five minutes to nip to the Asian grocer on the opposite side of the road to purchase milk and fresh bread.

Breakfasting with cereal, toast and a pot of tea, he turned on the radio and half listened to the music while he finished his coffee. Simon heard the news bulletin of an explosion within a house on the west side of the city, but his lie the previous night occupied his thoughts and he dismissed the story without paying much attention.

DI Burroughs had instructed he return to the office for nine, but glancing at the clock as it approached seven, decided he was better there than sitting about waiting to go to work.

Grabbing his jacket he was about to slip it on when he remembered.

Fetching the scribbled scrap of paper from his pocket he smiled and vowed that later today, if he were not arresting shoplifters, Miss Gracie McTear would be getting a surprise phone call.

Switching on the Criminal Intelligence office lights, DS Patsy Cline was her usual forty minutes early for the start of her shift and hanging her coat on the hook at the wall, yawned and more by routine than thought strode to the small anteroom the staff used as a rest rom. She switched on the electric kettle and checked the fridge to ensure the nightshift had bought milk. That done, she settled herself at her desk and with her second fag of that morning hanging from her lower lip, typed her unique password into the Police National Computer and signed on to the system. As the computer booted up, she noticed a small flag in the right hand corner of the screen, indicating a message awaited her. Patsy double clicked the message and squinting as she peered at the screen, unconsciously promising that this week without fail, she would attend for that eye test that she had promised herself since last November. The message informed Patsy that a confidential telex had been dispatched and awaited her at the Force Control Room, the recipient for all such confidential material.

Her curiosity aroused she left her desk and made her way to the fifth floor of the building and the hubbub of the Control Room located there, where the Duty Inspector required her to sign for the telex message that he had sealed within a plain, brown envelope.

Back at her desk, Patsy pored over the message and her eyebrows knitted when a name jumped out at her. To ensure she was not mistaken, she fetched the weekly Incidents of Note ledger and slid her finger across the pages, checking for the same name. Pursing her lips and conscious that maybe it was just a coincidence, she decided that nothing ventured, nothing gained and reached for the phone at her desk, but then glancing at the wall clock above her head, realised it was unlikely that anyone would be at the murder incident room yet.

Inhaling deeply, she blew the smoke away from her desk and deciding instead to leave a message, dialled the number for Pollok police office.

The police, similar to most large organisations, have both official and unofficial means of disseminating information. Officially, this is achieved by Force wide Daily Briefings, statements to the media for dissemination to the general public; the internal circulation of Force or Divisional orders, but more commonly by word of mouth from Inspectors or sergeants to their respective shifts.

The unofficial means of disseminating information is known as gossip.

Gordon McIntosh parked and locked his car in the rear yard at Pollok police office and strolling through the uniform bar towards the incident room was greeted with surprise by the duty Sergeant.

"Morning boss, I thought you were…." The sergeant started, then red-faced, grimaced.

"Don't believe everything you hear," he grinned at the sergeant's embarrassment, then pointing towards the incident room, asked, "Anybody in yet?"

"Aye, the young lad, Johnson."

"Thanks," McIntosh replied and pushed through the swing doors into the corridor that led to the incident room.

Simon Johnson had just boiled the kettle and turned with surprise to see his DCI enter the room.

"Don't ask," McIntosh grinned at him, pre-empting his questioning stare. "Suffice to say, I'm back. Now, before anyone else gets here, you've brought me up to speed regarding your interview with Ella McGuiness, understand?"

Simon with relief nodded in agreement and felt that a great weight lifted from his shoulders. "You'll have a coffee sir?"

McIntosh was about to reply when the door knocked and the duty Sergeant popped his head round it.

"Sorry boss, forgot to say," he handed a scrap of paper towards McIntosh, "a DS Cline from Criminal Intelligence at Pitt Street was on the blower and asked that you give her a call at your convenience. That's her number."

McIntosh frowned as he glanced at the clock, seeing it was just after seven. "When did she call; this morning?"

"Aye. She's at her desk now."

"Right," he nodded his thanks, dismissing the Sergeant and turning to Simon, said, "Two sugars son while I make this call," he said, dialling the internal extension number scribbled on the scrap of paper.

"DS Cline," answered the voice.

"Patsy, it's Gordon McIntosh, how the devil you doing these days? Still married to that drunken bum Iain?"

"Hello Gordon. Thanks for getting back to me and yes, still with Iain, but I keep him in his place by reminding him he's my *current* husband."

McIntosh chuckled and both spent a few minutes catching up on their respective lives since they last met.

"So, I remember now that you've always been an early bird, Patsy and I'm not surprised to find you at your desk, but what's so important that you need to speak with me at this time of the morning?"

She audibly took a deep breath and then said, "The murder of Alice Trelawney. It's not a common name round this area Gordon. The thing is I'm in receipt of an intelligence report from a Ports officer at Glasgow airport that records two London neds, a Moses Parker and Ronald Kyle, arriving just after midday on Saturday at Glasgow Airport where they were met by our very own Eddie Beattie and his boys. The report suggests that Beattie and Kyle seemed to be like old pals. The guy that forwarded the report sent it first to the Special Branch and they copied it to me.

According to what I'm reading," he heard the rustle of paper, "Beattie and his minders drove off in his Jag while the two London guys drove off in an old Transit van."

"Give me the van details," McIntosh instructed and snapping his fingers at Simon for a pen and paper, jotted the van details down as well as noting the two names. "How did you figure this might help my inquiry, Patsy?" he asked, while wondering how she had connected the dots.

"After I read the Ports report, I made inquiry with the Met Intelligence people in London about Parker and Kyle. They sent me a telex giving me the full script, chapter and verse about Parker and Kyle. Unbelievably, their lengthy report even included details of the new identity of a witness called Cris McGuire. Seems this McGuire had taken the stand in the Old Bailey against Kyle and who was later entered by the Met into their witness protection programme," he could almost envisage her shaking her head in disbelief.

"Cris Trelawney," he sighed, nodding as the door of the incident room opened to admit the sleepy-eyed and tousled Brian Davidson and Glenda Burroughs, who even that early in the morning, was dressed in an expensive looking cerise coloured skirted suit and looked as though she had just stepped out from a session at a beauty salon.

"Seems you are way ahead of me then, Gordon," Patsy chuckled. "That's him, Cris Trelawncy. It was the name Trelawney that rather jumped out of the report at me and I thought of the lassie's murder you are investigating, Alice Trelawney. It seemed to me to be too much of a coincidence, these two arriving in Glasgow and Kyle's connection with the name Trelawney. Is it?"

"No, you're bang on, Patsy," he admitted, nodding his head at the phone. It never ceased to surprise him that Patsy Cline was still stuck at her current rank. Maybe it was her choice, he wondered.

"It certainly puts the cat among the pigeons knowing that these two, Parker and Kyle are in Glasgow. I can tell you that they are a direct threat to the murdered girl's father, Cris Trelawney, who is up here to identify his daughter's body. I'm guessing you have already made a PNC check on the van registration number?"

"Aye, but it comes back as no current keeper recorded so I arranged for a lookout for it to have the current user identified, but nothing so far." There was a few seconds silence and then she continued, "I hope that's been a bit of use to you Gordon. Be sure and give my love to Mary," and hung up.

Replacing the handset, he turned to the others in the room as the door burst open to admit a red-faced Mark Renwick, whose open-mouthed surprise to see McIntosh was equalled only by his unshaven, dishevelled appearance.

"Sorry," he gasped and added, "Sir. Might I have a word? In private?"

Bemused, McIntosh nodded and followed him back through the door to the DI's room, where Renwick closed the door behind them both.

"Sorry," he repeated, "but I've just had bad news. There's been some sort of explosion at my parent's house." His voice sounded choked and his eyes flickered with unshed tears. "My mother's dead and my brother David, he's dead too."

"Dear God," replied a shocked McIntosh. Questions flooded into his head, but he had the sense to stop and ask, "Your father? Is he…."

"No, he's fine," replied Renwick, twisting his hands together and biting at his lower lip as the tears threatened to engulf him. "The thing is….I think I'd better go to him…"

"Of course," replied McIntosh, "I'll get someone to drive you…

"No, honest, I'll be fine," Renwick interjected and raised his hands as though in appeal, then his eyes narrowed, "Why are you here sir?"

"I'm back in charge, Mark, but first things first. Where is your father now; what hospital?"

"Ah, he's not at hospital. I mean, apparently he is uninjured. He's at Cranstonhill police office giving a statement."

McIntosh nodded, his face expressing sympathy, but unkindly thinking trust Dodger Renwick to survive and explosion without coming to harm, the slippery bastard.

Not wishing to delay his DI any further, McIntosh ushered Renwick from the office with the instruction that if he required anything at all, he was to contact the DCI as soon as possible, that nothing would be a problem.

"I'm sorry to leave you in the lurch like this sir," was Renwick's last words.

Again and disliking himself for it, McIntosh thought, but not as sorry as I am to see the back of you son.

Returning to the incident room, McIntosh gave the startled Burroughs, Davidson and Johnson and the half dozen other officers who had by that time arrived, Mark Renwick's news.

Instructing the detectives to grab a coffee, he invited Burroughs and Davidson to accompany him to the DI's room and closed the door behind them. To protect both Johnson and Burroughs, McIntosh continued the lie that prior to their arrival at the incident room, Simon Johnson had brought him up to speed regarding the breakthrough information from the shoplifter prisoner, but was disappointed at the lack of action they had tried to take in response to the information.

Nodding his head, he instructed, "Brian, get straight onto the phone and speak to whoever the boss is at this company down in Berkshire for a local address here. If there's any hiccup or they come out with the client confidentiality crap, tell them we'll have the local CID pay them a visit and that their account books had better be cleaner than a nun's underwear or else, get me?"

Davidson grinned and nodded, "Got that boss."

"When that's done Glenda, I want you to gather a team together and ready yourself to go after the suspect. However, as soon as you have the suspect's details, crave a Sheriff's warrant for the house and the car. This is our best opportunity so far to nail this bastard, so let's not have him slip away because we fucked up on our admin, okay?"

Burroughs grimly nodded.

"Have the warrant drawn up so all that needs to be added will be the name and house details. When you're in possession of the warrant, I want the suspect's house turned upside down. Organise the Scenes of Crime and Forensic to be standing by, but more importantly, I want the vehicle seized and torn apart for any evidence our victims were in that car."

"Got all that Gordon," she replied.

"What you planning to do boss?" asked Davidson.

McIntosh's brow knitted. The information Patsy Cline had passed was at the forefront of his mind. It was bad enough that Trelawney's daughter had been murdered on his patch, but by God he wasn't about to allow these London gangsters to then kill her father.

"I've a visit to pay," he calmly said, "and I'll take young Johnson with me, but don't be worrying, I won't be too far away."

Moses Parked rolled the van into the hotel car park and switched off the engine.

"How you going to explain that?" he pointed to Cris Trelawney's battered face. Cris gingerly touched at his bruises and tried to grin, but winced instead.

"If the cops ask, I'll tell them I slipped in the shower."

"Yeah, that'll work," Moses replied disbelievingly and grinned. "You'll need to tell them that after slipping the first time, you bounced up and down and banged your face and body another dozen or so times getting up."

"I'll think of something," Cris tiredly replied. "What about you, what are your plans Moses?"

"Me," the big man said, a faraway look on his face, "I think I've had enough of the Smoke. Me mum and me dad has gone now…"

"I'm sorry, I didn't realise…."

"No, it's all right mate, you couldn't have known. Remember," he sighed, "you've been out of touch for quite a while. Mum four years back with the big C and me dad? Well, he just couldn't do nothing without her and just kind of faded away, y'know?"

"Anyway, me and Shirley…" he turned towards Cris, "Of course, you wouldn't know. Me and Shirl hooked up about five years ago. I've got a nipper now, a little girl. Posey, she's three," he smiled, the image of his daughter entering his mind.

"I met Shirl when she was working for Ronnie, but when we got together, I put a stop to that," he said without explaining what Shirley did, but Cris noticed a trace of bitterness in Moses voice at the mention of Kyle's name.

"Shirl's like me, parents from the Caribbean; mine, you might recall came here from Saint Lucia and Shirl's folks, they went back last year for a holiday to Jamaica and stayed on. She misses them and so does the little 'un."

Moses sighed as if with regret. "So, there's really nothing to keep me and my woman here in the UK anymore, Cris. I've managed to put a few quid together so I'm thinking, with Ronnie gone, it'll create a gap and it might lead to some problems in the Smoke, some *takeover* bids, if you get my drift; so maybe this is as good a time as any for me to get my arse in gear and move on. We've talked about going back, maybe Saint Lucia and opening our own bar, that sort of thing." He smiled at Cris. "I hear the tourist trade out there is booming."

Cris nodded and then extended his hand. "Whatever you decide, Moses, I hope it works out for you."

Moses returned his handshake and as if in a final gesture, said, "I'm sorry again Cris, for… you know."

Cris smiled at him. "Life's moved on for me too, Moses. I'm grateful that you stepped up and you've given me the opportunity to enjoy it. I've got someone as well, so once I get clear of here, I'll be heading home. Goodbye, mate," he nodded and opened the van door.

He stood and watched without waving as Moses drove the van towards the hotel entrance, seeing the van pass by the Morris Ital car that was being driven by the young detective Johnson, with his boss McIntosh craning his head to watch the van depart.

Cris saw McIntosh pointing towards him and the car slowly crawled to a stop beside him.

"Morning Mister Trelawney," McIntosh pulled himself from the passenger seat and greeted him, then pointing at Cris's face, said, "Been in the wars, have we?"

"Could murder a coffee if you and your colleague are up for it?" he replied, "but first I'd better wash my face, I think."

McIntosh thought that Trelawney's face needed more than soap and hot water, but simply replied, "Lead on," and gestured towards the hotel door.

"I'm sure you have an interesting tale to tell us."

Brian Davidson replaced the handset in the cradle and notebook in hand, turned towards Glenda Burroughs. "There's good and not so good news, Glenda. The lease company have provided us with the registered keeper of the vehicle, but it's a double glazed window company located in," he glanced at his notepad, "King Street, Rutherglen. The King Street Window Replacement Group. The guy I spoke with," he pointed to his phone, "told me that it's a smallish outfit and his company have been leasing vehicles for this mob for the last seven years; three cars and six vans. He thinks, but he's not certain, that one car is for use by the manager while the sales team use the other cars. He's not sure how many salesmen they have."

"I don't suppose he was able to tell you if the car we're interested in is used by the manager?" she asked.

Davidson shook his head. "All he knows is the information he has on the lease agreement; three cars and six vans."

Disappointed that it was not as straight forward as she had hoped, Burroughs took a deep breath and said, "Right, here's what we'll do. We'll go in low profile, treat the call as just another line of inquiry. Jenny," she turned to a young, Serious Crime Squad detective, "I want you with me," and smiled. "It might do me some good to get out of the office. We'll call at this King Street office and find out who was using the vehicle on the nights we're interested; tell the manager something like it was seen in the city centre about blah, blah, blah time, yeah? With a bit of

169

luck, the manager might not consider two women as threatening as two male detectives."

Davidson nodded in agreement, smiling at Burroughs subterfuge. He risked a glance at the youthful faced Jenny who unknowingly had been the subject of some of his private fantasies.

"When Gordon gets back to the office," Burroughs interrupted his thoughts, "bring him up to speed and if Jenny and I get a result, I'll phone you the information as quickly as possible to allow you to get started with the Sheriff warrant application, okay?"

"Got that Glenda," he replied.

Dodger Renwick was convinced that he had satisfied the interviewing CID officers of his complete innocence in the death of his wife Mary and son David, that he had no knowledge of his son David's theft of munitions from the TA Barracks.

"I'm sorry, Mister Renwick," the horse-faced bitch of a DI had told him, "but your house is on ongoing crime scene and regretfully you will not be permitted access till our inquiries are complete and I'm guessing, at least today, if not tomorrow. However, I can arrange for some personal items, clothing for instance, to be brought to you. Do you have any family or friends, anywhere in the meantime where you can be accommodated?"

He did not think it prudent to suggest any number of brothels in the city boundary would suit him just fine, particularly as he was supposed to be the grieving husband and father and so requested instead they make arrangements at a city hotel, stressing a suite rather than a room; something befitting his councillor status, he loftily added.

Now here he sat, the panoramic hotel windows overlooking George Square three flights below with the City Chambers conveniently situated a mere one hundred and fifty yards distance. He still wore his dressing gown and slippers upon his feet, waiting with impatience on the police delivering his clothing.

A knock at the door startled him and snarling, went to open it, muttering, "About fucking time," under his breath.

To Dodger's surprise, it was the police, but not his clothing.

"Can I come in Dodger," ACC John Murray strolled past him without waiting on his invitation to enter, removing his uniform cap and placing the cap, swagger stick and brown leather gloves upon a side table.

"What the fuck are you doing here?" Dodger closed the door and thundered at Murray.

"Now, now Dodger, is that anyway to treat a close and trusted associate? Tell me, is there a small bar in this room then?" Murray replied and sat down on one of the comfortable armchairs by the window.

With ill-concealed grace, Dodger opened the mock Georgian cabinet door that hid the fridge and removed four miniature bottles of Grouse, pouring two bottles each into chunky crystal glasses.

"A little water, please," requested Murray, then accepted the glass and sipped at it.

"So, Dodger, what the fuck happened?"

Dodger settled his bulk into the armchair opposite Murray and shrugged.

"That idiot son of mine Davie must have brought some of his army stuff home and threatened me. *Me*," he exploded, "with one of they hand thingy's, what d'you call them…"

"Hand grenade."

"Aye, a hand grenade. He was drunk, the stupid bastard."

He paused as if rewinding the incident in his mind. "Martha must have heard him shouting at me. She came downstairs, came into the front room when he was holding the thing." He slowly shook his head, knowing that even though Murray was a corrupt and sleekit bastard, he was still a copper and he had better watch what he told him.

"I was standing right across the room and I tried to warn her," he lied, inwardly pleased that the story was becoming more convincing with the retelling. "Shouted that she get out, that she run, but she instead she moved towards Davie and tried to wrestle the fucking thing out of his hand."

He swept a hand across his face and shook his head as though the very memory was distressing him. "I don't know if she even heard me or just chose to ignore me. Anyway, when they were struggling, Davie dropped the thingy, the grenade," he corrected himself, "and I realised that it was about to explode. I don't even remember dropping to the floor, but the next thing there was a bang and a flash…."

Murray, who had just come from Cranstonhill police office after consulting with the investigating Detective Inspector, stared at him through narrowed eyes, convinced that he wasn't getting the full truth.

The DI who interviewed Dodger had told Murray she was suspicious that though Dodger was probably blameless in the death of his wife and son, she also suspected he wasn't telling the full truth. But, the DI had shrugged, without evidence and conscious that he was now a bereaved husband and parent, she was more than a little reluctant to put any pressure on him.

Murray, already smarting from the rebuke issued to him by the Chief Constable Tom Muirhead, had concurred that she had done the right thing. The last thing he needed right now, particularly with this fucking Papist thing the next day, was a high profile twat like Dodger, a relatively high profile City Councillor who had just lost his wife and son, complaining to the media about heavy-handed police tactics.

"What's your plan then Dodger? What are you intending now?"

Dodger shook his head. "It's too early to say, John. First though I need to get my things here, my clothes I mean," he raised his head expectantly. "Perhaps you might hurry that along please?"

"I'll see what I can do," Murray patiently replied.

171

"Then of course I'm supposed to be with the Council delegation tomorrow at the Bellahouston Park, meeting the Pope," he sounded pompous and immediately worried that he would miss out on a great photo opportunity; meeting with the Pope was an opportunity to attract votes from his Catholic constituents. Besides, he inwardly smirked, any talk about the Pope was sure to rile the bigoted Murray.

Murray snorted and replied, "Well, that aside, there's another little issue I'd like to discuss." He glanced sharply about him, as if he feared being overheard and in a lowered voice, said, "Regarding our mutual friend's interest in that piece of land in Shettleston; are we any further forward on that issue? My son-in-law's construction company is in danger of going to the wall, Dodger. He *needs* Eddie's building contract. When will your planning committee ensure that Eddie gets the land?"

Dodger sat back, comfortably relaxed now and smiled at Murray. "You've no need to worry on that score, John. It's like I told Eddie, I have the planning committee in my hand. It's just a matter of time…"

"How much time though? My daughter's husband's already overdrawn at the bank Dodger," he persisted.

"Next month, the end of June," he replied, enjoying the look of frustration that appeared on Murray's face.

Murray bit worriedly at the thumbnail on his right hand and then shook his head. "I don't know if the bank will support him till then. Damn!" he abruptly stood; a worried crease on his brow as he considered his son-in-law's financial predicament. If only he hadn't involved himself in making promises to the worthless bastard, he inwardly fumed.

"Right Dodger, I'll be off then," he said, placing his uniform cap upon his head and lifting his brown gloves from the side table.

"You'll remember about my clothes?"

"I'll see they get delivered," he nodded. "You just ensure you get the business done regarding that piece of land, okay?" and without a backward glance, left the room.

Dodger exhaled and reaching for his glass finished the remains of his whisky.
It was time for the first stage of his plan.

Lifting the phone from its cradle, he pressed zero for the hotel operator and said, "This is Councillor Renwick in Room 255. I'd like you to put me through to the newsroom of the 'Glasgow News', so as quick as you can please."

Cris Trelawney refused McIntosh's offer of an immediate lift to the casualty ward of the Southern General Hospital. Instead, he spent ten minutes freshening up in his en-suite room and returning downstairs, led the two detectives into the hotel restaurant where more than a dozen guests were at breakfast, most of whom stared with open curiosity at the arrival of the two suited men and the tall, athletically built man with the face resembling a pound of mince.

The wide-eyed, open-mouthed teenage waiter led them to an empty table and left to collect their order of coffee.

McIntosh tried again. "Want to tell me what happened?"

Cris didn't need a mirror to know he was badly beaten and with a half smile, gingerly touched at his face and replied, "It's noticeable, then?"

Even McIntosh had to grin. "Just a bit," he agreed.

There was a pause as the waiter returned with the tray upon which were three cups and saucers and a large pot of steaming coffee. Dismissing the young man with a smile or as close as he could manage, Cris turned to McIntosh.

"It was my intention to leave earlier this morning, but something came up that delayed me."

McIntosh decided it was past the time for playing games and replied, "We saw the van leaving. I figure the black man that was driving must be Moses Parker, correct?"

Cris nodded. He too had decided it was time for the truth and there was no point in trying to deceive McIntosh.

"I didn't see anyone else in the van, Mister Trelawney."

Cris swallowed hard and not without difficulty, his mouth and throat throbbing. He badly needed aspirin or Paracetamol to dull the aching pain.

"I can't tell you what you seen or didn't see Mister McIntosh," then his curiosity got the better of him and his eyes narrowed. "Why are you here, at this time of the morning I mean? Is there some news?"

McIntosh stared at him, unable to decide if Trelawney really was worth worrying about, then nodded.

"We are currently pursuing a positive line of inquiry…"

"That's police speak for you have a suspect, isn't it?" Cris replied, unable to hide the excitement in his voice or his bloodshot eyes.

McIntosh slowly nodded. "I don't want to raise your hopes or expectations, but yes; there might be a suspect. However, that's not why Simon and I came here this morning. We received information that your former associates Moses Parker and Ronald Kyle arrived on Saturday in Glasgow and met by a local man who is known to us; Eddie Beattie. Is that name familiar to you?"

Cris slowly shook his head. He didn't recall the name Beattie, but that wasn't unusual. He had never had a memory for names, but faces; he was good at faces. Besides that, the secretive Kyle had kept a number of cards close to his chest.

"Eddie Beattie, we believe, provided your associates with a van; the same van that we saw when we entered the hotel car park and being driven by Parker. Following our inquiry and subsequent discussion with you, Mister Trelawney, we had more than a reasonable belief that the purpose of Parker and Kyle's trip to Glasgow was to cause you harm."

He pointed at Cris's face again. "Seems we might have been correct with that theory, eh?"

"However," he continued, "if I'm guessing correctly, they got to you before we could alert you so you must understand that I am a little surprised to see you still alive."

Cris licked at his swollen lips. The next few minutes of discussion, he realised were crucial and he decided to hit back.

"What worries me, Mister McIntosh," he calmly replied, "is that your people up here arranged this hotel for me, yet in a city as large as Glasgow with, I'm guessing, dozens of hotels, I was so easily found by Parker."

McIntosh smiled. He was thinking the very same thought.

"That also occurred to me, Mister Trelawney. Do you have any thoughts on the issue; how they tracked you down, I mean?"

Cris shrugged as if he had no idea, but he still had to play his ace and didn't want to do so in front of the young copper. No, that was something he would discuss alone with McIntosh and nodding to Simon, said, "With the greatest respect, Mister, eh…"

"Johnson," Simon replied while McIntosh wondered where this was going.

"With the greatest respect, Mister Johnson, I understand that here in Scotland regarding your rules of evidence, you police operate under the two cop witness's thing; I'm sorry, I don't know what it's called."

"It's simply called corroboration, sir," replied a bemused Simon.

"Ah, corroboration. In that case, Mister Johnson," elbows on the table, he leaned across towards Simon and softly said, "would you possibly consider giving your boss here and me some time alone. There's a few things I'd like to say to Mister McIntosh that to be honest, I'd probably not prefer not having anyone else hear; no corroboration, I mean," he attempted a friendly smile that caused him to wince

Stunned, Simon glanced at McIntosh who was staring at Cris. "Boss?" he asked.

McIntosh, still staring curiously at Cris, nodded and replied, "Take your coffee out to the foyer son and grab a magazine or something. If I need you, I'll shout."

Feeling like a schoolboy that had been dismissed, Simon left the table.

Moses Parker crammed his and Ronnie's clothes into the two bags and then proceeded to wipe down the flat, paying particular attention to the kitchen and toilet areas. He knew how good the police Forensics were.

He recalled seeing a building skip round the corner near to where he had parked the van and decided that was where he was going to dump Ronnie's bag.

Big as he was, he was still shaking from the events of the previous night and still found it difficult to believe what he had done.

But he didn't regret it, he inwardly smiled.

Not one fucking bit.

With a final look round the flat, he locked the door and shoved the key through the letterbox, then quickly made his way down the stairs and into Duke Street.

Turning the corner into Bellfield Street and walking towards the van, he briefly stopped to heave Ronnie's bag into the skip.

When he rounded the skip, Moses stopped dead. Two uniformed cops were standing by the van, but fortunately with their backs to him.

One, a fair-haired female, was speaking into a radio and he rightly guessed they were checking the registration number.

Moses backed away, keeping the skip between him and the coppers and making his way back towards Duke Street, hailed a black Hackney cab.

"Glasgow Airport, please mate," he breathlessly said and then added, "There's an extra twenty quid in it for you if you get me there in time for my flight."

Sitting back in the comfortable seat, he blew through pursed lips then reflected on his narrow escape and grinned.

CHAPTER 24

Glenda Burroughs and DC Jenny Begley, who was driving, pulled up outside the window replacement company in King Street behind a dented and badly scraped Transit van that bore the logo on its side, 'King Street Window Replacement Group.'

The shop front had large windows on either side of an open door that badly needed a coat of paint. It did not escape Burroughs notice that for a window company, their own windows were stained and streaked with dirt.

"Remember Jenny," winked Burroughs, "we'll be all smiles and fluttering eyelashes. Don't want the bugger that we're looking for getting wind that he's a suspect, right?"

"Right ma'am," agreed Jenny with a grim smile.

As Burroughs pushed open the door of the showroom, a bell above their heads rang to announce their arrival and they stepped into a large foyer area with a number of windows of varying sizes displayed on freestanding frames. A table with three chairs arranged round it and piled with brochures on its top was to one side.

Burroughs first impression of the place was it looked seedy.

"Well, well," said a smiling man stepping out from behind a curtain that hung lopsidedly at the rear of the showroom, "what can I possibly do for you lovely ladies, eh?"

Burroughs judged the man, who wore his dark brown collar length hair neatly parted to be in his early twenties. Wearing a crisp white shirt and what seemed to be a company tie, he also wore sharply creased black suit trousers and was a complete contradiction to the shabby showroom.

Approaching the two detectives, he shrugged into his suit jacket.

"Hi there," Burroughs greeted him with a broad smile and flashing her warrant card, continued, "police. We're making inquires about one of your vehicles?"

With his suit jacket now on, she saw the name 'Gary' typed onto a piece of paper and inserted into a cheap plastic name badge that he wore on the jacket lapel.

"Eh, what vehicle are you talking about," he asked, sounding a little uncertain, "we have a fleet. Half a dozen Transits like the one outside, but that one's knackered at the minute. Then there's the two Escorts and a Mark four Cortina, but the Cortina is the boss's car and he's away touring in it just now; France I think."

"Not sure really," Burroughs pretended to search in her handbag for a piece of paper and bringing it out, said, "A Ford Escort, I think it is. Yeah, a Ford Escort, registration number W388RFC. That one of yours is it?" she asked, her eyes almost as wide as her smile and almost immediately guessing this was going to be easier than she anticipated.

Gary, for that's who he proved to be, was almost immediately smitten by the lovely blonde policewoman, regardless that she was more than a few years older than he was.

"Ah, yeah, it is," he grinned, displaying a perfect set of white teeth that last month had cost him a small fortune. "It'll be out the now with the salesman."

"Who is?"

"Eh, that will be Ricky, Richard Thomas I mean. He's our Southside sales executive."

"And is Mister Thomas the only person who uses the car," she asked, her face completely devoid of guile.

"Oh aye, I mean yes. The sales rep's have a lot of evening work to complete so they get to take the cars home. I'm the inside man, as it were, the office administrator," he joked, but still puzzled what this was leading to. Then, as if realising that maybe Gary was giving out too much information, he asked, "Where was Ricky's car seen again? I mean, why is it that you…"

"Can you tell me where Mister Thomas is at the minute? I mean, do you have a job record where he might be?"

"Ah, not really. You see, the rep's are all individually contracted. That is, they respond to inquiries that we receive here at the showroom or on our 0800 call inquiry line or to flyers that they issue to the areas they target. The usual routine is that they phone in each morning and I pass on prospective customers details. Well, that's the normal routine but," he winked, "with the boss being away on holiday, the last few days the guys have been kind of taking it easy, if you see what I mean."

"But you do keep employee details here at your office? Their contact phone numbers and addresses, yes?"

"Yes, of course," Gary replied then eyes narrowing, became very defensive. "Look, what's this all about? You said it had to do with a car now you're asking about one of my colleagues. Maybe you should really speak to my boss, but he'll not be back till next week."

Standing slightly behind Burroughs, Begley then heard the DI's voice change from seduction to a steely edge.

"Maybe instead you should phone your boss, wherever the fuck he is and tell him that you're hampering the CID with an ongoing investigation and that I'm taking you down to Rutherglen office where I'll detain you and charge you with perverting the course of justice."

Both Burroughs and the younger Begley knew she was bluffing, but they watched as Gary's face turned pale while his prominent Adams apple bounced in his throat like a disco dancer on speed. His shoulders sagged. Evidently, he didn't suspect the bluff.

"Look, I'm sorry, I didn't realise this was important," he almost pleaded. "What is it that you want to know?"

Five minutes later, having been courteously offered the use of the window firm's office phone by a now subservient Gary, Burroughs informed Brian Davidson at Pollok that their suspect was Richard Thomas, aged thirty-five, residing at 148 Shetland Drive in the Simshill area of Glasgow.

Gordon McIntosh opened both hands and stared at Cris Trelawney.

"Okay Mister Trelawney, just you and me now. Nothing that is said between us here will in anyway reflect badly back to you. You have my word."

Cris returned McIntosh's stare. A decade ago he would have openly laughed at a copper giving him his word, but there was something a bit different about this man.

He took a deep breath.

"You were right of course, Moses and Kyle did find me here at the hotel; took me away under the cover of darkness and used a shooter, a sawn off double barrelled shotgun as a persuader." He glanced down at the table and McIntosh saw his fists clench. "Do you recall the young receptionist, the pretty blonde one that works here?"

McIntosh did not really recall the lassie, but nodded anyway, his eyes betraying his curiosity.

"Kyle threatened that if I made a fuss, he would cut her throat and believe me Mister McIntosh, after what he did to my Daniela, I didn't doubt for a second that he would do it."

McIntosh involuntarily glanced towards the door of the restaurant, out to where the reception desk was.

"She's not on duty right now," Cris smiled.

"Anyway, you're right. They used the van to take me somewhere, I'm not sure where the location is; an old, disused warehouse type of place. Kyle had Moses tie me to a post and that's when he, Kyle I mean, did this to me," he pointed to his face.

"I still think you should see a doctor," McIntosh interrupted and offering Cris a clean white handkerchief from his jacket pocket, said, "Take this, your nose is bleeding again."

Cris took the handkerchief and gently dabbed at his swollen nose. "Thanks." Continuing to dab at his swollen nose, he continued.

"Kyle had his fun and then tried to take the shotgun from Moses to shoot me."

"But he didn't shoot you."

Cris smiled; a painful smile and stared into McIntosh's eyes. "No, but I would rather you worked that out for yourself Mister McIntosh."

"This man Parker, I'm guessing that he decided to intervene. What made him suddenly change his mind? What made him decided to stop Kyle from shooting you?"

Cris shook his head. "You have to understand, Ronnie Kyle wasn't just a bad man, he was an evil man. He was not beyond threatening his own team just to ensure their loyalty. There was one time," he suddenly licked at his swollen lips, "one of the team; a little guy called Dinger who Kyle used as a runner, nothing more. Dinger made a mistake, a stupid thing. He got drunk and got himself arrested. After doing a three-month stretch, he was released and when he got out, Kyle had it in his head out that Dinger's sentence should have warranted at least a year. Kyle suspected the little guy had been turned in prison, that the coppers now had an informant in the organisation."

He shook his head, "Kyle didn't go after Dinger; no, he had Dinger's elderly parents battered and hospitalised. Then he told Dinger that if anything were leaked his parents would end up in the cemetery. All because Kyle *suspected* Dinger might be an informant. That's how he assured loyalty, Mister McIntosh," then seeing the DCI's face, smiled sadly and added, "No, it wasn't me that beat the old couple."

"As for Moses Parker; I can only assume that even Moses had had enough of Kyle's madness and but for him, you would still be looking for me and Mister McIntosh, you wouldn't have found me either."

McIntosh softly exhaled. "That's why I only saw Parker in the van. Kyle isn't about anymore, is he?"

Cris did not immediately answer and then instead said, "I strikes me that you must have been a policeman for quite some time, Mister McIntosh. I'm guessing twenty years or more?"

"Almost thirty," he frowned and then, without realising why, confided, "I'm due to retire anytime now. This was to be my last case."

"Almost thirty years," Cris slowly repeated. "Well, I'm also guessing that in all those years you must have seen some awful sights and no doubt experienced some real frustration too, eh?"

"Some," admitted McIntosh.

"In all those years Mister McIntosh, were you ever able to discern the difference between what's called justice and what's right? Is there a difference?" he pursed his lips and shrugged his shoulders. "My Daniela, she was raped and murdered by Ronnie Kyle. Everyone, the police, the court, we all knew he was guilty, but the system, the so-called *justice* factor kicked in and he walked from court, a free man. Was that right? Then, even after all these years, the bastard comes after me simply because I stood up and for once in my miserable fucking life, told the truth; but the truth Mister McIntosh, that didn't matter. It was the *justice* that mattered and that was why he walked out of court; walked free to continue his drug dealing, prostitution racket and terrorising the people about him."

He rubbed his hands through his hair, still slightly matted with blood and arched his back.

"You won't find Ronnie Kyle, Mister McIntosh. Nobody will ever find him and let me tell you and I swear to you on anything you wish me to swear on, nobody will ever miss him."

He sat back and briefly closed his eyes and then slowly opening them said, "There's something else you should know."

In the foyer, Simon stood when he saw McIntosh exit the restaurant door, but was puzzled when the DCI held up a forefinger and then saw him use the receptionists' desk phone.

Replacing the handset, he walked over to Simon and said, "I want you to drive to Pitt Street and collect something for me from DS Patsy Cline from Criminal Intelligence. She'll meet you at the front door with the package and then get back here, okay?"

"Yes sir," Simon nodded as McIntosh returned to the restaurant.

Traffic on the M8 motorway was light and just over ten minutes later, Simon pulled up at the front door of police headquarters. The matronly woman standing with her back to the wall stared curiously at him then approached the driver's door.

"You young Simon?" she smiled at him.

He nodded and was about to speak when she handed him a plain, brown A4 sized envelope. He saw the flap was sealed and her scrawled signature across the flap to ensure if it was opened, McIntosh would know.

"Tell Gordon he's got my curiosity going and I'll expect a phone call," she grinned and turned towards the main doors.

When Simon returned to the hotel, the young man behind the reception desk, flustered and already stressed out by the newly arrived coach load of Catholic pilgrims who all vied for his attention was on the phone. Catching sight of Simon strolling through the front door, he beckoned Simon forward, who heard him say, "Hold on please, I think one of them is here in the foyer." Holding the phone in his hand, he asked, "Excuse me, are you one of the detectives visiting Mister Trelawney?"

The mob of guests that surrounded the reception desk as one quietened and turned to stare at Simon who startled, walked towards the desk and took the phone from the receptionists' hand.

"Hello?"

"The boss with you, Johnson?" Davidson curtly demanded.

"Yes Sarge, I mean, he's not right here. He's with Mister Trelawney in the restaurant."

"Tell him it's me with an update and fetch him to the phone."

"Ah, no can do, I'm afraid. He's instructed e on no account is he to be disturbed," he replied, irate at Davidson's tone and thought, I'm getting good at lying.

He smiled without humour at the frustration in Davidson's voice. "Right, well, as soon as you can, have him phone me here at Pollok, okay?"

179

"Right, I'll tell him, Sarge," Simon smoothly replied and handed the phone back to the receptionist, ignoring the curious stares of the many elderly guests who stood about him. As he returned to his seat, the guests quickly forgot about him and returned to their haranguing of the receptionist.

He reached for the magazine on the table, but quickly stood when he saw McIntosh and Mister Trelawney exit the restaurant and walk towards him.

"Simon," said the DCI, accepting the envelope from him, "contact Pollok and request DS Davidson to have Doctor Robertson attend here at the hotel and as soon as she can. If she asks why, he's to tell her it's a personal favour to me." As McIntosh made to turn away, he added, "Oh, and she's to bring her medical bag. When she arrives, bring her to Mister Trelawney's room."

"Yes sir," replied Simon, "but you should know that DS Davidson has just phoned. He's got an update and requested you contact him as soon as possible."

McIntosh frowned and rubbed at his chin.

"Right, in that case find out what the update is and let me know. Once that's done, you can wait here for Doctor Robertson, okay?"

Simon nodded.

"Good lad," McIntosh winked and turned to walk with Trelawney towards the door that led to the stairs.

Mark Renwick knocked upon the hotel door that was opened by his father, who wore a navy blue hooded tracksuit that just about encompassed his overweight bulk.

"Hello son," the grim-faced Dodger greeted Mark, "Come in."

To Dodger's surprise and embarrassment, Mark threw his arms about his father's neck and burst into tears. "I can't believe she's gone," he wailed and buried his face into his father's shoulder.

Dodger prised Mark from him and holding him by the arms, nodded towards the two men who stood in the hotel room. Through his tears, Mark saw one of the men, who wore a scruffy sports jacket, was holding a notebook while the other, who wore a safari type jacket with bulging pockets, had two cameras slung around his neck.

"These gentlemen are from the press," Dodger stiffly introduced them and ushering Mark towards a door, continued in an angry whisper, "There's the en-suite in there, so for fuck's sake, compose yourself and go and wash your face."

Mark stood back from his father, his face registering surprise and then shock. He realised almost immediately why the reporter and photographer were there. Even with the death of his wife and son, he knew, just knew that his father was already making capital from the tragedy.

Through narrowed eyes, he stared briefly at Dodger, then backing away from him and shaking his head in disgust, turned and opening the hotel door, slammed it behind him.

At the DI's direction, Jenny Begley drove the CID car towards Simshill.

"While we're out this way," Burroughs told the younger woman, "we might as well check to see if the suspect's car is parked up at the home address. Right," she bent her head down towards the Glasgow A to Z map on her lap, "Shetland Drive runs off Castle Road and directed Jenny towards Carmunnock Road.

As she drove, Jenny risked an admiring glance at Burroughs, guessing her to be aged about early to mid forties. Not yet turned thirty, Jenny knew without being pretentious that she was considered to be an attractive young woman and was not without her own admirers. If she could retain her looks in her forties as Burroughs undoubtedly has, she would be well pleased.

"Shetland Drive ma'am," she said, finally turning slowly into the road.

"Number 148 we're looking for. I'll tell you what, do a drive past and we'll see if the suspect's car's there. Then whether it is or not, you can take a walk past the house and do a quick recce, okay?"

"Right," agreed Jenny and then almost as quickly added, "There's number 148, but no car in the driveway and no garage."

"Okay," said Burroughs, "Park up at the end of the road. While you walk past the house, I'll get onto the radio and find out how Brian Davidson is getting on regarding the warrant. I'll also rustle up some bodies to watch the house."

As Jenny opened the driver's door, Burroughs reached across and tapped her on the arm. "Take your time, Jenny. There's no need to rush this. We don't want to spook anyone, okay?"

"Got that ma'am," replied Jenny and closed the car door. Slinging her handbag over her shoulder, she began walking towards number 148.

CHAPTER 25

Simon Johnson saw Doctor Robertson park her old, bashed Morris Marina car in the hotel car park and pulled open the glass front door, when she entered the foyer area.

"Hi Doctor," he smiled at her. "Mister McIntosh instructed me to take you straight up to the room."

"And you are?" she asked with a curious smile.

"I'm Simon Johnson, I'm an acting DC," he replied and offered to take her medical bag.

"What's this all about Mister Johnson?" she asked, handing the heavy bag to him.

"I think it's better that the DCI explain," he replied and led her towards the stairs. Outside Trelawney's room, Simon knocked the door that was pulled open by McIntosh.

Before he could greet Robertson, she coyly said with both hands across her breast, "I must remind you Mister McIntosh, I am a recently married woman. Imagine my surprise when I received your request to meet you at a hotel and then I'm led here to a room. I do hope you haven't any amoral intention towards me?"

McIntosh grinned at her sassiness and nodding that Simon return to the foyer, invited her into the room.

"Thanks for coming Doctor. I have a patient who flatly refuses to attend at hospital. I thought perhaps that you might be able to give him some first aid, some painkillers perhaps."

Cris Trelawney sat on the edge of the bed and attempted a smile at Robertson. "My, my," she moved towards him, standing over him while she gently took his face in her hands, "you have been in the wars, haven't you?"

She turned towards McIntosh and asked, "Is this gentleman a prisoner? What I mean is, will I be able to treat him without you being present?"

"It's okay Doctor," interrupted Cris, "I'm not under arrest or anything," he glanced with a grin at McIntosh and added, "at least I don't think I am. I don't mind if Mister McIntosh remains in the room."

"Right then," she glanced about the room and beckoned Cris to sit by the chair beside the vanity table, switching on the bright cosmetic wall light.

"Can you tell me how you came by these injuries," then as if answering her own question, added "no need. I'm guessing you suffered a beating, eh, Mister…."

"Just call me Cris," he replied.

McIntosh watched as over the next ten minutes, Robertson deftly cleaned and applied first aid to Cris's wounds and then using a small but powerful pencil torch, checked the inside of his mouth.

"You'll need a couple of stitches to the inside of your mouth and there seems to be a couple of cracked teeth, but that's a dental issue. I just don't have the equipment or the knowhow," she admitted. Turning, she began to rummage inside her medical bag and added, "What I will do is provide you with a powerful antiseptic mouthwash. It tastes absolutely vile, but should do the trick till you get to a dentist and," she turned her full glare upon Cris, "I mean as soon as possible. I will also strongly recommend that you also visit your own doctor. Do I make myself clear, Cris?"

"Yes Doctor," he meekly replied and when her back was turned, winked at the grinning McIntosh.

"Right, I've done as much as I can with your facial injuries," she said, her eyes narrowing, "but I noticed when you got up from the bed you favoured your left side. Remove your shirt please."

He did as was told then at her instruction, stood up from the chair. Gently she began robbing at his rib cage and unconsciously nodding, said, "I suspect from the bruising and your obvious wincing at my touch, that you have some damage to your ribs, possibly broken or at least badly bruised. I would also venture," she stared at his muscled torso as she gently prodded with her fingertips, "that you have some experience of physical encounters; boxing perhaps?"

"In my youth, but I like to keep in shape," he replied.

"Then it seems your fitness routine might have saved you from further serious injury Cris. I don't want to bind your ribs in case by tightening them, I exacerbate any internal damage, but I do suggest that when you visit your doctor, *as you will*," she stared meaningfully at him, "you get your ribs checked out. Just be careful and stay away from any further physical activity in the very near future.

182

However, that's *not* to say that you ignore my advice; get yourself attended to as soon as possible, okay?"

"Okay Doctor."

"Well," she turned towards McIntosh and began closing her medical bag, "not much more I can do here."

McIntosh saw her to the door and said, "I'd be grateful if you might keep this visit quiet, Doc. With regard your payment chit for attending…."

"Mum's the word, Mister McIntosh," and with her free hand she tapped the side of her nose then placed her hand on his arm. "Whatever you are doing, I know enough about you to know it's for the best," she smiled tightly at him and made her way to the stairs.

When he had closed the door, McIntosh turned towards Cris.

"Now then, there's good advice from a very smart young woman. Are you still certain you want to drive all the way home, particularly given the shape you're in?"

"Yes Mister McIntosh," he smiled at the older man's undoubted concern then his eyes narrowed. "What do you intend doing. I mean, about the information I gave you?"

McIntosh shrugged and stared hard at him. "I haven't made my mind up, but it's not something I can let go. However," he shrugged, "regarding the other matter, if a body turns up, then the police will be duty bound to investigate it, but from what you tell me it's unlikely that Mister Kyle will show up around here. Even in the event he is reported missing," he shrugged again, "I'm guessing that will be reported to the Metropolitan Police and it will be their inquiry. If they come looking for him here, what can we tell them? Besides, as you so succinctly put it, who will miss him?"

An awkward silence fell between them then McIntosh thrust out his hand that was clasped by Cris.

"As soon as possible, I'll inform you when your daughter can be released Mister Trelawney. If indeed our current inquiry does prove to be successful, I will inform you if we make an arrest. Whether or not the Procurator Fiscal cites you to attend any proceedings will be his decision. In the meantime, safe journey home."

Jenny Begley returned a little breathless, to the car and climbed into the passenger seat.

"I had to move up the road a bit," explained Burroughs. "There was a nosey wee woman in one of the houses where we were parked hiding behind her net curtains watching me. Didn't want the local uniform prowling down here and maybe spooking our suspect," she turned and grinned at Jenny. "So, see anything?"

"The curtains were wide open and I had a clear view inside the front room. A woman was standing in the middle of the floor, ironing I think. I thought I could see the television was on," she added. "There was a child's pushbike, probably a toddler's I think, in the front garden, but I didn't see any weans."

She reached into her handbag for a packet of mints. "What about the search warrant, ma'am, any news on that yet?"

Burroughs declined a mint and lit another cigarette, blowing the smoke out of the partially open window. "I had a radio message just before you got back. The search warrant is signed and is on its way here. There's a team from Pollok standing by as well as Scenes of Crime and a Forensic unit. Once they're in position we'll wait on the DCI's say so and hit the house."

Jenny was puzzled. "What's the DCI up to ma'am? Shouldn't he be here overseeing the operation?"

"What, you don't think I'm capable?" teased Burroughs.

"No, of course it's not that," replied a red-faced Jenny, "only given the nature of the inquiry..."

"I know, I'm only joking," admitted a smiling Burroughs and shook her head. "In fairness, there's not much more the DCI can do at the minute. He obviously feels that whatever he is doing is important, so having issued us with his instructions, we simply carry them out and I'm certain that we'll find out in due course exactly what he's up to."

Believing that she had satisfied the younger detective's curiosity, a thoughtful Burroughs *did* wonder exactly what Gordon McIntosh was up to.

Mark Renwick returned to his flat, still shaking from his encounter with his father.

His thoughts were all over the place.

He found it hard to believe that with the death of his mother and brother so fresh, his father was already soliciting the media; no doubt for the intention of supporting his campaign to be elected as a Member of Parliament.

It was as if his whole life had come down to that few seconds in the hotel room.

....for fuck's sake, compose yourself and go and wash your face....

He had been ashamed at his son's grief in front of the reporters; not the sudden loss of his wife and Davie, but at Marks's grief!

His father's support through his life, even during his career in the police; the whole thing was a lie; everything that he ever had done for Mark was to improve his own political ambition.

His son, his police officer son, was nothing more than a fucking paper puppet.

But now he knew the truth.

It was his father who was important.

His mum, Davie, him; they were all there simply to further Dodger's own career. Even his mum and Davie's deaths, he felt the tears well up in his eyes; even their deaths were of use to Dodger.

His rage overtook his grief and without realising what he intended, he found himself showering and dressing in clean clothes with the intention of returning to duty.

Alone in the incident room at Pollok, DS Brian Davidson was busy coordinating the separate agencies who were converging towards the address in Shetland Drive.

Sat at his desk, he was in the middle of updating the incident log when the phone rang.

"DS Davidson," he irritably snapped and then contritely added, "Sorry Mister Murray. I didn't know it was yourself sir."

"Is McIntosh there, DS Davidson?"

"No sir, I'm here by myself."

"Good," said the silky voiced Murray, "so Brian, tell me what's really happening and leave nothing out."

Simon Johnson turned from the roundabout into Brockburn Road, a quiet and pensive Gordon McIntosh seated beside him.

"Things seem to be moving very quickly, sir," he tried to open some conversation.

"Eh? Oh, aye, they do," nodded McIntosh. Then as if realising that the younger man was being polite, turned to him and said, "I know that you took one hell've chance young Simon; telling me about the arrested woman, I mean. It's not something I'll forget."

"It was actually DI Burroughs who suggested I speak with you sir," replied Simon, his face flushed at the praise, yet feeling guilty that he had doubted the wisdom of his actions.

"Aye, DI Burroughs," replied McIntosh. "Wise move," he added but, thought Simon, a little strangely.

He turned into the yard at Pollok office and parked the car.

"Grab yourself a cuppa first before you come through to the incident room, young man," ordered McIntosh and smiled. "In fact, take a ten minute break," and was about to close the door when Simon called him back.

"Your envelope sir," he said, handing it to McIntosh.

"Oh, aye, mustn't forget that, eh?" he replied, staring fixedly at the envelope in his hand.

It didn't escape a curious Simon's notice that the DCI seemed upset at what the envelope apparently contained. However, as he watched McIntosh stride through the back door he thought *ten minutes*.

Enough time to make a quick call.

The report writing room, a small office that contained four grey coloured metal cabinets sitting side by side, each drawer in the cabinets with a neatly printed label attached to the front and crammed with police forms covering every type of crime and offence. Scattered forms, some scribbled upon, lay untidily about the two desks under which were shoved two unforgiving wooden chairs and a dented grey metal bin overflowed in a corner of the room. The large notice board that hung crookedly on the wall had numerous posters attached; some that displayed Crime Prevention information while other posters and cards tacked there offered everything from contact numbers for holiday homes in the UK and abroad, menus for takeaway food outlets to one gaudily printed notice from a retired cop that offered local gardening services.

A torn and rather sorry looking printed notice instructed that officers ensured the room is kept tidy.

Simon was pleased to see the room was empty and sitting at a desk, pulled the old and chipped phone to him. Dialling nine for an outside line, he produced the scrap of paper from his jacket pocket and dialled the digits then waited pensively for the phone to be answered.

On the third ring a woman's voice said, "Hello?"

Suddenly finding himself dry mouthed, Simon blurted out, "Hello, is Gracie there please?"

"No she's not in the now. Who's calling?"

Guessing it was Gracie's mother, he replied, "Eh, my names Simon Johnson. Is that Missus McTear?"

"Aye, it is," replied the woman and he closed his eyes. She must think I'm an idiot, he thought.

"Can I leave my phone number for Gracie, please?"

"Wait till I get a pen…Simon you said?"

"Yes, Simon Johnson."

He heard the phone being placed down and a few seconds later, the woman said, "Give me your number then please, Simon."

He told the woman his home phone number and she asked, "Is there any message?"

He had not thought about a message and it occurred to him that Gracie McTear wouldn't have a clue who Simon Johnson was.

"Eh," he hadn't realised he was now standing, then with sudden inspiration said, "Can you tell her it's the man she met in th shopping centre; the man on the roll run."

"Ah," said Missus McTear with sudden understanding with unmistakable humour in her voice, "the young detective."

Abashed, he rightly guessed Gracie must have confided to her mother her encounters with him, when Missus McTear added, "I'll see she gets your message Simon."

Replacing the handset, he found himself smiling. He'd tracked her down as she had suggested he do, now it was up to Gracie McTear to get back to him and found himself hoping she did.

Brian Davidson greeted Gordon McIntosh and updated the DCI with news of the developing situation in Simshill. Halfway through the verbal report, both turned at the opening of the incident room door and stared in surprise at Mark Renwick. "Thought I'd get back to work, sir. Seemed to be the best therapy I could think of," he said to McIntosh's unspoken question, his eyes anxious and his face pale.

McIntosh simply nodded and to Davidson's surprise, he replied with a smile, "Glad to have you with us Mark. Things are moving fast and to be frank, I do need you here."

Renwick was taken aback. In the five months he had served as McIntosh's DI, this was the first time that he could recall his boss uttering any kind of appreciation towards him.

"Brian was just bringing me up to speed," McIntosh explained, "so listen in and you can catch up with the rest while I get some work done," and turning towards Davidson said, "go on Brian."

"Well," continued Davidson, glancing briefly at Renwick, "the teams are plotted up and standing by around Shetland Drive as we speak. There's no trace of the suspect's car at the house and when Glenda was at his place of business, the guy there said that he did not know where this Richard Thomas was supposed to be visiting today. Told Glenda that he thought Thomas might be out canvassing…"

"Canvassing? What does that entail and did he say what area?" interrupted Renwick.

Davidson shook his head. "Canvassing is apparently sticking flyers through letterboxes and no, he didn't know what area Thomas was working today."

He reached to the desk behind him for a notebook and glancing at it, continued, "I did a speculative check on the suspect's name and the only Richard Thomas we have recorded on the Scottish Criminal records Office that seems to fit the bill has just two previous convictions. Both conviction's are for RTA offences; one for speeding and the other for parking on a double yellow line," he grimaced.

"Neither offence justified him being photographed or fingerprinted, sir."

"However, I also did a speculative check on the address at Shetland Drive and it seems that within the last fourteen months, the police have been called there on three occasions to reported disturbances, the last occasion being just over one month previously. All the calls were anonymous and all three written off as no police action. That said," he glanced from McIntosh to Renwick, "the cops who attended the second call ensured it was recorded on the computer that the female occupant, Missus Paula Thomas, had a swollen mouth and while they suspected domestic violence, she refused to make any complaint."

Renwick turned to McIntosh. "Might be worth getting the details of the cops who attended the calls and have them submit statements, boss."

McIntosh nodded his agreement and said, "Good work Brian and yes Mark, that's a good idea. Get onto it Brian."

"Boss," acknowledged Davidson, writing a memo on his notebook while inwardly fuming that Renwick should fucking turn up and literally steal his thunder.

"Well," said a pleased McIntosh, "you guys seem to have matters in hand here. What I want now is when Thomas is detained he be brought to the Govan office where you and I," he nodded to Renwick, "will go now to wait on his arrival there. Brian, you continue to run the office here and congratulations; you did some good work today," he nodded at Davidson.

CHAPTER 26

The final preparation was under way for following day's visit by the Pope to Bellahouston Park.

Hundreds of council workers employed by the Parks and Recreation Department worked tirelessly in the increasingly humid weather to beautify the park with floral decoration while other teams struggled with portable metal barricades, designed to herd the expected thousands into areas where the visitors with their Pope could safely celebrate their Catholicism.

Scottish Ambulance personnel, ably assisted by their volunteer colleagues from the Red Cross, erected numerous tents in the expectation that many visitors, in particular the elderly, might succumb to the heat.

Also in attendance was the police in their dozens; senior officers directing their Inspectors who in turn directed their Sergeants. The constables, waiting patiently in their designated areas, nodded knowingly to each other and some paraphrased the military acronym FUBAR; that the situation was Fucked Up Beyond All Recognition.

All involved prepared for the worst and hoped for the best.

At the direct request of the Glasgow City Council, the local media refrained from any mention of the murder that had recently occurred within the Park, of the young woman Alice Trelawney.

However, the media were not being gracious, but reached an agreement that if they complied with the Council request every effort would be made to permit them better photographic opportunity than their English media colleagues.

In the Police Planning Department at Pitt Street, ACC John Murray sweated over minor details, finding fault and seeking someone to blame. His overworked and unappreciated staff muttered under their breath and flitted about the office in a vain attempt to keep out of his way.

Jenny Begley regretted her coffee intake that morning and as a result, was now bursting for a pee.

She glanced at her wristwatch noting that almost two hours had passed since she and the DI had been sitting waiting on the return of the suspect to his home address.

Every ten minutes, the detective secreted in the rear of the van parked along the road from the suspect's home address had radioed to inform his colleagues that there was no change; the suspect had not yet returned home.

Jenny was on the point of requesting the DI drive her to the nearest loo for a comfort break when a dark coloured Ford Escort flashed passed by at speed, hardly giving her or the DI time to note the registration number. However, less than a minute later the excited voice of the detective in the van informed his colleagues the suspect's car had just reversed into the driveway.

Burroughs turned with a grin to the younger woman and said, "Here we go," and starting the engine just as the van detective continued the male driver, presumed to be the suspect, was now out of the vehicle and into the house.

Within thirty seconds, a vanload of CID officers arrived and the driver parked his vehicle in such a manner to effectively block the driveway of number 148 Shetland Drive.

As a half dozen officers poured from the rear of the van, two designated officers quickly made their way to the rear of the property while the remainder, the Sheriff's warrant clutched in the hand of one, knocked loudly upon the front door. Glenda Burroughs pulled up as the officers were pouring through the front door and turning to Jenny Begley, instructed, "Get onto the radio to DCI McIntosh. Tell him we have the suspect at home and have now gained entry."

Simon Johnson was driving Gordon McIntosh and Mark Renwick to Orkney Street police office in Govan when the car radio called out the DCI's name to respond.

The message from DC Begley via the controller at the Force Control Room informed McIntosh of the arrest of the suspect and the entry gained to the house. McIntosh could not hide his delight and slapped the surprised Simon on the shoulder, then turning towards his DI seated in the rear seat, said, "When we get him to the office, Mark, you'll take the lead in the interview and report the case to the Procurator Fiscal, okay?"

Stunned, Renwick could only nod, shocked that in the twilight of his career, McIntosh would turn over such a significant arrest to him.

As if by way of explanation, McIntosh gruffly added, "He committed the first murder on your patch Mark. You're the senior CID officer at Pollok, so it's only right you have a crack at him," then turning back, stared through the windscreen.

Gordon McIntosh quietly exhaled. He knew that he had misjudged Mark Renwick's loyalties; indeed had strongly suspected that the young DI was touting information, but recent events had come to McIntosh's notice and now, in a fit of remorse had decided to give Renwick a break. Granted, the DI still had a lot to learn about CID procedure and in particular, his man management skills were a disaster, but persistently finding fault with him was not going to help. He fervently hoped with encouragement that these skills might develop in time.

"Thanks boss," Renwick quietly said from the back seat.

"I won't let you down."

DC Willie McNee took time off from the search of the house to stand in the roadway outside and light a much-needed fag. He watched as his Serious Crime Squad colleague Jenny Begley and another detective conducted a preliminary search of the suspect's Ford Escort while two uniformed cops, summoned to keep away any local interest, tied blue and white chequered tape across a nearby lamp-post and garden fence, effectively creating a no-go zone about the suspect's house. McNee inhaled deeply and turning saw an old, thin man standing at the front window of the semi-detached house that adjoined number 148. The old man was staring past McNee at the sight of two burly detectives compliantly leading the suspect Richard Thomas out into the street and then placing him in the rear of a CID vehicle that then sped off. A thought struck the rotund detective who nipping his fag between forefinger and thumb, returned it to his cigarette pack as he walked up the garden path to the old man's front door.

The door opened before McNee knocked upon it.

"Not before time, taking that bullying bastard away," frowned the stick-thin old man who stood there, grey thinning hair slicked back and a grey pencil moustache adorning his upper lip. McNee guessed the old man to be in his eighties and his erect stance caused him to think he was probably former military.

"You'll be a police officer then?"

"Aye sir, DC Willie McNee from the Serious Crime Squad, mister….?"

"Serious Crime Squad, eh? Mister McArthur's my name sonny. Come away in then and don't forget to wipe your feet," the old man replied and turned away.

McNee stifled a grin and closing the front door behind him, meekly followed the old man into the lounge where he was immediately impressed by the neat and orderly tidiness of the room. Old fashioned though the décor was, it was clearly apparent the place was spotlessly clean and a photograph on a wooden sideboard of a young McArthur wearing battledress with his young bride on his arm, confirmed McNee's earlier suspicion.

"So, you've arrested that bullying man at last, eh?" the old man shook his head. "Maybe now that young lassie might come to her senses and leave him; her and the bairn, I mean."

"You've had cause to worry about her then?" asked McNee.

McArthur nodded. "These walls," he pointed to the dividing wall between his property and number 148, "couldn't keep out a strong fart, let alone sound. I could hear him almost nightly. Shouting at her; abusing her." He took a deep breath and shook his head. "I was brought up in a society when it was taboo for anyone to interfere between a man and his wife, sonny, but things are changing and for the better I hope."

McNee detected a hesitation in the old man and asked, "Was there anything else, Mister McArthur?"

The old man took a deep breath and then said, "I phoned two or three times. Three times actually. To you people. When he was hitting her, I mean. I could hear it plain as anything. I'm ashamed to say I didn't give my name," he sighed.

"It's a terrible thing, sonny, getting old I mean. There was a day when I would have gone next door and sorted him out myself, but look at me now. Forty, even thirty years ago I would have challenged him. It's not right, a man hitting a woman. My Deidre, God rest her; she would have been fit for him right enough," he nodded his head, his thin lips tightening.

"You can't be blaming yourself for what goes on behind closed door, Mister McArthur," McNee tried to soothe the old man's feelings, but it was as if McArthur did not hear him.

"Out at all hours of the night, he is. I'm not a sleeper, sonny; not anymore at my age. I watch him in that car of his; screaming down the road then returning in the early hours."

McNee's ears pricked up. "Was this recently, Mister McArthur? Going out in his car, I mean. Did this happen within the last few days?"

"Oh, aye. Pretty regular in the recent weeks and certainly within the last few days anyway."

"Can you remember times?"

The old man tapped at his forehead and smiled. "My body might be giving up now I'm eighty-four, sonny, but I'm not senile yet. Of course I remember the days and the times. Why, is it important?"

McNee reached for his notebook and seeing an ashtray on a low table, fetched his cigarettes from his pocket. Offering one to McArthur, he smilingly asked, "What's the chance of a cuppa while I'm taking your statement, sir?"

Gordon McIntosh and Mark Renwick sat patiently awaiting the delivery of the prisoner to Orkney Street office.

While they waited within the DCI's office, Simon Johnson sat in the general office and read the latest crime bulletins, but his thoughts were on his phone call with Gracie McTear's mother.

God, she must think I'm an idiot.

The ringing of the wall phone at the CID clerks' desk startled him and he jumped up to answer it.

The Duty Inspector downstairs informed him that two Serious Crime Squad officers were at the charge bar with a prisoner and instructed him to inform Mister McIntosh.

"Yes sir, right away sir," he replied and breathlessly, hurried along the short corridor to inform the DCI.

"Once he's booked through, have him brought up here to be interviewed by the Detective Inspector, Simon," instructed McIntosh, who then turned towards his DI.

"Who would you like with you when you interview your prisoner, Mark?"

Before Renwick could reply, the phone on McIntosh's desk rung.

"DCI McIntosh," Renwick heard him reply and then watched as the DCI smiled before concluding the call with, "Right Glenda, get them here pronto and tell the troops from me, well done."

His smile continued when he told Renwick that the search of the house was so far proving negative, however, in the boot of the Ford Escort, beneath the spare wheel was discovered a thin bladed knife in a makeshift sheath and two pairs of women's panties.

"It will still need to be forensically examined, but there also seems to be what looks like some blood spotting on the carpet in the boot. Glenda and the young woman from the Serious Crime…."

"DC Begley," offered Renwick.

"Yes, Begley; they'll remain at the house after the search is completed. It seems there is a small child who is to be collected from a nursery, so they will accompany the wife there, pick up the child and then try to coax the wife to provide us with a formal statement. However, I've instructed that the knife and panties be brought here for you to confront the suspect with them."

He stared curiously at his DI. "You still up for the interview?"

Renwick nodded, though his stomach churned at the responsibility.

"Good. Any thoughts who you might wish to corroborate you with the interview?"

"To be frank sir, I've conducted dozens of interviews, but I've never interviewed a suspect for murder. I'd prefer someone with a bit of service, just to keep me right," he admitted.

McIntosh smiled, pleased that the previously blustering Mark Renwick was now displaying some humility and, if he was honest, a little surprised but liking the change in the younger man. His thoughts darkened and he regretted it seemed to have taken a family tragedy to bring about the change.

Then, as if with sudden inspiration, suggested, "I'm told that DC Willie McNee is a bit of a mouthy guy. I know he's got a fair bit of service under his belt. How about him?"

"He seems a fair choice sir. Can I use your room for the interview?"

"Of course," replied McIntosh, "I'll get out of your way and let you get organised. I will have Willie McNee bring up the knife and panties when he joins you. Good luck, Mark."

"Thanks sir."

DI Glenda Burroughs sat in the front passenger seat and smoked her twentieth cigarette of the day, surprising DC Jenny Begley that though such a heavy smoker, the DI never seemed to reek of tobacco as did some of her heavy smoking colleagues.

They both watched as Paula Thomas, her eyes red from weeping, returned across the nursery yard towards the CID car with a smiling, but struggling toddler in her arms.

Once they were seated in the rear of the car, Burroughs motioned for Jenny to drive and take the distraught woman and her child home.

Cris Trelawney's jaw still felt numb. Whatever the medicine the young blonde haired doctor had given him had some kick in it and gently, he used his tongue to probe the inside of his mouth. She had been right about the taste, but it was preferable to the pain, he decided.

He glanced at the needle, happy to stay just under the speed limit and was curiously pleased when at the Scotland/England border, the A74 became the M6. At last, he was home; back in England.

Seated behind the DCI's desk, his notebook opened in front of him and the production bags containing the knife and women's undergarments on the floor by his chair, Mark Renwick didn't know what to expect, but was surprised when DC Willie McNee led the still compliant and pale-faced prisoner Richard Thomas into the room.

To his surprise, the butterflies in his stomach seemed to have dissipated as he stared at the man who McNee bade sit in the seat facing him.

Short fair hair that was neatly combed to one side and clean-shaven, wearing a light blue shirt, navy blue suit and highly polished black shoes, Renwick guessed that Thomas' tie had been removed at the charge bar. His eyes narrowed as he stared at the prisoner and it occurred to Renwick that he did not look like the murderer of two young women.

Behind Thomas, Willie McNee dragged a chair nosily across the linoleum floor and the DI saw Thomas head bow and he flinched, as though waiting to be struck. Renwick paused for a few seconds, conscious that while McNee stared expectantly at him, the prisoner's head was still down and he would not meet Renwick's eyes.

"Mister Thomas," he softly began. "Look at me, please."

He waited the few seconds until Thomas glanced up at him.

"I am aware that you have been already been formally cautioned, but let me repeat that anything you say may be noted by me…."

In the general office, Gordon McIntosh again wondered if he had done the correct thing, permitting his DI to conduct the interview. Simon Johnson and other team members, animated by the arrest, quietly joked and laughed among themselves, conscious that the interview with the man they clearly believed to be the murderer was being conducted just a couple of offices away.

Some among the team who had served under DI Mark Renwick softly shook their heads and among themselves, whispered their disagreement and disappointment at their DCI's decision to permit Renwick to conduct the interview, but none had the courage to voice their dissent.

Those few detectives who were not involved in the murder inquiry, but had been assigned to deal with the day to day criminal inquiries sat quietly at their desks, reading or writing reports, answering the phone or grabbing their jackets to hurriedly attend incidents that required their presence. However, as divisional CID officers they shared the common goal with their inquiry team colleagues and they too anxiously waited for the interview to complete.

Tension in the room increased, even more coffee consumed and some run out of cigarettes as they nervously puffed their way through their pack, but were unwilling to head to the local shop to buy more for fear of missing the outcome of the interview. The loudly ticking wall clock neared the thirtieth minute of the interview when the door to the general office thrust open to admit a solemn-faced Mark Renwick.

The team remained silent as all eyes turned towards Gordon McIntosh, who said just one word. "Well?"

"He's burst to both murders sir," grinned Renwick.

A muted cheer filled the room as a relieved McIntosh vigorously shook his DI's hand.

Renwick held up a hand for silence and to everyone's surprise, continued, "More than that I think you as a team should all be congratulated."

He licked nervously at his lips, now with the full attention of everyone in the room upon him.

"Richard Thomas broke down during the interview and blamed his *inner demons*," said Renwick, theatrically waving the forefingers of both hands in the air, "and it was these *demons* that persuaded him that tonight he was going back out to kill another prostitute. Probably going for the mental defence," he grinned. "But the point is, ladies and gentlemen, your good work resulting in his arrest today has quite possibly saved a woman's life. Well done to you all."

Gordon McIntosh glanced about the room, seeing the pleasure that this simple statement had brought to the team and smiled. Maybe after all there was some hope for young Mark Renwick, he thought and made the decision that whether his DI agreed or not, he intended ordering Mark Renwick to take two weeks bereavement time off to try to come to terms with his tragic loss.

He inwardly sighed, knowing that if he required Renwick to take compassionate time off, he would effectively be leaving his divisional CID management team short. Mary would not be happy, for this would mean him having to carry on working for the time being, but curiously, *he* wasn't too unhappy at the thought. He caught Simon Johnson's attention and beckoning Simon to him, said, "When DI Burroughs arrives back here at Govan, have her meet with me in my office." Then almost as an afterthought, he fetched his wallet from an inside pocket and withdrawing two twenty pounds notes, asked the younger man to slip out and purchase a couple of bottles of whisky; the customary celebration at the conclusion of a successful murder inquiry.

Across the city, within a ground floor flat in Garscube Road, an area with a high incidence of unemployment, crime and social depravation, John Price, known to his associates as 'Wingy', whose nickname was awarded to him following the loss of his left arm, stared in helpless horror as the partially clothed Lizzie McLeish underwent a seizure.

Coughing and spluttering, her body convulsing uncontrollably, she began to violently vomit a white coloured, frothy phlegm and shuddered to her death on his stained and threadbare carpet.

Wingy could not know that the heroin he had supplied to Lizzie in exchange for sexual favour, adulterated beyond all recognition of the illegal drug it had once been, had shocked the unfortunate young woman's nervous system so badly that it induced colossal heart failure and destroyed her already fragile internal organs.

Panic-stricken and without thought of his actions other than the need to immediately remove her from his flat, Wingy hastily crammed Lizzie's disrobed clothing into her bag and pulled her arm through the bag handles. Grabbing the same arm, Wingy began dragging the almost weightless Lizzie towards the front door where he first peeked out to ensure the litter ridden close was empty.

Kicking the door wide open, Wingy continued to drag Lizzie's body towards the open rear exit of the close and with a quick glance to ensure no one was about, pulled her through the filth and discarded household waste towards the small, brick enclosed bin area.

It was unfortunate for Wingy that his elderly neighbour who resided above him had earlier heard then seen Lizzie knocking on Wingy's window.

While a fearful Wingy was using his only hand to cover the body with an old piece of carpet and bits of cardboard he had discovered in the bin area, the neighbour was already on her phone, relating his every move to the police officer at the Force Control Room in Pitt Street.

The face of Glasgow, like other cities throughout the developed world, is constantly changing, with derelict buildings torn down and replaced by new housing, factories or other constructions. City roads, often abandoned or neglected and others created to facilitate new housing estates or to develop and service industrial areas.

Whistling cheerfully while he worked, Angus MacKenzie, a tall, bearded Ayrshireman working at the Cambuslang site as a self-employed concrete pourer, opened the throttle that increased the rotational speed of the large drum on his concrete transport truck.

Reaching up, he pulled at the release mechanism of the circular metal tube, down which would pour the liquid concrete. Heaving the chute from its metal restraining clips, he positioned the mouth of the chute to discharge its grey, rapidly solidifying load over the deep but narrow trench that when filled and set hard, would become part of the foundation for the walls of the soon to be constructed primary school.

Glancing down into the trench, MacKenzie whistled tunelessly and looked about him while discreetly ignoring the lengthy bundle wrapped in the heavy-duty polythene and reminded himself that it was not always wise to be curious. While the trench rapidly filled with the quick-setting concrete, MacKenzie considered what finance he still owed towards paying off the second-hand concrete truck and calculated that the grand he got for this little job, so generously bunged to him by his old pal Eddie Beattie, would go some way towards the next couple of month's payments.

DC Jenny Begley drove the CID car into the rear courtyard at Orkney Street police office and switching off the engine, turned to Glenda Burroughs and asked, "What now, ma'am?"

Burroughs pursed her lipstick lips and softly blowing through them, replied, "First things first, let's find out how the interview went."

As she exited the passenger door, Simon Johnson, returning from a local off-licence with a plastic carrier bag in each hand, turned into the courtyard and greeted her.

"Heard the news ma'am? Thomas confessed to the murders," he grinned at her, still excited to be part of such a major inquiry and all within a few weeks of his CID secondment.

Burroughs returned his grin and turning to Jenny, said, "Told you, eh? Gordon McIntosh, the Glasgow Mountie; always gets his man."

Simon shook his head. "It wasn't the DCI who interviewed and burst Thomas, ma'am. It was DI Renwick."

Burroughs eyes opened with surprise; her first thought being why Gordon would trust Renwick with such an important interview.

Simon, walking ahead of the two women and using his shoulder to push open the heavy blue door that led into the charge bar, continued, "Oh, and the DCI asked if you would meet with him in his room when you arrive, ma'am."

Simon strode ahead of the two women, through the uniform muster room and up the narrow winding, wrought iron stairs to the first floor.

Jenny Begley followed him to the general office while Burroughs veered off to join McIntosh in his room.

He was sat behind his desk, his tie loosened, shirt cuffs turned back, suit jacket off and hung at the back of his chair.

As she closed the door behind her, she heard a muffled cheer from the general office at the arrival of Simon Johnson with the whisky.

"Hello, Glenda," said McIntosh, "sit down please."

It was something in his voice, the politeness that set her on edge. Instinctively, she knew something was amiss.

"I hear we've had a successful conclusion to the case," she smiled at him, reaching into her bag for her cigarettes and Zippo in an attempt to deflect him and gather her thoughts. Now why, she suddenly thought, do I fell ill at ease?

"Yes. Mark Renwick did well. Oh, I know we had the evidence of the knife and the woman's undergarments, but we both know from experience that a signed confession always goes down that wee bit better at the High Court."

"So, why is it that you wanted to see me, Gordon? You know we're missing our traditional dram with the rest of the team," she smiled at him.

He didn't return her smile. As he stared at her he saw that smart, poised and confident, she really was a beautiful woman. He recalled many times it was remarked that Glenda Burroughs was wasted as a cop; that she would easily have been a success in the fashion world.

He swallowed hard and prepared himself to destroy her career.

"I had a very interesting conversation earlier today with Cris Trelawney, before he returned home," he begun.

She continued to smile, waiting on him explaining.

"He told me something of his time working for Ronnie Kyle in London. Confided that Kyle had a number of Metropolitan police officers he was paying off; bunging them for information regarding when his clubs might be turned over and even better, when his rivals were due to be turned."

He fumbled in his pocket for his pack of cigarettes and placing one in his mouth, leaned over the desk when Glenda flipped open and lit it with her lighter. Inhaling deeply, he continued.

"One of the cops that Kyle had in his pocket was a CID officer, a DS called Harley. His nickname, according to Trelawney, was 'Handy'. Ever recall meeting anyone like that during your six month stint down in London?"

"The name doesn't ring any bells," she stared him in the eye.

"Trelawney, or McGuire as he was known then, told me that Harley was a frequent visitor to Kyle's clubs and sometimes brought women with him to the club. In fact, Trelawney recalls Harley bringing you a few times because he also recalled your good looks attracted a bit of attention from the male bouncers, who thought like Harley, you were a Metropolitan cop. It never occurred to anyone that you were a City of Glasgow cop on secondment. What Trelawney also told me was that as part of Harley's deal working for Kyle was the availability to him of the women who worked in the clubs. What Harley did not know was that in the club's private suites, Kyle secretly filmed him with some of these women. A sort of insurance against the cops turning on him, apparently. Seems he was a bit of a paranoid voyeur, was Mister Kyle."

She felt a cold chill run through her, but forced herself to remain calm.

McIntosh took another long pull at his cigarette.

"You recall the day that we met Trelawney at the hotel?"

She slowly nodded, not trusting herself to speak.

"He told me that he's pretty poor at remembering names, but he never forgets a face and admitted that he found you very attractive. That's what stirred up a memory, why he thought he recognised you and…"

"Where is this going, Gordon?" she snapped at him, deciding to take the offensive and both hands flat on the desk, rose to her feet. "If you are accusing me of something…."

He did not react as she had hoped, but merely raised a hand to quieten her and said, "It's in your interest to hear me out, Glenda."

Still staring at him, her mouth tightly set, she slowly sat down.

He could not see that in her lap her hands were tightly clenched to stop them from shaking.

"So, as I said, Trelawney thought he recognised you, but it was your blonde hair that threw him. He later recalled that when he had seen you last, you were brunette…."

"It's a woman's privilege to change her hair colour," she interrupted and tightly smiled at him.

"….and that you were brought to Kyle's club by this guy Harley."

"I visited a lot of clubs during my time in London. I don't recall the specific ones and I also met a lot of guys. I was then and still am a single woman, Gordon. I won't apologise to you or anyone who I see or who I date, okay?" her nostrils flared in self-righteous anger.

"About ten years ago, during the time you were there," he pointedly informed her, "Trelawney, was told that Kyle had a deal going on with an important customer; a drug deal that promised to net Kyle some hundreds of thousands of pounds. Trelawney was not keen on being involved in the drug trade and tried to warn Kyle off getting involved with drugs, but Kyle was seduced by the easy money to be made and ignored him. According to Trelawney, the customer was some big shot gangster from Glasgow, though Trelawney couldn't remember his name. Kyle told Trelawney that this man was so important that no matter what he or his girlfriend required, it was to be provided. Such was the Glasgow guy's importance to Kyle that Trelawney was sent to a jewellers in Hatton Gardens to collect gifts Kyle had ordered for both the Glasgow guy and his new girlfriend; a Scottish girlfriend, as it happens."

"The same night, the Glasgow guy and his girlfriend arrived at Kyle's club and were shown to a private suite that was exclusively for use by the most important guests. The best food, champagne and private entertainment was provided by Kyle for his special guests and he then presented the Glasgow guy and his girlfriend with their gifts; a gold Zippo lighter engraved with their respective initials. Just like that one there," he inclined his head towards her lighter that sat by her pack of cigarettes.

Her eyes widened and her nostrils flared in anger.

"And you think that this Glasgow guy's girlfriend was me, basing your premise on the assumption that about that time I was in London and," she scoffed lightly at him, "because I have a gold, engraved Zippo lighter?"

"Really, Gordon," she slowly shook her head and stared at him with sorrowful sadness. "You're far too long a detective to realise that what you have is nothing; a former criminal who *thinks* he might have recognised me, who *thinks* I might have been at Ronnie Kyle's club and who *thinks* I might be the girlfriend of a Glasgow drug dealer. Really?" she huffed at him.

"Trelawney recognised you Glenda because he had previously seen you in the company of this DS Harley, but you had then switched your…" he searched for the word, "*favours* to the Glasgow guy. He was quite specific about your being with this new guy and recalls that for the two nights Kyle entertained you as a couple, you stayed over in the private suite. In fact, he told me that when you and young Johnson visited him to inform him of Elizabeth Fisher's murder, he had remembered who you were and reminded you of those nights; even though you denied to him you knew what he was talking about."

"This is so much a fairy tale Gordon," her eyes blazed and she suddenly snapped at him, "I'm surprised that you even consider it worth the telling."

"It's worth the telling, Glenda," teeth bared, he snapped back at her, "because your actions almost led to Trelawney being murdered!"

Pale faced, she stared hard at him. "I don't know what the fuck you mean by that!"

He paused a few seconds to allow his allegation to sweep over her and then, calm now, he continued.

"Kyle was informed about Alice Trelawney's murder and travelled here to Glasgow to take his revenge on Cris Trelawney for giving evidence against him. When he arrived here he was met by his old pal Beattie who provided Kyle with transport and the address where Cris Trelawney could be found; the hotel address provided by you, Glenda."

"That's nonsense, Gordon," she replied, but he thought this time without conviction.

"No Glenda, not nonsense. Before he left, I showed Trelawney this," and from the brown envelope on the desk by his elbow, he withdrew an eight by six surveillance head-shot photograph that he turned towards her.

"Trelawney couldn't recall the name, but had no difficulty recognising the guy here as the Glaswegian you spent two nights with in Ronnie Kyle's club, all those years ago; the same man to whom you gave Cris Trelawney's location to pass onto Kyle. Eddie Beattie."

He paused and stared at her, her face ashen and her previous defiance now seeping from her like a deflated balloon.

"If that isn't enough, you tried to infer that Mark Renwick was touting information, sowed the seed of doubt in my mind because you already knew that I had little faith in his ability and, to my shame, it almost worked."

"So, who else knows about this?" she quietly asked, breathing so hard that her breasts seemed to reach out from her blouse with a life of their own.

"Apart from Cris Trelawney, no one else except me," he replied, shaking his head.

She bit at her lower lip and hesitatingly, said, "We could...." she paused and shrugged her shoulders, "if you're willing to keep quiet about this....we could come to some sort of arrangement, Gordon."

He smiled at her, a slow smile that conveyed his understanding of her offer.

"Thanks Glenda, but I already have a woman in my life."

She returned his smile, but a smile that was without warmth. "So then, what exactly do you intend doing with this information?"

"What do *I* intend?" he repeated and shook his head. "I don't intend doing anything. However, what *you* should seriously consider is resigning. Right now, today."

He sighed and inhaled deeply. He couldn't explain why, but he wanted to make this a little easier for her.

"You've done a lot of good work in your time as a police officer, Glenda. You've worked hard and done well in a job that until recent years quite publicly had a glass ceiling for women. You broke through that ceiling and achieved Detective Inspector rank and, if things hadn't turned out the way they've gone and with things getting better in the Force, there was every likelihood you might even have gone further."

He again shook his head. "But I can't ignore that you're touting to Eddie Beattie, regardless of your relationship with him. You deliberately put a witness in harms way, so here's your options; I say nothing and you resign today. That way you retain your dignity and your reputation and walk away with what pension rights you have accrued so far. Refuse that option and I have no choice; I contact the rubber heels at Pitt Street and turn over my information to them. If you choose that option, you're looking at not just a dishonourable dismissal, but more than likely, prison."

He could see her throat tighten and her eyes moisten then slowly nodding her head, she stood and turning, wordlessly walked towards the door and out the room.

Watching her leave McIntosh could not help himself and for a couple of heartbeats wondered, just wondered, what it might have been like had he taken up her offer.

Simon Johnson, sipping at his Irn-Bru, grinned with the rest of the team at Willie McNee's anecdotal story. This for him was a new experience, being present at the end of a successful murder inquiry and seeing the corks from both bottles being crushed and thrown into the waste bin. He was not really a drinker of spirits and resisted the good-natured jeers of the team when he refused to partake of a glass of whisky. Now standing by the general office door he watched curiously as unnoticed by the others, Glenda Burroughs hurried away down the wide stairs. He was about to call out to her, but stopped. He couldn't explain it, but her hurried steps suggested to him that something was amiss.

The hubbub within the office abated when Gordon McIntosh joined the throng, then resumed when he accepted a plastic tumbler with two fingers of whisky and toasted them all.

CHAPTER 27 – Tuesday 1 June 1982

From early that morning they came in their thousands, the very young carried on their parents back to the very old, wheeled or assisted by their family or carers and all descending upon the Bellahouston area of Glasgow. Most laden with bags or backpacking food and water and a large number carrying portable chairs in preparation for the long, hot day ahead.

Apart from a few dozen dissenters, all the visitors were in a cheery and hopeful mood, a party mood, arriving alone or with family, in parish groups with many singing their favourite hymns as they approached the gates to the Park.

On this exceptionally warm day every race and creed seemed to be represented and included those who, though not of the Catholic faith, were there because they believed in the goodness of the man they revered as a fellow Christian.

The police in their distinctive white uniform shirts and chequered caps and the stewards appointed by the local churches perspired at their designated posts while they directed the massive crowd to the staging areas; laughing and joking with them and keeping the visitors safe while taking time to enjoy the festive atmosphere and goodwill of those arriving.

Among the crowd strolled the plainclothes officers and detectives, summoned from every city division in response to intelligence reports from police forces throughout the UK that travelling gangs of pickpockets would also be attending the Park. Such was the diligence of these officers that pickings for the travelling thieves that day proved to be extremely poor.

At the southeast corner of the Park, near to the junction of Mosspark Boulevard and Dumbreck Road, a few dozen dissenters whose goal was to disrupt the days event found themselves outnumbered almost four to one by uniformed officers. Penned in with their backs to the metal railings of the park and surrounded on the remaining three sides by the large and intimidating Support Unit officers, the dissenters soon lost heart. Their cries of protests and pitiful homemade banners were hardly noticed and soon ignored by the happy throng, who instead were enthralled by the sight of the Pontiff in white celebrating mass at the newly created altar on the side of the grassy hill.

Simon Johnson, standing with a colleague on the blocked off roadway of the Boulevard, hardly noticed the thousands of worshipers, his thoughts instead filled with the recorded message that had arrived on his telephone answer machine. Gracie McTear had agreed to meet him and suggested if he was free that night, to call her and they would agree a time and a venue.

Gordon McIntosh, true to his word, contacted the Procurator Fiscal's department and made a personal appeal on behalf of the shoplifter Ella McGuiness, describing her as a valuable witness in the forthcoming murder trial of Richard Thomas.

The Depute Fiscal who took the call thought it rather unusual that a Detective Chief Inspector should make a plea for leniency in the case of a shoplifter, but he was astute enough to recognise McIntosh's experience in these issues and agreed with the request.

At her court appearance and at the direct request of the PF's department, the presiding judge granted McGuiness further time to pay off her fines and the warrants meantime cancelled.

Councillor John 'Dodger' Renwick's double bereavement was reported sympathetically by the media and in particular, the 'Glasgow News'.

The newspaper's three-page spread, complete with a photograph of the distraught Councillor sitting in a hotel armchair, his face drawn and his head held in both hands, reported the heart-breaking loss of his beloved wife Martha and his oldest son David.

When asked how the Councillor would deal with this very personal tragedy, he described his wife Martha as *'the rock upon which I stood'* tearfully insisting that he would continue to seek the Parliamentary seat for his Party, for he truly believed he would be failing his Martha if he did not do so. The Councillor also reminded the reporter it is his intention to carry on and serve his constituents as he had done so ably for many years.

As the article continued, Councillor Renwick boasted of his pride in his son David and of David's ambition to enlist and serve his country, particularly in light of the ongoing South Atlantic feud.

The heart-rending report included a sorrowful admission the Councillor and his wife who tried in vain to persuade David, having recently suspected their son of having undiagnosed mental health issues, to seek medical help. Though a close and loving family, both the Councillor and his beloved wife had been unaware of how deeply troubled their son had become and did not fully appreciate the extent of his failing mental health.

The issue of David bringing home a live hand grenade was something the Councillor was still trying to come to terms with and in a fit of confidence he disclosed the army were investigating this blatant breach of their procedures; a subtle inference that the real blame for David's unaccountable act of destruction lay at the military's door.

The article also included a brief reference to the Councillor's second son Mark, a detective with the police, but did not elaborate any further other than to suggest that Mark too was grieving for his family's loss.

The well-written and compassionate piece of journalism concluded that despite his own grief, Councillor Renwick believed it to be his civic duty to accompany his fellow Councillors and greet the Pope during the visit at Bellahouston Park as a representative of the people of Glasgow and more particularly, on behalf of his Christian constituents.

Sitting within his hotel room reading the early edition of the 'Glasgow News', Dodger was pleased and delighted with the article that portrayed him not simply as a grieving husband and father, but a victim of circumstances far beyond his control.

Yes, he unconsciously nodded while sipping at small whisky; the article was well worth the five hundred quid he had bunged the reporter.

All he needed now was to arrange that he arrange to be photographed being presented to the Pope, for Dodger believed that to be seen shaking hands with the world's most prominent Christian would do him no harm when the electorate went to the polls in the forthcoming election.

He squirmed his bulk comfortably into the soft lining of the armchair and, glancing at the wall clock, reasoned he still had time for a fresh cigar.

If all went well, he might even treat himself to another visit this evening to the flat at Nithsdale Road.

Closing his eyes, his thoughts turned again to the nubile, teenage girl.

CHAPTER 28

On the 8 June 1982 while preparing to unload soldiers from the Welsh Guards off the coast of the Falkland's, the Royal Fleet Auxiliary ship *Sir Galahad* was attacked by aircraft of the Argentine Air Force, who scored direct hits on the ship. The bombs caused massive damage and caused fires throughout the ship, resulting in the death of over forty sailors and soldiers.

Michael Johnson and his wife Alison received the news of their Royal Navy Lieutenant son Peter's death while watching footage of the attack in the lounge, at their home.

Distraught, Michael contacted the Duty Inspector at Govan police office, who in turn with compassion, broke the tragic news to Acting Detective Constable Simon Johnson, catching him as he was about to finish duty and meet for dinner with his new girlfriend, Gracie McTear.

During the weeks that followed, Gracie proved to be of tremendous support to Simon and it surprised neither family when a little over four months later, she agreed to move into his flat.

Just over four months later, Richard Thomas, aged 35 years, on the advice of his counsel, pled guilty to the murders of Alice Trelawney and Elizabeth Fisher and appeared for sentencing in Court 2 at the High Court of Justiciary, Lawnmarket, Edinburgh.

In a deal worked out with the Crown Prosecution Service, who were extremely conscious of the victims chosen profession, the CPS agreed that the charges of raping both women was deleted from the charge sheet; a decision that caused much controversy and drew a much publicised media backlash from a number of women's rights groups.

The accused defence team, headed by the eminent Mister Justin Kerrigan-McVey, had all but given up on their client, not least fumed Kerrigan-McVey because the idiot had retained indisputable Forensic evidence in the boot of his car as well following his arrest, written his own confession that included knowledge of the murders that only the killer must have known.

To top it all, Kerrigan-McVey had tried unsuccessfully to have his client's wife, Paula Thomas stand by her husband.

However, not only did Missus Thomas refuse the counsels personal plea, but he later learned she was negotiating with a popular women's magazine to sell her story that included details of beatings and sexual abuse at her husband's hand.

The decision to throw his client to the mercy of the His Lordship was not lightly taken; however, had Mister Kerrigan-McVey remotely suspected the eventual outcome of such a decision, he might have had cause to fight the case in court. However, as they say, hindsight is a wonderful thing.

His Lordship presiding, conscious of the publicity that surrounded the Yorkshire Ripper case in England, determined that no such monster would terrorise the ladies of the night in Scotland. From the bench, the judge berated Thomas for the evil man he was and to the shocked surprise of those present, sentenced the accused to two life sentences and each sentence to run consecutively.

At the announcement of the double sentencing, Thomas collapsed in the Dock while the reporters present run to the public phones. Almost immediately, His Lordship became the darling of the right wing and for weeks thereafter was much lauded by the media as an example of real Scottish justice at work.

Gordon McIntosh stood quietly smoking inside the foyer area of the High Court, waiting for Mark Renwick to come down the marble stairs.

"Hello Mark," he greeted him, his hand extended.

"Sir, I didn't expect to see you here," replied a surprised Renwick, genuinely pleased to see his old boss and shook his hand vigorously.

"Forget the sir, it's Gordon. I'm retired now, remember. So, how are you getting along?"

"Fine, yeah, fine. Pleased with the result," he jerked his head back up the stairs, "and to be honest, a little glad he didn't go to trial." He smiled. "I never did like giving evidence."

"It's about the closest any of us get to acting," McIntosh returned the smile as they began to walk together to the sunshine outside.

"So, why are you here? You weren't cited, were you?"

"No," McIntosh shook his head. "My wife and I are through for the day; shopping, she calls it. Torture I call it. I'm meeting her in," he glanced at his wristwatch, "twenty minutes in Jenner's tearoom. So, while I was here, thought I'd pop in while she's spending my money, see how you were getting on."

"Thanks for attending the funeral, Gordon. I didn't get the opportunity to speak…."

"No, I understand. It was a busy time for you. How is your father bearing up?"

"Ah, well, to be honest, I haven't seen much of him since then." He took a deep breath and slowly exhaled. "We kind of drifted apart. I'm afraid I don't really fit into his world, now he's on the campaign trail to become an MP and spending so much time at meetings here and there and in London."

An uncomfortable silence fell between them, broken when Renwick, his face betraying his curiosity, said, "If you don't mind me asking, the day we arrested Richard Thomas. Glenda Burroughs just seemed to be…I don't know; one minute she's there, the next she's gone. Retired, I heard. You have any idea what that was all about?"

McIntosh shrugged his shoulders. "All I know is she came into my office and said she had had enough of the polis and was leaving. You remember how obsessively secret she was about her private live life. It might have had something to do with that; I really don't know. "

Renwick shook his head. "A few stories were kicked about, the favourite being that her mystery man had persuaded her to run off with him. There was some speculation she travelled through Glasgow Airport on her way to Spain to run a pub, but I think it was just a story. You know what the polis is like; if they don't know the truth, they'll make something up," he grinned. "If she did run off with her boyfriend, all I can say is he is one lucky bloke. She was a looker right enough."

"Aye, Mark," McIntosh smilingly agreed, "she certainly was."

The calm waters in the bay of the fishing village of Hayle hardly disturbed the boat and gently lapped against the bow.

In the stern, Cris Trelawney, his newly clean-shaven face healed, stood in the centre, with Louise Davenport to one side with her hand proprietarily resting lightly on his arm.

Her son Jack stood silently on Cris's left.

Taking a deep breath he removed the lid from the urn and slowly poured the ashes over the side into the still waters.

"Goodbye, my lovely Alice," he whispered and almost as an afterthought, leaned over the gunwale and lowered the urn into the water and watched it slowly sink and disappear into the depths.

Needless to say, this story is a work of fiction.
If you have enjoyed the story, you may wish to visit the author's website at:
www.glasgowcrimefiction.co.uk

The author also welcomes feedback and can be contacted at:
george.donald.books@hotmail.co.uk

Printed in Great Britain
by Amazon.co.uk, Ltd.,
Marston Gate.